FINAL FANTASY XV

The Dawn of the Future

JUN EISHIMA

THE FINAL FANTASY XV DEVELOPMENT TEAM

TRANSLATED BY STEPHEN KOHLER

Story Synopsis

Departure for Altissia

Long has war raged between the Kingdom of Lucis, protector of the sacred Crystal, and the Empire of Niflheim, which has schemed endlessly to seize both the Crystal and all the world's lands. The greater part of Eos has fallen to imperial control, including much of the former territory of Lucis, but as Lucis nears total defeat, Niflheim suddenly extends an offer of peace. The empire will agree to a ceasefire, along with continued Lucian independence, on two conditions: that Lucis relinquish its claim to all lands beyond the walls of its capital city, and that its crown prince, Noctis Lucis Caelum, be wed to Lunafreya Nox Fleuret, Oracle and daughter of House Fleuret, ruling family of the imperially controlled province of Tenebrae. Regis Lucis Caelum, king of Lucis and father to Noctis, though having measured the true intent behind Niflheim's offer, is forced to accept the chance of an armistice, given the dire state of the war.

In compliance with the armistice terms, Noctis departs the Crown City accompanied by three friends and retainers: Gladiolus Amicitia, Prompto Argentum, and Ignis Scientia. Entrusted with the king's beloved vehicle, the Regalia, the party heads to Altissia, capital of the neighboring Accordo Protectorate, where the wedding is to take place.

Insomnia Falls

Noctis and his friends make their way toward the seaside town Galdin Quay in order to embark on a ship that will take them to Altissia. Shortly after they set out, the Regalia breaks down, and the party is forced to push the car to a nearby garage at Hammerhead. There they meet Cid Sophiar, a master mechanic and an old friend of Regis's, as well as Cindy Aurum, Cid's granddaughter. The duo's assistance soon has the Regalia repaired and the party back on the road.

However, when they finally arrive at the Galdin pier, a suspicious stranger informs Noctis that the ferries aren't running. The stranger's words prove to be true, and the royal entourage find themselves at a loss for how to proceed. A reporter named Dino Ghiranze catches their attention, offering to make a deal that will net them passage to Altissia.

The morning their ship is to depart, news arrives that the Crown City of Insomnia has fallen to the empire. King Regis is dead and the Crystal taken. The party temporarily abandons the trip to Altissia, instead rendezvousing with Cor Leonis, marshal of the Crownsguard, the military force tasked with the protection of Lucis. Cor explains Noctis's duty as the new monarch: he must visit the ancient tombs of his Lucian forebears and receive from them the power of kings.

The Power of Kings

As Noctis gathers the Royal Arms from the tombs with the help of his companions, he slowly grows in strength. He also begins to experience sudden and unexplained headaches. Visions accompany the throbbing pain, showing scenes of the Disc of Cauthess, site of the ancient Meteor that fell from the sky, and of Titan, the Archaean, who intercepted the astral shard's descent and has continued to brace it aloft ever since. Hoping to find and stop the source of the headaches, the party decides to investigate the Disc. As they approach the site, they once again encounter the suspicious stranger from Galdin Quay, who introduces himself as merely "Ardyn." Ardyn invites Noctis and his retinue to accompany him to the Disc, claiming he can see them safely through the location's imperial checkpoint.

With Ardyn's assistance, the group enters the Disc and Noctis draws near the Meteor, where he finds himself face-to-face with the Archaean. Noctis learns that the deity is the source of his headaches: Titan is attempting to convey a message about Noctis's calling as king. After a violent struggle and the sudden appearance of imperial forces, Titan is bested and the area around the Disc begins to quake violently. Just as certain death looms, Ardyn arrives via dropship, revealing himself to be Ardyn Izunia, chancellor of Niflheim, and offering to ferry Noctis and friends to safety.

An Unexpected Ally

Though delivered from immediate peril, the group is stranded in imperial territory and uncertain how to go about recovering the Regalia. Noctis receives a visit from Gentiana, one of the twenty-four Messengers that serve the Six, the gods of Eos. Gentiana reveals that the Oracle, Lunafreya, is forging covenants with the Six to awaken them from their long slumber and secure their support for the young king. She also explains that the empire fears the gods' powers and seeks to stop Noctis by ending his life. Noctis puts the search for the Regalia on hold, instead heading to Fociaugh Hollow to secure the blessing of Ramuh, the Fulgurian.

Soon after the Stormsender's pact is secured, the party learns that the Regalia has been spotted inside an imperial base. They infiltrate it only to be confronted by Ravus Nox Fleuret, Lunafreya's elder brother and high commander of the Imperial Army. Before the situation can escalate to violence, Ardyn intervenes, allowing the group to depart with the Regalia.

However, the taste of victory is short-lived, as the party learns on their return to Lestallum that Jared Hester, an elderly friend and retainer who aided Noctis's cause, has been killed by the empire as a warning to the fugitive king. The royal entourage infiltrates nearby Fort Vaullerey to whittle down imperial strength and deliver some justice for Jared. During the operation, they are accosted by Commodore Aranea Highwind. After an intense fight, Aranea mysteriously withdraws, and the operation ends without much gain.

Ardyn's Mysterious Motives

In order to make the sea crossing to Altissia, where Lunafreya awaits, Noctis and his companions head toward the site of an old hidden harbor at Cape Caem. There they rendezvous with Cindy, who informs them that the royal vessel there is in need of an overhaul, and that a certain material necessary for the repairs—a rare ore known as mythril—is proving difficult to obtain. Cindy asks Noctis to head to the Vesperpool, a nearby lake and the site of ruins said to contain the ore. But before Noctis can set out, Gladiolus asks to be allowed some time away to take care of another matter.

The party proceeds without Gladiolus, finding the Vesperpool under imperial occupation. In a coincidence now inviting no small degree of suspicion, Ardyn again appears to offer a hand. However, unclear motives notwithstanding, he is unquestionably furthering the party's goals. They are allowed into the ruins of Steyliff Grove so long as they travel with an escort: Aranea, the formidable foe they faced at Fort Vaullerey. Their minder turns out to be a dependable ally in the deep, and once the mythril is safely in hand, Aranea further offers to see the trio to their next destination via dropship, on instructions from the chancellor. The party experiences renewed concern over why Ardyn is so forthcoming in his aid, given his imperial alignment. Despite their doubts, they accept the help and are taken safely to Lestallum.

Parting with Lunafreya

The raw mythril needs to be treated before it can be used, and in exchange for that service, Noctis is tasked with clearing out daemons who have taken up residence in Lestallum's power plant. An anonymous hunter assists with the job. Noctis is impressed with the way this new partner always seems to have his back, eventually realizing that the man behind the helmet is Gladiolus, back from a quest to hone his strength. At long last, all the preparations for the sea voyage are complete, and Noctis departs for Altissia with his three retainers and Cid.

In Altissia, Lunafreya carries out the Oracle's rite of covenant with Leviathan, the Hydraean. The awakened god proceeds to attack Noctis—a trial to discover if he is worthy of the title of True King. The intense struggle leaves Noctis prostrate, and Lunafreya tries to rush to his aid, only for Ardyn to intervene and seal the Oracle's fate with the mortal thrust of a dagger. With the last of her strength, Lunafreya awakens in Noctis the full power of the Kings of Yore, allowing him to stand once more against Leviathan and overpower the god. Though victorious, the strain of using such power leaves Noctis unconscious, and while in a dreamlike state, he is told by Lunafreya that the gods have deemed him worthy and that her calling as Oracle is fulfilled. As the dream fades, she bids him a final farewell.

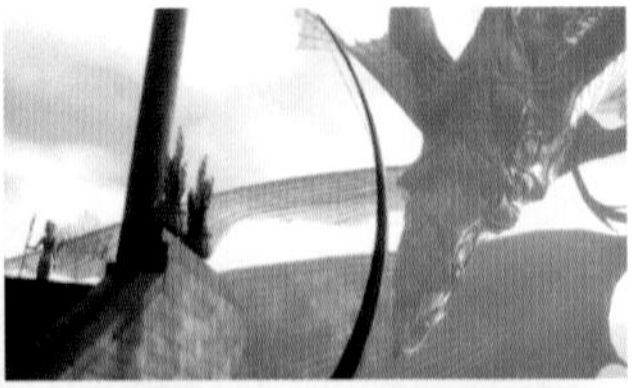

Gentiana's True Form

Though Noctis is finally in possession of the Ring of the Lucii, the conduit for the power of the Crystal itself, and has received the blessing of Leviathan, these things have come at great cost: Lunafreya's body has sunk to the ocean floor, and Ignis has lost his sight. However, Noctis is given little time to mourn, as the party must make its way to the imperial capital of Gralea to reclaim the stolen Crystal.

Along the way, Ardyn's meddling results in Prompto's separation from the group. Hoping to spare the other passengers further danger should the train be attacked again, Noctis and party make a stop at Tenebrae to allow everyone else to disembark. There, they run into a disillusioned Aranea, who provides them with the assistance of her two subordinates, Biggs Callux and Wedge Kincaid.

The train is forced to a halt at Ghorovas Rift. As the party tries to get it back in motion, Ardyn appears once more. Noctis confronts the chancellor, only for Gentiana to appear and freeze Ardyn with an icy touch. Gentiana then reveals herself to Noctis as Shiva, the Glacian, and shares with him the truth of the Star's past.

Ardyn's Intentions Revealed

The tale of the Star is also that of Shiva and Ifrit, the Infernian. Long ago, mankind received the gift of fire from Ifrit, enabling the ancient civilization of Solheim to flourish. For a time, god and man walked together in prosperity, but as civilization peaked, man grew arrogant, and Solheim sought to cast out its patron deity. Enraged by the betrayal, the Pyreburner endeavored to purge the world and all its inhabitants with flame. The rest of the Six stood on the side of man, resisting Ifrit's assault. In what would later be known as the Great War of Old, Solheim crumbled, and the bruised and battered gods retired into deep slumber, leaving mankind with the means to protect the Star themselves.

Shiva departs after entrusting Noctis with knowledge of the Star's past and present, along with her blessing as the Glacian, as promised to Lunafreya. Noctis smashes the frozen Ardyn to pieces, but the suspicious stranger lives on, bemusedly telling Noctis that his friend Prompto awaits in Gralea, along with the Crystal.

Also awaiting the party in Gralea is a horde of vicious daemons. Shortly after arriving, Noctis finds himself separated from his companions and unable to summon his Royal Arms. With no other recourse, he dons the Ring of Light, using its power to make his way through the city. Deep in the capital's stronghold of Zegnautus Keep, Noctis is able to rescue Prompto and reunite with his friends. They defeat Emperor Iedolas Aldercapt, as well as Ravus. Noctis then makes his way alone toward the Crystal. As soon as he places a hand upon it, Ardyn appears and reveals his true objective: revenge against the royal line of Lucis for sealing him away two thousand years ago after he saved their people by taking the scourge into himself. With Noctis ascended as the True King, Ardyn will finally be able to enact revenge by killing him. Noctis listens helplessly as his body is mysteriously drawn into the Crystal itself.

Characters

Ardyn Izunia (Ardyn Lucis Caelum)

Chancellor of the Niflheim Empire. Once meant to become the Founder King of Lucis two thousand years ago, Ardyn lost the Crystal's blessing because of the scourge riddling his body. He guides Noctis along the path to become the True King for a selfish purpose: to slay the ascended king and thus exact his revenge upon the royal line of Lucis, which sealed him away as an immortal monster.

Somnus Lucis Caelum

Founder King of Lucis and younger brother to Ardyn. Ascended to the throne in place of his scourge-ravaged brother. Pragmatic in nature and thus opposed to Ardyn's idealistic labors. As the older brother sought to save the afflicted one by one, the younger endeavored to rule in the manner he believed most befitted a king.

Verstael Besithia

The Niflheim Empire's chief of magitek research. A mad scientist for whom morals are no barrier to progress. Desires above all else to develop and command weapons of supreme power. With Ardyn's assistance, he provides the empire with an army of mass-produced magitek troopers and daemonic creations that serve to hasten the imperial annexation of foreign lands.

Aranea Highwind

Former commodore of Niflheim's 87th Airborne Division. Pilots a distinctive red dropship. Served in the imperial forces as a hired lance until she became disillusioned by the empire's dramatic expansion of daemon-derived technology. Since separating from the military, she travels freely, aiding victims of war and eliminating daemonic threats.

Biggs Callux

One of Aranea's two closest comrades. Has known "Lady A" since her early days as a mercenary, and was right beside her when she joined the imperial service and again when she resigned. Open and unreserved by nature, he's rather talkative with Noctis and party despite their once adversarial relationship.

Wedge Kincaid

Faithfully serves alongside Biggs under "Lady A's" command. Though often finding themselves amid the flames of war, the pair always seem to make it through safely—a testament to their skills on the battlefield. Unlike Biggs, Wedge is somewhat distant and sparing with his words, though occasionally he can grow quite loquacious.

Lunafreya Nox Fleuret

Daughter of House Fleuret, the royal family of Tenebrae. As the current Oracle, she is able to ease the suffering of the afflicted and commune with the Six. Her rite of covenant with the Hydraean at Altissia was disrupted when Ardyn thrust a dagger into her side. Once thought to rest in the slumber of death on the ocean floor, her fate now is not so certain.

Sol (Solara Antiquum)

A young girl who is occasionally quite stubborn but whose bearing betrays a noble upbringing. Of considerable importance to the Niflheim Empire, though initially not aware of her own status. On the day Gralea fell, her evacuation from the devastated capital was entrusted to Commander Loqi Tummelt by none other than His Imperial Majesty Iedolas Aldercapt.

Noctis Lucis Caelum

Heir apparent to the Kingdom of Lucis and the prophesied True King, destined to dispel the darkness that plagues the Star. Initially somewhat immature and inattentive toward others, he grows considerably over the course of the journey he takes with his three close companions. On infiltrating the imperial capital and placing a hand upon the stolen Crystal, he is mysteriously drawn into the sacred stone itself.

FINAL FANTASY XV

The Dawn of the Future

4th Printing

FINAL FANTASY XV

The Dawn of the Future

JUN EISHIMA
THE FINAL FANTASY XV DEVELOPMENT TEAM

TRANSLATED BY STEPHEN KOHLER

Contents

A Savior Lost

M.E. 756

The flurry of footfalls echoing along the cold catwalk came to an abrupt halt. A momentary shudder passed through the runner, who now stood before the sacred stone, bathed in its icy light. His black hair was shaggy, left to grow in any and every direction at will, and his shoulders hung slightly rounded, as if hinting at some wayward nature. His breathing was labored, heavy after his headlong sprint.

"Please . . . Help me stop the daemons." The words seemed wrenched from the boy's throat, his voice ragged. He reached out to touch the stone, but no sooner were his fingertips upon it than his desperate plea contorted into an astonished cry. The Crystal began to pull him in. His expression was frozen in shock.

The boy's observer drew close from behind, struggling to suppress a smile.

"Unharmed by the Light. The Chosen King, indeed."

The young scion was still so lacking. He was little more than a copycat of proper royalty, really. Yet the Crystal did not deny him. It was an irritating reality, further driven home when the boy turned to identify the voice coming from behind him. Oh, how familiar were the contours of that face. His was the very countenance of that ancient false king, never meant for the throne but drawing power from the Crystal nonetheless.

"Allow me to regale you with a tale," the observer said, offering a glimpse of history like scraps tossed to a dog. "In an age long past, an incurable scourge ravaged mankind. A tiny menace that twisted men into monsters, the likes of which you've seen."

The boy's eyes revealed how little he knew of the world. As the story began, a flicker of uncertainty flashed across them. But they quickly narrowed.

Good. Let the anger flow. Let it run unchecked. Wrap yourself in rage and gnash your teeth as you learn how powerless you truly are.

"In Lucis lived a savior that could cure the afflicted. His body would come to host myriad daemons, that countless lives be spared."

Thank you!

Without warning, a long-forgotten voice echoed in the observer's mind.

It was joined by another, this one choked with tears.

Oh, thank the gods. I'm my old self again.

Then more.

Lord Caelum, you have saved me!

Without your mercy, milord, I would have surely remained a hideous monster, struck down by the soldiers of our land.

It is only because of your kindness that I stand here today!

The observer shook his head slightly to dispel the flood. He'd presumed such words had been lost to time.

And what of it? he thought. *That chapter has long since drawn to its close. Should remnants linger, they are of no value or meaning to me.*

He smoothly resumed his tale, inner conflict unbetrayed by outward sign. "But a jealous king, one not yet chosen by the Crystal, ostracized and demonized this healer of the people. Making a true monster of him."

And here, the observer could no longer suppress his smile. The corners of his mouth curled up of their own accord, curved daggers that pierced through all the insufferable bitterness and aggravation that had plagued his life.

"I gave you my name earlier, but you should know that it was not the name given to me at birth."

All those who knew his true identity had long since departed this world. He was known now as Ardyn Izunia, imperial chancellor of Niflheim.

"Ardyn Lucis Caelum is my proper name."

On speaking his own name for the first time in ages, Ardyn was surprised by the potency of the hatred that surged within him. He'd taken it for granted, numbed to its constant, unwavering presence. Yet there it still writhed, that almost-forgotten intensity blacker than darkness itself.

Prince Noctis. His lips began to form the boy's name. He paused, then opted for more familiar address.

"Noct."

The boy's nickname. Uttering it spread a deliciously sinister warmth through him.

"Killing you as a mortal will bring me scant satisfaction. Claim the Crystal's power. Arise as its champion."

This was whom the Crystal had chosen, those fifteen years ago. Here was the young king who, with power of stone in hand, assumed the task of banishing darkness as calamity descended upon the world.

"Only once the Crystal and King are no more . . . can I know redemption."

All had been taken from the man they called Adagium. His brother, his own flesh and blood, had snatched away his hopes, his future, and the woman he loved. He'd lost everything, all because of that damn stone and cursed throne.

Would that it be gone from this world forevermore. Indeed, he would see it destroyed at his own hands. And along with it, everything else: the gods who forsook men without a thought, the Crystal that aided their divine cause, and the whole damn world smeared black with lies.

Ardyn longed only to see it all crumble. This was his sole remaining desire.

"Come back soon. I shall keep your friends company until you are ready."

Your friends. Noctis's face twisted as the words left Ardyn's mouth, his eyes reflecting every single bit of hatred and anger burning within him. And once again Ardyn was struck by a sense of familiarity. He had never experienced the pleasure of seeing such rage in Somnus, but the resemblance really was quite striking. Though his brother and the boy were mirrored in appearance, their personalities and patterns of behavior were night against day, their expressions a study in unending contrast. Still, the resemblance gave rise to a certain yearning in Ardyn: what a delight it would have been to see that duplicitous usurper's features contorted in torment just as Noctis's were now. How Ardyn had longed to watch, gaze ripe with malice, as his brother was erased from the world, powerless against fate.

Yet despite their endless disagreements and confrontations, not once had Ardyn seen his brother's face like this. The only expressions he remembered were those of annoyance, resignation, and disdain.

It was odd. Had he merely forgotten the rest? Had his brother's emotions slipped from his memory with the passage of millennia? Or was there some other explanation?

Brother.

From deep in his mind, he heard one more voice call out to him.

Long ago, when the words of the gods resonated in the hearts of men . . .
Two thousand years before the reign of the Chosen King . . .

"You understand nothing, Brother."

He'd not heard Somnus's voice for so long. The words his brother spoke seemed unusually cold.

"Willfully you disregard the duties of one charged to rule."

No, the chill would have been present for some time already. Anything resembling normal conversation between him and his younger brother had ceased long before then. How many years had it been since he last heard Somnus laugh? Ardyn grimly curled his fingers to count.

As children, they had been close. Between the many hours of study and training, they had enjoyed all manner of diversions together. They were particularly fond of chess. Somnus did not care for the game's prescribed handicap—one piece removed from the elder player's side for each year in excess of his opponent's age. He stubbornly insisted that victory meant nothing if not achieved on equal footing, and no matter how many losses he endured, his resolve never wavered. Ardyn had thought highly of his brother for being so intent, at such a young age, to see justice through.

And Somnus was always at his brother's side. No matter where Ardyn went, the younger boy was close behind. So inseparable were the pair that those who encountered either of them on rare days apart would jest that next they should witness rain falling from a clear sky.

But now . . .

"No, 'dear brother.' *You* are the one who does not understand."

Propriety be damned. He had to stop Somnus, no matter the means.

"Why do you give your men leave to slaughter?" he challenged. "Those they kill are neither beast nor foe. They are our countrymen."

"Countrymen?" Somnus scoffed. "What nonsense is this? They are *monsters*. Leave them be, and they'll start a slaughter of their own!"

"You're wrong. They are no monsters. The scourge is but a disease. Perhaps a bit vexing to treat, but a disease nonetheless. Though afflicted with the scourge, they are still men inside."

The Starscourge was indeed peculiar. Over the past few years, it had begun to spread among the populace. No medical art could cure it, nor could any tonic stem its progress. Those who fell ill were thrust into despair, realizing full well the fate that awaited them. Thus, the scourge was greatly feared among the people. Some declared it a curse; others deemed it punishment from the gods.

But in truth, it was neither curse nor punishment. It was certainly no retribution from the gods. Of that much Ardyn was certain. It was simply a disease. He knew as much *because* it could be cured, though not with any herb.

"Their assaults on others are born from the anguish of their affliction," he told his brother. "The souls inside remain free from blame. We must simply purge them of this disease before they reach that state. In doing so, we may save those nearby from harm."

The scourge brought transformation. The body grew black as jet, and the mind was lost to madness, causing the victim to lash out at anything nearby. Those most firmly in the clutches of the Starscourge were pronounced daemons and restrained before they were beyond control. Daemons were kept apart from the community . . . and eventually killed. Ardyn endeavored to treat the afflicted—to return them to their former selves—before that happened.

"I see no difference," Somnus spat.

"How is it not different?"

"Whether or not a plague is to blame, the fact remains that you alone are able to heal it. Not even the greatest physicians in our land can hope to imitate whatever it is that you do. Isn't that right, Brother?"

It was true. For reasons unknown, the gods had entrusted this healing power to Ardyn alone.

"Tell me, what can a single man hope to accomplish?" Somnus asked.

"Every life I touch means another soul delivered from the scourge."

"And as you save that one, how many others fall ill?" Somnus seemed to taunt him now. "Five? Ten? Ever will the scourge outpace you, Brother. You labor in vain."

"No, that's . . . " Ardyn faltered. *That's not true*, he'd wanted to say, but his brother's words stung as such.

"What will you do for the towns you are too late to save?" Somnus continued. "When the land is full of daemons, will you continue to try to treat them one by one? Better to end them now and stay ahead of the scourge before it brings ruin to us all."

"You speak of human lives!"

But Somnus smiled in triumph. To him, the argument was already won.

Ardyn continued to plead with Somnus, thinking of the men and women he'd seen struggling to hang on to the minds they felt slipping away, terrified by their own disfigured appearances.

"They have done nothing wrong!" And they hadn't. They simply bore the misfortune of some malady that had found its way into their bodies. "How can you strike them down when they are free from trespass?"

"Ever the dreamer," his brother sneered. "Sentimental hopes do not foundations form. To stand strong, a nation must be grounded in reality."

"And so you would take the easy way? The coward's path?"

Somnus's voice grew as hard as steel. "You try my patience, Brother. Indulge the people if you must, but I cannot allow you to lead them astray. Kin or not, I will not tolerate seeing my name and acts besmirched."

Ardyn did not respond. He could not. There was murder in his brother's eyes, and for the first time, Ardyn felt his own life might be in danger. A small part of him berated his own ignorance; these notions had clearly been brewing within his brother for some time. How could he have missed it? They were siblings. He should have known the man's mind and temperament better than any other. Somnus would look to any means to achieve his goals. So had he always done. Whatever he set his mind to, he saw it through to the end, no matter the cost.

Ardyn realized he had to flee, had to hide. He could not die just yet. Too many lives remained in the clutches of the scourge. They needed his help. He had to keep on living, regardless of all else, until the scourge ravaged their people no more. It was his calling to see the world cleansed.

"You look exhausted, my love. Are you all right?"

Graceful hands cupped his cheeks, as pleasant as the voice that accompanied them. Their touch was sweeter than the wind that combed through the golden wheat, warmer than the sunlight filtering between the green leaves as Ardyn sat in the shade of a great tree, resting against its trunk.

He spoke her name, eyes still closed. "Aera."

He felt his weariness lift. The haze in his mind vanished, like mist dispelled by the morning sun. True, the seeds of worry still lingered; his last conversation with Somnus had ended sourly, and it was possible to imagine that his life might be in danger. But with Aera's hands upon him, he found the determination to go on. He would hold his head high.

"Thank you, my love," he said. "But you needn't worry."

It was strange. Every time he was struck with longing to see her, she found her way to him. Ardyn opened his eyes. Her golden hair fluttered in the breeze, the light reflecting in her eyes. They were the color of the sea, the loveliest color he'd known in all his days.

"I thought that if I waited here, I might have a chance to see you."

"I felt the same."

Aera smiled. Seeing that smile was enough to fill his chest with warmth. But he thought also of the lives that had fallen to the scourge. Each of them were meant to know love one day. Each were meant to have a special someone who made their heart leap, whether their paths had crossed already or had yet to do so.

And what a wonderful feeling it was to stand with the one you loved, to face life together, hand in hand. Everyone should have the chance to know that happiness. It was an irrevocable right of life. That was the purpose of the powers entrusted to the two of them by the gods, her power to hear and his to heal. Together, he and Aera must see that no one lost their chance to know love.

"The gods blessed me with a power and a purpose: to cure people of what ails them. I must see their will be done."

Ardyn looked down at his outstretched hands. Aera laid hers upon them.

"Your devotion shall not go unnoticed. The gods will doubtless be watching over you."

Somnus had asked what one man could hope to accomplish against the Starscourge. But Ardyn was not alone. Aera was with him, and together they would carry on.

"It seems to me," Aera ventured, "that the cure for your exhaustion is comprised of two things, one of which is rest."

"And the other . . . ?"

Her cheeks flushed ever so slightly, and a trace of mischief danced through her eyes.

". . . is me," she finished.

Ardyn chuckled, then embraced his love.

"Oh, Aera," he said. "Pray be with me always."

At her nod, all his fear was gone. No matter what became of his flesh, he would carry out his calling until the end. No matter what Somnus said, he would not relent. If Somnus thought his words could stay Ardyn, he would be sorely disappointed.

"Milord! We have yet to locate your brother. However, we continue to scour the area, and—"

Somnus waved the man away, interrupting the report. He'd heard enough. Over half a month had passed since his last argument with Ardyn. His brother seemed to have determined that further talk would be fruitless, stealing away to gods knew where.

Irritation, resignation, scorn—Somnus bitterly recalled the final expressions he'd seen cross his brother's face. Ardyn was a man beloved by the people. They would have him as their king, leading their newly founded nation with the favor of the gods. Perhaps Ardyn's anger and frustration were a sign, reflecting feelings hidden in the hearts of the people.

However, despite the hope placed in him, Ardyn was woefully unsuited to rule. He lacked the ability to see the world for what it was. He was too trusting, not just of his fellow men but of the world itself. His eyes were ever fixed upon the good. Admirable, perhaps, but it kept him blind to less desirable truths.

Of beauty alone was no man or object sculpted. Kneaded in with the clay were cunning, ugliness, and filth. Was that not why the rule of law was needed? Such dark strains had to be kept in check. Was that not the duty of a king?

"That's precisely it," he muttered to himself. "The quality most needed in a king is a firm hand. To dote upon the people only ensures that the nation shall be forever weak."

And a nation had to be strong. It had to be secure. For the sake of its subjects, it had to be ready to repel any incursion. A clan of men gathered in one place did not a country make. But a clan was still all they had, and that under constant threat of these cursed daemons. The promise of safety required troops who were prepared to wipe evil from the world. Somnus was the one to raise those troops. To harden, hone, and lead them.

"My feckless brother is blind to the truth before his eyes . . . "

Ardyn always talked of another soul delivered, saved by his own two hands. But his method would not suffice to save them all. Only some saved meant many more were not, and in the end, Ardyn's path served only to put the choices of fate in the hands of man. His was the way of one who had never doubted his own position in the eyes of the gods. A man in whom all others placed trust and saw promise. A man chosen for everything. To Ardyn, the thoughts of those who had not been so blessed were and would always be a mystery. He would never know how it felt to be passed over in favor of another. He would never know how the forlorn gazed upon the chosen.

And so you would take the easy way? The coward's path?

Somnus scoffed. Why should ease be equated with cowardice? *His* was the way most just. He would not choose whom to deliver or cast aside from among those touched by the scourge. He would not foster despair and envy in those condemned to a horrid death. No one would be forced to wonder why they had been abandoned when others were not.

It was cold, yes. But it was fair.

Somnus stood to leave.

"Lord Caelum, shall I accompany you?"

He did not turn but replied, "Stay. I'll not need an escort."

The woman he sought would be in the sanctuary, the gods' words perhaps gracing her ears at this very moment. Aera, the Oracle. Aera, the woman of his brother's heart. Somnus needed to speak with her, and with haste. He had to ascertain the truth and then plot his course.

Somnus clenched his hands into fists. The thoughts hung heavy in his heart. But there was no other choice. It was something he needed to see through, even if it meant dirtying his own hands.

"I shall not ask forgiveness," he vowed to himself. "Nor do I expect to ever receive it."

Far beyond the fields of wheat rose a column of black smoke. Ardyn looked upon it, his expression strained. It was not hard to imagine what was burning there.

How could anyone be so callous?

In truth, he knew the answer to his query all too well. To Somnus, the innocents burning in the distance were no longer people. Perhaps the man even saw Ardyn as one among the monsters now. It would explain how easily he justified sending men to hunt down and kill his own brother.

The previous day had brought another close call. A single night's lodging, in a town already cleared of the scourge, and still the soldiers came. Ardyn had underestimated Somnus, and it had almost proved to be his undoing. The younger Caelum seemed to keep watch everywhere. Perhaps no settlement, no matter how small, was safe.

Fortunately, Ardyn had seen the dust kicked up in the distance by the soldiers' approach, and he ran. There was no doubt in his mind that had he tarried a moment longer, he would now be in custody, dragged back to the castle like a dog to be thrown at his brother's feet. It was the people's regard for him that kept him unharmed; they'd shown him a safe route, and he'd fled deep into the cover of the nearby woods.

Through the dim light beneath the trees, Ardyn ran like a beast hunted, until at last, when his strength gave out and he was unable to push his legs any farther, he huddled in the hollow trunk of a great sentinel of the forest. There, he waited for his pursuers to abandon their search. It was nearly dawn before he heard the distant piercing cry of a captain's whistle and the woods were finally free of the soldiers.

He continued to hide for some time, huddled motionless in his paltry shelter of bark… Oh, how weary he felt. The past few days had been spent healing several unfortunates deep in the clutches of the scourge, and that had taken its toll.

At the root of the plague they knew as the Starscourge was some manner of parasite.

Somehow, it found its way into hosts, where it wreaked its havoc. Eventually, the hosts lost their minds to the scourge. Those gone that far were pronounced daemons and reviled.

But thanks to the blessing of the gods, Ardyn's hands knew how to draw out the root of the scourge. They pulled the darkness from the victim's body and brought it into Ardyn's own. Cleared of the disease, the patients regained consciousness. Their skin, once black as jet and exuding the scourge's dark miasma, would regain its former hue. And Ardyn would carry on, host to another bit of scourge himself.

He was no stranger to the experience of the disease. In fact, he may have understood it more fully than anyone else. In addition to the ability to absorb it, the gods had given him a mind unaffected by the scourge's insidious influence. They had not, however, seen fit to bless him also with the power to cleanse himself. The scourge ever remained, never lessened, simply drawn from others and into him. Each time Ardyn saved another soul, he was forced to accept that pain and suffering as his own.

At first, he'd felt no more than a faint malaise. But with time, it grew to become a most unpleasant sensation and then finally a clear and piercing agony. The larger the swarm of organisms within him, the harder they were to suppress. They thrashed about until he thought they might tear a hole through his skin. They felt *alive*, like some manner of parasite worming inside him.

For now, the scourge remained in check. But he knew not whether his body would continue to hold as he drew yet more in.

What can a single man hope to accomplish? Somnus's words clawed at his mind. All too well did he know the loneliness of his struggle.

How many more victims would he be able to heal before he succumbed? How long would he be able to endure the pain?

What will you do for the towns you are too late to save? When the land is full of daemons, will you continue to try to treat them one by one?

Once more, Ardyn cast his gaze across the fields of wheat, at the smoke of countless lives brought to an end for naught more than the misfortune of having known the scourge. First beaten and abused, now they were reduced to ash and scattered to the wind, with no rites spoken over them.

Ardyn shook his head. Such atrocities must not be allowed to go unanswered. He had to keep moving forward. There were people seeking his help. He was needed at their side.

He tried to rise and leave the shelter of the forest, determined to continue on his way. But his body, riddled with scourge, would not obey. He pitched forward, unable to throw out a hand in time to arrest his fall. And then he was on the ground, lying with his face in the dirt. No strength came to his limbs. He felt the tiny creatures squirming around beneath his skin. It was hard to draw breath.

Finally, his vision grew dark. Black. The same color as the daemons themselves . . .

"Stop, Lord Caelum!"

Somnus did not reply. He shoved the female attendant aside and put a hand on the sanctuary door.

"The Oracle mustn't be disturbed! No one must interfere with the ritual!"

He brushed away another set of grasping hands and pushed his way inside. He knew the precepts. The Oracle was here, listening to the words of the gods in the hour of their people's need, and she mustn't be disturbed. He would dare to do so regardless.

As other lords voiced their support for House Caelum to lead the realm, the gods, too, sought to select a ruler from among the house's men. An absolute sovereign to sit atop the throne of the world's first kingdom. There were two candidates.

"Lord Caelum, please! You mustn't!"

Somnus closed the door behind him, shutting out the attendant's shrill cries. Aera, kneeling in prayer at the altar, lifted her head to see who had entered. Her expression was a mix of surprise and confusion.

"Hail, Oracle."

At seeing Somnus, her features hardened with suspicion.

Somnus continued, unfazed. "What say the gods?"

Aera did not answer, so Somnus shifted his approach. "The Crystal, then?"

"The Crystal has no will of its own," she finally replied, tone flat.

Did she intend to evade his questions? Perhaps she could see right through him. Or perhaps the Crystal had provided no answers. It mattered not. Neither would impede his plan.

"Spare me the nuances of its workings. I only care to hear the message."

"... Very well. If you desire it, Somnus, you shall have my trust ..."

Her gaze fell upon him, calm and true. Somnus met her eyes. He would not look away. He would deliver his words with confidence, even if they were riddled with lies.

"I am to be your brother in marriage. Need I desire to have your trust?"

Aera's gaze grew more piercing yet. "I am the Oracle, tasked with making the will of the gods known."

She paused, letting him feel the weight of what might transpire. She had a duty to uphold. The truths handed down by the gods were not something to divulge lightly.

"Of that I am well aware. I am not so bold as to defy the will of the gods. However . . . "

Here, Somnus paused, at the point of no return.

No, he thought. *I will not turn back. This is a decision already made.*

"However," he continued, "my brother's whereabouts are currently unknown. The rift between us is of my own making, and if I do not see it bridged, the gods' words shall fail to reach his ears. Surely you see how finding him would aid both my cause and his—as well as your own calling, Oracle."

Her gaze had been so sharp, he thought it might bore straight into his skull and see the truth buried there. But his entreaty made it waver and fall. Somnus imagined the nights Area spent without sleep, wracked with worry for her beloved. The brief moment of uncertainty was all he needed.

"I would send for my brother," Somnus announced.

"You know he would not come."

"If my envoy bears a message from the gods, he will believe. He will come."

Aera's gaze lowered still farther. After a moment, she looked back up, staring directly into his eyes. She seemed to have reached a decision.

Ardyn awoke. His mind was thick with confusion. He found himself indoors, lying in a bed. The room felt vaguely familiar, and yet not.

"Oh, thank the gods. Lord Caelum, I'm so glad to see you awake."

A young woman peered down at him. Her face, full of concern, jogged his memory. He'd been in this room several days ago. The same woman had lain here, hands and feet bound, growling like a wild animal. She had been badly afflicted with the scourge, and Ardyn had healed her.

"My father and I," she said, "found you collapsed on the ground when we were on our way to town. You can imagine our surprise."

Ardyn recalled fleeing from the troops sent by Somnus and concealing himself in the forest. But everything beyond that was blank. He must have wandered around blindly during that lost time, ending up near the same town from which he'd fled.

"You . . . saved me?" he asked.

"You give us far too much credit, milord. We merely loaded you onto our cart and brought you here. Pray forgive us such a crude means of transporting you."

The woman's shoulders slumped. Her cheeks, now back to their former healthy hue, flushed with embarrassment. Ardyn remembered their pallor after he'd removed the scourge. It had concerned him at the time, and he was glad to see her looking so well now. Back then, pale as she was, her parents' eyes still had welled up with tears, overflowing with joy when they saw their daughter's mind restored. That alone had been reward enough. Drawing in the Starscourge was a small price to pay in exchange for a chance to bring such happiness to others.

"I owe you a great debt for your kindness."

"Not at all, milord," she said with a smile. She'd taught him anew what it meant to help those who suffered. There was no time to laze about in bed. He had to move on. But when Ardyn tried to lift himself up, the world began to spin.

"Lord Caelum! Please, you mustn't! You have yet to regain your strength!"

"There's no time to wait," he said. "So many others are out there, still in anguish . . . "

"And in such a state, I'm afraid you'll be of no use to them."

"Nevertheless, I must go. I must help the people."

The sound of armored boots treading the earth came from outside. The young woman's parents burst through the door. Ardyn needed only to see the looks on their faces to know whose men were approaching.

"Hurry, milord!" the mother implored. "You must flee!"

"Troops from the castle. They're almost upon us!"

Somnus's men yet again. Ardyn managed to steady himself and rise to his feet. He cared not about preserving his own life, except that his death meant an end to the people's only means of deliverance. He recalled the column of black smoke, and his heart grew heavy once more. He readied himself to face the troops, but the young woman slipped past his side and rushed outside first.

"What business have you here?" she demanded. "Lord Caelum is ill!"

She stood braced in the doorway, arms flung wide, showing no trace of fear despite the soldiers now surrounding the building. Her small frame exuded uncanny courage. *No one gets past*, she seemed to say. *Not a step closer to Lord Caelum than where I stand.*

Ardyn placed a hand on her shoulder and drew her back inside. She reminded him of Aera, though physically they did not look the least bit alike. It was the girl's spirit, so like Aera's on that day they'd vowed together to deliver the people from the scourge. When he'd seen that resolve in Aera, he'd felt that as long as she were with him, he'd be able to continue, no matter how difficult the journey grew.

"Lord Caelum?" the young woman asked.

"Please, that's enough. You've done so much for me already."

He would not burden this household any further. He could not bear the thought of their happiness being stripped away again so soon after he'd managed to restore it. They would not suffer on his behalf, even if that choice meant suffering of his own.

"But, milord!"

"I will not forget your kindness to me," he said, and walked through the doorway, each step unsteady.

Outside, he caught sight of a banner emblazoned with that all-too-familiar crest. Beneath it stood men in armor bearing the same. He could have never imagined the day would come when the symbol of his own house would signify the enemy.

What order had Somnus issued? Kill on sight? Or perhaps he wanted his brother taken alive, to be brought captive back to the castle?

The men did neither.

"Lord Ardyn Lucis Caelum, son of House Caelum!"

Ardyn could not believe what he was seeing. These were the same men who had chased him through the dark of the woods one night prior. Now they knelt before him.

"Last night, the word of the gods was heard. Ardyn Lucis Caelum, you have been chosen to serve as king!"

A cheer rose up around them. Ardyn realized that the villagers had been watching the exchange from afar.

The members of House Caelum and their retinues were gathered in the Crystal's sanctuary. All were present, from Somnus and Aera down to the lowest-ranked soldier, all in full ceremonial garb.

"Lord Ardyn Lucis Caelum, son of House Caelum!"

The ranks lifted their swords in unison. The crowd opened a path for Ardyn as he approached the Crystal's altar.

Somnus, kneeling at the forefront, abruptly stood.

"That will be enough. The charade stops here."

Somnus wore a look Ardyn had never seen before—one he would not have believed possible of his stubbornly fair-minded younger brother.

"I'm ashamed to call you my kin," Somnus began. "Is there no low to which you will not stoop? You flee and cower in the shadows, then stride back here as if you were a hero. Do you truly covet the throne so desperately?"

Ardyn was stunned. It was his brother who had sent the men and their message. The same men who had, not a day earlier, been out to take Ardyn's life. Who was Somnus to speak like this?

"I was merely on a journey to heal the people," Ardyn said. "I have no thirst for power. I do not seek control over the land." Then he added, "Unlike you, 'dear brother.'"

Ardyn had not once desired to sit the throne. Such power was only a means to an end. If the title of king bestowed the authority to reach more of the people and end their suffering, if it meant that no one could interfere with his calling, he would take it. That was all. That was why, when told he'd been chosen, he'd returned home.

"Ever does that mouth of yours twist the truth in your favor," Somnus spat. A flash of blue, and he stood with sword in hand.

Ardyn found himself confronted by the gift of blades, as bestowed by the gods upon House Caelum. Weapons summoned at will, now brandished by brother against brother. Ardyn knew he could stay Somnus if he must; the power was split evenly between them.

"It was me, Brother. I was chosen by the gods!" Somnus raised his sword high and brought it crashing down.

Ardyn prepared to catch the blade with his own, when another voice rang out.

"Stop!"

Aera leapt before him.

"Aera!" he shouted.

Her body caught the flash of steel, and she fell. And to Ardyn's eyes, the whole world was bathed in red.

Cold. Dark. Pain. They were everything. There was nothing else.

He was in a place deep underground, one never to be graced with the sun's rays. Thick chains held him fast a dozen times over, allowing him not even the tiniest movement. And beyond the chains, beyond the walls of his stone cell, the sea extended in every direction. There was no escape from this place.

Angelgard. An island long revered by man. A place where the gods used to gather. The tides and winds pulled strong here, as if they were incorporeal guards stationed to keep mortals away. Days fit for a ship's landing came but a few times a year, he'd heard. Even if he managed to break the chains and force his way free of the stone, he'd have no means to return to the mainland.

Why?

For some time after his imprisonment, it was the only question that ran through his mind.

Why am I here? Why am I still alive?

He saw the weapons—spear and sword—still lodged in his flank. As they'd slipped in, red blood gushed out, as it would with any mortal man. But the blood stopped far too quickly, and the wounds closed up. *Around* the steel still lodged in his body.

"He's become the monster I knew he would be . . . "

Somnus's final jeer echoed in his mind.

No. The daemons were not monsters. They were simply victims afflicted with disease. That they returned to normal when the scourge was lifted from them was proof enough.

To save them, he'd simply had to remove the scourge residing within them. But what of himself? What of the scourge residing in the man who healed others? Filled with more Starscourge for every soul he saved. What would happen to him?

Ardyn had felt in some vague way that he'd not be able to contain the scourge within him forever. That if he continued to absorb the darkness from others, he'd eventually lose his mind and lash out at those around him. He, too, would one day be a daemon.

"Your devotion shall not go unnoticed. The gods will doubtless be watching over you."

Yes, Aera. The will of the gods must not be questioned. They work in mysterious ways—ways which our feeble minds could never fathom. So, too, did I believe.

"Stop!" she had screamed, before the blade ended her life.

Aera, no! Oh, how foolish you were. Why did you lay down your life to protect me? Me, the monster who can never be struck down.

Worse still for her to die at the hands of a coward. A man able to raise his sword without a trace of guilt against an opponent unarmed and unaware. How could such a man be allowed to sit the throne?

Thus was sown the first seed of doubt about the gods and their ways. When Ardyn held Aera as she slipped from the world, as he climbed the altar stairs and reached a hand to the Crystal, he'd felt so certain. A man who slaughtered innocent lives was fit not for ascension to the throne but to be cast down by bolts of judgment.

Gods, now is the time to deliver thy wrath! Please let us see your true will!

With all his strength he'd prayed. Surely this sacred stone bestowed by the gods would set everything right. Surely it would light the true path forward. It had to.

But Ardyn's wish was rejected. The Crystal's harsh light knocked both he and Aera away.

"By the authority of the crown," Somnus had proclaimed, "I, Somnus of House Caelum, hereby announce the establishment of the new and righteous Kingdom of Lucis. Know ye that henceforth, anyone who turns their sword against Lucis shall not live to see another day!"

Ardyn lay crumpled on the ground as Somnus, suffused with the pride of victory, struck him with those words. He did not even think to stand. He couldn't. He lay motionless, with no desire to move.

If this was the will of the gods, to name a king who massacred his own people at the mere suspicion of scourge, had all Ardyn's labors meant anything at all?

"See that this traitor is dealt with at once!"

"Traitor"? Must you still carry on this charade? It was your plan all along to kill me. So desperate were you to have me draw my sword that you ended Aera's life.

Somnus had killed her, their devoted Oracle so attentive to the will of the gods, all to see his own mad ambitions through. And *still* the gods did not punish him.

Could the gods truly be so blind? Is the heaven in which I placed all my faith filled with fools? Or was Somnus so cunning that he deceived the gods on high?

Had Somnus known? Perhaps his grab for the crown preempted the Oracle's revelation. It seemed ample reason to see her mouth forever silenced. But if he had yet to hear the will of the gods, then why the ruse? Aera surely would have voiced her upset as Somnus arranged the ceremony. Which meant . . . the gods must have chosen Somnus.

How had Aera felt when she learned of the gods' will?

"The gods will doubtless be watching over you."

No, Aera. The man the gods chose pays no heed to his people. He thinks not but to sate his own desires. We two will not be watched over. The gods have abandoned us.

Or perhaps Somnus had no need to deceive the gods, and they simply cared not at all. Why should a god show concern over life and death among men? The fact that one man alone possessed the power to stay the scourge, or that a murderer sat the throne—perhaps all such things were but idle diversions to the gods.

Was it only for heaven's amusement then that Somnus had ascended, Aera had died, and Ardyn now spent his days as a monster locked away in darkness? If so, life was a farce. Somnus was out there, his throne more comfortable with each passing year, reveling in his power and doing as he pleased. All the while, his subjects suffered, ignored in the shadows.

But . . . what of it if they suffered? What made them worthy of care and protection, that Ardyn should lay down his own life to provide for theirs? Somnus's men had looked upon him with eyes full of fear and disgust. "Monster," they'd spat, as they thrust their blades in him with no trace of hesitation. Monster, indeed. Doubtlessly even the people whose illness he'd healed would treat him the same once he turned into a daemon. "Ardyn the Savior," they'd cheered, "Lord Ardyn Lucis Caelum, destined to be our king." Hands that had once clapped for him would grasp for stones to hurl at him and drive him away. It had been a mistake, perhaps, to try to deliver them from the scourge. Maybe everything he'd known and done, from the very beginning, had been in error.

Anger festered in him, of a kind different than what had ignited on Aera's death. This was a quiet rage. It grew bit by bit, threatening to consume him from within, until there came a day when nothing but rage was left.

Down here, he would have all the time in the world to brood. To foster his hatred.

M.E. ???

Ardyn knew not how much time had passed, how many years he'd hung in chains. Decades, perhaps. Surely it couldn't have been centuries.

Oh, Aera. I'm so weary. There is nothing here. No windows through which light may shine. No doors opening to the outside world. Only cold walls of stone on every side.

Once Ardyn had been securely bound in his prison, Somnus had sealed up the only entrance with layers of stone.

Living on in that empty place, unmoving, merely existing, had grown so tiresome that Ardyn began to yearn for death. It was torture anew—another thing he longed for but would never have.

Please, my love, do not let melancholy cloud your face . . . Yes. I know, I know. You are but an illusion. It is my mind alone bringing such sorrow to your brow. But I'm afraid there is naught else for me to do here.

If only you'd lived. If only Somnus's sword had not found you, and we'd fled to some faraway land to grow old together.

No, in the end, he'd have suffered all the same. Though she could pass into death, he could not, and the day would still have come when he held her lifeless form, weeping like a fool. Because he chose to absorb the scourge and bring succor to others, now he hung in darkness alone. An endless suffering for he who sought to end suffering. The greatest of ironies, all because of the preposterous power thrust upon him by the gods.

"Forgive me."

Aera? Why are you apologizing? You've done nothing wrong.

"Forgive me."

No. Stop. You mustn't say that. Please, my love. I would remember your smiling face. Smile for me, lest I forget that face forevermore.

"Forgive me."

No. Why can't I remember? Why can't I call your happiness to mind?

"That's hardly a surprise." Now it was Somnus's voice. "You're a monster, Brother. Happiness is beyond you."

Curse you, Somnus! Begone! Why do you still plague my mind?

"Foolish woman."

Silence! Enough with your arrogance. Enough with your constant disparagement of those you think beneath you. I know you for what you've always been. Do you?

"And why should a king not look down on those he rules? The quality most needed of a king is the ability to subjugate. To dote upon the people only ensures that the nation shall be forever weak."

Begone!

"I was chosen by the gods, Brother! *Me!*"

Why did this specter continue to haunt him? Somnus's was the face he least wanted to see. Everything in this dark prison was but a figment of his mind. So why would his brother not go away? How did he always manage to return of his own accord?

"You would turn your blade against the king?"

Yes, he most certainly would. If the king and the gods that named him could be felled, he would most surely do it. But so many years had passed already.

Dear brother, he began.

You are already dead.

He hung for ages in that endless, boring existence. If only someone would come to kill him, to bring an end to this interminable tedium. He craved death's sweet release. He wished to be gone from the world, to be free from the endless workings of his mind.

Anyone. I care not who. Please end me. If it can be done, end this entire world.

I'm so very tired...

M.E. 721

There was a rasping sound, like steel working against stone. A slight wrinkle formed on Ardyn's brow. *Leave me in peace*, he'd meant to mumble, but his throat produced only a hoarse moan.

The rasping ceased and silence returned, but only for a moment. Next he heard boots marching across the ground. Dozens of them... No. Of course there had been no sound, Ardyn chided himself. It was a figment of his imagination, one among the countless that haunted him every day.

After hanging imprisoned for so long, constantly mulling over the events of the past, imagination and reality had become blurred in his mind, and the line between the two was difficult to draw. On the many occasions he was visited by Aera's figure and voice, he was certain he felt her breath and the warmth of her body.

Thus, the footsteps and the voices they carried were easy to dismiss as a fantasy or dream.

"Good, Brother," Somnus said. "You know your fate well. No man shall ever set foot in this place. I have decreed it so."

Still his brother's voice came. Still he failed to banish it or drive it away. Nothing vexed him more thoroughly.

There were more footsteps, closer this time. Shouts accompanied them.

"Watch it!"

"This way!"

"Keep your eyes open!"

What was all this *noise*?

When Ardyn's gaze drifted upward, lazily, still without any real interest, it was met with a sudden, blinding pain. A stream of searing torture assaulted his eyes.

Light.

For the first time in how many hundreds of years—no, much longer still—he was bathed in the uncaring, relentless wash of light. His other senses suggested men present in the cell, surrounding him, but he could not confirm by sight, as his eyes remained squeezed shut against the glare.

"He's alive!"

Ardyn heard a laugh.

"Just as the ancient texts told!"

Of what did this man speak? Who *was* he?

"Who . . . ?" With great effort, Ardyn forced the one word out. Its tenor was unfamiliar. Either his throat had warped with the long years of silence, or more likely, he'd simply forgotten the sound of his own voice.

Suddenly, he was falling facedown. The chains and restraints had been severed, and Ardyn, unable to support his own weight, went crashing unceremoniously to the ground. His arms and legs lay limp, unresponsive to his will.

Then, in another instant, he felt pain in his chest and flank. The weapons embedded there were being pried free. It was a rough, ripping sensation, underscoring the fact that the blades had become one with his flesh as the ancient wounds healed over.

"Take him away!" The command came from the same man who had laughed earlier. The order—and its tone—made his position in relation to the others clear.

Ardyn felt his body rise. Hands gripped him from either side.

"Don't touch me..." he said.

He wanted to brush the hands away, but not a one of his fingers would heed his mind's commands. Concentrating every bit of strength in his body, he could barely manage to raise his head slightly. It was a pathetic display.

Still, when his eyes finally grew accustomed to the light, the new angle allowed him glimpses of the men who had brought an end to his isolation. The two carrying him seemed to be rank-and-file soldiers. They were clad in curious garb, unlike anything he'd seen before. But they carried themselves in the manner of trained troops. Of that he was sure.

Somnus would have been long dead. Perhaps the men were under the orders of one of his brother's heirs.

From some distance away came another voice, this one strange, somehow inhuman.

"Status report." It was accompanied by a crackling noise, like kindling in a growing fire. The noise and the voice's hollow quality made it difficult to sift out the words.

"We'll have the medical team ready as planned. We're ju—!"

There was a noise like distant thunder, then silence.

"Shit. Move!"

What the cause for upset was, Ardyn could not fathom, but he felt the men at his sides quicken their pace. The edges of the light at his feet began to blur. Cold crept across the uncovered skin of his shoulders and torso. He gathered his strength and lifted his head a bit higher, now able to see almost straight ahead.

They were headed toward a rectangular opening—it was a door to the outside. The *outside*. He could *see* it. New sounds echoed from beyond the doorway. Heavy objects colliding with each other. Shrieks of pain.

"We knew they'd come. Keep moving forward," the leader ordered, his voice low.

Who else was here that this man had expected to encounter?

The next instant, the world stretched out around him on all sides. The sky was the color of ink swirling its way through a vessel of water. It might have been dawn, or perhaps it was day and the weather harsh. Still, it felt unbearably bright to eyes accustomed to an eternity of darkness.

A little farther ahead, several figures stood facing them, clad in black, with weapons held at the ready. At their feet lay several men in armor identical to that of the soldiers at Ardyn's sides.

Suddenly, the hands were gone, and he was pitching forward again. He heard the men to either side of him groan as they both crumpled to the ground. Their defeat had come so easily, Ardyn wasn't sure if it was a sign of their weakness or their enemies' strength. They *were* enemies . . . weren't they? Clearly there were two factions at play here, but Ardyn had no idea which was friend and which foe.

He found the strength to rise from the ground and observe his surroundings, more annoyed than curious. One of the men clad in black barked out, "Adagium sighted!"

Another word he didn't understand.

"Get it back in the cell—no matter what."

Ah, they're speaking of me, he realized. *Is that what they call me? "Adagium"?*

"We can't let that thing off this island!"

Tiny objects zipped through the air, rushing toward him. Pain streaked through his side.

"Stop . . . " he moaned.

His chest seared with agony. It was some manner of assault he'd not encountered before, but the pain itself was the same as he'd experienced so long ago.

"Cease this . . . " he pleaded.

His flesh tore, his guts spasmed. These were sensations he hadn't felt in ages. Sensations he'd desperately wanted to banish from memory.

"Cease this at once!"

Anger welled up from deep inside him. He felt the fresh wounds closing. A man with short swords clenched in both hands rushed at him, and Ardyn's arms rose to intercept the blow. It should have been a fruitless defense: Ardyn had no weapon but his bare fists. Instead, he flung his attacker away. The man's body spiraled through the air, swords spinning away in opposite directions.

"Unbelievable. He really is a monster . . . "

In a flash, Ardyn found himself on top of this other soldier—the one who had called him a monster—and was pummeling him into the ground. He'd heard the insult so many times he ought to have been numb to it, yet at its sound his blood boiled.

"Who did this to me?" he demanded.

Why did he have this monstrous strength? He had never wished for such a thing.

"For what sins must I atone?!"

Rage filled him, and another man who happened to enter his field of view found himself its target. Ardyn made a fist, into which seemed to flow every bit of anger he possessed. His knuckles drove deep into the man's body. His bloodcurdling cry echoed in their surroundings.

Then time stopped.

To Ardyn alone, the world was frozen. The barren stone landscape of Angelgard was replaced with a new scene, a summer day bright enough to leave him dizzy. Large white boxes were neatly aligned atop gray earth. Pillars in the ground flickered with red and green lights in curious shapes. It was strange. Baffling. And stranger still was the means by which the images came. He saw them not with his eyes: they arrived directly in his mind.

"These memories are not my own . . . Could they be *his*?"

His wife stood beside him, a smile on her face. A small hand clutched his own. He felt another small weight and the warmth it exuded draped across his back. It was his family. It was . . . the family of this man beneath him.

Other memories came in succession. A deluge of scenes.

Lucis.

Insomnia.

The king.

"Graaaugh!" Ardyn could do naught but shriek and stare. This man—this soldier—was a subject of the kingdom built by Somnus. The Kingdom of Lucis, now ruled by its 112th king, Mors Lucis Caelum. Descendant of House Caelum. No. Descendant of *Somnus*. "This man . . . belongs to . . . "

Ardyn's vision shifted once again. The flood of images had stopped, and now, under his gaze, lay the man he'd beaten to the ground. Except he was a man no more. From black sleeves protruded hands equally as black. Diseased skin with which Ardyn was well acquainted, along with the languid black haze he knew it to emit.

"I didn't purge him of the scourge; I bestowed it upon him . . . " he said to himself in disbelief.

He looked down at his own hands. When he'd driven them into the man's body, they'd seemed suffused with his anger. He could still feel it. And that concentrated rage seemed to have turned this man into a daemon. His mind reeled at the prospect.

His entire life, he'd labored to deliver the people from the scourge's grip. Even if it meant becoming a monster himself, every life touched still meant another soul delivered.

Now, rather than saving a soul, he'd infected one. Now, his body was a vessel that poured the scourge into another. It was too great a contradiction for his mind to accept.

"Incredible!"

Beside him, clapping his hands in a decidedly exaggerated fashion, was the pretentious man who had ordered Ardyn taken from the prison of stone. He seemed to have withdrawn to a safe distance during the scuffle, waiting to see how things unfolded.

"His power's unbelievable!"

Ardyn studied the man more closely. His silver hair was carefully slicked back, and his uniform heavily adorned. He very clearly was of a different pedigree than the men he commanded.

As the man strolled closer, he threw his arms wide. His features retained a dignified reserve, but his eyes radiated a strange intensity. This was a man to whom morals meant nothing, one of those who dreamt of atrocious schemes and cared not what price they carried. He was a man of Somnus's ilk, and Ardyn wanted nothing to do with him. Ardyn tried to move away but found his limbs unresponsive once again.

"Hey!" the man exclaimed as Ardyn fell.

But his voice was already far away, and blackness closed in on all sides.

M.E. 722

His eyes opened to a familiar vista. Ears of wheat gently bowed in the wind, the field extending as far as he could see. Above them stretched the evening sky. Aera stood beneath the outstretched boughs of their tree.

Oh, Aera, how I longed to see you. The real *you. Not the pathetic imitation conjured by my mind. How I begged for one more chance to be with you. Come, let us sit in the shade and talk as we used to do. There is so much I have to tell you.*

But as he ran toward her, she was not smiling as she should have been.

"Aera!"

She was somber, gazing at something over his shoulder. Ardyn turned. Somnus was there.

"Forgive me, Brother. But the throne seats only one!"

Why do you still go on about the throne? Unless . . . you were never meant to sit there?

"Stop!"

A longsword flashed into Somnus's raised hand, and Aera threw herself in front of the blade as it came crashing down. Crimson welled from the wound. Ardyn stood frozen, unable to do anything at all.

"Why . . . ?"

This last whispered word came not from Ardyn's mouth but Aera's. It seemed strange. Shouldn't he be the one to ask why? But he felt certain that back there in the sanctuary, it had been Aera who spoke that word. What had she meant?

Ah, of course. This is a dream. The same dream as always. I've seen it so many times, it's more vivid than reality. An ancient tale, still unfolding right before my eyes. Her body in my arms, growing cold.

"Gods, no! Aera . . . !"

He awoke with a start. A dream that was all too real was now replaced by a reality that could have easily been a dream. The ceiling above him shone with an unnatural luster. The bed in which he lay did not smell like a bed. The room around him was cluttered with furniture. Every object in sight was much too gray and had shapes that were far too straight and uniform.

Ardyn rose from the bed, but the strange room did not vanish. That alone seemed to prove that this was not a dream. A sigh escaped his lips. Would he never be free from this unfathomable world?

"Ardyn Izunia." A metallic voice rang out with such perfect timing, he had to imagine its owner waiting patiently for the sleeping man to wake. Ardyn flicked his gaze about, searching for the speaker, but he was alone. Then he remembered: it was one of this world's many devices meant to carry voices from afar. The contraptions had been absolutely baffling to him at first, but time saw him develop a modicum of familiarity with them.

"Chief Besithia would like to see you."

What drudgery. Of course Chief Besithia wished to see him. The man always did, and every interaction was a chore. Verstael fancied himself single-handedly responsible for waking the ancient monster sealed at Angelgard and returning it to the modern world. Worse yet, he now assumed his new pet to be at his constant beck and call. From the moment Ardyn had been carried into the facility, the poking, prodding, and questioning had been ceaseless. He'd have refused, had his weary body and mind not deemed resistance the greater nuisance.

I wish he'd give up, Ardyn thought, *and leave me be. There isn't anyone I wish to speak with. There isn't anything I wish to do or any place I wish to go. I'd be content enough back in the monotony of that stone prison.*

He did not, however, make any of those thoughts known. Trying to do so would have been a tedium of its own.

"Might as well head out."

Each footfall was accompanied by a faint, hollow tap. He'd somehow managed to accustom himself to the dreadfully uncomfortable shoes everyone wore. But the clothes still irked him. They cinched at his waist, constricting around him in a way quite unlike any other garment he'd known. Any movement of his arms was accompanied by an unpleasant tugging at the shoulders. He felt restrained. Pinned down. As he continued down the hallway, he grumbled to himself, "I daresay this outfit wasn't tailor-made."

He knew that such comments would scarce resolve his complaints. Such garb was common—even expected—by the people of this "year 722 of the Modern Era." Ardyn passed through a great sliding doorway made of some material even colder than the walls of his ancient stone cell: just one more strange and off-putting experience for him that, to everyone else in this world, was so regular as to pass unnoticed.

The troopers posted at seemingly every door and in every hallway were all clad in the same uniform, faces indistinguishable under the same masked helmet. It made the people, too, seem strange and unnerving, as if they were not men at all, and this place devoid of all life beyond Ardyn himself. Perhaps that, too, contributed to the ever-present blurring between reality and dream.

He trudged through a long corridor until he reached the doors at its end. This "research lab" of theirs was a place of simple, straightforward design.

When he opened the doors, he found a room empty of researchers save Verstael, who sat stiffly in a high-backed chair at a dining room table. The man extended a hand without rising, his movements theatrical as always. Repeated exposure to the man's mannerisms and speech had not bred familiarity so much as barely suppressed irritation.

"Come. Have a seat," Verstael invited.

The spacious table was laden with a lavish array of dishes. "I thought we might enjoy a nice chat over dinner."

Ardyn lowered himself into a seat at Verstael's urging, but he was uninterested in the food. He'd been served countless meals since his arrival, and as with the garb, he found them strange and unpalatable. The things piled atop each plate looked unapologetically artificial. Bread rolls in a nearby basket were the only items he saw that he felt certain were edible.

"Are you not going to eat?" Verstael asked.

When Ardyn didn't respond, the man continued, unperturbed. "You've been asleep for years. Learning to appreciate the waking world again will take time."

Ardyn had no appetite. He saw no reason to force himself to consume objectionable food. After all, he did not risk death for lack of it.

"How long has it been since you brought me here?" he asked.

"Two hundred and four days," Verstael responded. "Roughly seven months or so."

The revelation surprised him. Had it really been that long? Ardyn reflected on what had happened since his arrival. Aside from periods spent under observation, attached to the strange equipment that filled the facility, he'd spent the majority of his time asleep. Perhaps that was how the days had passed so quickly.

"Then again," Verstael mused, "the Lucians had you locked away in that prison for nearly two millennia. I'd be more surprised if you *hadn't* lost all concept of time.

"You must loathe those Lucians for what they did to you," he added.

Ardyn gave only an irritated sigh in response.

It was not that he did not care, but he had little need of a lecture on the subject. Verstael had neither ties to nor understanding of the matter. Ardyn found his smug air distasteful, and he had no desire for the man's sympathy.

"Was your examination of me a fruitful one?" he asked.

Verstael and his researchers had poked and prodded to their heart's content. *Something* better have come of it.

"Oh yes. You've proven far more fascinating than expected. No wonder they kept you locked away. To think the powers of a daemon could dwell within the heart of a man. It's incredible!"

Verstael was all too excited to explain, as if he'd been waiting desperately for Ardyn to broach the subject.

"The Starscourge doesn't sap your life force. It gives you more! Your cells can regenerate themselves, and you can daemonify other life-forms as well. There's no doubt. You are—"

"A monster," Ardyn finished.

"Not a monster. A *marvel*."

All a matter of wording, Ardyn thought.

Whatever words were used to describe him, it did not change the fact that Ardyn was something other than human.

"I can't wait to unravel all your mysteries," Verstael continued.

"What is it you want from me, anyhow? What about me interests you so?" Ardyn asked.

"We need those powers that you possess. With your strength on our side, we could finally put an end to the gruesome war with Lucis."

An end to the war. Put more bluntly, the goal was to see all of Lucis's lands under the empire's control. The man never could settle for direct expression.

"You, too, must desire the fall of the kingdom that cast you into exile?"

Verstael seemed to peer into his mind as he spoke, and Ardyn found it incredibly disconcerting. He stood from the table and turned his back on the other man.

"My desires are all in the past." Ardyn's reply was curt.

When he'd first learned how long he'd spent in the depths of Angelgard, he was stunned. It was no longer an issue of whether Somnus was alive or dead; this world wasn't even aware of what had transpired all those centuries ago. The Kingdom of Lucis had no record of a man named Ardyn Lucis Caelum ever existing. So what did he stand to gain by dredging it all back up? And even if he'd wanted to, what means did he have to take action?

"The man who wronged you may have died long ago, but his descendants live on to this day. Surely you must bear them some feelings of ill will?" Verstael prodded.

Ardyn turned to glare at the man and the infuriating smirk he wore.

"My feelings are none of your concern."

He took no care to hide the scorn in his voice, but Verstael seemed unfazed. Quite the opposite, he appeared to believe Ardyn's response an indication that he'd been right all along.

"Come along," Verstael said, rising from the table. "There's something you should see."

Ardyn could have chosen to ignore him. To walk away without another word. He couldn't imagine a thing in this world now able to catch his interest. Yet he followed obediently as Verstael made his way down the facility's other hallways.

"I found something most interesting on the Rock of Ravatogh," the chief said.

Something I should see. Something most interesting. The fact that Verstael was able to entice him suggested that, somewhere deep inside, Ardyn still possessed some spark of curiosity. He'd spent two millennia locked away on that lonely island. And though the days outside wore on, for Ardyn time had been at an unchanging standstill. It would have been a lie to claim he had no interest whatsoever in the world's course over all those centuries.

"This way."

And many of the objects that filled Verstael's laboratory were admittedly striking. There was a miniature panorama fashioned after the face of the Star itself, a thing quite beyond the drawn atlases Ardyn had known in his own time. Verstael had called it a "model," describing it as "how the gods must feel, looking down upon our world." On examining it, Ardyn had found Angelgard. The island where he'd spent two thousand years in captivity was but a speck, hardly larger than a pebble in the grand scale of the world. The mainland shore that had seemed so impossibly far away was now separated from the island by just a thin line of blue. All the lands Ardyn had known in his own time—his entire world—occupied but a fraction of Verstael's modern map.

Aside from the model, there were the specimens—daemons harvested for study—and great paintings, stretching from floor to ceiling on the laboratory's vast walls, that depicted the events of the *Cosmogony*. The displays were all grand, but they never seemed to have visitors to entertain or enlighten other than Ardyn. They seemed to exist largely for Verstael's own amusement.

Soon the corridor narrowed and canted downward at a steep slope. Ardyn felt as if he were walking through a giant, angled tube. It was a strange, unsettling sensation.

"Right down here," Verstael coaxed.

They reached a dead end to the tube, and Verstael placed his hand upon the metal surface with a knowing smile. There was a shriek of shifting metal, and the dead end was no more. It was like no door Ardyn had seen before, but it was a door nonetheless.

On the other side was a vast, open space. Verstael strode in and stopped, gazing at something beyond and below. Ardyn realized the room was divided in half by a long, transparent wall. He'd seen such partitions in other areas of the facility. Usually they were placed at right angles, forming boxes to house the labs' many specimens: creatures stripped of their flesh, bare skeletons, and other such oddities.

This one must have served a similar function on a larger scale. But there was another type of object he'd not encountered before: huge cylinders extended at a downward angle from opposite walls. They each expelled a steady stream of white mist.

Ardyn drew closer to the partition. Peering in, he discerned a large, humanlike shape lying flat on the ground, shrouded in the mist. The shape may have been human, but he'd known no man even half so large.

"Is that . . . ?" Ardyn began, only to trail off.

Verstael grinned. "Ifrit, the Infernian."

For a moment, Ardyn thought he'd misheard. The huge figure, however, seemed of a size befitting an Astral. The being that lay there would have had no trouble crushing a man in just one of its enormous fists.

"You subjugated a god . . . and brought him here?"

"He was sound asleep, just like the legends said he'd be, so we put him on ice."

After the War of the Astrals, the gods, having used up all their strength, were said to have fallen into a deep slumber. The spot where the Goddess of Ice lay became a region of bitter cold; the bed of the Infernian, a mountain spitting fire.

"Do you think you could turn him?" Verstael asked.

Ardyn's eyes widened. Turn a *god* into a daemon? It was absurd. Beyond fantasy. Something only a madman could conceive of.

Verstael continued to probe. "You're able to keep the memories of those you daemonify, yes?"

At some point during the many hours he'd been under observation, Ardyn had spoken plainly of his experience on Angelgard, when the memories of the daemonified soldier had flooded into his mind. Perhaps it was a detail he should have kept to himself.

"If you manage to daemonify a deity, you could learn truths no mere mortal could ever dream of knowing. It's certainly an enticing offer, isn't it?"

"How so?" Ardyn asked dryly.

"You'll access two thousand years of his memories, and if you can control him, he'll be a weapon of supreme power. Just think. You could exact sweet revenge through divine retribution!"

Ardyn cut him off. "How do *you* know what I want?"

Revenge? On Somnus's descendants? The very idea was absurd.

"I don't," Verstael responded. "But I know you have no other options."

Ardyn did not care. Anger and hatred still burned within him, as strong as ever. But too many years had passed. He was centuries removed from the age he knew. Nothing he did now would matter.

"Suit yourself. This was not the only thing I had to share."

At Verstael's urging, Ardyn proceeded down another corridor. Nothing sparked his interest. Everything was gray and bland and devoid of life. All of it had so little to do with himself. Still, this seemed somehow better than returning to his room. He half listened to the scientist's ramblings as he slowly trailed behind.

The bottommost level was a large hangar area. From its size, Ardyn guessed it was used not only to store but also to test the weapons and large mechanized suits Verstael adored so much. It stretched on and on, several times the size of the room housing the dormant fire god. The ceiling, too, was several times higher, and in that vast space, Verstael's animated voice began to echo, much to Ardyn's annoyance.

"Do you spend *every* waking moment thinking about daemons?" he asked the man.

Ardyn had meant it as a jab, but Verstael responded with a broad smile and deep nod. "Aren't they wondrous creatures? I *adore* their strength! So utterly does a daemonified entity surpass the pitiful constraints of a human. I envy you."

"You *envy* me?" Ardyn asked.

"A human life is too short to truly understand all there is to know about the world. If my time on this star spanned millennia like yours, oh, the things I would do!"

Ardyn would have gladly handed over the burden of eternity if he could. But scarcely had the thought formed in his mind before it was disrupted by a crashing sound and the sudden sight of several black shapes dropping to the ground. The intruders rose, and Ardyn knew them for what they were: the same forces that had attempted to intercept his extraction from Angelgard. The Lucian Royal Guard. Soon more were arriving in the hangar, warping in one by one from somewhere outside.

"Lucians! But how?!" Verstael spat, face twisted with malice, but the soldiers ignored him.

They moved quickly, surrounding Ardyn.

"So you've come to kill me, have you?" he asked. It was a question that hardly needed an answer; he remembered the words of those he'd encountered on the island. *Get it back in the cage—no matter what.*

"Or die trying," a woman's voice answered all the same. Her features were obscured, and she resembled Somnus not in the slightest, yet suddenly Ardyn found himself staring at Somnus's face.

Maybe the association was logical. She was, after all, a Lucian—a subject of the kingdom established by Somnus and watched over by his successors.

But it was more than that. Though the weapon she brandished was a far cry from a longsword, her movements were strangely familiar. When she rushed in to strike, he saw his brother's footwork. His brother's hands. Why? Why did she seem like . . . ?

"Because it *is* me, Brother. I'm here, come to kill you."

It was Somnus's voice. Again. The same voice that had taunted and tortured him in the depths of Angelgard.

"Just as you would kill me. Right, Brother? Well, I'm afraid to say you'll never know the satisfaction of taking my life."

"Silence!" Ardyn screamed.

He raised his arm to block the incoming blade. Pain ripped its way through his flesh, but he did not care. The wound would close soon enough.

"I'm already dead, and have been for some time," Somnus continued.

With a violent shake, Ardyn dislodged the sword from his arm. It went clattering across the floor—along with its black-clad wielder. She still wore Somnus's face.

"Though I may be gone, my legacy lives on in Lucis!" his brother taunted. "It lives on in the minds and hearts of the soldiers before you."

"Enough of this! Begone!"

Ardyn's red blade flashed into his hand, and he slashed at the soldier. From her chest—from *Somnus's* chest—came a fountain of blood, and then she lay in a heap on the ground.

Another Somnus rushed him from behind.

"While you were lost in slumber, I was busy building a kingdom! What sort of legacy have *you* left behind, Brother?"

"Silence! Away with you!"

He matched blows with Somnus after Somnus, blade swung with such ferocity that it lodged in the floor at his feet and gouged chunks from the walls. Still his brother would not disappear. "Where's that backup?!" a voice shouted, far away and faint.

An explosion roared through the facility. The lights went out, but the darkness was momentary, soon dispelled by the glow of red flames spouting through a great hole in the far wall.

"Blast! The cooling unit!"

Light from the flames flickered across Verstael's anxious expression. His eyes were wide, and for a moment, Ardyn forgot about the soldiers all wearing his brother's face. He followed the researcher's gaze.

There was something unnatural about the flames. Pouring through the gaping rent in the wall, they were now scorching the high ceiling of the hangar. They twisted and writhed as if they possessed a will of their own. The black smoke billowed upward, filling the room, and as the flame and smoke intertwined, they formed the nebulous shape of a giant arm.

There was a splintering noise, and the fire spread farther. The giant arm broke through more of the wall, and a body wreathed in flames passed through, landing on the floor of the hangar. In its other hand it held a giant, fiery sword.

"He's awakened!"

Ardyn finally understood the reason for Verstael's panic. The explosion must have been the sound of the cooling unit rupturing. With the ice melted, there was nothing left to restrain the Infernian.

"We must stop him before he destroys everything!" Verstael yelped.

There's little chance of that, thought Ardyn. This was a god. Verstael and the others were now dealing with something quite apart from a once-human monster.

The Pyreburner spoke, his words strange and haunting. The language was impossible to parse, but the god's tone was clearly not a friendly one. His giant blade came smashing down, engulfing the floor of the hangar in a sea of flames. In an instant, the Lucians in their black garb were naught but ash.

Out of the corner of his eye, Ardyn saw Verstael bolting away, a shrill shriek escaping his lungs as he fled. The fact that he was running at all was a testament to the malevolent man's luck.

Ardyn stared up at the Infernian, making to neither flee nor fight. Verstael's earlier words floated to the forefront of his mind.

Do you think you could turn him? Just think. You could exact sweet revenge through divine retribution!

With the passing of two millennia, Ardyn had thought his lust for revenge long withered. Somnus was dead. Killing his descendants seemed to serve little purpose.

But his mind and heart were at odds. The anger and hatred had never left him; still they smoldered deep in his breast. That was why the Somnus of his mind—the illusion that had taunted him—said the things it did. *My legacy lives on in Lucis. It lives on in the minds and hearts of the soldiers before you.* Somewhere deep inside him, Ardyn longed to see an end to the Lucian line.

He was so wrapped up in these thoughts that he failed to notice the motion of the god's flaming hand. It was too late to run. Soon he was in the grip of a fist that could crush a man with no effort. There would be no escape. No matter how much he struggled, he would not break free of this grasp. Ardyn had only one means to resist.

"Power . . ."

He funneled the darkness—the *rage*—into the palm of his hand.

"O Infernian, grant me the power to take Somnus, his people, and his cursed kingdom . . ."

The same sensation he felt when he'd turned those soldiers into daemons surged through his arm. The Pyreburner's great frame shook. Soon Ardyn felt his own body ablaze, ignited by the Astral's unquenchable heat. Yet Ardyn's hold did not slacken. His fingers dug into the deity's arm.

" . . . and burn them all to the ground!"

The Infernian fell to his knees. "Fool!"

The cryptic sounds coming from the Astral's mouth began to convey meaning. The words of the gods were no longer a mystery to Ardyn.

The hand clutching him slackened, and he was cast to the floor. No doubt the process would take far more time with a god than it would with a man, but the scourge was beginning to take hold.

"You dare to subjugate the divine?!"

Ifrit's memories flowed into Ardyn's mind. He witnessed the moment when man was given fire, and the days when civilization enjoyed the Infernian's patronage. Solheim dawned and flourished, its technology ascendant. Man grew arrogant. Then betrayal. Rage. The Great War of Old. The Six subsiding into slumber.

Beyond that, there were memories of the Crystal. Ardyn was fascinated to learn that it not only relayed the words of the gods to the Oracle, but also served as means for the sleeping gods to observe the human world. The realization came in bits and pieces, as he observed faint images that could not have been lived by the Infernian himself.

He saw Aera, kneeling before the Crystal. She wore an expression unlike any he'd known in his countless imaginings at Angelgard. It bothered him that there was any side to her he didn't know.

"Aera!" he called, though she could not hear.

The head bowed in prayer tipped back suddenly, as if with a gasp. Her face seemed to radiate joy. Her eyes were wide, and her cheeks were flushed pink.

When Ardyn caught the image reflected in her pupils, he was stunned.

"No . . . How could that be?"

It was his own face swimming in her eyes. There could be no doubt. Aera was seeing his image in the Crystal. The meaning was clear.

"I was the one chosen to be king . . . ?"

The gods had not selected Somnus.

"Why . . . ?"

It was the word she'd spoken during that final confrontation in the castle. It had played back endlessly in his mind, a swirling uncertainty that finally made sense. Her final, soft utterance as her life slipped away. The question she'd asked when the Crystal rejected Ardyn's outstretched hand.

This was what she'd not been able to understand. Why had the Crystal turned away the man chosen to be the Founder King?

Two thousand years' pondering had bestowed on him some clues. Clearly the gods had, at one time, settled on the man who cared for his suffering people. They'd seen him most fit to serve as king. But as he absorbed more and more of the scourge into his body, he became something other than a man. He acquired strength not meant for mortals, a power so unnatural that it offended the Crystal. Or perhaps it was the scourge itself that the Crystal could not suffer.

In any case, the choice of the gods and approval of the Crystal were in contest. Perhaps it was an oversight on the gods' part; perhaps they cared so little for man that the error slipped by unnoticed.

It was a development not likely foreseen by Somnus either. To him, it must have appeared as a great stroke of fortune. Surely the people assembled there saw what transpired and deduced that Ardyn had not been chosen. All that would have remained for Somnus was to silence the only other voice aware of the truth. With the Oracle gone, there would be no one left to convey the knowledge that Somnus had never been granted the gods' favor.

The Crystal faded from view, and Ardyn found himself standing amid a vast expanse of flame. If what he'd witnessed was the truth, then that meant…

"It was Somnus's lie that killed you!"

Aera floated before his eyes once more. At some point in his cell on Angelgard, he'd lost the ability to envision her smiling. Now, too, her face was clouded with sadness.

"Forgive me."

Why do you apologize? It was all a trap laid by Somnus.

"I defied the will of the gods and revealed to Somnus you had been chosen to be king."

No. It was Somnus's cunning. His scheming pried the revelation from your lips.

"It's *my* fault. I'm the one who ruined your future!"

You were deceived! That is all! You've no sins to atone for!

But no matter how strongly he objected, she refused to acknowledge his protests, as if even now, in death, she remained entangled in Somnus's wiles.

"In the names of the gods above… fulfill your calling, Ardyn, and punish me for my sins! Kill me!"

Why was *she* the one to suffer pangs of guilt? The one who must pay was Somnus, not Aera. Somnus was the one who deserved death!

"Too bad," his brother announced. "I'm already dead, and have been for some time."

Another Somnus appeared before his eyes. Another trick of the mind he could neither kill nor send away. This was the man who had deceived everyone, who had killed Aera and usurped the throne. No number of deaths dealt to him could ever be enough to see justice served. Yet he would never die at Ardyn's hands. How could such a travesty be allowed to stand?

"This monster may not be able to destroy you, but I'll see to it that I destroy everything you built!"

The nation. The bloodline. He'd destroy it all. Just as the name Ardyn Lucis Caelum had been expunged from history, he'd see to it that Somnus Lucis Caelum and everything connected to him was eradicated.

In an age past, Ardyn had believed himself called upon by the gods to save the people. Now, he'd have to kill them.

"Hear me, gods above! No longer shall I supplicate you for pardon."

Gone was the obligation to obey the gods who failed to see through Somnus's deception.

It was the gods who had allowed Lucis to flourish, who brought no punishment down upon it.

"No longer shall I sojourn toward the light. Nay . . . the path I intend to tread is paved with blood and darkness."

His faith had been unwavering. He'd lived for the people. Now he saw what a fool he'd been. His faith belonged with no one else. He'd seek strength only for himself, labor to see only his own desires filled.

And the only desire he had was for revenge.

He would agree to Verstael's proposition and aid the man with whatever he desired. It would be a means to see the end of the Caelum bloodline and the destruction of the Kingdom of Lucis.

"No longer shall I seek your guidance. This path is mine to tread alone."

As Ardyn thought of Lucis and all the many ways it would be brought to ruin, a great burst of laughter welled forth from deep within him. It was some time before the laughter stopped.

"Verstael, this is the man of whom you spoke?"

"Yes. Ardyn Izunia, Your Radiance. He has proven to be of vital importance to our technological progress."

Ardyn kneeled respectfully, his head bowed. An audience with Iedolas Aldercapt, emperor of Niflheim, was not a thing granted lightly. Yet the emperor's gaze wandered aimlessly. He seemed to have little interest in his visitors or their news.

Just a short time ago, the response would have undoubtedly been quite different. House Aldercapt had long aspired to see the glories of Solheim restored to the world, and of all its members who had sat the throne, Iedolas was the most ardent proponent of magitek development. Merely a hint of a plan to speed production of their prized new infantry should have been enough to secure his rapt attention.

The lukewarm response was likely tied to tragedy: his empress had passed, freed now from the burden of her mortal coil but leaving her husband alone and despondent. They'd had only one child between them—a boy not yet a year in age, and thus much too young to soothe his father's sorrow.

Still, in a sense, Iedolas's despair was quite fortunate for Ardyn. The man was beloved by his people as being both wise and just—perhaps more the former than the latter. He endeavored to rule over the people fairly, but his real talent lay in shrewdly guiding the growth and development of his nation. In other words, he was calm and his decisions were rational. It was a fact that, until now, had been a slight inconvenience to Ardyn.

But when a man has lost something that cannot be replaced, his judgment tends to suffer. Reason knows no greater enemy than a sense of loss.

Ardyn wanted desperately for Iedolas to covet more, to greedily grasp for things beyond his means. On that point, he and Verstael were in full accord. The researcher was eager to see more of the empire's budget dedicated to military expansion, and Ardyn wished the emperor to grow more bold in his conquests—and thereby hasten the downfall of Lucis.

"The studies we conduct on the daemons bring us great advances in development, Your Radiance. But we are equally indebted to this man for the materials and information he provides."

At Verstael's grand introduction, Iedolas finally deigned to look Ardyn over. However, in all likelihood, he felt less interest in someone of Verstael's recommendation than annoyance with the researcher's incessant talk.

"Your Majesty." Ardyn stood, interrupting Verstael before he could launch into further address.

The scientist shot him an irritated look. *This is not*, he seemed to say, *what we agreed upon.*

"Pardon my candor, but I wonder if perhaps Your Majesty might have interest in a way to stave off death?"

Ardyn was taking a chance by disposing with formality, but he'd decided it was the best way to pique the emperor's interest. Since his wife's death, the man had undoubtedly been addressed with the utmost delicacy by all who approached him.

"Stave off death, you say?" Iedolas raised an eyebrow.

Hook, line, and sinker. There was nothing more effective than the loss of a loved one to kindle a hatred of death and the desire to cheat it somehow. Wise and just Iedolas might be, but in the end, he was still a man. His loss and yearning would drive him to take action, no matter how rash.

"Yes, Your Majesty. In truth, study of the daemons and the scourge will open the door to more than just might. It is a key element to discovering the secret to immortality."

Ardyn peered into the emperor's face. He'd dispensed with protocol altogether.

"Just think," he continued. "A body that cannot perish. The means to reign for time everlasting. Doesn't that sound magnificent?"

In Iedolas's eyes, until then dull and lifeless, a fire began to burn.

M.E. 725

With the prospect of immortality dangled before his eyes, Iedolas agreed to most everything that was proposed. Ardyn found it an almost trivial matter to lead the man around as he wished.

Ardyn provided the daemons and Verstael conducted the research. The discoveries and inventions were progressing more rapidly than ever before, and soon they were creating myriad new machines of war. Never for a moment did Iedolas doubt that the techniques used to fashion weaponry would one day also pave the way to his fountain of youth. So the money kept flowing, copious, to keep the research moving forward.

Ardyn had already been installed as chancellor, which brought him freedom to travel both within the empire and without, along with ample amounts of authority.

He urged the emperor to take an aggressive stance on Lucis. Countless numbers of Niflheim's magitek creations were sent to the front lines, managing even to take down a portion of the Wall. Lucis was forced to pull the barrier back to Insomnia's borders, so that the king could see it strong enough to resist further assaults. The empire then moved its forward forces to occupy the lands at Insomnia's doorstep, and with those new bases as footholds, Ardyn ventured forth, daemonifying the former subjects of Lucis with the scourge and thus adding to his store of knowledge about the kingdom.

The murder of innocent lives brought him no feelings of guilt. The objections and criticisms he'd once cast at Somnus were gone, along with the self that had voiced them. Now, to kill was an act of no great import.

He was steadily climbing toward his goal of vengeance, on a stairway built with the blackened bodies of the Lucian people.

M.E. 734

His driver was not a particularly talkative man. It struck him as unusual. Most taxi drivers chattered on incessantly from the moment you entered the car, as if afraid to let you get another word in once you'd given your destination. The passenger ended up spending the ride with his mouth shut out of necessity, not volition.

"In other news . . . "

Because this driver was of so few words, Ardyn could hear the radio broadcast in perfect, uninterrupted clarity.

" . . . a member of the border patrol has been reported MIA since sometime before dawn this morning."

It was a mildly inconvenient time for this particular story to break. Ardyn decided a bit of prudence might be wise. Men with guarded tongues often boasted sharp ears.

"The missing officer has been identified as twenty-eight-year-old Mars Sapientia."

He rubbed at the tiny splatter of blood on the ID badge at his chest. For such men, sometimes it was not only their ears that were sharp. Ardyn briefly considered keeping a hand over the name on his badge for the remainder of the ride. Perhaps he could cross his arms and keep the badge concealed with that casual gesture. In the end, he did not try. A person's memory was a fickle thing, plagued by uncertainties. Ardyn knew that better than any. A name repeated over the radio would be gone from a listener's mind in minutes. No, an awkward attempt at concealing the badge would draw more attention than not.

"Although Officer Sapientia allegedly reported for duty at his appointed time, fellow officers say he disappeared soon after and has not been sighted since."

At the reporter's last line, he wanted to laugh, but carefully held back. The border patrol could search all they wanted. They'd not find their poor officer. The real owner of the guise he now wore had been a daemon for hours. Mars Sapientia no longer existed as a human.

Ardyn did not remember when he'd found himself capable of this particular trick or how, but over time, adopting the appearance of others had become second nature to him. Maintaining the guise of Officer Sapientia was no particular strain, and it was something he intended to keep up for the duration of the day's events.

Should he happen to run into any of the officer's acquaintances, the knowledge he'd gained from the man as he transferred the scourge would keep the secret safe. Even Mars's closest friends wouldn't be able to see through the ruse. Ardyn knew everything about him, down to the tiniest quirks.

Suddenly there was light, as the car came out of the long tunnel into the sunlit city. Ardyn grimaced slightly and turned away from the window. He normally took great pains to keep the sunlight from his skin, but the typical uniform of the border patrol left his face exposed. Well, that wasn't quite right—a regulation faceguard would have been standard with the uniform, but it would have seemed a rather conspicuous choice inside the taxi. Ardyn leaned forward, pretending to be absorbed in the sights of Insomnia straight ahead, and in doing so, kept himself that much farther from the window and the rays that streamed in.

He'd not walked the streets of Insomnia before, but he knew the city well, its layout absorbed bit by bit with each soldier of Lucis who fell at his hands. Most men in the border patrol had set foot here at some point, and among Ardyn's "informants," there was even a man who had once been granted an audience with King Mors. Others had fought on the front lines under the command of Crown Prince Regis.

Or rather, *King* Regis. Mors had passed some five years ago, and it was Regis who now sat the throne. Ardyn smiled at the irony. He perhaps knew more about the Crown City and its doings than any of the kingdom's residents.

"What about you?"

It was the driver's voice that interrupted his reverie. The man's words took a moment to register.

"Shouldn't you be lookin' for your buddy?"

Of course. The missing soldier. So the driver had been paying attention to the radio broadcast after all. He'd failed, however, to notice the name on Ardyn's badge. Typical.

"Oh no," Ardyn replied casually. "I'm on special assignment."

The taxi was already cruising through downtown Insomnia. This seemed as good a spot as any.

"Pull up over there, if you would."

No sooner was the door open than he found himself plunged into the bustle of the city. There was laughter, faint strains of music, the sound of cars rushing this way and that. Ardyn climbed out. The sunlight stung. It was a revoltingly fine day.

"Home sweet home at last."

Two thousand years. Not a trace remained of anything he'd ever known. Gone were the golden fields of wheat, the birdsong, and the smell of soil carried upon the breeze. Instead, he saw skyscrapers and streets of gray, lined by rows of trees spaced with artificial precision. And everywhere the kingdom's banners flew overhead.

"So this is the city Somnus built," he mused to himself.

People thronged the roads and plazas, eagerly celebrating the founding of his brother's kingdom.

"Built on the back of his own flesh and blood."

All those around him were caught up in the atmosphere of revelry, spirits high, so oblivious to the truth of their homeland. Everything they knew and cherished was built atop a foundation of lies and betrayal. How little they knew of their history. How little they knew of *anything.*

"Just look at them, free of care and unaware of the war beyond their Wall," he sniffed. "What need is there to worry when brick and mortar blind them to the suffering outside?"

Surely the residents of the district of Galahd in Cavaugh had once thought the same. Never had they imagined a day might come when their happy home would no longer be protected by the Wall. Yet, nine years ago, the barrier keeping Lucis's enemies at bay was scaled back to the ramparts of the Crown City, and Galahd enjoyed the protection of the Wall no more. Demise was ever a swift thing. It might arrive without warning, yet even if there were signs, no one ever paid them heed. The creature known as man was all too eager to avert his eyes from the unpleasant.

"Trapped within these walls, they cannot even see how wide the world truly is."

Beneath this sliver of blue crowded by skyscrapers, the citizens of Insomnia chattered away with empty heads. They'd never known hunger. They'd never known cold. They hadn't even faced the terror of disease. They were fools to the last, and nary a thought had entered their minds beyond where they might turn for their next moment of excitement, their next laugh.

"What a dismal existence."

Amid the laughter and music came the chirp of a loudspeaker. "Welcome to the Founder's Day Festival. In a moment, the parade will begin making its way through the city."

Ardyn smiled. He'd show them something more exciting than rank after rank marching down the streets. Soon the whole city would dance in red. A garland of flames for every man, woman, and child. Together, they would celebrate Insomnia's demise.

"Now let the fireworks begin!"

His right hand shot into the air, to summon forth Ifrit, the God of Fire. Soon fear would fill the city. The Infernian would be a storybook myth no longer. The people would stare upon the god with their own eyes, and then they would tremble and scatter in glorious panic.

Yet nothing happened. The citizens around him continued their merriment, vapid expressions intact.

"Oh dear," Ardyn mumbled.

In fact, no one had even paid his now-embarrassing display the slightest attention. Well, almost no one. There was a single small child staring at him, a look of confusion on her face as Ardyn stood with arm still upstretched.

"That's odd."

Ardyn tilted his head, but the mystery was soon solved. A chorus of screams arose—but from a wholly unexpected direction. The ground rumbled in the distance, and he heard the shattering of glass and shriek of twisting metal coming from buildings nearing collapse. From a side street in the distance licked tongues of unearthly flame. And then the Pyreburner was there, on the grand boulevard for all to see, fire curling around his colossal form and the massive blade he wielded in one hand.

"Oh, cursed be the wavering whims of the gods," he moaned. Though a daemon under Ardyn's control, the Astral yet managed to carry out commands only in the ways he saw fit. He refused to come obediently when summoned and seemed always a wild stallion, ready to throw off the reins and run mad at the slightest opportunity.

"Oops," Ardyn said, jumping to one side.

Jagged bits of rubble pierced the spot where he'd just stood. The Infernian continued to attack whatever portion of the city was closest to hand. The daemon god seemed wholly unconcerned as to whether the wreckage would fly in Ardyn's direction.

Tides of flame surged across road and plaza, charring black anyone whose flight was not sufficiently swift. Shrieks of panic no longer filled the air. Now Ardyn listened to the agony of death: anyone near enough to hear was either forever silenced or soon to be so.

"Now, then," he said. "It would seem the Infernian has things taken care of over here."

Ardyn proceeded down the boulevard, opposite the path of the fleeing citizens, mentally listing off the next steps to take. His to-do list distressingly long.

"Ah. I almost forgot."

He turned and caught sight of a stalwart member of the Crownsguard, doing his best to stay his own hysteria and direct the flow of panicked citizens. Ardyn flagged the man down, asking, "Could I borrow that?"

The man's look of disbelief was soon replaced with anguish as his body collapsed to the ground in a black haze. Not a soul around seemed to notice. They were all too absorbed in their own flight from the flames to care what happened to anyone else. Ardyn picked up the fallen soldier's radio and checked to see it was on.

"Ah, so glad to finally find one," he mused. Officer Sapientia had, much to Ardyn's dismay, carried a different model—one not attuned to the frequencies used within the city walls. "Good. It's all coming in loud and clear."

Every channel was a confusion of yelling and barked orders. It grated on his ears and also brought its own delight. Ifrit had only just arrived. It would be a while before anyone grasped the full situation, and longer still until any organized response would form. Confusion among the city's leadership was patently apparent.

"Do enjoy yourself, my infernal friend," he said, waving cordially. "You seem to have everything well in hand here, so I'll go on ahead to prepare."

Phantasmal leaps brought him easily to the top of a nearby building. From that high vantage, the extent of the inferno was easy to see. And what a wonderful sight it was. But he had other business to attend to. The memories of a certain technician, recently deceased, informed him that elevation was key when hijacking a broadcast signal. Gigantic screens mounted throughout the city all showed a close-up of a female news anchor. Her eyes darted about nervously and her mouth was tight as she delivered her report: "Attention, all citizens. An enormous, unidentified life-form has appeared near the Citadel. The creature has begun emitting flames, turning the area around the Citadel to a sea of fire. All citizens must evacuate immediately. I repeat: Attention, all citizens . . . "

The screens flickered blank, and then the woman's words were replaced by another, deeper voice.

"Testing, one, two, three. Is this thing on?"

Another flicker, and now it was Officer Mars Sapientia on display throughout the city. *Ah, that wasn't so difficult.* Ardyn smiled to himself. It was quite amusing to see himself on-screen, speaking with another's voice and likeness. It certainly made for a novel experience.

"Greetings, people of the Kingdom of Lucis! Do forgive me for interrupting the festivities, but I must tell you this day of rapturous revelry shall be your last."

He saw one citizen stop, bewildered by these new words, only to be quickly engulfed by the flames around him.

"Call it 'divine retribution,'" Ardyn continued. "False kings and fraudulent nations are fated to perish."

The Infernian's great blade sliced through yet another building, and a cascade of rubble crushed several lives below.

Ardyn smiled. "Sins of the past must not go unpunished. The time of reckoning is at hand!"

The smell of scorched debris and burning flesh reached him on his high perch. Today marked the final day of the history of Lucis and the first day of his retribution upon the world.

"Well, time to set to work. I beg you, good king and people: do struggle. It will make this far more satisfying for me."

Now they would watch as he undid a nation grown vast in his two-thousand-year absence. And it would take only a single day. Nay, it would take but a few *hours*.

The screen flickered again, returning to the female anchor, her face now stricken with astonishment. That, too, would be gone soon. Either the monitors would crack and burn, or the woman herself would be charred black. It was hard to say which might come first, but that knowledge was assuredly only minutes away.

"Attention, all units. This is your captain speaking. Code red. I repeat, code red. Follow your commanders' orders and get the situation under control."

One clear voice rang out amid the turmoil on the Crownsguard frequencies. The initial confusion seemed to have passed.

"Every word, clear as day," Ardyn said, admiring the stolen radio. "The wonders of technology!"

The radio chirped again. "Clarus here." *Clarus*. Ardyn had heard the name somewhere before. No . . . he'd *seen* it somewhere before, among someone's stolen memories. This voice must belong to the leader of the Crownsguard, Clarus Amicitia.

"Have you identified the creature?" Clarus asked.

A subordinate replied, "Not yet, but we believe it to be daemonic in nature."

"A daemon?!" Clarus exclaimed. "But how could it possibly withstand the daylight? Why is it here now?"

Why? Because I summoned it, Ardyn thought, stifling a laugh.

"For now, help the citizens evacuate. The Royal Guard will take care of the giant."

"Absolutely, sir."

He'd wanted to spend a little more time on his perch above the city, looking down on the suffering below, but it seemed he could afford to dawdle no longer.

"Evacuate? Well, we can't have that, now, can we?"

Every last subject of Lucis had to die. There could be no survivors.

"Yoo-hoo! Oh, Ifrit!"

The Infernian drew near, and Ardyn dove, plummeting back to ground level. Between the two of them, the Crownsguard mobilizing at their current location wouldn't have a chance to reach the fleeing civilians. Slay those trained to organize the evacuation, and there wouldn't be much of an evacuation left to stop.

The strokes of the Pyreburner's great blade tore through the guards' ranks, leaving the better part of their number ablaze.

"My, but the gods' might does inspire." He beamed, as Ifrit continued to ravage soldier and city. "Though I must admit, they're not much for detail work."

A lucky few soldiers managed to avoid each strike, but their luck was short-lived. In the god's wake came Ardyn, who dispatched the remaining troops one by one, their movements so dull and predictable that to him, they might as well have been standing still.

"The Crownsguard is almost wiped out, sir. Target is still on the move."

"Special forces are on the way. Try to hold out until they arrive!"

"Special forces" undoubtedly referred to the Royal Guard. He'd encountered them before on Angelgard, and again at Verstael's facility. Clad in black, with faces obscured, they were also combatants of significantly greater skill than their Crownsguard brethren. Ardyn realized they'd be a bit of a nuisance once they arrived. He was anxious to have the rest of the fodder mopped up before that happened.

No sooner were the last of the Crownsguard units downed than several black-clad soldiers warped in. A new voice came over the radio. "Engaging the target."

At Ardyn's first blow, the same voice spoke again, its timbre changed. "He's so strong." Ardyn heard the words twice, once with a slight delay. He realized the soldier he was hearing on the radio was the same man he was attacking just then.

"Sending backup!" Clarus barked. "Don't let him get away!" But by the time the order came, the man was dead.

"So sorry to disappoint," Ardyn mused, "but I think I've had enough of being restrained for one lifetime."

He felt another enemy at his back and dodged the incoming blow without turning. Then he was circling, shadowstepping in a great arc to get behind his assailant. Or rather, assailants. As Ardyn closed in, he realized there were several. Not that it mattered. They'd die all the same.

"Currently engaging the target," a reinforcement from the Crownsguard chimed in as he reached the area.

"Are you quite certain you have time to be talking right now?"

But the man continued to report as he and Ardyn clashed. "Sir . . . I don't think he's one of us!"

"See? You're leaving me all kinds of openings." And then this man, too, was dead.

Not that it would have mattered if he'd stayed silent and entirely focused on the fight. The outcome would have been the same.

"Then what the hell is he?" Clarus demanded over the radio.

What am I? Ardyn thought in response. *Why, I'm me!* Would it have even been possible to explain? Better to leave simple minds blissfully unaware of the complexities of immortal life.

Another crackle of static. "Sir, we've identified the giant! It's the Infernian—Ifrit, the Infernian!"

"An Astral?!"

"My, does information flow at a leisurely pace in Lucis," Ardyn quipped. They all fought with movements heavy and cumbersome, like men flailing underwater, and it seemed their minds moved just as slowly.

"Yes, sir. One of our officers seems to be controlling the Infernian, but we can't get an ID on him."

"What?!" Clarus shouted. "Find out who he is at once!"

"And to think I wished to savor their struggle," Ardyn sighed. "Oh well. I suppose I can't expect a legacy such as my brother's to produce the greatest minds of the day."

He pummeled another man into the ground, then looked up. The battle seemed to be over, all enemy combatants dispatched. What an underwhelming start. He pondered where to go next. Was it better to finish off the other Crownsguard squads doubtlessly mobilizing in sectors all across the city? Or perhaps he ought to let them organize an evacuation after all; let them gather the entire populace in one convenient location for swift and total annihilation.

Another transmission sounded, this one different from the others.

"There seems to be some kind of disturbance. What's going on?"

Ardyn checked the radio, but it was silent. He shifted to look at another device he'd brought along—an imperial transceiver. Of course. The voice belonged to Verstael, presumably still positioned just beyond the Wall.

"Why, whatever do you mean?" Ardyn smiled as he responded.

"Fine, I'll not ask," Verstael said. "Now, I need you to locate and destroy the devices amplifying the Wall."

"As you wish. Just sit back and enjoy the show."

If they could manage to bring down the Wall, Ardyn could leave the slaughter of ordinary citizens to the imperial army.

Hard to argue with efficiency, he thought. Then aloud, "Now, where in the world might those dastardly devices be . . . ?"

He'd merely been speaking to himself, but Verstael seemed to take the question as addressed to him. "I've marked the location of all the devices they're using to amplify the Wall."

The transceiver's screen displayed an aerial view of the city. Several red circles dotted the map.

"They seem to be positioned on rooftops around the city. Find them and destroy them."

"With pleasure," Ardyn replied. "I'll be sure to keep you abreast of my progress."

Then, with the transceiver carefully muted this time, he sighed. "No rest for the wicked."

He examined the screen, determining the best route to reach the first device. The answer was the rooftops. Up high, he'd be able to avoid the Crownsguard grunts scrambling among the city streets. One less annoyance to deal with. He sighted the tallest building nearby and leapt with phantasmal force to the top.

As he warped along, he developed a sliver of appreciation for the densely-packed buildings. Down below on the city streets, they had felt cramped and claustrophobic, but now they afforded unexpected freedom and ease in his quest to find the amplifiers.

As he neared the first marked point, an unusual bit of architecture entered his view. It had to be the structure housing the amplifier. It was of elaborate design, looking somewhat akin to a small temple or pavilion, and nearly every surface was covered with intricately patterned carvings. Inside stood a large stone figure, which seemed to glare from its post as Ardyn drew near. The statue seemed familiar. Ardyn recalled something resembling it in one of his many borrowed memories.

"The Fierce, is it?" Ardyn chuckled.

Tonitrus Lucis Caelum. One of the Kings of Yore. As for when, exactly, he was part of his nation's history, the borrowed memory did not say. Perhaps it was a mystery that would remain ever unsolved.

"In any case, what terrible taste in headgear." Ardyn shrugged, then turned to inspect the fixtures positioned at each of the structure's four corners. They seemed to be some manner of repository meant to channel magical energy. Smashing them would undoubtedly disrupt the amplifier. Ardyn moved in a circle, taking them out one by one, but his destruction of the fourth was met with an unexpected bellow.

"I have sworn to vanquish all who would besmirch this sacred place."

The deep, booming voice came from inside the structure. When Ardyn lifted his eyes, he beheld the speaker: the great stone figure shuddering to life atop its dais, its surface glowing with otherworldly light.

"Oh dear," Ardyn sighed. "The kingdom's defense budget is surely nothing to scoff at."

He'd assumed the Wall was designed exclusively to repel external assaults. After all, if no enemy could get inside the city to begin with, why bother mounting more of the Crystal's defenses on the inside? It seemed a reasonable enough assumption. More importantly, not a single one of the many daemonified soldiers had offered up memories suggesting otherwise. It only served to underscore how uninformed underlings always were. The details of real importance were leagues above their pay grades.

A lattice of light flashed into place on every side of the rooftop. It was the same hexagonal grid design of the Wall itself, on a miniature scale. Clearly, this was meant to bar the escape of anyone who tampered with the amplifier.

The stone Guardian lurched forward. It slammed its mace into a portion of rooftop occupied by Ardyn not a split second before. Its weapon was immense—one blow would have sufficed to smash any mere human to a pulp—yet the Guardian's movements were sluggish. The power of an attack meant nothing if it never connected. Ardyn would soon be victorious, and he wouldn't even have to break a sweat; all he had to do was devote a fraction of his attention to avoiding the mace.

Moreover, with the Starscourge able to infect both flesh and stone, his arsenal was as robust as ever. Whether man or statue, the Guardian's fate at Ardyn's hands would be the same.

The battle did not take long. When it was over, the statue fashioned after the Fierce faltered, light fading from its surface, and then the stone itself crumbled and vanished into thin air. The grid of blue light surrounding the rooftop vanished, too, and Ardyn was free to move on.

As he made his way, he heard more chatter from the Crownsguard radio.

"Sir! One of the Wall amplifiers has been destroyed!" The young officer's voice was panicked.

Clarus's response came quickly. "But why would he target them? Is this a Niff attack?"

Goodness, Ardyn thought. *You're still all the way back there?* He found it hard to believe that *this* was the man leading the kingdom's esteemed Crownsguard. Could he be any more obtuse?

"We haven't sighted any imperial soldiers inside or outside the Wall, sir."

"Then they must have sent him to do their dirty work," Clarus replied. "Stop him at once!"

Ardyn chuckled. At least they seemed to be on the right track. He began heading toward the next marker. There were seven amplifiers in all. But the thought of dancing the same dance six more times seemed a bit wearisome. At least all seven were installed within the relative vicinity of the Citadel. It wouldn't take long to move from one to the next.

The next device involved a bit more effort. This time, the stone Guardian was not alone. With it were several of the Royal Guard. They were more nimble than the regular fodder, but their attacks had grown predictable; they engaged him in the exact same manner as when he'd dealt with them on the island and at Verstael's facility.

"Oh, how I tire of entertaining you," he moaned.

He needn't fear death at their hands, but the attacks they landed were admittedly painful. And their cries of fear and surprise quickly grew stale—over and over, the same shouts of "Monster!" and "He's not human!" that he'd heard from countless mouths already. It was a bother he'd have sooner avoided.

Still, for all the burden they posed, the harvest was great. The Royal Guard represented the best of the best—the information they had access to was far beyond that of the normal troops. A captain among them might even sit in on an occasional briefing about the most sensitive of topics. The memories Ardyn gained this time around included several terms he'd neither read nor heard before.

"Most interesting. It seems they've another line of defense waiting to deploy."

The Wall of Lucis and its efficacy at deflecting invasion was known far and wide. This new bit of information seemed to be about another capability. "The Old Wall," they called it. A wall in name, perhaps, but in function it seemed something else entirely.

"In times of crisis, they call upon the Kings of Yore to come to their aid." Ardyn hummed in mock admiration. "Bless their souls."

So the ancient kings lay in wait, ready to defend the land. When things looked dire, they'd materialize to drive Lucis's enemies away.

Of course, the information provided by the memory was secondhand. Even the king's personal guard seemed to know little about the Old Wall, and the now-daemonified soldier hadn't actually *seen* it. Perhaps no one had. Perhaps it hadn't been activated in ages. Still, the information seemed detailed enough to trust.

"If they summon the Old Wall, perhaps I'll see that long-lost brother of mine."

His body shivered with delight at the unimagined possibility. Somnus was dead. Therefore, there was no hope of confronting him directly. Ardyn had come to accept the destruction of Somnus's line and nation as a poor consolation, but now... This was the chance to get what he truly wanted. If his brother's spirit could be called forth, it could be crushed. *He* could crush it. Ardyn looked down at his outstretched hands. With those very hands, he might yet kill Somnus!

Strength and glee filled his body anew. He leapt from rooftop to rooftop, his new objective clear: bring the kingdom to the brink of collapse, and thereby create a crisis ripe for the Old Wall to intervene.

"He's going after the Wall amplifiers, sir!"

"He took out another one?!" Clarus responded. "I'll station reinforcements around the amplifiers."

"Sir!" the underling replied.

As Ardyn obliterated each subsequent Guardian and operative, the messages between members of the kingdom's guard continued to flow. Each victory inched him closer to his goal. How many devices were left? While contacting Verstael, he counted out on his fingers the number of towers he'd vanquished thus far.

"Are you there? Can you hear me?" Ardyn spoke into the transceiver. "Almost done. How does it look?"

The empire's plan had been simple: disable the Wall from the inside, then launch a general attack with the imperial infantry. Ardyn's part seemed to be nearing completion.

"Quite promising," Verstael's response came. "We should be able to break through the barrier with a well-timed assault. You ought to evacuate, lest you get caught in the crossfire."

Meanwhile, another statue had lurched to life, and Ardyn was engaged in another fight.

"Yes, but there's something I must attend to first," he said into the transceiver as the combat raged on.

Once this Guardian was laid to rest, it was time to see the Old Wall summoned. And to do that, he'd need to pay a special visit to someone.

"I've got a king to kill," he announced to Verstael.

"What?" the chief's tone grew shrill. "That wasn't part of the plan!"

"I've finished my work; now it's time to play."

"But we—"

Ardyn cut him off. "No 'buts.' You just stick to your plan and keep the boys in black busy for me."

He cut the transmission and silenced the device. The infantry could manage the destruction of Insomnia and the massacre of its citizens. Ardyn had a new priority.

"Yes," he crooned to himself. "It's time to play."

He dove down to the rows of trees lining the roads below, then hopped from one to the next, humming as he went, ripping banners and snapping flagpoles of Founder's Day decorations he encountered along the way. Rubbish, all of it. A nearby loudspeaker blared a single word, over and over: "Evacuate! Evacuate!" He smashed it to silence its inane parroting.

His earlier time spent thinning the Crownsguard's numbers had paid off in spades. There was hardly a soul in sight. No one would challenge him or slow his own little festival of destruction.

"Such a mess," he laughed. "Whoever is going to clean it up?"

The answer, he mused, was "no one." From this day forth, Insomnia would be a ghost town. There would be nothing left to maintain.

"Oh my. What big walls you have!" Ardyn said, standing at the front gates of the Citadel. "All the better to look down upon his enslaved subjects from."

Not a guard was in sight. It would have been unthinkable at any other time but for the chaos. Every free hand, and then some, was needed to attempt to stay the Infernian and organize the civilian evacuation.

"Priorities, priorities." Ardyn chuckled. "This is what you get when the men you command can't even stop to think for themselves."

He pushed through the gates and strode into the large, unobstructed courtyard that led up to the Citadel proper. A glance was enough to see that it wasn't only the gates that were unmanned: the Citadel's entire guard detail had been dispatched elsewhere.

"Time to call in a favor with the king and have him summon my beloved brother," he said, making his way across the courtyard. Just then, someone emerged from the Citadel doors. Ardyn made no effort to turn or flee; he was but a simple soldier on duty. His presence wouldn't invite the slightest suspicion. Or so he thought.

"Something wrong, Officer?" The tone was sharp, as was the stare. As the speaker drew close, Ardyn recognized him.

"Ah, you must be His Majesty."

"I'm pleased to make your acquaintance," the man replied, but the implication of his tone was clear: *I don't know you, and I don't trust you.*

Numerous memories had featured this face and the gentle smile it apparently was known to wear. Others showed it bearing a solemn dignity well beyond its years. But not one soldier of the kingdom—or at least none of those into whose minds Ardyn had delved—had been forced to confront the monarch he saw now, a man with a cutting gaze, ready to do away with any opponent.

"Why are you here?" the king demanded.

As the 113th of his line, undoubtedly naught but a trace of Somnus's blood flowed through his veins. Little of him reminded Ardyn of his brother. But details be damned, this man—Regis—was a king of Lucis, and that alone was enough reason for him to die.

"Why, for you!" Ardyn declared. His crimson Arms flicked through the air, headed straight for Regis. The apparitional arsenal of their shared heritage. *This* was the proper means to kill a man of Somnus's line.

Regis's own blue blades were instantly summoned forth in response. The two men stood like that for a brief moment, Ardyn's weapons at Regis's throat, Regis's at Ardyn's.

"The Royal Arms! Who are you?!"

The clash had undoubtedly unnerved Regis. Set against the king was his own power—the spectral weapons bestowed by the gods, subject to the command of House Caelum alone. Only those born to the royal family could wield them, or the trusted individuals to whom they imparted a portion of that power. And now here stood a common soldier, unidentified and wielding the Arms of Kings.

Yet those of the royal house should be at least *somewhat* aware of the ancient truth they'd carefully wrapped away in lies.

"You ought to know," Ardyn taunted, "being a man of royal blood yourself."

"Adagium!"

As Ardyn anticipated, Regis had immediately understood, drawing from memory the name of the monster entombed on Angelgard. There was no one left in the kingdom who knew the name "Ardyn Lucis Caelum," but "Adagium" they did know. What cruel irony that Niflheim should now stand closer to the truth of that ancient era than Lucis itself.

Whether or not Lucis knew the truth of its own history, it would suffer all the same. But it would bring Ardyn greater pleasure if they understood by whose hand their end had come.

"In the flesh," Ardyn replied with a chuckle. "Here to bring the bloodline of Lucis to an end!"

"Hear me, Adagium! On my honor as king, I will vanquish you!"

"Oh dear. What an awful thing to say to your own flesh and blood."

The Royal Arms still hung in the air, each set of weapons straining to bite flesh but stayed by the force of the other. Suddenly the arrays of red and blue were dispelled, and the men turned to blade in hand to further the fight. Regis moved with speed and precision, wielding his sword with all the valor Ardyn had observed in his stolen memories. The king's skill with the blade might have excelled that of Somnus himself. Ardyn could easily imagine Regis on the front lines as Crown Prince, alongside his men in the thick of battle.

But as the king exchanged blows with Ardyn, his surprise grew apparent.

"Such power . . . !" he gasped.

"Yes, I'm afraid that trait seems to have skipped a generation or two."

Battling the Royal Guard had been a bore. The Crownsguard foot soldiers were even worse. But Regis put up a proper fight. It was exhilarating. The kingly barrage would have proven fatal had Ardyn been a man of mortal flesh. Still, Regis's movements lagged just a moment behind those of his undying opponent.

"This monster must be contained . . . " the king gasped as the fight raged on. "He's too dangerous. He must be stopped!"

"Must I? Really? By whom, may I ask?"

Ardyn's body was immortal. Nothing could fell it, not even a king of Lucis. Even if he were stabbed in the chest, or his throat torn out, though blood would gush forth for a moment, the ragged edges of the wounds would quickly knit together, his flesh made smooth and whole once again.

But for Regis, every nick and scratch would sap his strength. Each blow landed upon him would slow him down, and in the end, no matter how great the power granted to him by the gods, his mortal body would know its limit.

"What's the matter?" Ardyn smiled. "Can't keep up?"

Ardyn whirled, a circling shadow of miasma, reforming behind the king. He thrust forth his hand. One sure grasp and the scourge would flow. Oh, what a pleasure it would be to turn Regis into a daemon before striking him down. The king was unfortunately swift, however, and Ardyn's fingers closed on air.

But though his grab may have missed, his blade struck true. It opened a great gash in Regis's side, and the fight was over.

Anguish filled the defeated king's eyes. "I swore to protect my people..."

He groaned and pressed one hand to the wound, as if he might stop the flow of blood. He staggered, and although he did not fall, neither did he manage to stand and raise his blade.

"Done already?" Ardyn taunted. "But the fun's just begun."

Do you hear, dear brother? his mind added. *The king of Lucis groans in agony. Do you see? Your scion is a wretch, brought to his knees in disgrace.*

Ardyn towered above Regis and issued his command.

"Summon the Old Wall."

Regis stared up in disbelief. Ardyn kicked him, and the king's bloodied body tumbled across the flagstones of the courtyard. Regis came to rest faceup, his features contorted with strain, as if he were determined to lift himself back to his feet. If that was indeed his goal, the struggle was in vain: his body remained motionless on the ground.

"How do you know about that?" Regis's words came in broken gasps.

"I've heard the souls of *kings* reside within those statues," Ardyn said. "Of course, that's only hearsay. Why not summon the Wall so we can see for ourselves?"

Regis's hands trembled. He began to curl one into a grip, but it quickly fell limp again. It seemed the man could not summon forth the Royal Arms.

"What I wouldn't give for a chance to speak with the Founder King himself!"

Ardyn kicked Regis's bleeding flank once more, then shouted to the sky, "Come out, Somnus! The longer you wait, the longer he'll suffer!"

Nothing. Not a trace of the Old Wall. Not a trace of Somnus. Ardyn's anger turned savage. He kicked the downed king again, driving his heel into the man's chest. He continued until his ferocious assault had bruised every inch of Regis's body, then he stepped back.

Where was Somnus? Why wouldn't he appear? Was this a game to him? Perhaps he thought he was calling a bluff, certain his brother was incapable of murder. If so, he was wrong. Ardyn was a savior no longer. The kindly Lord Caelum who was beloved by the people of his age was no more.

"Huh?"

Regis had stopped moving.

"Is he dead?" Ardyn wondered aloud. He bent, placing a hand on Regis's wrist to check for a pulse.

"Oh dear. Perhaps I don't know my own strength."

And then a blinding light flared from the king's body. Ardyn stepped back involuntarily. It was the ring. That same ring, now passed through generations of Somnus's line. The gift from the gods to the rulers of Lucis sat securely on the downed man's right hand. The ring's beam widened and began to trace a silhouette in the air. Ardyn's assault had worked after all. The Old Wall was coming to defend the king.

"Well?" he drawled. "I'm waiting."

The spreading light took on a human shape—a towering giant clad in armor—upon which Ardyn gazed with a triumphant grin.

A giant voice boomed down at him. "Brother!"

"Somnus! Haven't seen you for years," Ardyn replied. "Two thousand, in fact."

The giant manifested by the ring was outfitted not unlike the amplifiers' Guardians, with thick plates of armor and a giant weapon. In this case, a sword.

"What's wrong, 'dear brother'? Too afraid to put down your expensive toy and face me yourself?" He sneered. His brother acted in death as he did in life. No fair fights. Never relying on his own strength alone. "I won't let you forget what you did to me."

"You were tainted," Somnus boomed. "Unfit to sit the throne. That is why the Crystal rejected you."

The man was a fool if he thought his words would save him.

"The Crystal. Is that who exiled me as a monster and erased me from the face of history?" Ardyn shouted back.

"Please, Brother. Return to the darkness from whence you came."

"Now? But I'm having so much fun! To think I'd get the pleasure of killing you myself!"

There was no need for further discussion. Not that there ever had been—Ardyn was not interested in any excuses his brother might wish to provide. Blades summoned forth from the Armiger now rained down on Somnus's apparition.

In a distant past, Ardyn had similarly drawn his sword in anger. But back then, his point had faltered, failing to pierce his brother's heart. He knew not what stayed his hand back then. It was a mistake he'd relived over and over while chained in the darkness. But here, beyond his wildest dreams, was a chance to right it.

Ardyn slashed again and again at the great stone legs, then warped up high to strike at the giant's face. Each attack fed his lust.

A small part of him still yearned to put fist to flesh. Would that he could take out his anger upon Somnus the man, one blow at a time, until his hands were numb with fatigue.

The giant stepped back in the face of Ardyn's assault. "This is preposterous... How could one so impure possess such power?!"

Power from impurity? Ardyn mused. *Hardly. This strength was born of hatred. What you feel is two thousand years of longing to see you dead by my own two hands.*

"I was right to have sealed you away. You truly are a monster, Brother."

"Yes. A monster, indeed."

In life, Ardyn had ever yielded to the gods' commands. He'd been willing to give everything to aid his people. Yet the only fruits of his devotion were this inhuman power and immortal body. And with naught else left to him, those were the tools he would use to exact his revenge.

Swords alone would not suffice. Let Somnus burn in the fires of retribution. Let him writhe and wail in pain.

"O Infernian, lend me your strength," Ardyn intoned. "Help me burn this wretched nation to the ground."

Astral hellfire enveloped Somnus. Scorching tongues of flame lapped at the giant stone figure, its limbs cracking and groaning from the sudden heat. Ardyn leapt into the air, concentrating every bit of anger and hatred he'd ever harbored into one final blow.

"This is where it ends," he said as steel met stone. And then, at long last, Somnus's knees buckled, and the giant form was crashing to the ground, its blinding blue light diffused and fading. A great laugh erupted from Ardyn's lungs. His eyes were squeezed shut in delight. When the laughter finally subsided and his eyes were open again, he saw Somnus was no longer encased in stone. The figure on its knees before him was his brother as he'd known him two thousand years ago.

"At long last, 'dear brother,' vengeance is mine."

"The gods blessed you as their chosen," Somnus began. "The people adored you as their savior. I was neither powerful nor popular... just envious, perhaps. I yearned desperately to be special, yet I had nothing to set me apart. Nothing at all!"

"Until you stole it from me."

Somnus lowered his gaze.

"What I did to you was unforgivable, but I did it for the future of our kingdom—of our people. Our line has done everything in our power to protect our people, just as the gods bade. I was merely fulfilling my calling."

"Our line"? I think you meant yours. You and the one hundred and twelve kings who followed. I suppose you think you've done a wonderful job carrying out the gods' bidding.

He remembered Aera's words. *Your devotion shall not go unnoticed. The gods will doubtless be watching over you.* He and Aera had been the ones to abide by the will of the gods. Not Somnus.

"And here I thought *I* was the blessed one," he spat, "but it was you all along."

It was not only the throne that had been stolen from him. Not just his future. Somnus had taken all that and more. Ardyn had lost everything he'd ever known.

His brother's reply was soft. "I dare not ask for your forgiveness, but I do ask for your understanding."

Ardyn's fury boiled over.

"What?!" he demanded.

Did Somnus think he could apologize? That his words could erase the past? That he could change anything at all?

"You took everything from me—*everything*—and you ask for my understanding?"

The humbled request. The lowered gaze. Pathetic gestures acted out for his own sake, just like everything he'd ever done in life. Now he felt remorse for his past crimes? Was he so desperate to erase the guilt that plagued him?

To hell with him!

Ardyn grabbed at his brother but caught only air. Somnus's form began to dissipate as the statue's had.

"I pray your soul find repose, Brother."

Repose? Repose? *How dare he proffer such garbage.* He *was the one to cause all this!*

He wished to hurl more words of hatred at his brother, but it was too late. Somnus was already gone. Ardyn stood alone in the city.

His brother's death was supposed to be the answer. Killing Somnus was supposed to bring the relief he'd craved through centuries spent in solitude. But now that Somnus and his great stone puppet were toppled, Ardyn felt not even a flicker of joy in his heart. All he found inside was grave exhaustion and an unbearable emptiness.

Why? This wasn't the ending I imagined to my tale of vengeance.

Ardyn wasn't certain how or why he had ended up back at the site of the previous battle. His mind was clouded, his body moving of its own volition. But when he looked down, Regis lay at his feet.

Of course. My revenge is not yet complete. I must end Somnus's line, destroy his legacy. Perhaps Regis's death will fill some part of this void in me.

Ardyn summoned his sword, hand tight on the grip. One quick thrust, straight through the downed man's heart, and it would be over. The king would lie dead on the stones of the courtyard. Ardyn lifted his sword overhead, poised for the killing blow.

Ardyn Lucis Caelum . . .

An inhuman voice, awful and immense. It seemed to come from everywhere at once.

I command thee to halt and kneel before me.

Each word was a cacophony that crashed into his mind. Ardyn pitched forward as countless towering blades rained down from above. They drove deep into the flagstones of the courtyard, forming a great circle around Regis's unconscious form. The intent was clear: no harm would come to the king.

From high above came a dizzying light, and the world was washed in white. Ardyn looked toward the heavens, squinting through the glare, and beheld something of greater size, strength, and presence than he'd ever known descend upon the earth.

On my honor as the Bladekeeper, Bahamut, I shall not let thee become a slayer of kings.

The Draconian. The God of War. Bahamut. Whilst the rest of the Six slumbered after the Great War of Old, this god alone vanished to a place unknown.

"Why . . . ? Why do the gods deny me my revenge?!"

As Ardyn cried out his dismay, his surroundings shifted without warning. He was no longer in the world but suspended in some strange void. He stood, though not on ground, and in every direction he saw light the color of night sky and ocean depths intermingled. It was a place far removed from reality, so much so that Ardyn could not think to question where he was.

In that void, he faced the God of War.

Because thou hast been chosen to serve a different purpose. To spread darkness throughout the world is thy true calling.

Calling. It was a word engraved upon his heart, but one he'd not had in mind for some time. It caught him off guard. All he could manage to do was parrot back a single word. "Darkness?"

Soon, the True King will be born unto Lucis. He shall lead the people as their beacon of hope and drive away the darkness.

In turn, thou shalt be his sacrifice—the limitless shadow that ushers in the light.

"Why must I continue to suffer? Have I not already sacrificed enough?!"

Bahamut continued, unfazed and uninterrupted, not seeming to care whether his words were understood or not.

When the True King awakens, summoning the power of his forebears, he shall at last relieve thee of thy suffering.

It dawned on Ardyn that he had no need to ask. The things of which the Draconian spoke poured into his mind, played out as moving scenes as clear as anything Ardyn had witnessed with his own two eyes.

The birth of Regis's son. The child who would be known as Noctis. The Crystal, which would name that child the Chosen King. Ardyn himself crossing swords with the boy grown to a young man. In the same courtyard where he'd clashed with Regis just moments ago, Ardyn would be defeated by Noctis. Noctis would sit on the throne of Lucis and offer up his life, using the power of the ring to open the door to the Beyond.

The Beyond. It was a mysterious realm linked to their world by way of the Crystal, unreachable by mortal flesh. Two thousand years ago, Ardyn's soul had become trapped there, separated from his body, when the Crystal cast him away.

He'd thought his immortality had been granted by the Starscourge that coursed through him. In truth, his spirit was trapped in the Beyond, while his body remained in the mortal realm, soulless and cursed to walk the earth until the True King arrived. And when Noctis was ready, he would cross over to this realm through the power of the ring and put Ardyn to rest once and for all.

Then the line of Lucis shall come to an end, and the revenge thou seekest shall finally be found.

So it is ordained, and so it shall be.

Ardyn would be gone forevermore, as would Noctis, Lucis's True King and also its last. The line would end with him. And in exchange for Noctis's sacrifice, the Crystal, now host to all the Starscourge that had plagued the world, would shatter. Eos would be cleansed.

A glimpse of a world to which light had returned flashed before Ardyn's eyes. Then it was gone, along with the Bladekeeper's other visions, and Ardyn was again in the place that was at once like dark sky and deep sea.

He stared at Bahamut. "You say I am not the savior of man, but his sacrificial lamb. And that I live only to die by the hand of the heir to an ill-gotten throne."

Two millennia ago, Ardyn had believed with all his heart that to save others was his calling. He'd been ready to embrace death, if it were in service to others and brought an end to suffering. He'd thought it a mission of which only he was capable, and thus he'd been prepared to sacrifice everything.

But even at that time, he had not thought to lay down his life without a struggle or fight.

During his long time on Angelgard, he'd come to think the gods fools. They had bestowed but a single man with the power to stop the scourge. They had failed to imagine the Crystal's rejection of the one whom they had chosen to be king, and Ardyn had despised them for it. But now, to hear that everything that had occurred was but a means to spawn a monster fit for sacrifice . . . It was a cunning cruelty far beyond that of mortal minds.

"*That* is the fate the gods have chosen to bestow upon me?!"

The very same.

Defy thy destiny if thou dare, but know that it would grant thee a life of darkness unending, devoid of death's reprieve.

What say thee, Adagium?

The war god's words echoed in his mind, merciless and cruel. Everything that had befallen him had been Somnus's fault; he'd been so sure of it. It was the crowning achievement of his brother's cunning, carried on by generations of his successors, a scheme that robbed him and Aera of their happiness and future. It had cheated them of everything—even their purpose in life.

But now the truth was laid bare. The trap had been set by not Somnus but the Draconian. Lift the lid on the chessmen's case, and Somnus lay there, too, another pitiful pawn in the gods' cruel game.

The fate bestowed upon a man cannot be changed.

Now go. Fulfill thy calling.

"Not once have I begged the gods for such a blessing. And I do not intend to kneel before you now!"

Ardyn summoned his own blades and flung them at Bahamut. When the weapon points connected with the god's giant form, Ardyn infused them with daemonic fury. But all his assault managed was a tiny scratch across the giant masked face.

Thine impudence shall prove thine undoing, foolish mortal. Pitiful creature.

By the time Ardyn was conscious of the counterattack, it had already landed, and his body was hurtling backward. He could not move to retaliate. Pain seared through him as the war god's great blades lanced deep into his arms and legs.

It was not a physical pain alone. Ardyn had felt an anguish like this once before, in the sanctuary with Somnus, when his brother and countrymen had thrust their weapons into him. The Draconian's assault brought those feelings back, this time with a relentless, deep intensity many times beyond what he'd suffered at Somnus's hands. Each wound burned with agony as it opened in his flesh.

If thou wilt fight against fate, so shall it be.

His vision blurred with the torment. A pale figure appeared before him. The pure-white, immaculate garments seemed familiar, as did the hair, with its faint gold luster. He then saw that it was Aera and that she bore the Trident in her hands.

"Ghosts do naught but haunt my tortured soul," he whispered.

It was an illusion of the war god's making. He would not be fooled.

Once Aera was lost, he'd brought her face to mind again and again, desperate not to lose its details. Every little mannerism. Every movement. Every sound of her voice. He'd recounted every minute thing about her until it was all etched in his memory forever. No illusion could fool him. The woman before him was not Aera.

"Enough of this," he gasped between bolts of pain.

Aera stepped near. The Trident of the Oracle was before him. The woman's expression was flat.

The threat was clear. Obey, or lose everything.

"If this is the fate you thrust upon me, I shall see it back to you," he said.

Aera stared at him with cold, unfeeling eyes.

"I will not yiel—!"

The Trident pierced his bowels. He screamed as he was visited by agony anew, one that was far greater than any real pain. His breath caught in his throat. Between thrusts, he saw blood black as night dripping from the tines. He knew in his mind that this, too, was an illusion. Aera, the Trident, the spilling blood, and all the agony he felt—they were all conjured by the Draconian. But his mind could not push them away.

"Pierce my heart if you must, but you will never kill my resolve."

He told himself that the pain was nothing. That he would not succumb to the god's foul tactics. He would no longer be toyed with. What was another eternity in darkness when he'd endured one already?

"The path men tread was never meant for me," he growled, and suddenly he was filled with a ferocious strength. He raged like a beast—a *monster*—and the blades lodged in his limbs snapped and broke to pieces. His spectral Arms again appeared around him, and he cut the false Aera to the ground.

Doth man know no recourse but the blade? Return to thy world. Embrace thy suffering.

The space at his feet shattered, and he was falling. Falling with no end in sight.

"Where am I?"

The world was murky and gray. He knew not whether he'd spent only a moment in that strange emptiness, or an eternity.

"Am I alive? Does it matter? Perhaps not."

There was something familiar about the place. When he strained his eyes, he could make out the stone walls. The cramped space. The broken shackles and rent chains on the floor below. It was Angelgard. The cell.

"Nothing matters—none of it. Not the 'blessed' gods above nor the accursed kings below. To hell with them all!"

He stood. Unlike the day of his discovery by Verstael, his limbs felt strong and sure. The way to the surface still gaped open, and Ardyn's step did not waver as he made his way out.

"All that matters is I have my revenge."

No longer would he bow to the whims of others. He would be the master, and all others his puppets. He'd toy with them, more cunning and cruel than even the gods.

"I will spread this scourge across the earth, lure out this 'King of Light,' and kill him. Then, the entire world of Eos will be drenched in the darkness of despair for time eternal."

It was not enough for Somnus alone to suffer. There were others upon whom vengeance must be wrought.

"And then, I shall fell the gods."

In time, the day would come. He would tear off Bahamut's mask, break his swords, and see him crawl across the ground in shame. The gods would bear the greatest humiliation they could ever know.

No matter how many decades or centuries might pass, what eons beyond imagining might be needed to draw his plan together, he would see it done and executed. That alone he vowed to himself.

And for the first time in two long millennia, Ardyn felt truly fortunate to have a body that would not know death.

M.E. 736

N*octis Lucis Caelum is born.*

M.E. 741

C*rown Prince Noctis, heir apparent to the throne of Lucis, is revealed as the True King.*

His is a face known to Ardyn, seen in the vision shared by Bahamut seven years ago in which Regis, to whom the revelation was delivered by the Kings of Yore, holds the small boy in his arms. The child's face bears an unmistakable similarity to that of Somnus. The same picture-perfect scene is doubtlessly cherished by all throughout the Citadel.

Regis establishes the Kingsglaive, a reformed Royal Guard to serve under his direct command and ensure the safety of the Chosen King.

All continues to proceed according to fate—or rather, the will of the Draconian.

M.E. 745

Shiva, the Glacian, awakens in Ghorovas Rift, in the region of Vogliupe. She begins an assault on Niflheim, engaging with the imperial forces at their border. Niflheim is ultimately victorious, but at the cost of the greater part of their military forces.

For Ardyn, the goddess's attack is an unexpected stroke of providence. He had been gently prodding Verstael along a new line of research, in hopes of creating a new type of daemon-infused magiteknology tailored for engagements against the gods. The encounter with Shiva provides a perfect opportunity to test and confirm the weapons' efficacy. Whether similar results might be expected against the Draconian, none can say. Still, the progress made is undeniable.

M.E. 755

A cease-fire is declared between Niflheim and Lucis. Ardyn visits Lucis personally to negotiate the end to hostilities. The Regis he encounters there, twenty-one years after their last meeting, looks astonishingly haggard and gray for his age. His efforts to stay the imperial incursion by way of sustaining the Wall and the city's other defenses seem to have taken a great toll upon him.

M.E. 756

Insomnia falls.

The Niflheim Empire's plan goes off without a hitch. The day before the invasion, Ardyn enjoys a first encounter with Prince Noctis at Galdin Quay. Seen in the flesh, the young prince is the spitting image of Somnus. So close is their appearance that Ardyn is filled with zeal anew: he is determined to see the boy suffer in every conceivable manner before his ascension as True King and ultimate demise.

Later that same year, Noctis is pulled in by the Crystal to begin his awakening as the Chosen King.

M.E. 766

The Crown City was shrouded in darkness, covered in night like every other corner of the star.

Oh, how long it had been. And how curious that it should have felt long at all. Thirty-two years since the Draconian's decree. Thirty-two years since the discovery of that incomprehensible destiny thrust upon him. After two millennia in that cursed stone cell, those years should have felt like a brief moment, passed with hardly a notice. Instead, they had dragged on, a wait of unbearable length.

Once the day was gone and the world knew only night, the areas surrounding the Citadel were a place where daemons lurked and men dared not draw near. There, upon the throne now claimed as his own,

Ardyn waited with singular purpose, ever eager to receive the man bearing the Crystal's blessing and the title of True King.

Do hurry, Noct, was his constant wish. *I am ever so anxious to see you again.*

Thus Ardyn sat in unwavering desire, waiting for the one fated to approach his throne. When the day finally came, and the doors were pushed wide by hands wearied beyond their years, he knew precisely how he'd begin.

"I'm afraid you're out of luck."

The observation was true not only for the guest but for the speaker, too.

"The one you hope to see," Ardyn continued, "is not here."

Nor is the one I *wish to see*, he added, though not aloud.

The visitor before him was not the one he had long awaited. This was something quite different from the reunion the God of War had promised. A laugh Ardyn could not suppress rose from his chest. It seemed the gods could not dictate the future with the precision that they claimed. Either that, or the fate they decreed had gone off course. It was a reunion that could not be explained in any other way.

"Ah, but do pardon my surprise," he said, "at this most unexpected development."

There she stood, in defiance of death. A death of which he was certain, for it had come at his own hands, that day in Altissia.

"How very nice it is to see you again, Lady Lunafreya."

The Beginning of the End

The sound of popcorn kernels crunching between Aranea's teeth reverberated through her skull. She tasted salt and stale oil and little else. She'd have been happy to ascribe the underwhelming flavor to dulled senses—gods knew how long it had been since she last slept—but honestly, the popcorn was just disgusting. It was almost impressive in a way. Who would have thought the City on the Sea could boast food so repulsive?

In any case, it was obvious now why the popcorn had gone virtually untouched. A wry smile crossed her lips. During the cleanup, they'd found bags of the stuff, along with tins of chocolates and cookies that had similarly been spared a watery fate. They'd been picking over the remains of a street vendor's stall, and the owner of the place, an absolute saint of a confectioner, hadn't uttered a word of discontent as they handed out the salvaged merchandise to little onlookers—kids who hadn't made it out of Altissia, but who'd somehow survived the devastation.

While the other treats had disappeared quickly, filling hungry young bellies, the popcorn remained. But the bags were sealed, and it didn't seem right to throw away perfectly edible food, so Aranea had taken the stuff back with her, only to realize later how contemptible it really was.

Her location wasn't helping. Popcorn was a snack best suited for movie theaters and amusement parks, for times of fun and relaxation. Not so much for scarfing down while sleep-deprived in the cockpit of an imperial dropship.

Theaters and theme parks. Aranea sighed. There weren't many of those left in Niflheim. Nor were there the audiences or visitors to fill them. There was a time when such diversions weren't unusual, back when the empire still had a shred of dignity to its name.

When had her country gone so far downhill? As Aranea pondered the question, words from her childhood floated to mind.

At this rate, what's going to become of the empire?

The emperor is acting so peculiar these days.

She'd overheard plenty of comments like that when she was small.

Never was there a more wise and just ruler. But now . . .

A sigh had accompanied those words.

His Radiance is the ruler we've always adored. It's his advisors. Fools to the last. They're the ones to blame.

I say it's the military. Too much ambition at the top. All eyes on the borders and none at home.

Another sigh. Such was the mood that permeated her earliest memories of childhood. Still, the city had been brimming with life at the time, and to a child the decline was not yet apparent. There were playgrounds for her and the other children to enjoy, and the adults had their own favorite haunts, places for a quick drink or a long, leisurely glass.

By the time she'd taken up the life of a mercenary, the playgrounds were vanishing, their old equipment deemed unsafe and carted away. The emptied lots lay dormant for a while, before being repurposed as armories or stockpiles. Theaters and athletic fields were the next to go, and then the neighborhood shops. Trade in stylish clothes, trinkets, and other luxuries vanished almost overnight. Children's toys and picture books grew rare. In short, if something wasn't an absolute essential, it became all but impossible to find.

Still, the empire continued to speak of itself in terms of grandeur. New territories were being annexed all the time, and soon Niflheim's rule would span all of Eos. It led one to wonder why imperial subjects endured such spartan lives. There was endless talk of glory, yet little glory to be had at home. And it was unlikely things would ever improve—any sum that found its way to the imperial treasury was quickly funneled into whatever bizarre experiment the military researchers dreamed up next.

To be sure, those experiments had endowed Niflheim with unparalleled might. But it was hard to think so highly of them now that legions of daemons led the forward assaults. It was hard to feel eager for progress when it came at the price of endless accidents and disappearances. When personnel at some far-off research lab vanished without trace or official inquiry, that was bad enough. But when the public never heard a whisper about it, something was rotten. The government had an iron grip on the flow of information, and it wasn't hesitating to squeeze.

It's his advisors. Fools to the last. Which frowning face from her childhood had foreseen this? Who had possessed the prescience to assert that the empire's troubles would result from its military ambition? She wondered what they might say now about the sorry state of their homeland today . . . if they were even still alive.

Aranea sighed.

Or rather, she intended to sigh. Instead, it came out as a yawn. From her two o'clock came an echoing yawn, and from her ten yet another. Biggs and Wedge sat ahead of her, equally bleary-eyed and begrudging the handfuls of popcorn they downed.

Even if they had attempted to get a decent sleep, they would have been thwarted by the constant vibration and earsplitting rumble of the magitek engine. It was the last sound you wanted around you when you were trying to relax. Of course, relaxation wasn't exactly advisable while operating an airborne dropship. So the three of them continued their battle against exhaustion, with victory always an uncertain prospect.

Sleep wasn't even a particularly formidable enemy. Aranea had fought it countless times before. Rather, the problem was the current means of doing so. It took every bit of her willpower to cram the next fistful of disgusting popcorn into her mouth. If she'd had any other options, she'd have sealed the popcorn away in an airtight container and thrown it into the furthest corner of the cargo hold. Thirty years without having to endure the greasy reek of synthetic butter again would have still been far too soon.

Wedge gave a small grunt; they must have been drawing near Gralea's airspace. They'd be on the ground in minutes, back at base, and it'd be mission complete for the Third Army Corps's 87th Airborne Division. *Nothing unusual to report.* She swore to herself that would be the extent of her debriefing. If the brass were expecting any more detail, then tough luck.

Biggs was counting down on his fingers in an exaggerated manner. *Three*... *Two*... *One*... When he reached the end of his count, he stopped and turned around.

"Congratulations! We just set a new record for overtime logged."

Ah. So that's what he'd been doing. That was Biggs for you—eyes on the inane. It was typical for him to pay attention to absurd little details and trivialities, though he always claimed there wasn't anything trivial about them at all. Aranea had to admit that the man's quips had eased more than a few tense situations, and that he could be relied on for the three of them to share a good laugh.

"We're on hour thirty-six since this mission started," he added. No laughter accompanied his comment this time.

Aranea rubbed a finger against her brow and replied, "Hits you like a ton of bricks, doesn't it? I think I'm about done with assignments where they won't even give us a damn break."

Thirty-six. Hearing the actual number only made the exhaustion weigh heavier, something she wouldn't have guessed possible. Recalling the events of their record-breaking mission was even worse—every second they'd spent in Altissia was one more tiny weight dragging her down.

The situation was hard to wrap one's head around. "Recovery efforts," they'd been told at the briefing, "from the damage caused by the Hydraean." Even once they were on-site, it was still difficult to comprehend. The once beautiful City on the Sea was devastated. The buildings with their ornately decorated walls were now nothing more than piles of stone and mud. The covered bridges had collapsed, their supports snapped and roof peaks jutting from the water. Even neighborhoods that had escaped the brunt of the Astral's rage were still ruined by flooding.

They'd spent the entire time without sleep or even breaks, cleaning up debris and pulling submerged gondolas and assault craft out of the water. The gondoliers had managed to escape. Those manning the assault craft hadn't been so lucky. Each ship that was winched from the water had the bodies of its crew members still inside.

"The troops don't seem too happy lately," she heard Biggs say. "Lot of 'em are startin' to wonder if command thinks they're disposable."

"No different than one of their toys," Aranea replied. "Just a number on a report. Same as a magitek trooper. Or a daemon."

An MT or a daemon could be force-marched until its strength gave out, and it would never utter a word of complaint. But the soldiers on the recovery effort were living, breathing people. They tired. They needed sleep. They couldn't shovel muck and lift debris forever.

And it was hazardous work to boot. The majority of Altissia's citizens had been evacuated and were safe outside the city, but Aranea and the others were still reeling from the scale of the casualties racked up during the Hydraean's rampage. They'd all lost friends and comrades, and the conditions were shit, so it didn't seem out of line to drop a complaint or two. Or three. Or four, or five, six, seven . . .

"Even lower than that," Biggs intoned, without so much as raising an eyebrow.

"Lower than what? Lower than a daemon?"

"You think I'm wrong?"

"Nah," Aranea shrugged. "You're probably right."

She'd have been hard-pressed to argue anything else. Unlike the MTs and daemons, which were still relatively expensive to produce, mercenaries came cheap. Find the ones desperate for their next paycheck, scoop them up for next to nothing, and throw them at a low-level problem. That was the logic of the top brass. They didn't even bother trying to hide it anymore.

"Still, work is work," she added. "I'll see the job done, but . . . I gotta tell ya, I'm pretty sick of military life."

Aranea gave another sigh that transformed into a yawn. Biggs and Wedge soon followed suit. It was a bizarre little song sung in round, with yawns instead of words.

"Too tired to get worked up about it, though," she grumbled.

She had to hang on only a little longer. In less than a minute, familiar sights would roll into view below, and then they'd be prepping for landing. After the devastation they'd witnessed in Altissia, the rundown landscape of Gralea might as well have been paradise on Eos.

"Fancy a taste to celebrate a job well done?"

A flask was thrust in Aranea's direction.

"I'll pass, thanks," she said with a small wave of one hand.

She figured she could probably down a bit of the stuff, but she also knew full well that alcohol wasn't what she needed right now.

"I'm more interested in a nice, soft bed right," she added. Clean, starched sheets with that delectable stiffness, and a firm pillow with just the right amount of give. Space to stretch out her arms and legs to her heart's content. Bliss.

Her reverie was interrupted by the sound of a distant explosion and the violent pitch and roll of the ship. Suddenly, the world was upside down. Biggs's flask went flying, and just after it, a flurry of popcorn fluttered through the air like snow. The ship's shrill alarm hammered on her ears.

"Close call on the port side," Wedge's voice came from directly above her. Aranea realized she was sprawled out on the deck.

"What do you mean 'a close call'?" Biggs demanded. "We're in imperial airspace, aren't we?"

Questions later. Actions now. Rubbing the sore spot on back of her head with her left hand, Aranea sat up and reached for the comm with her right.

"All units scatter! Evasive maneuvers!" she barked.

"Roger, evasive maneuvers." The reply rolled in from several voices in succession.

Aranea climbed to her feet, her mind already focused on their next steps. With any luck, they'd have bought themselves a moment of safety. Now it was time to figure out what the hell was out there.

When it came into view on their screens, her eyes widened. The thing was massive. They could see it wading through the capital's skyscrapers on its two gargantuan legs, orders of magnitude larger than any of the daemon-based tech they'd seen before. Regardless of its size, its imperial origin was as clear as day. "Just what we needed," she said. "Another big-ass magitek armor."

Biggs chimed in, "I've heard about this thing. Think it's called Diamond Weapon. Or somethin' like that."

The name didn't take long to place.

"So this is what they deployed in Insomnia."

A magitek armor with enough destructive force to lay waste to the Crown City overnight. No doubt whatever hangar the empire used to store it was equipped with an extensive array of restraints and precautions. Yet here it was, loose in the imperial capital. It just went to show that no amount of planning could account for everything. Perhaps they hadn't foreseen how powerful the thing really was. Maybe it had grown anxious for a bit of freedom and tore its way outside.

At any rate, based on the current imperial response, it looked like there wasn't much hope of getting it back under control. Conventional MAs surrounded Diamond Weapon on all sides, laying into the hulking giant with everything they had. It was clear they'd given up on any attempt to secure the daemon-infused monstrosity. They were out to destroy it.

Closer inspection revealed the plating on Diamond Weapon's upper arms and chest was already stripped away, exposing its innards. Though command referred to it as a magitek weapon, it still writhed like a beast in pain, roaring, swinging its massive arms and stomping its feet against the ground with the impact of each new volley.

Aranea couldn't get over the size of the thing. Even its *actions* were massive. Each of its movements sent nearby high-rises shaking and crashing to the ground. Its path through the city was marked by a trail of empty craters where entire blocks of buildings once stood.

Diamond Weapon roared again, and this time a segment of its head began to glow. It was a big red orb-like protrusion that looked like some kind of bulging tumor. "Cores," the researchers called them. The cornerstone of daemon-infused magitek design.

The bulbous core grew brighter and brighter. Then there was a great flash, which condensed into a wicked red beam. The beam started at one end of the imperial combatants below and swept across the field of battle, mowing down one MA after another, until the ground forces were no more. Aranea would have kept staring in rapt horror, mouth open in shock, but for the weapon's next target: the beam flicked up into the air, streaking toward the airborne division's inbound ships.

Messages from friendly craft bombarded the comm.

"Incoming enemy fire!"

"We're hit!"

"Jerk 1, Jerk 2, damage critical!"

"This is Amigo 2. We're taking heavy damage!"

There were more shrieks of terror than status reports. Airships were spewing flames, plummeting from the sky. More lives being snuffed out. More comrades lost. She felt the slow pulse of anger rising in her blood. "Come on, boys. We're going to take Tiny out."

She kicked her seat and headed back toward the cargo hold. Biggs hollered after her, the confusion in his voice shading into full-on consternation. "Uh, Lady A? That's just the sleep deprivation talking, right? I know you don't mean it, 'cause that would be crazy."

Of course she meant it. And sleep-deprived or not, she wasn't crazy.

"Maybe this is all just a dream," Biggs continued. "Someone tell me I'm having a bad dream."

"Then it's time to wake up. Let's go."

Her head felt like it was made of lead, and her body was desperately crying out for rest, but what they were seeing on the viewscreen was all too real, and someone had to stop it.

"Wedge. You're on helm," she ordered, as she grabbed the Stoss Spear in one hand. Her longtime companion. One faithful, piercing point, rigged up with a magitek engine for enhanced performance and output on the battlefield. Here was a bit of magitek she *didn't* mind.

She adjusted the frequency on her comm and sent a message to all ships in the 87th Airborne. "Listen up, people! I'm gonna need you all to stay on this thing as long as you're able. Got that?"

She received several replies of "Roger," plus Biggs's comment of "Lost her mind, I tell ya."

And with that, Aranea threw open the hatch and dove out.

The wind roared in her ears. She saw the capital's ramparts directly below. Gauging her altitude by eye, she made slight adjustments to the Stoss's inertial dampener. One straight dash along the wall would be enough to bring her next to Diamond Weapon, and then it'd be goodbye, Tiny.

But a crosswind blindsided her. Suddenly thrown off course, she lost the timing for the Stoss's retrofire. This wasn't going to end well. By the time she realized where she was going to land, she was only a split second away from crashing into a storehouse. She felt the shock of the impact and heard the splintering of the roof materials. Then there was darkness and the smell of dirt.

Using her spear and free arm, she shoved away the rubble surrounding her. Finally, light and fresh air were hers once again. She looked up as she pulled herself the rest of the way from the wreckage muttering, "Well, that was graceful . . . "

The roof now boasted an impressively large hole. The light streaming in revealed a silver lining to this little debacle: at least she'd ruined a military storehouse rather than a civilian one.

"Daemons. I really can't stand 'em." She sighed.

Like them or not, she'd still have to deal with them. She stood and brushed the dust off her armor.

"Let's get this over with."

And thus began the single worst day of Aranea's life.

The complete destruction of the imperial capital. Those were the words that flashed through her mind as she assessed the damage. That's how bad the situation looked. From her position atop the rampart, she saw flames and black smoke rising from every corner of the city, as well as countless collapsed buildings and sunken roads. The shadows she observed darting among piles of rubble were almost certainly daemons. They weren't particularly large, but their sheer number would make them a nuisance to deal with.

She caught the sound of a looped recording playing on one of the public announcement speakers mounted throughout the city. "An evacuation order has been issued for all areas of the imperial capital. All civilians must proceed to their designated refuge stations." The voice cut out at irregular intervals. This particular speaker had probably taken a beating.

Just as the thought struck, a splintering sound echoed from the same direction as the speaker. She caught sight of a large daemon ripping through a building, and she muttered, "Lucky for him, I've got bigger issues to deal with first."

Diamond Weapon was the priority. If that giant monstrosity couldn't be stopped, Gralea would be annihilated. It'd be like Insomnia all over again. Wouldn't matter how much of the rabble she mopped up if the biggest threat remained.

"Lady A? You read me?" Biggs's voice crackled over the comm.

"I read you," she responded, then broke into a sprint along the rampart.

"'Fraid we've had a bit of an unscheduled landing," Biggs said. "We'll get her back up in the air, but it'll take some time. How are things on your end?"

"I'm managing."

In truth, she felt surprisingly good for having body-slammed a roof. She was a bit put out that the threat of sleep still loomed large despite the wake-up call.

"You got any way to check if the aerial safety net system is still up?" she asked.

Between the dismal state of the roads and the daemon infestation, she wasn't going to get anywhere fast at ground level. All the time in the world wouldn't have been enough to reach Diamond Weapon if she had to scramble over rubble and dispatch daemons one by one. It'd be a lot quicker if she were able to jump straight from the rampart to a building, and from there continue rooftop to rooftop.

"Looks like you're in luck. The system's up and running," came

Biggs's reply. "Jump to your heart's content. No need to worry if you botch a landing up there."

"Roger," she said, then made a leap for a nearby rooftop. Biggs's intel was solid: her jump overshot the building she was aiming for, but she felt the net activate at her feet. She took a second bound, which propelled her far enough to catch the ledge of the adjacent rooftop. Thank the gods for the net. The system had become standard on high-rise rooftops some time ago, back when the empire still cared about things like safety during routine maintenance tasks and creating alternate evacuation routes. Today, it looked like the net would be keeping her alive.

Of course, considering the current state of Gralea, who knew how long the system would remain up. It seemed wise to keep moving, and to be quick about it. The Stoss would keep her alive in case of an actual fall—or *another* fall, rather—but the daemon situation down on the streets wasn't going to change anytime soon. Engagements with the enemy would be best kept to a minimum.

All in all, the plan seemed straightforward enough—until the flying daemons showed up.

Aranea winced. "Oh, great. So now I've gotta deal with you all, too?"

Too bad the safety net, for all its ingenuity, never accounted for the possibility of something unpleasant flying *up* from below. It would activate to keep Aranea from falling, but it wouldn't serve as a ceiling to keep the flying daemons at bay.

"Well," she sighed, "let's get this over with."

She flicked the Stoss's output to max and flung herself high into the air. At the apex of her ascent, she angled her spearpoint straight down at one of the pursuing daemons. The momentum of her fall drove the weapon deep through its body. Then a step on the antigravity field. Another jump. Fall. Impale. Repeat.

With the daemon corpses still skewered on her spear like a kebab, she swung the Stoss in a wide arc, cutting another flying creature clean in two. The corpses soon vanished in a cloud of dark miasma.

"I *really* can't stand daemons," she muttered.

Aranea straightened up and resumed her rooftop trek. In the city streets below, she caught glimpses of rogue MTs thrashing about alongside the daemons. The control system normally keeping them in line must have been put out of commission.

She grimaced. "This is what they get for building an army out of those things."

An MT or a daemon could be force-marched until its legs gave out, and it'd never utter a word of complaint. But while that might make for a convenient, low-maintenance army, the second there was any trouble with the systems keeping them in line, they'd transform from assets into threats. An army of living, breathing humans might require rest and food, and they might complain when conditions were poor, but at least they could be reasoned with and wouldn't go berserk at the slightest provocation.

"And an army of humans won't start slaughtering their own countrymen for no reason," she murmured.

She spotted a human corpse, head clearly smashed in not by falling debris but by an MT fist. It unsettled her, and she quickly averted her eyes.

But the scene sparked a question in her mind. Diamond Weapon wasn't the only one running amok. The standard troopers were out of control, too, and on top of that, there was the sudden daemon infestation. It seemed a stretch to call all the whole shitstorm a coincidence. Sure, Gralea saw its share of daemons. One or two might pop up in a neighborhood, only to be eradicated or contained in short order. But they never appeared in numbers like this. What she saw now was a far cry from a couple of daemons gone unnoticed while the military had its hands full with Diamond Weapon.

She'd heard that the research facility spawned its own daemons these days, for ready availability during experiments. Maybe that could explain the numbers; they could have all escaped from the facility. But for that to happen right at the same moment when both Diamond Weapon and all the MTs went haywire?

"Wait. What if . . . " she began. The idea that occurred to her was disturbing in the extreme . . . but it didn't seem beyond the realm of possibility. She felt a shiver run down her spine.

The comm interrupted her thoughts. It was Biggs.

"Repairs all finished. We're headed your way to provide support."

"Thanks. I could use it."

For each rooftop she crossed, she didn't seem to be getting any closer to Diamond Weapon. It looked like the creature was moving in random directions, and closing in on it was proving to be a more difficult task than she'd anticipated.

"Wandering around like some giant three-year-old lost in a department store," she sighed. She'd looked after a child about that age once, in the distant past. The memory somehow had floated to mind, prompting the comparison.

The monstrous entity turned again, now moving in the general direction of the residential district. She needed to hurry. If she didn't close the gap and put a stop to the thing soon . . . She shuddered. The most densely packed section of the city, it was almost certain to be filled with residents still struggling to evacuate. Perhaps they could use the cannon on the dropship; rain some lead down on Diamond Weapon and chivvy it along a different path.

The comm crackled again. A hint of panic had entered Biggs's voice.

"We're seeing civilians still in the city. Loads of 'em!"

Damn. It was one supposition she'd have been happy to be wrong about. Soldiers should have been on the ground, directing people out of the city. Instead, the imperial idea of an "evacuation" was to loop a message over emergency speakers. And now even *that* pathetic bit of assistance was vanishing. Daemons and rogue MTs were putting the blaring speakers out of commission one by one. No wonder the city was still full of civilians. She paused on the rooftop she was currently on to assess the situation.

"What do we do?" Biggs asked.

"Well, we're not leaving them to fend for themselves."

"Right, then. Time to do a few favors," Biggs said. "Boy, are they gonna owe us once this is all over."

"You two round up the people on the ground and see them to somewhere safe. Send the word out to the other units to give you a hand. I'll take care of Tiny myself."

They'd spent endless hours in Altissia cleaning up wreckage and recovering the dead. It had been devastating work, and she wasn't eager to replay that scene. These residents were still alive. They needed help getting out of the city. It was work a hundred times more preferable, even if it came with more risk.

Aranea took a running start, fired up the Stoss's engine, and was back on the chase, flinging herself toward Diamond Weapon. No sooner did her feet hit one surface than they were leaping toward the next. Then, finally, she was leaving the tops of buildings behind, this time jumping onto the elevated ring road that encircled Gralea.

Diamond Weapon was finally in range of the Stoss.

"Y'know, for a big fella, you sure do get around a lot," she muttered.

The city had already suffered enough; it was critical to minimize further damage. A quick immobilization would be key, and the best way to do that would be a single clean shot to whatever component controlled the thing's actions. *So if I was a giant magitek armor, where would I keep my brain?* she thought, scanning the massive form. The core on its head seemed as likely a target as any. Even if the core didn't have a control function, taking it out would at least neutralize a major threat. The scorched remains of the imperial ground forces were a testament to that.

"All right, Tiny. Time for your spanking." Aranea steadied the Stoss, ready to deliver a quick, sharp thrust to the core, when the roar of igniting thrusters drowned out every other sound. A wave of incredible heat washed over her, and she threw an arm over her face to shield it from the blast. Then the ground was sloping away beneath her, and she was sliding, tumbling downward along with a collapsing segment of the elevated roadway. In one corner of her lopsided, shaking, sliding view of the city, Diamond Weapon blasted off into the sky.

A second later, the sliding was replaced with the gut-twisting sensation of freefall. Aranea frantically angled the Stoss and engaged the retrofire, using the momentum it generated to right herself. A brief touch of boots to ground, and then she was flying upward again, and not a moment too soon. The beams of the sagging roadway split, and tons of concrete smashed into the spot she'd just leapt away from.

She scanned the city as she completed her arc through the air. Diamond Weapon was now atop Zegnautus Keep, right at the center of the capital. Infuriatingly, its flight had preempted her attack by seconds.

"You all right down there?" Biggs asked.

She recalled giving an incomprehensible yell as the road had begun to collapse. Oops. Biggs must have caught it over the comm. He was probably wondering what on Eos was going on.

"Don't worry about it. I'm fine. How are things over there?"

"We've rounded up all the civilians we can find."

"Any safe place around here you can put them?"

Even as she said that, she knew there wasn't. Licks of flame danced in every quarter, and daemons stalked the streets like they owned the place. After such rapid deterioration, there didn't seem to be a single safe place left in Gralea.

"We might have to fly them out of the capital altogether," Biggs said.

"Sounds about right."

Who knew how many dropships they had left or how many evacuees they'd be able to carry? Aranea ran a quick mental count. Even assuming the best-case scenario, the situation seemed dire, and she doubted it would get any better.

"What's your current location?"

"Right up alongside Zegnautus."

It was a smart move, as long as Tiny didn't change its mind and head back down. Building codes in the areas adjacent to the Keep had always been strict. No high-rises nearby to interfere with takeoff and landing. Better visibility than the residential district, too. They wouldn't have to worry about being caught off guard by daemons or rogue MTs. It was a good place to gather the evacuees until they figured out what to do with them.

"Got it. I'm heading your way," she responded.

And Zegnautus Keep was exactly where Aranea wanted to be, too. Diamond Weapon was up there, and it was finally standing still.

She found Biggs and Wedge among the empty lots at the base of the Keep. With them, several other troops were gathered, one aboard an MA on daemon cleanup duty, and another attempting to soothe a wailing child.

Biggs had referred to them as just "civilians" over the comm. More precisely, they were all children. The oldest looked like she'd maybe just hit double digits at best. It might have seemed strange to find only children and no adults, but Aranea had experienced something similar before. The adults must have seen to the children's safety, then gone to try to hold off the daemons and MTs. She felt sure of it, remembering voices from the distant past.

Daemons are coming! Get the kids into the shelter!

You wait here, understand? Be extra quiet.

Aranea bit her lip.

"How about Tiny? Still up on his perch?" she asked, forcing herself to sound cheerful. This wasn't the time or place for melancholy.

"Seems ready to go to roost," Biggs said.

For an enemy positioned like that, the standard tactic would be to approach from above. But she wanted the dropship ready for a swift withdrawal. They'd be better off keeping the ship prepped and ready down here, in case it was needed. She sighed. That meant she'd be hoofing it through the Keep's tortuous hallways and dealing with its elaborate security measures, the kinds of things that made you want to throw your hands in the air and give up. But it was the only other way to get to Diamond Weapon.

"Biggs, you keep leading the evacuation. Wedge, I need you down here running support. Keep the dropship hot in case we need it. Copy?"

A child's wail preempted either man's response. Aranea turned and spotted the crying boy. She walked over and placed a hand on his head. He was depressingly young. Young enough to be clinging to his mother's legs. No comforting words came to mind—to offer them now and stay his tears might only prove more cruel once the day was done. Based on the city's current state, there seemed little chance his parents were still breathing.

Still, little chance was a world of difference from none. Aranea ruffled his hair, then crouched down to look him in the eye.

"Listen up, little man. Right now, we've gotta concentrate on getting away. Don't cry just yet."

The child's nose ran. He sniffled and wiped tears away with the back of one hand. Aranea's chest burned. It was unforgivable, making a child of such tender years sob like this. She hated the military for leaving him in this situation—and she hated herself for being part of the organization. She gritted her teeth and turned back to her men.

"Let's get this show on the road already. We need to transport these kids out of the capital. And there might still be other survivors roaming the streets. Pick up whoever you can on the way out."

"Roger," Biggs replied. "Be careful, Lady A. No telling what you'll be up against in there."

She nodded. She was no stranger to the Keep, but her visits had been restricted to only certain sections. Many had been off-limits, their purpose and contents classified, and the details of the structure's layout had been barred to her. Rank notwithstanding, the clearance her mercenary status gave her was about as useful as spit in a rainstorm.

"I'll be counting on you, Wedge."

With her beloved Stoss holstered securely at her back, Aranea set off to brave the Keep.

Inside the elevator, Aranea's battle against exhaustion raged on. If the lift had gone from the ground level all the way to the top, it would've been a safe bet that she'd be sound asleep by the time the doors opened again. But even on this relatively short trip to one of the intermediate levels, she found herself slumped on the floor, the doors at her back, when the elevator dinged its arrival.

Thus, after the doors slid open, her dramatic entry into the Keep was a moment spent splayed out on the floor, admiring the ceiling.

"Damn . . . I *really* need to get some sleep."

At this rate, she was worried about nodding off during the confrontation with Diamond Weapon. Aranea raised both palms and gave her cheeks a hard slap.

"Wish I could find a place to splash some cold water on my face."

The Keep did her one better: over the hallway speakers came the unsettling voice of Chancellor Ardyn Izunia.

"Citizens of the empire," Izunia said. "I thank you for the great kindness you have shown me. And thus it is with deep sympathy and regret that I make this announcement. For today, you see, the illustrious history of your beloved homeland comes to an end."

Sleep's tenacious tendrils were instantly gone. It seemed the chancellor was speaking not only to the occupants of the Keep, but to the entire capital below.

"My, how unfortunate that His Radiance never managed to produce another heir."

What was that supposed to mean? An entire nation had to end because the throne sat vacant?

"That creep could use a good smack in the face."

Irritation lent Aranea's legs an unexpected new burst of strength. Her heels slammed against the corridor floor faster than ever.

All things considered, Emperor Iedolas Aldercapt was a man of little fortune in terms of family. Thirty-five years ago, his empress bore him a son, only to lose her own life shortly thereafter. From what Aranea had heard, the woman's constitution wasn't up to the strain of childbirth, and the delivery took a toll from which she never recovered.

The emperor might have been loath to spark a debate about succession, or maybe it was simply out of love for his departed wife, but in any case, Niflheim hadn't had another empress. It was a decision that would haunt Iedolas years later, when his sole heir perished on the field of battle.

Izunia carried on over the PA. "In truth, your dear emperor desired life everlasting. He would have liked to reign over his domain for all eternity."

Hmph, Aranea thought. *No heir, so instead just eliminate the need for one.* What a ridiculous notion. To be human was to await death. With a fool that blind at the helm, it was little wonder their nation had drifted so far astray.

"Being the magnanimous individual that I am, I offered to help," Izunia continued in his singsong way. "I cast a little spell on him."

A spell? That didn't sound good—not least of all if it came from hands as sinister as the chancellor's. What was Izunia implying?

"But I'm afraid he'll soon learn that immortality carries a price."

Whatever this spell was, it was clearly something better left undone.

From what Aranea had heard, Ardyn Izunia had shown up in the empire thirty-four years ago, and rumor said the man's appearance was all but simultaneous with a shift in the emperor's character, from selfless statesman to selfish despot in a few years flat. Some people had tried to give the emperor the benefit of the doubt, asserting that the tragic loss of his beloved empress had been hard for him. But Aranea wasn't above pinning blame on the man they now called Chancellor.

The only talk that circulated about Izunia suggested that he was up to no good. If someone got on his bad side, they were gone, with no explanation and no clues. All the while, the taxpayers' hard-earned money was constantly funneled into his unsettling projects. Perhaps that alone wouldn't have made for much of a story—such decisions were the prerogative of any ruler—but what really bothered Aranea about the man was one particular rumor she'd heard. Apparently, Izunia held some sort of sway over the daemons, or worse, he might be capable of spawning the things himself. The soldier who told her as much swore up and down that he'd watched it happen with his own eyes. Even if that wasn't true, it was an indisputable fact that the empire's understanding of the daemons had improved by leaps and bounds since Izunia's arrival.

However, she couldn't deny that research on the creatures and their uses had already been going on for some time previous to Izunia's appearance. The man spearheading Niflheim's daemonic research, Chief Verstael Besithia, had been secure in his position for years before Izunia showed up.

That left her with slim evidence at best, but still the suspicion lingered. Izunia carried on, traipsing through imperial affairs in his disarmingly carefree way. And Aranea could never shake the feeling there was something else lurking behind that ever-present smile. She was sure the man had other intentions, and he was damn careful never to give any hint of what they might be.

Aranea continued her sprint, hoping to leave the foreboding thoughts behind. To the end of the corridor, up the elevator to the highest floor it would go. Down the next corridor and up again. And again. There was a rhythm to it, along with a constant frustration about why whoever designed the place couldn't have built one damn shaft all the way to the top.

"Well, don't keep them all waiting," the disturbing voice sang again over the speakers. "Don't you have any last words for your beloved subjects?"

Last words?

An image formed in her mind of what Izunia was up to and who he was with.

Next came a different voice. It trembled as it spoke.

"Sol . . . heim . . . "

It was a voice Aranea knew well. She wished it had been another.

"The sun of Solheim . . . will rise once more . . . "

This final, hoarse whisper trailed off, replaced by an anguished groan. Aranea stopped cold. Then the groan faded away, too, and there was nothing but silence.

After a moment, a sad murmur sounded over the comm.

"Lady A? Was that . . . who I think it was?"

She hadn't heard Wedge speak full sentences over the comm in days or more. It seemed a fitting sign of how disquieting the broadcast had been.

"Seems like it." Her reply was brief, almost curt.

What the hell had happened? And what exactly was this "spell" Izunia had mentioned?

She was making her way toward the last elevator—the one that would finally see her to the top of the Keep—when she felt compelled to take a slight detour. The current floor would have a surveillance room. The Keep's security cameras might shed some light on what had occurred.

She was retracing her steps down the corridor when another thought struck her: why the hell was security so light? She'd crossed paths with a few rogue MTs, but they'd been random encounters. It had been easy to lurk in the shadows and wait while they passed, or to run up behind them for a surprise takedown. The things used to be stationed at every door and hallway. If they'd all gone rogue, the Keep should have been crawling with malfunctioning troops. What had happened to them all?

Based on numbers alone, one explanation seemed logical: the Keep was the source of the rogue MTs rampaging in the city streets below. But given the structure's winding layout, how had unprogrammed MTs made their way down to the city in unison? It would take far too much coordination for a bunch of malfunctioning machines.

She spoke the conclusion out loud. "Someone must have led them out."

It was the only way the puzzle pieces fit together. And based on what she had just heard, it seemed obvious enough who the prime suspect was. It didn't take a detective to figure out what had happened.

"Not a soul in sight," she said with a sigh on entering the surveillance room. It should have been manned by several MT control officers. Instead, it was eerily quiet. Clearly, the human officers charged with monitoring and managing the Keep had been run out—or worse.

Aranea flipped the switches for every camera in the Keep. The room's monitors flickered to life, filling with square after square of footage as the security cameras came online. She couldn't see a single human officer across the entire display.

She found the camera for the throne room on the top floor and selected its feed to enlarge on the main screen. Her fears had been spot-on.

"By the Six . . ."

Any further words eluded her. Sprawled across the rich, leather-upholstered seat was a body, bent backward as if snapped at the spine. Its skin was black as ink, its eyes wide open, with trails of ebony tears still glistening on its cheeks. But despite the discoloration and disfigurement, there was no mistaking His Imperial Majesty Iedolas Aldercapt dead upon his throne.

That he was dead was quick enough to ascertain, but the means of death was less so. Whatever had happened to the man, it wasn't anything within the normal bounds of human experience. His robes hung in shreds from his shoulders. That the emperor himself seemed to have clawed at them with enough force enough to rip them apart hinted at the extent of his agony. It looked like Ardyn Izunia's spell was as poisonous as the man himself.

Aranea bowed her head in a brief moment of silence, then flipped the surveillance system off. It had cost her a bit of time, but at least she knew the truth. Now she needed to focus. A certain weapon of mass destruction awaited her. Time for a charming rooftop date.

"The only good daemon is a dead one," she muttered, dashing back to the end of the corridor and into the elevator.

This time, no trace of sleep haunted her. The moment the elevator reached the top and a crack appeared between the doors, she jammed her way through. She was already halfway down the final short corridor when she heard them fully open. She vaulted up the stairway and positioned herself in front of the door leading outside.

"Hope you're ready to die," she growled.

With the Stoss Spear clenched in one fist, she kicked open the door, only to pause in confusion.

"Huh?"

Nothing. The vast expanse of Zegnautus Keep stretched out before her, but there was no trace of Diamond Weapon.

She cast her gaze upward and finally caught sight of it, high in the sky, suspended from what looked to be an imperial dreadnought. The weapon's rampage seemed to have ended. It hung limply beneath the airship, completely still.

"Are you kidding me?!"

The airship's magitek engines roared, and it began speeding away, bulky payload in tow. Aranea returned the Stoss to its holster.

"Unbelievable. Lost it again."

Far below the receding dreadnought, she saw dozens of dropships, many engulfed in flames. A great horde of flying daemons swarmed them, occasionally slamming into a hull or flitting in front of a ship to bar its way. It seemed almost playful, but the results were decidedly not. The pilots veered, slamming into friendlies, and then more ships were up in flames. Several of the burning craft were in downward spirals, trails of black smoke marking their descents. Aranea found herself reminded of a fireworks display she'd once seen as a child and then grimaced at the irreverent comparison.

The ground toward which the flaming ships plummeted was itself a sea of fire. Explosions flared, buildings toppled and gave rise to new gouts of flame. The empire was crumbling. For Aranea, the truth had yet to sink in. She'd come to terms with the fact that her nation was in decline. The play was in its final act, and any reasonable mind could see that. But it was still jarring to have the curtains drawn so suddenly.

"Such a waste. Wouldn't you agree, Commodore?"

Once more, she heard that unpleasant voice, this time coming from right behind her. Imperial Chancellor Ardyn Izunia.

She'd always suspected that everything somehow traced back to this man and his actions. She had thought it was largely a matter of incompetence, that his failure to carry out the duties of his post had set the empire on this course. But now it seemed the truth was so much worse. Who would have imagined him explicitly orchestrating the downfall of his own nation? Here he was on the rooftop, nonchalantly watching the giant magitek armor being carried off into the distance. He had to be the one who freed Diamond Weapon from its hangar, who set the facility's daemons loose on the city, and who carefully marched the MTs down from Zegnautus Keep before sending them rogue. All to destroy Gralea.

"Truly, such a dreadful waste," he repeated.

Aranea's hand flew to the Stoss's grip. By the time she spun to face him, the spear was out, leveled point-blank at his face. No human being would be able to dodge at that range before she'd managed a thrust.

"Oh dear me. Do watch where you point that thing."

The tone of Izunia's voice was light, mocking. Then he darted forward. His speed was unnatural. By the time she realized he'd sidestepped the point of her spear, his attack had already hit her. Something slammed into her flank with enough force to send her flying. She landed on her back, then felt another blow drive the air from her lungs. She had no idea what kind of weapon had delivered the hit. All she knew was that it had knocked the wind out of her. Her back and shoulders spasmed, and she began coughing violently, unable to stop.

With great effort, she managed to right herself. Still, the coughing continued.

"Anyone ever tell you that you hit like a baby?" she finally managed.

Izunia looked on, amused. They'd just been at point-blank range, but now the man was half a dozen spearlengths away. What kind of weapon did he wield that could fling her around so easily?

For his part, the chancellor didn't seem interested in fighting. He turned his back on her, gazing at the airship as it glided off into the distance.

Between lingering coughs, Aranea spoke. "What's your plan for Tiny?"

She didn't bother asking if he was the one issuing its orders. Diamond Weapon was up there, being carted around by an imperial dreadnought, and Emperor Iedolas was dead. Who else was around to give the command?

Izunia turned once more to look at her.

"Just sending it off to have a little fun," he said with a wink. He pulled a bright red apple from one sleeve and began tossing it into the air. Why the hell he was carrying a piece of fruit around, she could only guess, but the apple wasn't the only red she saw.

"To Tenebrae," he added.

"If you're out to take over the empire, why attack Tenebrae?"

"Who said anything about taking over? Look at the place! It's in a *dreadful* state. Daemons everywhere." Izunia gave an exaggerated shrug, then brought the apple to his mouth for a loud bite. Aranea longed to escort him off the side of the Keep.

"So you just want to see it all burn?"

"Emphasis on *all*, my dear. Every last thing on this miserable little star."

Hardly any time had passed since he had destroyed Insomnia. Today it was Gralea. Tenebrae would be next.

"I always figured you were insane," Aranea said. "I just didn't realize you were *this* crazy."

Suddenly everything was absurd, and she hated it all. She couldn't believe how many years she'd allowed herself to be ordered around, to toil for the sake of this fool who was dancing mad. She was disgusted with herself that he had been able to evade her attack so easily, that he had struck her down in a heartbeat. She hated that she was his subordinate, serving under his command.

The mad fool took another bite of apple. He seemed terribly pleased with himself.

"I wonder if His Highness is already aboard the train?" he mused aloud, clearly referring to Prince Noctis of Lucis. Or rather, with the youth's father now departed, *King* Noctis.

Noctis. Right. She'd spent a night not too long ago guiding the prince and his buddies. They'd all enjoyed a little stint of spelunking at Steyliff Grove, at the order of the same man who stood before her now.

Just then, the comm broke in.

"Lady A!"

"Biggs. You all right?"

"A-OK. Our passengers are all nice and cozy, too."

She felt a flood of relief pour through her. It was the best news she'd had all day.

"Plenty to eat on this thing. Medical supplies, too. Only problem is the course is locked in, and we can't make any changes, not even a single turn. The vehicle's on autopilot, as it were. But don't worry, I'm sure we'll make do."

"Say again about the autopilot?"

"Hey, nothin' for you to worry about! We're on a superexpress. Nonstop ride. Leavin' the capital far behind!"

An autopilot that wouldn't turn off but also didn't pose an immediate problem. Superexpress. Nonstop ride.

"Don't tell me. You're on a train."

"Bingo!"

Aranea had a bad feeling. There were only so many lines extending from the capital. And of those, fewer still were in any sort of operable state.

"And let me guess. You're headed for Tenebrae."

"Bingo again! You're on a hot streak today, Lady A!"

Biggs let out a big, bellowing laugh. Aranea wanted to clutch her head and scream. Their evacuees were out of the frying pan and speeding straight into the fire.

"Listen, Biggs, I hate to be the one to tell you this," she said, "but our friend Tiny's taken to the skies. And he's headed the same way you are."

"Ha ha h—Uh, sorry? Say again?"

"Tenebrae's next on the docket for Diamond Weapon."

Biggs's tone soured. "Can't say I saw *that* coming," he groused.

And she couldn't blame him. Who could have guessed that the giant magitek armor would bother going all the way to Tenebrae to "have a little fun"? It was a plan that could only come out of the mind of a madman. Like the one standing before her now.

"Wedge!" she called out.

She wasn't about to let the children she'd saved run straight into the same danger as before. First, she needed to chase down that train.

"Wedge! Do you read? Where are you?!"

An agonizing moment passed before the terse reply "Dropship." She sensed the tension in his voice.

"What's your status?"

"Being chased. Swarm of daemons."

Aranea groaned. She knew she should be thankful for the simple fact that their ship had not been downed or destroyed like so many others. But the ship already being up in the air meant that her plan wouldn't make it off the ground. It would've been so simple: Wedge would fly up to her, she'd hop on board, and the two of them would go racing after the train.

"Uh... Is this thing on?" Another transmission crackled through the comm, this one from Biggs, though it wasn't for her. "Attention, all passengers. We've got a bit of a, um, situation."

The reception was poor, and it was hard to hear him through all the static, but he seemed to be making a general announcement on the train.

"It looks like the brake lever's snapped. There wouldn't happen to be anybody on board with a tube of industrial adhesive, would there?"

Biggs's words were a little slurred. He'd clearly had a nip or two, which Aranea wasn't the least bit surprised by. He had a tendency to crack under pressure. Normally optimistic and composed, he'd grow skittish and fretful when the going got tough. He was aware of the problem himself, but nonetheless he often went for a swig of liquid courage when larger threats loomed. Today, though, the alcohol didn't seem to be helping.

Aranea glanced up to find Izunia watching her with a thin smile on his face. He'd been listening to the entire exchange, and it seemed to amuse him.

Irritation surged through her. "You know what you could use? A good beating." She struggled to her feet. "How about I put you down and stop all these damn daemons once and for all."

She'd hoped her words might bring the slightest hint of dismay to Izunia's face. That alone would've been cause for celebration. But the man didn't even give her that.

"Why not try? I've even got a little prize for you, if you manage to best me."

Izunia extended the apple toward her. The gesture and his grin made her sick. The jagged bite torn out of the apple was turned in her direction. Deliberately, she assumed.

"Afraid I'm not much for sloppy seconds," she said, swatting his hand away and stepping past him. She took a glimpse over the edge of the Keep: still the same cityscape painted in flame and smoke below.

"And anyway, we have more pressing business," Aranea continued. "I think my subordinates and I are just about done playing soldier."

"Is that so?"

"Mind if we tender our resignation to you? You know, seeing as His Radiance isn't with us anymore."

"I suppose I could oblige," Izunia said. "What prompted the decision, if I may ask?"

Aranea was surprised he hadn't figured it out for himself. She thought she'd made it obvious enough.

"It's simple: I really can't stand you."

She winked, then dove off the edge.

She was hurtling through the air when Wedge's next transmission arrived.

"Think I can shake 'em. Train line?"

He'd apparently kept an ear on her conversation with Biggs while outmaneuvering the daemons. Good. This would get them in position to chase down the runaway train.

"On my way now," she replied.

As the ground rushed up toward her, Aranea engaged the Stoss's retrofire to brake her descent. Her landing would be perfectly timed. Or at least it wouldn't be a wipe-out.

"Oof!" The air left her lungs as she slammed into the ground, a wave of pain rushing from the bottom of her soles to the top of her head. She'd lessened the impact somewhat, but that didn't mean it was a soft, comfy landing. In any case, she was still alive, and that seemed about as good as she could hope for given the distance from the top of the Keep to the ground.

All she had to do now was sprint the remaining distance to the rendezvous point. But as if fate were determined to deny her any imminent victory, no matter how small, the comm crackled to life again.

First there was just static. Gut-sinking static. Finally a voice came through. "Aranea!"

Of all the times . . . She was ready to throw back her head and start yelling curses at the sky.

"Where have you been?! You have a job to do! Stop messing about and help fight off these daemons!"

Loqi Tummelt. Arguably the most annoying man in the entire imperial army, if not the entire world. Sure, making commander in his early twenties was a real achievement and implied he had *some* talent, but as far as Aranea could tell, he produced more noise than actual results. And gods, he was always so *uptight*.

"It is the duty of all a nation's people to defend the homeland!"

How did one pair of human lungs manage to produce that kind of volume? It was like a direct assault on her eardrums. She flicked off the comm—no time to deal with Little Lord Hotblood—and focused on sprinting with everything she had. Anything less wasn't gonna cut it in a chase after a superexpress train.

But Loqi wouldn't let go. As she neared the train line, she heard his voice again.

"Aranea!" This time it blared over a loudspeaker rather than the comm. He'd apparently stuck to her the entire way, like stink to a chocobo. She cursed herself for not thinking to turn off her coordinate data when she silenced the comm. Too late now.

She turned a corner, and there he was in his giant, obnoxious armor. Blocking her way in all his MA-X Cuirass glory.

"Some guys just can't take a hint, huh?"

She was tempted to lay into him out of sheer frustration but managed to keep the venom in check. Of all the times to make a nuisance of himself, why had Loqi decided to do so now? Before she could think about it any further, there was a loud boom. Reflex propelled her to safety before her thoughts caught up with her body. A crater was smoking in the ground just shy of where she'd been standing. The Cuirass was *firing* on her.

"What the hell are you doing?!" she shouted.

"I would ask you the same!" his reply boomed. "Do you expect me to stand idly by in the face of your dereliction?!"

Her head was throbbing. The MA's speakers were too damn loud and the situation too damn ludicrous. The whole day was a shit sundae, and Loqi was the cherry on top.

"All right," she snapped. "You wanna play? Then let's play."

She drew the Stoss and thrust it at the Cuirass. If her words wouldn't make him back down, she'd let her spear do the talking.

Her spearpoint slammed into the cybersuit's left leg, rocking it off balance. She followed immediately with another thrust. The quickest way to put the MA out of commission was a concentrated assault on one leg. But several thrusts later, Loqi still wasn't going down. It was a damn testament to the custom plating he'd rigged his armor with. The maneuverability of the Stoss was unmatched, but for all it excelled in that regard, it lacked in raw power. She was going to have trouble delivering a finishing blow to a heavy opponent like this.

And her mounting exhaustion wasn't helping. *Hour thirty-six.* At this point, her overtime hours were racking up overtime. If she didn't finish this quickly, she might not be able to finish it at all. Just as she began to mull this distressing new realization over, she heard a shout.

"Look out! Above you!"

The voice came from the MA's speakers, but it wasn't Loqi. He was young, but not *that* young.

Aranea looked up.

"Oh great," she muttered. Loqi's cry of dismay came in unison.

A winged daemon was incoming on a steep dive. Aranea leapt to meet it with the Stoss, skewering it through the middle, only for the corpse to explode off to either side. The Cuirass's guns seemed to have found their mark, too.

In any case, the daemon was dead. Attack averted.

"Looks like you owe me one, Blondie," Aranea drawled, right atop Loqi's haughty assertion, "You do realize you'd be dead right now if not for me, yes?"

And all of a sudden, the whole situation seemed utterly ridiculous. The world was falling apart, and here they were, squabbling over battlefield credit like a couple of green cadets. Aranea felt the fight drain out of her with that realization, and she holstered the Stoss. Just as the spear clicked tight in its catches, the cockpit of the Cuirass popped open. Apparently, their little two-step wasn't over. Loqi seemed to think their coincidental timing just as absurd as she did, and she found herself laughing along with him.

"It seems my accusation was unwarranted."

"Finally figured that out, huh?"

Took you long enough, she was about to add, but stopped short. Loqi wasn't alone in the cockpit: he held a small girl in his arms. Her presence solved the mystery of who had shouted the warning earlier, but it also posed an even greater one—who *was* she?

"Tell me, then," Loqi asked. "Where are you headed in such a rush?"

"Got some business to take care of in Tenebrae."

Loqi carefully lowered the girl to the ground. "I suppose it's all that's left to us now."

"What do you mean?"

"The last safe haven in the empire."

"For the moment, anyway," she responded.

Pretty soon, they wouldn't have even that. Diamond Weapon's flight and the impending danger surged back to the forefront of her mind.

"We never should have used daemons in the way we did," Loqi said. "Now it seems we're finally paying the price." His words possessed an edge of self-derision.

Aranea couldn't have agreed with him more.

"And I'd wager that this nation was set on the path of its own destruction the very day that man arrived in the capital."

The chancellor. Perhaps Niflheim's fate had been sealed years ago, well before she and Loqi were born. Perhaps the moment Ardyn Izunia had stepped onto their land, welcomed with open arms, this end had been inevitable.

"We could use an extra hand in Tenebrae, you know," Aranea found herself saying.

Loqi sniffed. "My place is here," he replied, "in the heart of the empire to which my life is sworn."

What a time to be harping on that, she thought. Maybe that was what marked the difference between a former mercenary and a soldier born to the role. To Loqi, this was his heritage. House Tummelt had proudly provided Niflheim with generation after generation of officers and leaders. Maybe that was a thing worthy of respect in its own way. Not that it made it any easier for her to comprehend.

"If the capital is to fall, then I shall go down with—"

"I wanna fight, too!" the girl interrupted.

She looked to be about seven, maybe eight. She seemed healthy, and her eyes were bright and inquisitive. Even at a glance, Aranea could easily perceive the confidence and willpower the girl carried within her.

"No. Out of the question," Loqi replied.

"But I can help! I'll beat up the daemons with you!"

"Listen to me," Loqi said. "I am taking great pains to see to your—"

"I never asked you to," she pouted.

"And yet I am duty bound to do so. I must give everything I have to see to your safety, and to—"

And to the empire's, he'd undoubtedly planned to say, but this time Aranea was the one to cut him off.

"Enough. What is this, a battle of wits, loser takes all?"

Both Loqi and the girl turned to look at her.

"Tell me, Blondie. How well can you pilot that thing when she's in there with you, crowding the cockpit?"

Loqi fumbled for a response.

"And you, kid. Come talk to me in about a decade if you're serious about killing some daemons."

The girl's lips tightened. Aranea saw something she recognized in the expression. She'd probably made the exact same face, a long time ago. In fact, she would have been right around the same age. That was when the daemons had shown up. A whole pack of them, ravaging the only home she'd ever known.

The children had been quickly herded into the village church and told to hide in the basement. To stay there and keep quiet. Then the adults—Aranea's parents among them—readied their weapons and prepared to fight.

I wanna go, too! I can help! I can fight!

She'd shouted after them, desperate not to be left behind. She had felt it in her bones that once her parents walked out that door, she'd never see them again.

No. Out of the question.

It was exactly how one of the adults back then had responded, tone firm but face betraying anguish. She knew it had been one of the villagers, and she could remember the voice, but beyond that, few details came into focus.

Ha. Let's talk about it when you're a decade older.

It was her father who had said that.

Listen to your father, her mother had added. *Wait here. The younger children need you. Look after them. Understand?*

The gentle firmness of their expressions cut off any further protest. As Aranea watched them go, it took everything she had to fight back the tears.

"I don't know who the kid is to you, but I take it she's important," she said to Loqi, back in the moment.

The girl stood with Loqi's great mantle wrapped around her, enveloped in its folds. There was little risk of anything penetrating the armor plating of a heavy MA like the Cuirass, but as the suit jerked around, an extra occupant in the cockpit could easily end up being buffeted against the hard interior surfaces. The thick fabric of the mantle was probably Loqi's way of keeping the girl uninjured.

"I am under the direct orders of His Radiance, to be executed with utmost discretion," Loqi proclaimed. "My duty is to secure this girl and ensure her safety."

"Seems like a pretty good reason to get her the hell away from this war zone," Aranea responded. "You ever think of that?"

When Loqi had lifted the girl down from the cockpit, he'd done it with great care. He held the girl like he was handling a piece of delicate glasswork. Obviously, she was important to somebody for some reason.

"You can put your own life on the line, but you shouldn't bet someone else's."

Aranea glanced over her shoulder. Sure enough, there were more daemons inbound. Flying ones, and too damn many of them. They were still in the center of the danger zone, and if Diamond Weapon was going to be stopped, she needed to get the hell out of there.

Wedge came in over the comm. "Sorry for the wait."

Perfect timing. Aranea held a hand out to the girl. "C'mon, kiddo. Let's leave this fight up to our big, bold hero."

She heard the dropship approaching overhead, and then it was smoothly descending to their position. The girl stepped forward, uncertain. Aranea reached out and picked her up.

She looked back at Loqi. "Let's just say you owe me for this one too."

"Thank you, Aranea."

Granted, she *was* leaving the poor sap and his Cuirass alone with a boatload of daemons. That probably meant they were already even.

"She is in your hands," Loqi said.

Aranea turned and gave what was probably the last imperial salute she'd ever give. Her resignation had already been tendered, and she was a soldier no more. If she hadn't had the comm right next to her, she might have missed Loqi's next words. They were soft but certain. "It has been an honor to serve with you."

Aranea held her salute, watching him, but made a point of giving him no verbal response. The dropship hatch yawned open, and she leapt inside, still clutching the girl. She saw Loqi returning her salute.

"Tenebrae," she ordered Wedge. "Let's go!"

Aranea closed the hatch and put the girl down in an empty seat. No more deaths today. Not the girl, not Biggs or the kids on the train, and not a single one of the people going about their lives in Tenebrae.

Their craft shot forward. The last thing she saw below was the Cuirass, firing machine-gun rounds wildly into the oncoming wave of daemons. She thought she caught Loqi's voice blaring over the MA's speakers. *The sun will rise once more. Glory be to the Niflheim Empire!*

She turned her attention forward. "Wedge, we're gonna beat that monster into the ground."

It was the only way to save everyone. They couldn't afford to fail.

"This will be our final mission," she added. "So let's make it good."

The dropship accelerated into a sharp climb, shaking off the last few daemons hot on their tail, and they were on their way.

Once the ship was out of Gralean airspace, they set a straight-line course for Tenebrae. They passed over the white monotony of snowdrifts for a while, then the vast expanse of the sea, until finally they were above dark earth and forest.

They skillfully dodged or shot down the occasional flying daemon. Fortunately, the things were few in number, so they couldn't cause too much trouble. Most of their disgusting friends were probably still busy tearing up the capital.

Wedge was uncharacteristically talkative during the ride. The man usually didn't say much, but every once in a while the words came rushing out of him like water from a busted dam.

"Wouldn't have guessed it from him," he said. "Loqi, of all people, signin' off like that."

It seemed that Wedge had caught the commander's faint message, too.

"Sure isn't something we'd ever catch *you* sayin,'" he added.

"Damn right. Who talks like that?" she replied. "And to people you serve with every day. Honestly."

That was reason number two why she hadn't responded when Loqi said it. Reason number one was a bit more macabre.

"Stuff like that'll jinx you," Aranea continued. "It's the kind of thing people say before they up and die."

Considering the situation they'd left Loqi in, letting his message go unanswered and presumably unheard seemed the optimistic response.

Wedge started to say something else, but she cut him off, eager to leave the topic behind. "Wedge, how many times have I told you to cut it out with the garlic already? Could you *please* not eat that stuff when you're aboard the ship?! It *reeks* in here! And not just of garlic! You smell like a half-empty beer bottle that's been sitting out all day!"

Normally, and in no small contrast to Biggs, Wedge was a man of few words. He was cautious and apprehensive by nature, but there were two things that could flip his switch: a situation that was looking dire, or a couple of drinks down his throat. Either would loosen his tongue and embolden his actions, the former in particular being exasperating—once he was going, he wouldn't shut up.

During their escape from Gralea, when Wedge had found himself stuck between a rock and a hard pack of daemons, he'd probably thrown back a few spirits to lift his own. You know, the normal thing to do when being chased by enemies, weaving through a dense cityscape at high airspeeds. And of course, no drink was complete for Wedge without his favorite snack: pickled garlic.

But her lecture didn't have much effect.

"Wooo! Feelin' pretty good right now!" he exclaimed.

"Oh for gods' sake."

"Yeehaw!"

"Wedge, shut up. I'm serious."

Aranea looked over at their young passenger. The girl sat rigidly in her seat, her mouth firmly shut. It might have been unease or lingering shock or maybe just an attempt not to breathe in the stink of garlic and booze. With her mouth shut tight, at least there wasn't any worry about her biting her tongue with a sudden movement of the ship.

With her hard, blank expression, and wrapped up in Loqi's mantle, she didn't appear to be a typical cosseted little noble girl. Still, she was used to being picked up and held. Aranea had felt it when she had taken the girl in her arms. Whoever raised her had clearly doted on her.

And what was it Loqi had said? *Direct orders of His Radiance.* What was *that* supposed to imply? Just as the threads were beginning to draw together in her mind, Wedge interrupted her thoughts.

"We got 'em now! Tiny and the airship, dead ahead!"

He glanced over his shoulder at their passenger. "Hang on tight, little lady!"

Wedge slammed on the throttle. The force of the acceleration pressed them all back into their seats. As the speck of the dreadnought quickly grew larger on the display, Wedge started rambling. "The core on its head. That's what makes it go. Which means all we gotta do is punch a hole in the core. The whole thing'll go down. But there's a problem. Up here it'll be like throwing pins at a thumbtack. So we'll have to knock the dreadnought outta the sky. Could pin 'im down for us. Keep things nice and local. And if we're real lucky, we might get the whole ship to blow up in Tiny's face. Wouldn't that be a real show?"

He didn't seem to notice whether Aranea was following or not.

"Wedge!" she yelled. "Focus! What's the plan?"

He sniffed. "We take down the ship."

"Got it."

It was all she needed to hear. She got on the autocannon control and started shooting, finger hard on the trigger. But the dropship's firepower was no match for the dreadnought's armor—Aranea could have fired the cannon for days and left not a scratch on the other ship's thick hull.

Wedge pushed the dropship into a nosedive, and then, with their stomachs still in their throats, burned into a steep ascent. It looked like he'd reached the same conclusion.

"Lady A! Target the ship's engines!"

"I'm on it!"

The second the dropship's nose came up far enough for a target lock, she had the cannon on full blast. No need to worry about retaliatory fire for the moment. She could leave that up to Wedge. He'd be able to evade it well enough. Her job was to rip the dreadnought a new asshole.

"Straight down the tailpipe!"

"That's what I'm doing!"

They were in a race against time to stop the thing before it reached

Tenebrae, and now, more crucially, before they ran out of fuel and ammo.

Crash, damn it! Crash! she screamed internally as she continued firing.

"Crash!"

Or rather, she'd meant it to be internal.

"Crash!" Wedge joined in.

"Crash!" Now all three of them were chanting it.

"Bad news, Lady A! We're almost out of fuel!"

She heard the panic in his voice. The ship jerked violently.

"Crash, already!"

"We're going down!"

They were slowly losing altitude, and now she was out of rounds. But luck hadn't forsaken them quite yet. Not entirely, anyway.

The dreadnought's cannons fell silent. The incoming fire ceased. And then the mammoth ship was listing. Metal screamed and flames burst from the superstructure as the craft began its downward spiral, Diamond Weapon still dangling in its harness below. The lush forests of Tenebrae lay ahead of them.

They watched as Diamond Weapon slammed into the ground. Dust geysered into the air and hung suspended, blocking their view. It was impossible to see what had become of the airship—or of the monster.

"Did we get 'im?"

Wind gently tugged at the veil of dust, and the dreadnought was slowly revealed. It lay on its side, half-demolished.

In its shadow, something moved.

They heard a piercing roar as Diamond Weapon rose from the wreckage.

"Oh for the love of..."

Aranea slammed a fist against the gun controls. They had no ammunition left, and at this point they were running on fumes. Wedge was managing to keep the ship on a stable, if low, flight path, but there was no way he could coax from it the kind of mobility they'd need to fight a daemon-infused superweapon.

"Wedge. I want you to head for Tenebrae. Stop Biggs's train. There's enough fuel left for that, right?"

The fight against Diamond Weapon wasn't over yet. She still had one card left to play.

"Get the civilians out of the area. Evacuate whomever you can."

She stood.

"What about you?" Wedge asked, his eyes wary.

"I got a date with Tiny."

"Huh? But we're all outta rounds. We don't have any weapons left to shoot it with."

"Still got one left."

She slung the Stoss onto her back. "This helluva big shot right here."

Aranea patted the spear, her longtime companion of so many battles past, and offered up a silent plea. *Don't let me down now.*

She opened the ship's rear hatch. The howling wind ripped at her body. They were close enough to Diamond Weapon now that she could make it. At this range she wouldn't have to worry about being blown off course.

She tuned the comm to the 87th's general channel and wondered how many were still alive to hear her message.

"Attention, all units! This might be the last thing I ever say to all of you, so listen up. I've resigned my command and the squadron is disbanded. As of today, we're no longer in service to the empire."

From the cockpit, Wedge was yelling at her to come back inside, but she ignored him. She kicked off from the lip of the hatch, into a dive straight at Diamond Weapon's head. The dropship, Wedge at its helm, continued to speed on toward Tenebrae.

As she plummeted, she uttered one last quiet line into the comm. "I just want you all to know . . . It's been an honor to serve with you." And then her spear was out, and she was closing in on the target. Just a hair off her intended trajectory. Well within tolerance.

"Hey, Tiny! I got a present for you!"

The monster's massive head was directly below her. The disgustingly colored tumor of a core on its brow was dull and lightless, thank the Six. She didn't want to have to deal with the same lethal crimson beam that left Gralea's ground forces a smoldering heap.

The Stoss struck true, right into the core's center. Diamond Weapon roared in reaction. At such close range, the sound was unbearable. It felt like it might rattle her skull apart. But with both hands on the spear, she had no way to cover her ears. The only thing she could think to do to get her mind off the pain was scream back. She fired the Stoss's thrusters to dig in as deep as she could and yelled back at the monster until her throat was raw.

She'd hoped that one dive might be enough, that she'd take out the core and be done with it. Unfortunately, the empire's giant pet seemed to be engineered a bit tougher than that.

Diamond Weapon twisted its giant body and tossed its head from side to side. Aranea clung to the Stoss, still lodged deep in the core. She flicked its controls, changing the spearpoint into a hook shape for an extra bit of anchorage.

Even with that, she was barely hanging on. Her body was thrown up, down, left, right as the monster thrashed, the force of its movement making her as nauseated as a cadet on a maiden airship flight. It took all of Aranea's effort to keep clinging to the Stoss's shaft, and so her guard was down when Diamond Weapon swiped one huge arm up toward its head, as if swatting away an obnoxious fly. She was hurtling downward before she knew what hit her.

She landed right in the guts of the downed dreadnought. Her back slammed against the hard armor plating—the same armor that had deflected all her earlier cannon fire. Her vision went white. The back of her head throbbed and burned. She thought she might vomit.

But she couldn't just lie there. She had to get up. Aranea gathered her remaining strength, trying to jump back to her feet. Instead, all she managed to do was to roll to one side.

As pathetic as it was, the roll saved her life. One giant fist came smashing down beside her.

Aranea stared, horrified, at where the monster's blow had crumpled the heavy armor plating like paper. With a single strike, Diamond Weapon had inflicted more damage than the full, sustained firepower of an imperial dropship. This time, she stood. *Gotta stop this thing*, she thought. *Can't let it reach Tenebrae.*

She angled her spearpoint skyward and jumped high.

"Never imagined myself going toe-to-toe with a giant magitek weapon," she shouted into the rushing wind. "Just goes to show, you never know what life's gonna throw at you!"

Her spear bored into one of exposed areas in the monster's midsection, and she silently thanked the ground forces for chipping away the armor on its chest and upper arms. The Stoss couldn't generate enough altitude for her to reach Diamond Weapon's head in a single jump, so it looked like she was in for some free-climbing. She hoped at the same time she might find a way to slow down the thing's limbs.

When she finally made it to the upper arm, she let out a frustrated grunt. The Stoss was planted firm and deep, but she was at a dead end. She couldn't find any route to get higher. Worse, Diamond Weapon's giant hands continued to flail at her. She leapt down, withdrawing to the safety of the ground to regroup for another attempt.

"Let's try that again," she said. A high jump, and she made it to the chest, spear anchored deep. Another jump, and she scaled the upper arm. The shoulder was next, but in swooped a giant hand, swatting her away, and she was back on the ground, game reset.

But she was getting the hang of things.

"Y'know, it'd be real nice," she began, leaping up once again, "if you'd just die already."

Diamond Weapon's arm swept in. She jumped again, before it could knock her away. This time, she just might make it.

"Hrrraaaugh!" Her war cry echoed as her spear drove into the core. She hadn't connected right at the middle, but it was a solid hit nonetheless. She flicked the controls on the Stoss, transforming the speartip to its hook shape, and then she thrust in again. The spearpoint began to rotate rapidly, churning that section of the core's rotten red tumor mass to mush.

Her body lurched downward as Diamond Weapon staggered, her assault seeming to have an effect. She kicked one boot against the core, thrusting herself away from the monster before its arm could knock her down again.

The ground was rushing up at her fast, but the Stoss was slow to respond, and she couldn't change the spear's mode back in time to engage the retrofire. The hard landing sent her tumbling across the ground. Diamond Weapon's arm was overhead before she could get back up. So this was the end.

"Almost had it," she muttered.

Granted, it had been pretty rash to take on a colossal superweapon while armed with a single spear. Still, she'd done her best. And her best hadn't been too bad, she thought, shutting her eyes against her impending doom.

But the blow never arrived. She heard a sound like machine-gun fire, and her eyes flew open. The arm should have been right on top of her, but it was nowhere to be found.

Voices crackled over her comm. "Heads up, Lady A!"

"Sorry for the wait."

Two magitek armors slammed down in front of her, machine guns rattling. She saw Diamond Weapon beyond them, its ass planted squarely on the ground.

"Biggs! Wedge! What are you doing back here?!"

What had happened with the train? Were the people all right?

The answers came before she could ask. "Don't worry! All the passengers were safely evacuated!"

Wedge was the one speaking. He must have still been feeling the buzz of his earlier drinks. She could tell, even over the comm. She chuckled and stood.

"All of them," Wedge added, "except for one lout who wanted to come along and play hero, that is."

Aranea let out a snort. Biggs couldn't even muster a comeback, so he changed the subject. "You two ready to put an end to this?"

She lifted her spear in lieu of a spoken answer. Diamond Weapon was already struggling to its feet. No more time for banter. They had to get serious.

"It's almost down! We just need to give it one more push!"

Biggs and Wedge laid into the monster's plating with their guns, and she went after the parts left exposed once the armor was stripped away. If they could knock it back down on the ground, it'd be just a short jump with the Stoss. She'd be right between the eyes, perfectly positioned for a direct hit at the core.

"Legs! Focus on the legs!" she shouted.

She saw the muzzle flash of the two MAs' guns, now pointed low. The plates on Diamond Weapon's left shin came loose, and the monster's hulking form began to limp. It roared and flailed, kicking up huge clouds of dust. Visibility went to nil. The monster's temper tantrum had created a smokescreen that lay across the entire battlefield. Fat chance of finding the core down on the ground like that.

"Biggs," she shouted into the comm. "Got a favor to ask. How's your throwing arm?"

If the free-climbing part of the competition was over, maybe it was time for the javelin.

Biggs caught on quick. "Good to go! Hop on!"

Flung with the force of the MA, she was a missile on its way through the cloud of dust. When she could see again, Diamond Weapon's face was right in front of her. She'd reached the apex of her trajectory level with the monster's head. She opened the Stoss's throttle to max, hoping to maintain enough velocity for the strike.

"Just remember who started this," she yelled as the spearpoint drove in. About a third of the core had been destroyed by her previous attack. Time to put the rest of the damn orb into the blender.

She tended to avoid using the Stoss's overdrive function, since it was rough on the machine, but if there was ever a time of need, this was it.

"Open wide!"

One more thrust. The spearpoint was wrapped in a red light that burned like flame. It spun at high speed, drilling deep into the partially destroyed core. She pushed hard, driving it deeper still. With the engine limiter off, the body of the Stoss was getting very hot, very fast. Her hands felt like they were being held above scalding water. Then came the acrid stench of her gloves melting. But she wasn't going to stop. Not now.

The body of the spear began to vibrate and grew hotter yet. Suddenly, the material at her spearpoint swelled into a white-hot bubble and . . . boom. The explosion ignited Diamond Weapon's core and sent fragments arcing six ways to hell. Aranea didn't even have time to rejoice. She'd been caught in the wave of the explosion, too, and now she was hurtling toward the earth, with no Stoss to stop her fall.

"Lady A!" someone shouted.

Biggs. The arm of his suit stretched toward her. A touching gesture, but it was going to fall more than a bit short if he'd meant to actually catch her.

"We've got you!" Wedge yelled.

Then the second MA was leaping onto the arm of the first, and Biggs sent Wedge's machine flying toward her trajectory. Aranea stretched her own arm out, reaching desperately.

"Wedge!" she screamed back.

The moment the cybersuit's appendage closed on her singed glove, the shock wave hit. Diamond Weapon's explosion dwarfed that of her tiny magitek spear. She clung to the MA's arm as they were slammed into the ground. The smell of burning daemon and scorched earth flooded her nostrils.

A great big goodbye from Tiny, and all three of us going with it, she thought bitterly.

And then she blacked out.

When she awoke to darkness, her first thought was, *There's no way that didn't kill me.* But she tasted grit in her mouth, and her face was pressed into stinking mud. She tested her arms and legs. They moved, but she couldn't get up. She didn't even know which way up was. There was little other choice than to flail her limbs and see where that took her.

It was a bit like swimming in place. The weight on her back shifted, cueing her that she was facedown. She pushed down with her palms and knees. Her body inched forward. Again. She was crawling her way free, one laborious push at a time. The area before her eyes grew lighter.

And then she was out of the mound of mud under which she'd been buried. She coughed repeatedly, hacking up the dirt lining the inside of her mouth with each convulsion.

She turned in a slow circle, still coughing. The wreckage of the two MAs lay nearby. They were well beyond repair. Not too far off, she saw the remains of a big billboard.

The Most Relaxing Stay of Your Life
Tenebrae Highland Resort
Straight Ahead

The letters were stripped away or faded in places, but from age, not from the explosion. Tenebrae hadn't been a hot resort destination for residents of the empire since before the occupation of Fenestala Manor.

As for the sign's message, it was an irony not lost on her.

"Most relaxing stay of my life, huh? Could use that right about now."

She looked around. "Biggs? Wedge?"

"Over here." She heard a groan.

Then another, pathetic moan. "Any chance I could get a hand?"

Each voice came from directly below a mound of mud and rubble. At each, a small section of mud parted, enough for a single hand to pop out. The first was thick and rough. Biggs. The other, with its knobby knuckles, definitely belonged to Wedge. Aranea grabbed each in turn and helped the men pull themselves up out of the debris.

"Looks like it's mission accomplished, boys," she said, with a long sigh of relief. Biggs and Wedge both coughed and spat on the ground, their saliva brown with mud and sand. They'd all been to hell and back, but at least they were still alive. The evacuees were safe, too. Aranea shook her head in disbelief. *All's well that ends well, I guess.*

A grin lit up Biggs's face, and he cleared his throat.

"I just want you all to know . . . It's been an honor to serve with you," he said, voice pitched an octave too high.

Aranea turned away, hoping to hide her flushed cheeks. Seems they'd heard the little parting message she'd given during her dive.

"She ever say anything like that before?" Biggs asked, nudging Wedge with an elbow.

"Don't think so."

"Those're some pretty heavy words."

"Got that right. The kind of thing people say before they up and die on you."

Their skit finished, the two lapsed into a fit of chuckles.

They're never going to let me live this down, Aranea realized, her lips pursed tight.

And they were still at it.

"Hmm. Sky's clear, but it feels like we might get a spot of rain," Biggs jested.

"Real thunderstorm, I reckon," Wedge chimed in.

"Ha ha, very funny. Now give it a rest, would you?"

But her words were drowned out by a piercing shriek overhead. Daemons. Flying ones. Probably inbound from Gralea.

Seemed about right, given their luck.

"Well," Biggs said. "Here comes our thunderstorm."

"I knew there was gonna be trouble," Wedge added.

They both looked at their commodore, with matching irritated looks on their faces.

"Oh, what, so this is *my* fault?"

But there was no time for the blame game. The three scrambled to the wreckage of the two MAs, grabbing anything that looked like it might serve as a weapon. They had to stop the daemons, keep them away from the civilians in Tenebrae.

"When the hell are we gonna get some sleep?" Aranea groaned.

It looked like the worst day of her life wasn't quite over yet.

When they'd eked out a victory against the last pack of flying daemons, killing what they could and sending the rest scattering back the way they came, it was nearly evening. They made for the dropship, dragging themselves along, bodies battered and limp like old rags. They got the craft into the air, and then they were heading toward the people they'd saved in Tenebrae, the children they'd evacuated on the train, and the girl entrusted to them by Loqi.

When they arrived, no sooner did the girl's eyes fall on Aranea than they were filling with great big tears. It was another scene that seemed all too familiar, an unpleasant echo from a dark corner of Aranea's past. Before she was even aware of her actions, she'd scooped the girl up into a tight hug and was walking over to settle on one of the benches, running a gentle hand over her hair.

"I was so scared," the girl whispered.

"It's all right now. You're okay."

"Everyone . . . went away, or died, and . . . "

Aranea felt the small body trembling in her arms. She knew that fear. She knew that sadness. She wouldn't have wished it on anyone else in the world, least of all the young girl before her now.

She'd been so eager to wipe every last daemon from the face of the star, she'd not even been able to wait the full ten years to hit her legal age of majority before she joined the mercenary forces. And there hadn't been anyone left around her to tell her to wait, to not be so reckless.

But her life had gone smoothly enough, all things considered. She met Biggs and Wedge, gained new comrades in arms, and eventually made enough of a name for herself in the imperial service to earn a bit of rank. It had been rough when the empire started toying around with daemons, though. It didn't feel right owing allegiance to an army employing the same monsters she'd wanted to destroy. She'd strayed a bit from her one great aim in life, but she went on nonetheless.

"Tell me. What's your name?" Aranea asked. It was a detail she'd overlooked in all the rush.

"Sol," the girl replied. "Solara Antiquum."

"Sol, huh? Not a bad name."

It had an air of dignity to it, bringing to mind that grand, ancient civilization the nation of Niflheim aspired to.

"I want to be strong."

Aranea smiled. That was another thing she remembered herself saying, all those years ago.

"Like you," the girl continued.

"Like me?"

Sol nodded, her face earnest.

"I'm not really that strong. I barely even managed to make it through today. Thought I might break down at any moment."

The girl paused, clearly processing the information, before asking, "Honest?"

"Honest. It's a good thing a certain little someone showed up to inspire me. What was that you said back there? 'I wanna fight, too'?"

As Aranea said it, she playfully tapped Sol's nose.

"Couldn't let myself get shown up by a little pipsqueak like you."

Sol gave a bashful smile, and Aranea breathed a silent sigh of relief. It was the first smile she'd seen from the girl. It looked like she was going to be all right.

When Aranea finally lifted Sol off her lap and set her down, a small sparkle caught her eye. It gave her a start. She hadn't noticed the brooch before, thanks to the blanketing folds of Loqi's mantle. In fact, she hadn't noticed the girl's outfit at all. Sol wore fine clothes, well-tailored and obviously expensive. The design of the brooch was more than just familiar: it was a symbol practically burned into the mind of any member of the imperial forces. The crest of House Aldercapt.

What had Loqi said back there?

Direct orders of His Radiance, to be executed with utmost discretion.

The possibility had occurred to her, faintly, aboard the dropship. Iedolas had lost his son in battle several years ago. Officially, there was no heir to the imperial throne. The emperor was dead, and the line of succession had come to an end . . . unless there was a child nobody knew about. An illegitimate child born to the imperial prince.

And her name, Sol.

The sun will rise once more.

Those had been the emperor's final words.

Maybe Iedolas hadn't fully trusted his chancellor. After all, Izunia had that air about him, like he was concealing some kind of secret. Or a thousand secrets, more like. It would make sense if the emperor decided to keep quiet about his only living heir. When Ardyn Izunia had finally bared his fangs, the emperor must have given the order to Loqi to find and secure the child.

"Listen to me, sweetheart," she said.

Aranea didn't know where or how the girl had spent her days until now. But there was no question in Aranea's mind that the people in Sol's life had loved her dearly.

"You've got a great big life ahead of you. Let's see that you make the most of it."

It was what all of them would have wanted, from the people who'd lovingly raised her since the day she was born, to those who laid down their lives to see that she could live hers.

Aranea hugged the girl once again.

M.E. 766

Lady A, you seen the little miss?"

"She took off a couple of hours ago. Why?"

"She did?"

"Yeah. Said she was meeting you two over at Beta Point. I guess if you're here, she must've run into Biggs on the way. Give him a shout over the comm."

"I, uh . . ." Wedge said, concern painted on his face. Something smelled like trouble.

"I was just over at Beta," he continued. "Biggs is the only one there. And I'm pretty sure . . ."

Aranea realized she'd been had.

Hmph. Clever little twerp, she thought, as she recalled the conversation she'd had with Sol two hours ago.

"I'll be fine," the girl had said. "I'll be with experienced hunters. And we're not even going that far. I don't need Biggs and Wedge babysitting me."

"It's precisely *because* they're experienced that I want Biggs and Wedge along. Meldacio's people have a job to do. They don't have time to be looking after you."

"When are you gonna quit treating me like a child?!"

"You want to go clear out daemons with the rest of them? Come talk to me in a decade."

"I've *already* waited a decade!"

They had a lot in common. Aranea had thought so since the beginning. What she hadn't counted on was raising the girl to be even more strong-willed than she was herself. But teens would be teens. They have to start lashing out at some point.

"The life of a foster parent is a hard one," she sighed, looking at Wedge.

Aranea hadn't had any parents left to rebel against when she reached adolescence, but she'd probably made life plenty difficult for the villagers and mercs who'd looked after her. Still, this wasn't the past. For one thing, when Aranea was a teen, the world still had daylight. Things had been peaceful, more or less. A little girl playing grown-up among mercenaries had a decent chance of making it without getting herself killed.

Now that Eos was locked in perpetual night and daemons roamed around wherever the hell they pleased, irresponsible decisions were more often than not served up with a nice, cold side of death. The fact that Sol was a few years older than Aranea had been when she'd started fighting didn't bring any peace of mind.

That was why, even when there was a whole group of hunters going out on a patrol, Aranea made certain to send Biggs and Wedge along. But apparently, Sol had grown sick of her little security detail. She'd cooked up a plan complete with fake rendezvous details to ditch them. This was a first.

When are you gonna quit treating me like a child?! The girl's tone had been defiant.

"Never would've pegged myself as an overprotective parent," Aranea said.

"What's overprotective about it? Parents are supposed to worry about their kids. Why am I even saying this? I gotta get out there. I gotta find her!"

A slight smile formed on Aranea's lips. At least she wasn't the *most* overprotective adult in Sol's life. That title belonged to another. Two others, in fact.

"I gotta get a message over to Biggs, and then . . . Oh geez. Listen, Lady A. I'll see you later, all right?"

"Thanks, Wedge. I owe you one."

The man left in a fluster, and then, for the moment, Aranea found herself alone.

"Guess it's 'bout time to radio in the day's report," she told herself.

But when she stepped over to the transceiver, she realized it was earlier than she'd thought. She still had some time, and an idea formed about how to burn it.

"Hmph. How long has it been since I last made that?" she wondered out loud.

There was one more can of beans left, and if she put some of that dehydrated meat to soak now, there'd be just enough time to reconstitute it. It'd be a little sparser than usual, and she'd be making do with only what they had on hand, but still, it would be a home-cooked dinner. Her famous cassoulet.

More often than not, nights at the outposts meant eating straight out of a can. It was nice to enjoy a proper meal together every once in a while. There was always the chance that Sol wouldn't be back until tomorrow, but if so, she could reheat and serve it again. Cassoulet was just as good the next day, if not better. Sol would come home to a clean bed and a big bowl of her favorite food—after she got an earful for running off on her own, that is.

Aranea opened the little cabinet and began pulling out ingredients, humming as she set about the task.

Choosing Freedom

The ocean's depths are much like the sky. As light passes through water, the playful shimmers trace the same graceful arcs as petals falling through the air. A dance of beauty, but one mingled with a trace of sadness.

Luna.

She heard her beloved's voice calling her name. Whether real or merely an illusion conjured by her overwhelming desire to see him again, she could not tell. He was there, far off in the water, his image wavering and softly distorted by the current, as if revealing him to be no more than a mirage born of longing.

His lips formed her name once more.

Luna!

Shouting her name, brow knit with desperation, he was seemingly on the verge of tears. She had seen him like this once before, on a day twelve years ago, when they'd still been children, when they'd only barely met. His expression and words now were a perfect echo of what they'd been then. His arm, too, was again outstretched, as if he might bridge the great and growing distance between them.

That was the day when the peace in her home of Tenebrae was suddenly shattered. Soldiers of the Niflheim Empire stormed Fenestala Manor and captured it, and then she was running, being pulled along by the hand. Failure to escape meant death—not for her, but for one much more important than her. Prince Noctis.

The title of Oracle was not yet hers, but still she understood the duties with which she would be tasked. She was to aid the king of Lucis—the *future* king. That was her calling, as bestowed upon her by the gods, and she would see it fulfilled even if that meant casting her own life aside.

They will not be able to escape with me slowing them down. If he does not have to protect me as well, I know for certain His Majesty will be able to bring Noctis to safety.

She released her grip on King Regis's hand. She was not afraid. There was only the ache of sadness at knowing she might never see Noctis again. But that was a small price to pay if it meant the prince would live.

She watched as he was carried off into the distance. Not wanting to forget a single moment, she kept her head held high, eyes trained upon him and ears open. She saw his outstretched arm, reaching for her, and heard his desperate cries. She watched, unmoving, even as the imperial host swarmed around her.

Now, here in the ocean, she saw the face of the young boy, the same one long burned into the backs of her eyes. And superimposed upon it was the face of the adult.

The time has come for us to part.

For some reason, it was harder this time than it had been before. The old grief ached, ready to tear a hole straight through her. Why was it so difficult? She was older now. She'd come of age. Quite some time had passed since her ascension.

So why did she feel like this? Why did she wish to cry like a small child?

She bit her lip. Her king's last memory would not be of tear-stained cheeks. He would remember her happy.

Gathering together every ounce of willpower she possessed, she put a gentle smile on her lips and silently stretched her arm out toward his. A blue flower was lightly clasped in her hand, one of the sylleblossoms she loved so much.

I give this flower to you. This is sure to be our final moment.

When the world falls down around you, and hope is lost, when you find yourself alone, amid a lightless place, look to the distance. Know that I am there, and that I watch over you always.

Farewell, dear Noctis.

He flailed in the water. Their outstretched hands drifted apart. It was so like that other day, all those years ago, and yet this time they drew apart slowly, almost gently. She felt grateful to the sea, for there, immersed in its water, her tears could not be seen.

And with that same gentle momentum, she continued to sink, deeper and deeper, to a place that would never know the rays of the sun.

I can cry now, she told herself, *for no matter how loudly I wail, I needn't worry that Noctis might hear*.

A kind voice interrupted her thoughts. "Let not sorrow overwhelm."

She knew the voice well, for it had been at her side since she was very young.

"Sleep now, just for a little while," Gentiana continued.

Gentle fingertips softly lowered her eyelids, as they'd done so many times in the past. Somehow, Gentiana always knew. It had been a mysterious constant of her childhood: whenever Luna woke late at night, troubled by frightening dreams, the Messenger was there. Mother and Ravus would be sound asleep, but Gentiana would be at her bedside, coaxing her back into slumber.

She still ached with grief, but the loneliness and worry lifted as though they'd never been there. Tranquility bathed her mind under Gentiana's soothing hands, and she allowed herself to be carried away by sleep.

It was a mysterious sleep, not unlike a shallow afternoon repose. She hung in the space between dream and consciousness, and everything radiated warmth. Thought no longer held shape. Time was forgotten. There was nothing left but the tender, nebulous hands of warmth gently cupped around her.

How much time passed like that?

Suddenly, she felt her body rising. It was not a comforting sensation. Instead, it was a stark, jolting difference from the hazy warmth of before. Slightly disorienting, like being woken up. No. She *was* waking. She felt a distinct weight against her eyelids and forced them open. A wave of prickling sensations and then pain came rolling in. Her mouth opened, hungry for air, only to find foul-tasting liquid. She realized she was underwater and flailed her arms about, grateful to find firm ground below and the surface not far away. She sat up, freeing herself from the water's embrace, and coughed repeatedly.

The shallows in which she found herself would have been difficult to describe as clean by any measure. Her eyes stung, streaming tears as she blinked the water's dirty residue away.

"Where am I?" she asked aloud, half to prove to herself this was not another dream. One hand came to her throat as she spoke. The clear vibration of the words brought further proof. This was reality, true and certain.

Finally, when her eyes were clear, she looked about. The world was dim and her surroundings hard to discern. The air was cloyingly humid, and she heard the sound of something else—something not liquid—spilling to the ground at intervals.

"Is that sand?"

If not sand, it was certainly of similar quality. Fine grains of something rained down from above. Her eyes slowly grew accustomed to the dimness, and she looked about. There was a hewn ceiling but no windows, as far as she could tell. Not far away, she could see the edge of the shallow body of water she was now sitting in.

Where in the world was she? It was not a building, but neither did she feel herself to be in some purely natural cavern. She couldn't say for certain because of the darkness, but some aspects seemed familiar. The thick odor, somewhere between moss and mold, and the way the chill hung in the air brought memories of long ago. A place she'd once visited had been like this. It, too, had been dim, but not so oppressive. Perhaps given the light of several braziers, the similarity would become more apparent. What had that underground tomb been called?

"Reciele." Just as the name came to her lips, another memory flashed to mind. She saw the chancellor of Niflheim, Ardyn Izunia, eyes full of anger and hatred, and in his hand, a dagger.

"I'm . . . alive?"

It seemed impossible. She remembered the indescribable pain as the dagger was driven into her side. She remembered the blood gushing from the wound and the fear as her consciousness slipped away.

A hand unconsciously moved to her flank, where the blade would have entered. At the site of the wound, she found an unnatural concavity of skin pulled tight, surrounded by a raised ridge of scar tissue. So her memory of being stabbed by Ardyn was truth. How, then, was she here, alive and well?

An involuntary shudder coursed through her body, not prompted by such macabre thoughts, but rather by simple cold. Her arms trembled, goose bumps forming across her skin. When she attempted to rub warmth into them, she realized her clothes were soaked. She looked down. This was the dress she'd worn the day she was stabbed. It clung to her skin, torn in several places, stained and ruined.

How could this be? She was supposed to be dead, but here she was, somehow transported to some mysterious underground space. It was all too much to fathom.

"It's freezing," she said to herself. Her voice was small and wavering. Her teeth chattered. Pushing all her questions aside for later, she stood. She'd need to get out of here before she could do anything else.

The world spun. She let out a small gasp, then found herself collapsed back on the ground, her left shoulder having taken the brunt of the fall. Standing hadn't been as easy as she'd thought. In fact, it was almost as if she'd forgotten how to walk at all. She rubbed her shoulder and tried once more, slowly and carefully.

With a hand on one wall, she shuffled forward. She could feel a draft, and the direction in which the air flowed. If she followed that, she'd find her way outside.

After a few steps, strength seemed to return to her legs. As she walked, the heels of her boots clacked against the flagstones, and the sound continued to echo across the stone surfaces of the rooms and corridors. A little farther, and she felt certain she'd find a long stone stairway leading to the surface. Either that or a short slope leading upward to a higher level. All the tombs were built like this. They had to be, to accomodate the ceremonies when the dead were carried down to their final resting place. As Oracle, she'd visited a number of such places in order to perform the rites.

Although the layout was not unfamiliar, this time there was no one leading the way with light in hand. Doubt formed in her mind; suddenly, it seemed unlikely that her outward journey would be straightforward. She might wander here, lost in the darkness, for some time.

A sudden rustling noise reached her ears, along with a sensation of something like dry leaves underfoot. The clear, unsettling sound interrupted the steady clack of her heels and forced her to a halt. She stooped and groped at the ground, discovering the object at her feet to be an old, crumpled newspaper. Next to it was a small bundle, like withered branches. A bouquet, most likely, brought as an offering to the dead who rested here. The newspaper must have been wrapped around the flowers.

Lunafreya felt a flush of anger at the irresponsible soul who had left an offering on the floor rather than seeing it properly to the intended grave. She took the erstwhile bouquet and situated it properly on the stone coffin near where she stood, though not without some guilt. A gift of dry, withered stems seemed ill consolation for a departed soul.

She began neatly folding the newspaper, intending to dispose of it once she reached the outside. It wouldn't do to leave rubbish behind in a tomb. When her eyes fell on a small photograph on one page, though, her hands paused.

"... Noctis?" she gasped. Despite the photo's size, there was no mistaking his face. But in the darkness of the tomb, she couldn't hope to make out the words of the article. All she caught when she strained her eyes to read were scattered phrases: "third year since the disappearance of" and "king of Lucis." When she looked to find the date at the top of the page, she realized it had been torn away.

"Noctis? Missing?" she whispered. "That cannot be." She tried to calm herself. She hadn't read the article properly yet. Perhaps it was not Noctis who had disappeared.

"Three years ago, His Majesty King Regis would have been alive and well," she reassured herself. "If the article was about the king, then ..."

But how could she be sure Regis was king at the time the article was printed? Three years ago from when? From today? When was today? How much time had passed?

Another chill ran down her spine. Something vile was trying to crawl its way up her leg. She wanted to leave this place at once. She wanted desperately to be outside. She had to hurry.

When she turned to continue on her way, she felt a tremor at her back. From over her shoulder, she saw a burst of debris rain down from the ceiling. Then another, and another. Each time, the quantity seemed to increase, a steady mix of gravel, dirt, and who knew what else. Something up above was trying to break through the ceiling. What that something was, she had not the faintest clue.

Then the intruder was seeping in: some black, wispy thing that floated in the air, reminiscent of a worn and dirtied rag, and yet far more massive. As it broke through, it unfurled itself to fill the narrow passage, blocking her view of the newly formed hole, as well as the way from whence she'd come. A knot formed in Lunafreya's stomach. Her fears were soon confirmed. From the eerie dark mass stretched a huge pair of hands—if they could truly be called hands at all. Pale, bluish-white bone curved in great arcs, forming scythe-like claws. The havoc those claws could wreak was obvious at merely a glance.

If there was a god of death in the world, this was undoubtedly the form it would take. But in truth, she knew it for neither reaper or beast: it was a daemon. Some type she'd not encountered before, but a daemon nonetheless. She could faintly make out the telltale black miasma exuded from its billowing figure.

Even when she'd ascertained as much, her body somehow failed to react. She had to run. If she did not, the creature would prove reaper enough. She knew this, but her legs only trembled, failing to afford her even one step to safety. She stood transfixed by the daemon's two glowing eyes, like holes gouged out of darkness. As her body shook, she felt a scream rise within her chest. It tore from her throat, and then Lunafreya's curse of stasis was gone. She turned and ran, thinking of nothing but running as fast as she could.

Up the incline of the tunnel, through the dark corridors, running, running, without a spare moment even to look back at her pursuer. If she slowed even slightly, she would be overtaken, and once she was in the grasp of those curved claws, it would all be over.

Up. The only answer was up. Get to the surface, and if her luck was any good, it would be daytime and the daemon would be unable to follow. She still knew not whether the tomb was one she'd visited in the past, but it didn't matter. The layout would be similar. There would be sloped tunnels, stairways, and small rooms cut into the stone, with crossroads running between them.

A daemon so large would not be able to squeeze through the crossroads. It might not even be able to push its way through one of the narrow stairways. As long as she stayed away from open spaces, she might have a chance. She might distance herself from the pursuer while still in the tomb.

Finally, she spotted a narrow corridor, just wide enough for a single human to pass through. She darted in, then dared to spare a second to flick a glance over one shoulder. Just as she'd hoped, the massive black form hung unmoving at the mouth of the passage, a curtain blocking her view of anything beyond. *It must be stuck*, she thought. *It cannot pursue any farther*.

She breathed a sigh, certain for a moment that she was safe. But her relief was premature. A roar shook the corridor. Bits of rock showered down from overhead. Lunafreya's blood froze. This was the same monster that had ripped its way through a ceiling of stone. What desperation had allowed her to imagine a corridor any manner of refuge? The daemon seemed perfectly content to break the walls apart to reach her. If not shredded by its claws, she'd be buried under the rubble. Either way meant death.

She continued to run, hell-bent on escape. The corridor sloped upward. Beyond that, she neither knew nor cared about the tomb's layout any longer. As long as she was moving up—as long as she was getting closer to the surface—nothing else mattered.

Dull thuds echoed from behind her. No corridor or wall was going to stop the monster. She had to get outside.

The ground at her feet shook violently. She tumbled but felt no pain. There was no time. Any pause invited death. The daemon's thrashing brought still more stones loose. Jagged shards fell from above and the stairs began to crumble beneath her feet, but she pressed on, scrambling along somewhere between a run and a crawl.

Then the oppressive smell of stone and dirt was gone. A chill wind brushed across her skin. Outside. She'd made it. No sooner did her mind register the fact than another tremor, accompanied by the deafening thunder of falling stone, sent her facedown to the ground.

The roar subsided, and Lunafreya nervously glanced back. The stairway into the earth was gone. The entire tunnel leading down into the tomb must have collapsed from the intensity of the daemon's rampage. Nothing remained to suggest she'd just emerged from an underground complex or that one had ever existed in this place at all.

No. That wasn't quite true. This place was, without a doubt, a gravesite. A short distance away rested a water basin made of stone, and next to that grew a large, old tree and a plot of small flowers. This was a spot to rest for those who came bearing offerings to place upon the graves of those they'd lost.

Half of the tree's branches were gone. They had been wrenched off and broken, and now they lay scattered among the roots as if telling the tale of some huge, rampaging beast that had passed by this place. Lunafreya picked up one of the fallen branches that appeared longer and sturdier than the others. She grasped it tightly in her hand. It was not much more than a stick, but its length rivaled her own height, and it would serve as a makeshift weapon for the time being. It was far better than walking through a nighttime gravesite unarmed.

She began to walk, intending to hurry toward some safer location, when she realized she was missing one boot. It must have been lost during her panicked flight from the tomb. Just one of a pair would hardly serve swift progress, so the only option seemed to be to abandon it and proceed barefoot. She would just have to find replacements somewhere along the way, preferably before some sharp stone or fragment of glass found its way into her soles. Perhaps by morning she'd have made it to some place well inhabited enough to offer shops.

The last thought prompted her to cast a casual glance upward. That was when the realization hit. Something was off. She slowly turned around, sweeping her gaze across the sky, straining her eyes against the blackness.

"Is it not night?" she wondered aloud.

The dimness overhead suggested otherwise. It was not the dark brought on by dusk. There were no stars. There was no moon. But neither was it the black of a moonless night. The entire world was bathed in a gloomy, unnatural gray. When she looked harder, she saw flecks swirling through the darkened sky. It was unnerving. They were far too similar to another black mist she knew: the particles of miasma that emanated from daemonic bodies.

A shudder passed through her as she whispered, "What is going on?"

In one direction, she saw an endless expanse of ice. In another, a vast, empty desert. Farther afield was a forest of familiar profile. If those were the woods of her homeland of Tenebrae, then she had to be somewhere along the border of Succarpe and Eusciello.

How odd. There was no trace of anyone else. The strip of land sandwiched between desert and tundra was not suited for planting, but she'd long heard it functioned as a transit artery. She stood along a major throughway. Trucks and other vehicles should have been passing by day and night, and yet there was nothing but silence. Not even an imperial dropship overhead.

Third year since the disappearance of... The newspaper's words rose in her mind.

She'd expended her life to form the covenants with the gods, and to see the Ring of the Lucii to its rightful heir. Everything she'd done was for the sake of the True King and to ensure the future of their star. So what did this gray sky mean? In the span between the events in Altissia and now, what could have happened to their world?

A roar shook the dim surroundings. She turned to find dust billowing from the remnants of the tomb—a tomb she'd thought crumbled and closed forevermore. Clumps of dirt and debris flew through the air, and then it was back: grim death unfurled itself once more, tattered rags fluttering wide overhead.

It was unthinkable. The collapse of the underground tomb should have surely been enough to see the daemon trapped and destroyed. With the entrance gone, she had breathed a sigh of relief, certain that the immediate threat was past. Now that relief went spiraling away like debris from the tomb. The daemon had emerged. Its hunt was not over.

With precious moments already lost to thought, Lunafreya spun away, clods of dirt spraying from beneath her feet as massive claws swung behind her. It was a close call—the arc of the claws had passed no more than a hairbreadth from her back. Luck and naught else had kept her from being ripped to shreds. She might not be so fortunate the next time.

Suddenly, she was glad to be barefoot, able to run much faster over the soil than she'd have ever managed in the high heels she had worn the day she'd been stabbed. She sprinted with all her might. The daemon caught the top of one shoulder, nearly pulling her to the ground, but her luck held and she was somehow able to shake free. The blow sent her tumbling, but she sprang back up and continued to run. If she could make it to one of the main roads . . . She prayed for there to be at least one passing truck. It didn't matter where it was headed. If she could hitch a ride, she'd be safe, away from this awful place.

She thought she heard the faint rumbling of an engine. The road had to be near. The muscles in her legs screamed in protest, but she carried on, unheeding.

And then the ground was gone. Her feet found no purchase, and her body plummeted through empty air. Whether she'd gone straight over some ridge or met some sloping path, she did not know, but the world spun. Her body rolled and finally thudded to a halt. The sound of the engine drew closer. It was her third stroke of luck in an otherwise unfortunate day. She had found her road and was now sprawled across it. She heard the screech of brakes and saw a motorcycle come to a halt mere inches from her nose. To one side of the wheel in her face, she spotted an attached sidecar.

Lunafreya scrambled to her feet and threw herself into the unoccupied sidecar. The daemon was still in pursuit. There wasn't time to ask permission.

"What are you doing?!" the driver demanded.

Lunafreya couldn't make out any features beneath helmet and goggles, but the driver's voice was clearly that of a young woman. Her garb seemed to indicate that she was a hunter. Lunafreya tried to respond, but her breaths came too heavy for clear words.

"I'm . . . I'm sorry, but . . . "

The driver audibly clicked her tongue. Lunafreya simply huddled deeper into the seat. Then the motorcycle and sidecar were in motion.

The daemon's claws were not far behind.

"Damn it!" the driver cursed. "I can't get this thing to go any faster with all the *extra weight*!"

"Right. Extra weight. What should I dump?" Lunafreya said, her hands groping at the items underfoot.

"Hey! No! I meant—"

But Lunafreya already had the corner of a cloth bag in hand—a particularly large one crammed in the floor of the sidecar. She tugged it free and threw it in the face of the pursuing daemon, knowing it was in vain, but desperate for any means to slow the monster down by even the tiniest bit.

The bag's contents spilled out over the roadway. Canned food. Hardly something to deem extra weight, she thought.

"I was talking about *you*!" the driver shouted over the roar of the engine. "*You're* the extra weight!"

"Oh no," Lunafreya muttered. "I'm sorry."

The imposed ride brought guilt enough. Now she'd managed to cause her unwilling companion further trouble. That her actions were taken in haste was no excuse. The vehicle had a new load to bear, and the traveler was now without rations on which she'd doubtless been counting. Lunafreya tightly gripped the long tree branch from the gravesite. She would not be any more of a burden. She'd made it this far on her own—more or less. In truth, she had no confidence in her odds. She'd been no match for the pursuing daemon either in or out of the tomb. But there was no other choice now. She'd have to face it.

Lunafreya grabbed the lip of the sidecar, intending to hop out. But a hand pulled her back in, and she dropped ungracefully onto the seat once more.

"Enough!"

Enough with the dramatics, the driver seemed to mean. Lunafreya had been accepted along for the ride.

"Just hang on tight and keep your mouth shut. It's gonna be bumpy, and I don't want you biting your tongue."

The engine revved higher, and Lunafreya was pressed back into her seat by the force of acceleration. The wind whipped against her, her hair streaming behind her like a veil. For a moment, it seemed like this burst of speed might see them to safety. But that hope was soon shattered.

Lunafreya sensed the bluish-white hands reaching from behind. Then, before her mind could even process the attack, she was being lifted from the sidecar and slammed against the roadway. They'd hardly made it any distance down the road.

Her left half felt heavy, numb. She gritted her teeth against the pain and rose to her feet. The motorcycle had already skidded to a stop, its rider hopping out, a shotgun in hand. From the way the younger woman held herself, it was clear she was no stranger to battle.

"Get back. I'll deal with this," commanded the rider.

Lunafreya shook her head in protest. This stranger was helping her when she could have kept going. If she hadn't stopped, she might have gotten away safely. Lunafreya owed it to her to help fight.

"What, you gonna give me a hand, then?"

Lunafreya nodded. "Yes. I can fight."

Inside, her confidence hardly measured up to her words. Would she truly be able to help against a daemon so ferocious? Still, she felt that she had to fight. The stranger might know how to hold her own, but she'd not yet witnessed the strength and terror of this daemon as Lunafreya had. This was not an opponent that could be taken down alone, without the aid of comrades.

To Lunafreya's relief, the branch from the gravesite had rolled to a stop at her feet. Picking it up and hanging on to it had seemed somewhat silly at the time; now she thanked her past self from the bottom of her heart. But when she bent to retrieve it, the stranger gave a snort of disbelief. "You've gotta be kidding me.

"You're gonna fight using that?" the stranger continued. "Is your head on straight? Look, just don't get in my way, all right?"

Lunafreya recalled her lessons. Years ago, as part of her training as Oracle, she'd learned how to fight with a polearm. She gripped her branch, adopting the proper stance for a spear, readying herself for the coming battle.

Just do as you were taught, she told herself. *Imagine that this branch is the Trident.*

"Here it comes!" the stranger shouted.

A report from the shotgun drowned out Lunafreya's response. The massive, writhing black form twisted in the air. Lunafreya jabbed at it with the branch, aiming for the incoming claws. She felt her blow land, then thrust again. Once more, she felt it firmly connect. Her hits were landing. She was helping—or so she thought. Then too many things were happening at once, and when she could again make sense of the world, it was her own body sprawled across the ground rather than the daemon's.

She scrambled to her feet, flustered. The shotgun sounded again, from mere steps away. The daemon's movements were unbelievably swift, and little of the weapon's shot was finding its mark. Lunafreya leveled her branch and charged once more. If she could grab the daemon's attention, she might provide her ally with an opening. Even a single moment might be enough.

A shock ran up both her arms and she let out a short cry of surprise. The branch, which should have been firmly in her grip, was spiraling away through the air, and the daemon's claws were swiping in.

"No!" she cried out loud. And in her mind, *I don't want to die! I refuse to. Not here. Not without any answers! Not without managing to help!*

Lunafreya flung both arms forward. She knew it was a futile gesture. This wasn't some harmless beast that might be driven away with her bare hands. And yet she stretched forth her arms anyway, filled with all her will and determination not to give in to death.

She braced for the pain of being shredded apart, vividly recalling the agony she'd experienced before at the threshold of death. She shut her eyes.

The sensation that arrived was something else entirely.

"Shouldn't I be . . . ?" she whispered to herself.

It was not pain. It was more of a tingling sensation, running from her fingertips up through her arms. When Lunafreya opened her eyes, the daemon was shrinking back, writhing as if in pain of its own.

"What happened?"

More reports from the shotgun, and the daemon's accompanying roars of pain shook the surrounding dimness. It seemed she'd somehow succeeded in stopping the daemon's movements, but she wasn't quite sure how. It was all beyond comprehension.

But she decided to try once more. Whatever it was she'd done, she had some idea of the sensation that had accompanied it, and a vague sense of how to make it happen again. The daemon hung in the air, its motions slowed. She moved in close, fighting back the fear. This was not a time to hesitate. She extended her right hand, mind focused on the tips of her fingers.

Remember what you felt, she commanded herself, but there was hardly a need. It came again almost automatically. The same puzzling force flowed freely through her arm. There was no need to coax it forth—if anything, it was smothering, overbearing, as if with a will of its own. And now with it came a clear, deep ache, spreading from her chest to the pit of her stomach. Lunafreya held her breath and weathered the pain.

The gun sounded several more times, and the daemon was writhing on the ground. Its features began to blur.

We're defeating it, Lunafreya thought to herself. *It's almost over.*

The sensation in her arms shifted. Before, it was as if something was flowing through them. Now it was a far more disturbing feeling, as if hundreds of tiny insects were crawling about beneath her skin. A guttural noise tried to force its way through her gritted teeth.

The daemon continued to squirm on the ground. Just a little more, and it would be gone. There was a grating screech, like metal against metal. She'd see this monster dead. She swore it to herself.

"Hey!" the stranger shouted. "Ease up! You're gonna get yourself killed!"

Lunafreya ignored the words of caution and stretched her hands toward the daemon once more. She steeled herself against a growing nausea.

The stranger yelled, "Above you!"

Lunafreya looked up. The claws were bearing down. Too close. She wouldn't be able to avoid them this time. The bluish-white scythes gouged deep into her upper arm. The pain ripped through her, an experience far worse than the crawling in her skin. And then, mere moments after delivering the devastating wound, the daemon dispersed into a spray of black particles. It was defeated.

The threat finally vanquished, Lunafreya's tensed muscles relaxed. But her relief was cut short by another wave of crushing pain. She fell to her knees.

"Are you all right?!" the stranger shouted.

Lunafreya nodded a lie. No, she was not all right, not in any sense of the words. The agony of her wound consumed her. Bile rose in her throat.

"Hang on. I'll find something to stop the bl—"

The stranger's words cut short with an audible gasp of surprise. Lunafreya's own breath caught, too. Blood should have been pooling below her arm, but the flow had already stopped. Instead, the gaping wound emitted a sickly purple glow, along with telltale black flecks. The skin closed over before their very eyes.

"What the hell just happened?" the stranger demanded, voice suddenly ripe with mistrust.

Lunafreya could hardly blame the woman. They'd both seen black flecks like that before. The sight of them could only lead to one line of thought: Miasma. Daemons. Suddenly Lunafreya was against the ground, the barrel of a pistol hard against her cheek.

"What are you? Some kind of monster?"

After what she'd observed of her own body, Lunafreya found it difficult to argue otherwise. Her silence brought a harsh jab of the gun.

"I asked you a question. What the hell are you? Answer me!"

Lunafreya didn't know what to say. But if she failed to speak at all, her fate was apparent.

"I'm . . ."

She trailed off, unsure how to continue. Her mind was muddled. And then the feel of cold metal was gone, and she heard the thump of a body hitting the hard surface of the road. Lunafreya hurried to right herself.

"Miss? Are you all right?"

The stranger had clearly been full of murderous rage. Now she was crumpled on the ground, body limp. Lunafreya put a hand to the woman's throat and found a stable pulse. She removed the woman's goggles and saw slight twitches of movement under her eyelids.

The stranger must have fainted from the hits she'd taken during the fight. Lunafreya loosened the collar of the woman's jacket, taking care not to jar her body.

She spread a hand, thinking to ease the stranger's discomfort with her powers as Oracle, then hesitated. The way she'd brought down the daemon—what *was* that power? It was bizarre and unsettling. What if it happened again now? Did she still have her powers of healing at all?

Lunafreya looked down at the palms of her hands. She ran her gaze along her arms. The gouges in her flesh had been deep, but now not even a scar remained. The wounds had healed over so cleanly it was as if they'd never been there at all. She had encountered no curative power like it before. In fact, she hesitated to think of it as curative at all. There had been those awful black particles, clustered over the site of the wound. Could they truly be what she thought they were?

Lunafreya had no answers. And one mystery still troubled her above all others.

"Why am I alive?" she wondered to herself again.

In that darkness that was not night, Lunafreya's hopes, too, seemed bleak.

The young woman was a walking armory. Lunafreya was half disturbed and half amazed. When she unfastened the stranger's jacket, intending to check her over for wounds in need of attention, she found an astonishing amount of weaponry. Her eyes involuntarily darted over it all: spare magazines, several knives she could only assume were meant for throwing, grenades hooked to a belt, and numerous cylindrical containers of varied sizes, whose purpose Lunafreya could not begin to fathom. On the woman's shoulders were several holsters, a gun carefully secured in each.

Given the stranger's tone before fainting, confiscating the weapons seemed the reasonable precaution to take. Lunafreya was not anxious to find a gun pressed to her head again. But the quantity of weapons and munitions posed a problem. Even if she were to take them, where would she hide them all?

In the end, she resigned herself to not tampering with the stranger's belongings. She might find herself staring down a barrel once more, but she'd cross that bridge when she came to it.

Eventually, the stranger woke. Her first action was predictable: she quickly distanced herself from Lunafreya and readied one of her many guns.

"Who the hell are you? What do you want?" she demanded.

The fact that she hadn't shot first and asked questions later was promising. She had even asked for Lunafreya's name. There seemed to be a small glimmer of hope.

"My name is Lunafreya Nox Fleuret."

The stranger continued to glare at her, but Lunafreya noticed a small, uncertain shift in her gaze.

"That's . . . That's the name of the Oracle. The one who's been dead for ten years."

So I did, in fact, die, Lunafreya thought. But aloud, she found herself questioning the claim.

"A decade ago?" she asked.

The question reminded her of another pressing uncertainty. She withdrew from her dress the bit of newspaper from earlier, unfolded and smoothed it out, then held it aloft.

"Please tell me, do you know anything about this?"

Perhaps the young woman could shed some light on the article's contents. Gun still leveled, she approached close enough to snatch the paper from Lunafreya's hands, then stepped back and studied it warily.

"Weird thing to ask," she muttered. Then, "Geez. Weird thing to carry around, too. If they're saying the king's been gone for three years, this must be, what . . . six or seven years old?"

"The king is gone?" Lunafreya's thoughts whirled. *Noctis, missing? How? Why?*

The stranger continued, "Yeah. Nobody's seen a trace of him for a solid decade."

Lunafreya felt herself grow dizzy, on the verge of fainting from this new revelation. It seemed impossible. Her last memory was of Altissia. The covenant with Leviathan. She'd been prepared to sacrifice her life that the king might receive the Tidemother's blessing. Lunafreya had already realized the weakness in her body. She knew the ritual would mean the end for her, even had Ardyn Izunia not come with dagger in hand.

But death had not mattered. She'd opened the way for the future of their star. The king would dispel the darkness that plagued Eos. The promise would be fulfilled.

But now . . .

She looked up. Darkness shrouded the sky. This was not the black of night. It was sinister. Ominous. What had happened to their world?

The rider's patience was wearing thin. "Are you really the Oracle?" she demanded. "Or are you some daemon posing as a human? If you're really who and what you say you are, give me some proof."

"I do not know that I have any," Lunafreya responded.

She pressed a hand to the scar in her flank. Even over the cloth of her garments, it was easy to feel the raised flesh. There was no pain from the wound, though it seemed so recent in memory. If this wasn't the scar from her stabbing, what was it?

"I don't know anything," Lunafreya confessed. "Why I'm here, what this power is, or why I'm alive."

She cupped her hands and covered her face. Just one answer. That was all she wanted. But she'd received nothing. No one could explain what was going on.

"Look," the stranger said, voice suddenly soft. "I just wanna know one thing."

Lunafreya looked up at her.

"Can I trust you?"

Once again, Lunafreya stared down a barrel of steel. But the stranger's eyes were no longer those of a killer. The question was sincere.

"I am afraid I cannot say with certainty," Lunafreya responded.

"Why not?"

"I have no way to prove to you that I am who I say."

She did not want to lie. The stranger stared at her, and she felt compelled to stare right back. Lunafreya held her eyes open wide.

The gun barrel lowered. But instead of relief, Lunafreya felt her knees begin to tremble. She'd been so on edge, she hadn't even recognized her own fear.

"Just remember this," the stranger added. "One wrong move, and you're dead."

Then the gun was back in its holster. A small sigh escaped Lunafreya's lips.

"If you want to show me you're trustworthy, I could use a hand pushing the bike. This looks like more of a repair job than I can handle here on the road."

The driver looked back at Lunafreya and added, "This *is* mostly your fault, y'know."

"I'd be happy to," Lunafreya responded, "Miss, um . . . "

She realized she had not yet asked the stranger's name.

"Sol," the stranger answered.

It was unclear whether that was a surname or given name, or perhaps some manner of nickname, but Lunafreya nodded.

"C'mon then, Lady Oracle. Let's get going."

She hoped, at the very least, they'd found trust enough for the stranger not to give a false name.

Sol was breathing hard.

"You're . . . a lot stronger . . . than I would've guessed," she remarked, flicking a glance at the self-proclaimed Oracle as they pushed the poor, busted three-wheeler down the road.

"That's . . . very kind of you . . . to say."

The stranger—Lunafreya—was speaking in the same short, concentrated bursts. They were both gasping for air, a clear sign of the effort it was taking to push the vehicle along the road.

She's a lot stronger than she looks, Sol thought, feeling a bit perplexed.

When she'd asked the woman to give her a hand, her expectations weren't exactly high. Pushing the bike was obviously going to be an effort well beyond her. Not that the woman's shabby attire was doing her any favors, but from the way she spoke and conducted herself, Sol could tell she'd had a pretty posh upbringing.

Still, when they righted the motorcycle and its sidecar, and when they began rolling it down the road, Sol quickly realized the woman was pulling her own weight.

Come to think of it, she'd held her own, more or less, during the fight with the Deathgaze, too. She'd held her little stick as if it were a real polearm, and her movements were those of someone trained to fight.

Frankly, the woman was suspicious with a capital "s." Who went around claiming to be the *Oracle*? And that spell or whatever she'd used against the daemon. And the *wound*. Now here she was, blithely pushing away like nothing had happened, like a Deathgaze hadn't just sunk its claws right into her arm. Sol had been staring straight at the wound when it closed up. It was weird. *Creepy as hell*, she thought.

On the outside, Sol was doing her best to keep a straight face. "How about . . . a bit . . . of a break?" she asked the woman.

"Yes, please," came the response, voice thick with exhaustion. They stopped, each leaning against the bike, then sliding down to sit on the ground. Sol was careful to keep her arm positioned for a quick draw if needed.

This was the second time they'd stopped to rest. Sol glanced once more at the bike. The Deathgaze had managed to mangle it pretty bad. No amount of roadside tinkering was going to get it moving like this. They needed access to spare parts, as well as the space and time to make the repairs. Pushing it to the nearest temporary outpost was the only choice they had.

Not that it was a bad choice. It was the right thing to do, and part of what the outposts were set up for in the first place. Aside from functioning as bases from which to conduct reconnaissance and strikes against the daemons, they were dotted throughout the former imperial territories as makeshift shelters for anyone who found themselves in unexpected circumstances.

She'd told the so-called Oracle that Wael outpost was just a stone's throw away. In reality, that was mostly to keep the woman from getting any funny ideas. It seemed reasonable enough to think she'd go along with things quietly if she believed Sol's comrades weren't too far away.

When they'd had a minute to catch their breaths, Lunafreya asked, "Might I ask, do you often travel by yourself?"

"Are you nuts? Of course not. It just worked out that way today."

It wasn't a lie. Traipsing around daemon-infested territory on your own was gambling with your life. The kind of thing only a mad fool would do.

Yeah, Sol thought. *It just worked out that way.*

More precisely, she'd had an unfortunate run-in with a pack of daemons. She'd taken the things on and, in the process, ranged a little farther out than she'd intended. When she realized what had happened, she was pretty far separated from her squad. Naturally, she'd immediately headed toward the rendezvous point. It would have been fine if she hadn't been sidelined by an Oracle and a Deathgaze along the way.

Anyway, the important thing now was getting to the nearest outpost. Fixing the bike was the next priority, even if it meant heading in the opposite direction of the rendezvous.

"It seems strange that there isn't any other traffic along here," Lunafreya ventured.

When they'd had their first break and Sol had stopped the bike right in the middle of the road and sat down, the Oracle had asked, "Shouldn't we at least push it to the shoulder?" She'd said it with a completely straight face, too. That had been the first clue that maybe she wasn't full of it, maybe she really had been living under a rock for the past ten years.

"Didn't you hear me last time?" Sol responded. "It's empty out here. Lestallum's the only town we have left."

Sol had explained that because of the daemons, the world was in a state of perpetual night. The corners of the Oracle's mouth tightened at the news. And when Sol told her how daemons ran wild in Insomnia—that it was more or less a nest for the things—the woman's face visibly paled. To top it off, Sol mentioned a rumor she'd heard, that the king had been pulled inside the Crystal itself. At that, the Oracle began to tremble, as if she might faint altogether.

"So," she continued in the present, as if explaining to a child, "if there aren't any people, there aren't any cars."

Admittedly, there was *some* traffic in the areas outside of Lestallum. Trucks still had to haul materials from one location to another, and hunters hit the road for recon missions or to take out particular packs of daemons that needed quelling. But that didn't amount to a large number of vehicles, and the farther out you went, the fewer there were. The former expanse of the empire wasn't exactly on the doorstep of modern civilization.

So the idea of a car cruising down the highway, blaring its horn at a couple of travelers sitting in the middle of the road, was a scene that could have been straight out of a fairy tale.

Sol turned to look at her companion. "Assuming you're the real Oracle and everything you've said is true, that you did actually die ten years ago and came back to life . . . "

Speaking of fairy tales, she thought.

" . . . it still doesn't add up. We're talking ten whole years. You had to be doing *something* during that whole time."

Lunafreya remained silent, crestfallen. Sol sighed. This was the real world. *Not* a fairyland.

"Whatever," Sol said. "Break time's over. Let's get some more effort out of those arms, Lady Oracle."

The stranger stood up, looking determined once more. It seemed like her spirit might match her unanticipated physical strength. Clearly, there was more to this woman than met the eye.

"Not much farther to Wael," Sol announced.

This time, it wasn't a lie.

"Ready . . . steady . . . push!"

Right around the time they'd developed a nice rhythm and the motorcycle was rolling along at a steady clip, Lunafreya saw a stretch of road ahead lined by several wooden structures. Sol nodded her head toward it. So this was the temporary outpost she'd spoken of, Wael. They'd made it.

According to Sol, nobody lived out here in the remnants of the Niflheim Empire, but the Hunters and the Kingsglaive were still active. It seemed they came out this way for reconnaissance or to conduct surveys of the land and daemons. Wael was one foothold from which they could carry out those duties.

When they drew close to the buildings, Lunafreya could see that everything was old and worn—all except the doors and their locks. The outpost seemed to consist solely of repurposed structures. These buildings must have been abandoned residences that the Hunters and others had salvaged for their own needs.

Lunafreya breathed a sigh of relief at the thought that their long walk was over. Sol had lent her a pair of boots when they began pushing. She was grateful to have them, but the fit wasn't quite right and the way the leather chafed against her bare skin made it difficult to walk. She'd been determined to do her part in pushing the motorcycle, but in truth, her feet were sore and she was exhausted.

They parked the motorcycle, and Sol produced a keycard to open the door of one of the buildings. From her confident movements, Lunafreya perceived it wasn't the first time she'd been to this particular outpost.

"Hey! Anyone here?" Sol shouted.

Then after a pause, "Guess not."

Sol flicked on the lights and gave a small shrug. None of the windows had been illuminated as they'd rolled in. Apparently, Sol was right. No one else was here.

From the way Sol had spoken, Lunafreya assumed the young woman's companions would be waiting for her at the outpost. Perhaps it was simply her way of making Lunafreya feel a bit less forlorn—just like how she'd continually described the distance to Wael as "a stone's throw away" when for most of the trek it had been anything but.

"Hello? Cindy?" Sol stood with a small device in hand. "Finally! It's about time you picked up."

The device was thin, flat, and rectangular. It must have been some kind of transceiver. And whoever "Cindy" was, Sol seemed ecstatic to be talking to her.

In fact, she realized, Sol had been trying to reach this person for some time. Before they'd started pushing the motorcycle, and again during each of their breaks, she had fiddled with the same transceiver, apparently trying to get through to this Cindy. Each time the transmission failed to go through, Sol had made a sour face and muttered, "Why isn't she picking up?" Then she'd put the transceiver away with a sigh.

Whatever the case, Lunafreya could guess at a few things: Cindy was versed in whatever knowledge they'd require to get the motorcycle running, and Sol desperately needed Cindy's help.

"Yeah. That's right," Sol was saying. "Wham. Right down onto the pavement. And now she's not making a peep. I don't even know where to start."

It seemed her assumptions had been correct. Sol moved back outside to the parked motorcycle, and Lunafreya followed at a slight distance. She'd promised to help. It didn't feel right to stay behind in the building, resting by herself.

But it occurred to her that perhaps she ought to hang back a bit longer, so as not to accidentally appear to be listening in on the conversation. Just then, she heard a familiar bark. She turned around to find a black dog bounding toward her, excitedly wagging his tail.

"Umbra!" Lunafreya exclaimed.

She hurried over to meet the dog and immediately began running her hands through his warm, soft fur. His poofy tail swished excitedly from side to side. The sight of it made her glad, but it also brought to mind another tail, this one white.

"If it's just you, I suppose that means Pryna . . . "

The other dog had remained beside Lunafreya until the very end in Altissia. Again and again she'd commanded Pryna to flee, but the dog had stayed stubbornly by Lunafreya's side. Her absence now surely meant that she'd sunk into the sea alongside her master's wounded body.

Lunafreya looked at Umbra. "I'm sorry. I wish I could take you back with me, but . . . "

Umbra just wagged his tail in response, as if to say he understood.

"Thank you," Lunafreya murmured, as she stroked his ruff.

"What about Noctis?" she asked.

Umbra continued to wag his tail. He gave a spirited bark. It seemed Noctis was safe. Still, Umbra wasn't carrying their notebook.

"The notebook," she asked him. "Does Noctis have it?"

She desperately longed to write a message, to tell Noctis that she was alive and well. She tried to think of something she could use in the notebook's place, then remembered what she'd seen inside the outpost building.

"Stay here for me, Umbra," she said and turned back to enter the building. There had been notebooks and scraps of paper on a table there, along with a number of mismatched pens and pencils.

"I'm sorry to use this without permission," she said, not knowing the objects' owner and thus not exactly sure to whom she was apologizing. Still, she felt compelled to express her remorse aloud. She picked up a notebook slightly smaller than the one she and Noctis had used, as well as a pen.

In a rushed scrawl, she wrote, *I'm safe*. She would have liked to add the date, but she'd forgotten to ask Sol about the current month and year.

She dashed back outside to find Umbra faithfully waiting just beside the entrance to the building.

"Please," she asked the Messenger. "See that Noctis gets this."

Umbra had always managed to convey the notebook safely to Noctis before, no matter where he was. Even when Lunafreya had been cloistered in the training grounds, and when she'd been hiding away in Altissia, still the dog had managed to relay their messages without trouble. So this new message would surely find its way as well.

"Please hurry!" she pleaded, but Umbra stayed firmly planted in place, shaking his head from side to side.

I can't, he seemed to be saying.

"Why won't you go?" she asked.

But Umbra only stared back in silence. Though the dog did not speak with the words of man, he was still a Messenger of the gods. If he refused her plea, there must have been some reasonable explanation.

"You cannot," she surmised. "But tell me. Noctis is safe, yes?" she asked again, at which point Umbra nuzzled against her.

Everything will be okay, he seemed to say. *Please don't worry.*

"Do you mean to say it is not yet time for us to reunite?"

Umbra's tail began waving more vigorously than before. She gently embraced the dog's warm body.

"Then I shall wait," she said. "Thank you, Umbra."

Umbra gave one more wag, tail held high, and then he was gone. Lunafreya let out a small sigh. It was the first familiar face she'd seen in this new world into which she'd been thrust so bewilderingly.

Speaking of which, where was Gentiana?

She felt certain Gentiana had been there at the end, right as she slipped into the slumber of death below the waves at Altissia. It would have brought so much comfort to see her again. Until Umbra's appearance, it hadn't seemed a possibility. Perhaps Gentiana, too, was aware that the Oracle had returned to life. And if Umbra could visit, surely Gentiana would be able to as well.

Lunafreya thought of the many things she wished she could tell Gentiana regarding what had transpired, and of the many questions she wanted to ask. The outpost was not far from Tenebrae. Surely a visit was not out of the question. The thought sparked new strength and determination within her.

When Lunafreya turned back toward the motorcycle, Sol was still speaking with the woman named Cindy.

Sol had been ready to thank the gods when she finally got through to Cindy. The bike was in bad shape. She'd been worried half to death that it might be beyond repair, that it would have to be scrapped altogether. But Cindy, ever the genius mechanic, was making everything all right again.

And she was doing it all over the phone, to boot. Cindy had rattled off questions on how the bike was behaving, which Sol answered as best she could. The answers must have been good enough, because Cindy almost immediately seemed to understand what was wrong and started giving instructions for how to get the bike up and running again.

And the level of *detail*! Cindy had it all covered, right down to which parts weren't kept on hand at the outposts, and what Sol could use as substitutes for their repair.

"Yeah, I think I've got it," Sol said, once she'd located everything they'd need. "Thanks, Cindy. You're a lifesaver."

And Cindy had replied, in her usual upbeat tone, "Aw, honey. Don't you worry about it."

"Hey, while I've got you," Sol ventured, her voice suddenly hushed, "something kinda weird happened. Wonder if I could get your opinion."

Sol glanced over her shoulder. The Oracle was busy playing with some stray that had found its way to the outpost. She didn't seem to be paying the least bit of attention to the call with Cindy. Perfect.

"I ran into someone. The Oracle."

"Say again?" Cindy said, her voice shooting up an octave. A reasonable response, to be fair. There wasn't a soul on the Star that didn't know the Oracle died in Altissia ten years ago.

"That's who she claims to be, anyway," Sol continued. "Think there's any chance she's for real?"

Cindy fell silent. It took a while for her response to finally come.

"Well, honestly, I don't know what to think" was all she said.

That seemed like a reasonable reaction to Sol, too. She didn't know what to think, either, even with the supposed Oracle standing right before her eyes.

"Anyway, wonder if you could pass the word on to, y'know, Gladio and the rest of 'em," Sol said. "Sooner's probably better than later."

She intentionally tiptoed around titles, referring to the Shield by name and avoiding the word "Kingsglaive," too. Cindy would know what she meant and get word out to those in charge at Lestallum.

Out of the corner of her eye, Sol noticed the Oracle looking in her direction. The dog was nowhere to be seen. It must have run off. Time to wrap things up, before the woman got suspicious.

"Okay, then, I'll talk to you later. Thanks again, Cindy," she said, and ended the call before Cindy could reply to the request.

"Hey," she turned to the stranger. "Sorry to keep you waiting."

Sol casually waved the woman over, and the Oracle hurried near.

"My friend Cindy gave me the rundown on how to fix up the bike. I've never had a crash this bad, so some of this is kinda new to me."

There was a good way and a bad way for a bike to fall. A good fall didn't leave more than a few scratches on the rider or the bike. Sol had always been a natural, ever since'd she started riding. She'd taken some spills, but never bad enough to really mess the vehicle up. So she'd never had to learn how to do serious repair work.

"I truly am sorry," the Oracle said, her shoulders slumping slightly. She seemed to have taken Sol's earlier jab to heart and really did feel responsible for the accident.

"Show it, don't say it. Sit tight over there while I get things ready. Then you can give me a hand."

"Certainly," the Oracle nodded with the innocence of a child. Her lack of concern probably indicated just how little she knew about bike repair. This was gonna require muscle, and by the end of it, their hands would be filthy, coated in dirt and grease. Sol laughed to herself. Once the Oracle found out what the job required, she'd probably break down in tears.

That's what Sol figured, anyway, but she couldn't have been further off the mark. The Oracle didn't flinch in the slightest at getting her hands dirty. She obviously didn't have much experience working on machines, but she wasn't completely useless either. Actually, Sol had to admit, she was kind of nice to have around. A quick learner, too.

If you want to get a good sense of a person's character, work alongside 'em. A little boring, back-breaking work'll show you exactly who they are.

How long ago had she been given that advice? Not too long, Sol decided. It would've been after she was finally recognized more or less as an adult in her own right, when the two of them could start speaking on equal terms.

Good advice, sure, but the person who gave it still couldn't stop treating Sol like a child. Just that morning, Sol had gotten fed up enough to shout at her.

"All right. Lookin' pretty good," Sol announced. "The rest is fine tuning. You can leave that up to me."

Sol looked up. It was night already. It'd been years since you could find the sun to track the time, but the color of the sky still got a bit darker as night set in.

"Let's call it a day," she said.

More than anything else, she wanted some dinner.

Lunafreya had thought she was accustomed to traveling. Her calling as the Oracle had taken her to places all across the land, conducting every imaginable ritual and rite, blessing the havens, easing the pain of the ill and wounded. The work had been unquestionably demanding.

However, as the Oracle, she'd always traveled in the company of others. Her safety on the road was assured, and wherever she stopped warm meals and comfortable accommodations always awaited her. She hadn't had to face daemons in battle herself. Nor had she ever slept in an unoccupied building, wrapped up in a dusty blanket. These experiences were new.

It was also the first time she'd eaten straight from a can, fork thrust directly into the unheated and decidedly unusual contents. According to the label, she'd dined on vegetable and meat stew, but the taste was rather removed from that description. It wasn't that it was bad, but it gave her pause. The bewilderment accompanying her first bite must have been apparent, for Sol smirked and said, "Is it not to the Lady Oracle's liking?"

Sol's guns were never far. She no longer watched Lunafreya with obvious, constant caution, but neither had she fostered any degree of trust. That, too, was a new experience. Never in Lunafreya's life had she been treated with such clear suspicion. The title of Oracle alone had always elicited a measure of trust and openness from anyone she encountered. Even the imperial forces, who regarded her with little warmth, had never been openly disrespectful, and Lunafreya had never felt the need to go out of her way to dispel a sense of mistrust from those in the employ of the empire.

Thus, when confronted with suspicion, she had no idea how to react. She did not know the proper overtures to overcome Sol's mistrust. Lunafreya had never envisioned a need for such skills or knowledge.

As she prepared for bed, her mind still was weighed down with concern. It felt as though she might not manage even a moment's sleep. But when her head met the pillow, she realized how weary her body was from the day's events, and the moment her eyes closed, she drifted off.

Lunafreya Nox Fleuret.

Lunafreya's eyes opened at the sound of her name. The voice was one hard to imagine coming from a human, and her surroundings were far too luminous for the mortal realm. Even a decade ago, before the perpetual darkness, there had been no place on Eos so bright. And it wasn't just the light. She hung weightless in a space of emptiness extending as far as the eye could see, and the emptiness itself glowed like some great jewel. This was most assuredly no part of the reality she knew. This was a place of dreams or visions.

Hearken unto the voice of the Bladekeeper, Bahamut.

The Bladekeeper?

As a child, she had often listened to Gentiana recounting tales of the Star. They were the stories of the Hexatheon, the six gods of Eos, of which Bahamut was one.

As Gentiana told it, all members of the Six were as gods to mortals, but even among them Bahamut stood apart. Titan, the Archaean; Ifrit, the Infernian; Ramuh, the Fulgurian; Leviathan, the Hydraean; and Shiva, the Glacian: these five ruled over the natural elements of their world, existing alongside the Star itself. But the Draconian was different. He existed alongside the heavens encircling the Star. Gentiana never outright stated as much, but her tone seemed to suggest that Bahamut occupied a position superior to the rest.

And now here Lunafreya was, being directly addressed by the Bladekeeper.

A new calling awaits the Oracle.

As the voice boomed, the space around Lunafreya began to shift. What had been empty void before was now darkened landscape. Within that landscape she observed the Citadel. In a courtyard which she faintly remembered, Noctis and Ardyn stood with blades crossed.

Noctis seemed much older than that day they parted in Altissia. Did that mean she was seeing a vision of the future? The scene was silent, but she could still almost hear the ringing of the two men's weapons striking against each other. At times the swords spit sparks. At times they found their marks, and their blades and the arcs they drew were painted with blood. For a moment, she thought the two men might go on fighting forever.

When it finally did come to an end, this swordfight that was a duel to the death, the one on the ground was Ardyn. But the battle between him and Noctis was not yet over. Darkness still hung thick over Insomnia.

"This cannot be . . . " Lunafreya murmured.

The scenes that came next defied everything she believed true of their lives and fates. Deep within the Citadel, Noctis sat upon the throne as the True King, calling forth the power of the Ring of the Lucii, summoning the souls of his ancestors. Thirteen Kings of Yore encircled Noctis, weapons held raised and ready. Each in turn thrust spectral steel into Noctis's flesh.

Tears formed in Lunafreya's eyes as she watched. "Noctis!" she screamed. "Why?!"

No words accompanied the scene that unfolded, but nonetheless Lunafreya found herself provided with an answer. The ring served not only to call forth the souls of the departed into the mortal realm, it also allowed its wielder to travel together with those souls—to cross over into the Beyond, the realm linked to their world by way of the Crystal, which had existed since time immemorial. And over its boundary could traverse no mortal flesh.

Lunafreya watched as Noctis, stripped of flesh and no longer of this world, traveled to the Beyond using the power of the ring. There he sought out Ardyn's trapped soul and destroyed it.

However, use of the ring had always come at a price—the powers it bestowed cost the wielder's life. After defeating Ardyn, Noctis's own form shattered. He vanished in that space beyond and was gone forevermore.

This was the calling of the True King: to bring an end to the bearer of darkness through the sacrifice of his own existence.

"But that . . . That is . . . " Lunafreya could not finish.

She'd been asked by King Regis to see the Ring of the Lucii safely to his son. Keeping that promise, she believed, would ensure a future for their star. So she'd run desperately to escape Insomnia as the city went up in flames. She slipped in among the throngs of evacuees and quietly made her way toward Altissia. Never had she imagined that the object for which she'd risked so much would ultimately take her beloved's life.

She had sacrificed her life, only for the man she loved to lose his as well. That, it seemed, had been the Oracle's calling.

All strength left her body, and she collapsed to her knees. If only she'd known . . . If only she'd realized the truth of her actions and the end they would bring . . .

Thus was ordained the fate of man. Thus was the Chosen meant to fulfill his calling.

Lunafreya's head snapped up.

Was?

Had something changed?

The Noctis of her vision was not as she'd known him in life. He was older, more wearied. If the Noctis she'd seen fighting with Ardyn was some vision of a future meant to be, perhaps the Bladekeeper's words implied that fate's course had changed. Noctis would no longer be able to fulfill his intended calling. But if that were true, what had happened to stand in his way?

The color of the space around her shifted yet again. Darkness became the flames of a raging fire. Ardyn stood, and before him Ifrit, the Infernian, knelt in subjugation. The chancellor's body was no longer that of a man. His skin was jet black, his entire form shrouded in the dark miasma of the daemons.

The impudent Accursed would resist his fate. Eyes blind to will divine, he submits to the base desires of his iniquitous heart.

The impure power the Usurper wields grows great, such that even the power of the ring suffices not to drive him away.

The Ardyn who had crossed swords with Noctis in the Citadel courtyard had seemed yet human. The Ardyn she saw before her now, commanding the Pyreburner, was anything but. So this was the power of darkness brought to a peak.

Go forth with haste to Insomnia and stay the Usurper.

For this purpose are new life and strength granted. Such is the Oracle's new calling.

Lunafreya put a hand once more to the scar in her side. This body, dead once at Ardyn's hands, and this power, strong enough to stay the mightiest daemons—they were both gifts bestowed unto her by the God of War.

And with them, I am to defeat Ardyn? Me? Am I even capable of such a feat?

But if fate ordained had changed, perhaps that meant Noctis would no longer need to use the ring. He'd seemed to be in such agony when it happened. If she ventured forth as the Draconian commanded, perhaps Noctis would not have to suffer. He would not shatter into pieces in the world beyond. He would not cease to exist.

If Noctis could be saved, it was worth trying to see this new calling through.

When Lunafreya rose in the morning, the sensation wasn't any different from all the other times she'd woken. Only this time, there was no morning light to greet her. The world outside the windows was still immersed in perpetual darkness.

She remembered with perfect clarity every word of her conversation with the Draconian. But no matter how she tried, she could not remember the god's form or visage. Somehow, that confirmed to her that what she'd seen had not been an ordinary dream or a product of her imagination.

"A new calling," she said softly to herself.

As the words left her mouth, she felt a surge of motivation to see it through. She sprang up, ready to act. On the floor next to where she'd slept she saw a small pile of folded black cloth. When she picked it up, she discovered it to be a full set of clothing. It hadn't been there when she went to sleep. Perhaps its presence suggested she was welcome to change into it?

As she pondered what to do, the door opened and Sol peeked in.

"You finally up?" Sol asked.

"Oh. Yes. Good morning." Lunafreya responded. She paused, then asked, "About these clothes . . . "

"You looked like you could use a change. I dunno if they'll fit, but it's better than walking around in what you've got on now."

Over the course of the previous day, her soaked dress had finally managed to dry. Still, it was torn in several places and smeared with dirt. It had, in a sense, seen ten years of use, so it was hardly surprising that it might be literally a bit worse for wear. She thanked Sol and quickly changed.

Black was a color she'd never worn before. As Oracle, it was only proper for her to perform rites in formal white. On her journeys, too, she'd always chosen to wear white. Come to think of it, even her casual wardrobe had been filled exclusively with whites and off-whites.

The new clothes thus seemed rather peculiar on her, once she'd changed and was looking herself over. The stretchable fabric was admittedly comfortable, and she suspected it would prove easy to move about in. Yet the clothing was still somehow hard to accept. It made her uneasy. She wondered if she might ever shake the feeling that she was wearing borrowed garb.

The first words out of Sol's mouth on seeing her were, "Looks good on you." Then she added, "A lot better than that old dress."

It may have been self-serving, but she let Sol's compliment assuage her unease. Until this moment, she'd paid little attention to her apparel. It was strange and somewhat exhilarating to learn how a new outfit could bring with it an entirely different mood.

Lunafreya was on a journey like nothing she'd experienced in her past, and she was making it in clothes wholly different from anything she'd worn before. But this new fate had been thrust upon her, and it stood to reason that new experiences and a new appearance would come with it.

"I'm done tuning the bike. Once you've got some food in you, we're heading out," Sol said.

It seemed Sol had woken up far earlier than Lunafreya.

"I'm sorry. I promised to help you."

"No big deal. Figured I'd get the repairs done early and skip on out of here. Y'know, leave you behind."

Sol said it with a straight face, but if she'd truly intended to abandon Lunafreya, it seemed unlikely she'd have gone to the trouble of finding her a change of clothes.

"Miss Sol, I wonder if I might ask a favor," Lunafreya ventured.

She straightened and looked the other woman directly in the eye.

"I should like to accompany you a bit longer. There is a destination I must reach."

To fulfill this new calling, Lunafreya knew she would need assistance. Over the relatively short distance from the underground tomb to Wael, that truth had become all too apparent. Compared to Sol, she fell far short in so many ways. Sol had means to get around and was experienced in combat. And it wasn't only the obvious things. The previous night, Lunafreya had realized she did not know how to open cans of food for herself with a knife, let alone how to start a fire.

Sol had the learned skills of a person well-traveled in lands from which civilization had vanished. She knew so many things that Lunafreya could never have hoped to gain in her days of warm welcome at every place to which she journeyed.

"Not that I expect you to see me all the way there," Lunafreya clarified. "I should simply like to stay with you as long as our paths are shared."

Even a short while would be welcome. She would journey alongside Sol and learn as much as she could. Her travels as Oracle might have failed to teach her how to subsist on her own, but it was not too late to begin learning now.

"Where are we talking about?" Sol asked, her tone curt. She peered at Lunafreya with suspicion.

"I need to get to Insomnia."

"The Crown City? You've gotta be kidding. I told you, that place might as well be a breeding ground for daemons. What business could the prim and proper Lady Oracle have in a place like that?"

"Please. I would ask you stop calling me that. My name is Lunafreya."

Every time Sol referred to her as "Lady Oracle," Lunafreya was acutely reminded of the wall that stood between them. Yesterday, she'd made no protest at the distant, cold means of address; Sol was, after all, a simple passerby with whom she shared no relationship. But now things would have to be different.

"Sure. Whatever you want," Sol replied. "But Lunafreya's still kind of a mouthful."

"Then, please call me Luna."

When she said it aloud, that familiar young face floated once more to mind. *Lunafreya*. Her name had been too long for him then as well.

He'd stumbled over it, until finally they'd both settled on his simply calling her Luna.

"Okay. Luna it is. Then you can quit calling me Miss. Just Sol is fine."

"Agreed," Lunafreya responded. "Thank you, Sol."

"So what do you have planned once you get to Insomnia?"

"I will fight. I will challenge Ardyn."

"Ardyn? Don't tell me you're talking about Ardyn Izunia," Sol said, one eyebrow raised.

When Lunafreya nodded in response, Sol first stared blankly. After that initial moment of shock, her words were incredulous and mixed with laughter. "*You?* You're gonna take down Ardyn? That's a joke if I've ever heard one."

Lunafreya simply regarded Sol in silence. She had no delusions that Ardyn would be an easy opponent to fell. But if she did not fight . . . If she did not stop Ardyn, the darkness that shrouded their star would ever remain.

After a moment, Sol registered her expression and stopped laughing. "Whoa. You're serious, aren't you?"

She seemed to hesitate, and then mumbled to herself, "You've gotta be kidding me."

But Lunafreya was most decidedly not kidding. The sentiment seemed to convey itself, and Sol's next words, accompanied with a small sigh, were "Fine. Whatever.

"First we head to Lestallum," she continued. "Your little trip to Insomnia comes after that. That good with you?"

"Of course," Lunafreya nodded.

She knew a sea crossing would be necessary to make it from the former empire to Insomnia. If Sol was taking her to Lestallum, it meant help and companionship through the crossing as well. It was far more than Lunafreya could have hoped for.

She bowed her head and added, "It will be a great help, thank you. I shall be most indebted."

A look of distaste crossed Sol's face.

"Is something wrong?" Lunafreya asked.

"Forget about it."

Sol turned away, her eyes clearly contradicting her words. Lunafreya felt as if she'd said something wrong, but she had no idea what it might have been.

"I found one! This is one of them, yes?" Luna held a can aloft, seeming quite pleased with herself. The two had driven back to the spot where the Oracle had thrown out the "extra weight" in their panicked flight from the Deathgaze. On the road, food was precious. They really couldn't afford to leave it.

Along the way, Sol had also given Luna a chance to try driving the bike. It wasn't the kind of thing someone could pick up in a day or two, but they had a long trip ahead. There would be plenty of time for Luna to learn, and it'd be a lot easier on both of them once switching off became a viable option.

Sol was able to identify the stretch of road where the bag had been lost. But what proved to be the really painstaking work was tracking down the cans themselves, which had rolled off in all directions.

Luna labored without a single word of complaint. She probably felt responsible, which she pretty much was, since she'd been the one to fling the bag out of the sidecar in the first place. So Luna hunted in concentrated silence, save for her triumphant outbursts on each find.

"Here's another!" she exclaimed.

She was quick. In the time it took Sol to find one can, Luna would pick up three or four.

"Geez. You're . . . "

Good at finding things, Sol had begun to say, but she clamped her mouth shut.

"What was that?" the Oracle asked.

"Nothing. Forget about it."

As the words formed, it had occurred to Sol just exactly what would make someone—or some*thing*—so quick at locating the cans. Visual acuity in low light conditions. In other words, seeing well at night. Just the kind of thing daemons were good at.

When they'd had the encounter with the Deathgaze, Luna had seemed to be pulling or absorbing some kind of energy from the monster. And the particles that rose off her open wound—for the brief span of time it had been open at all—were just like those of a daemon.

And now, here was another daemon-like skill. Hunting things in the dark. It fit right in with the other odd feats the Oracle was apparently capable of.

But it didn't seem right to jump to the conclusion that Luna was an enemy just because she had powers in common with the daemons. Sol had made sure to visibly lower her guard a few times the previous evening to see if her new companion might go for a surprise attack. She'd seen no indication of a desire to try.

And of course, to top it all off, there was the woman's ludicrous claim that she intended to face off against Ardyn Izunia himself.

How were you supposed to react to something like that? Sol was still wrestling with the question as their search for the wayward cans wrapped up.

After that, they hopped back on the bike, and when they'd ridden for about an hour, they were met with bits of white falling gracefully from the sky.

"Not a cloud in sight, but we've got a flurry," Sol observed. It was said to happen around here, along this little swathe of land sandwiched between the desert and the mountains locked in eternal winter, but only at this particular time of year, when temperatures were low and the air was dry. Strong wind lifted snow from the peaks and carried it to fall like a winter flurry over the land below, creating the bizarre sight of snow falling from a clear sky.

"Heh. I guess it's probably nothing new to you, being from Tenebrae and all."

"I have known of it, yes, but this is my first time seeing it with my own eyes," Luna responded. "It was described to me as resembling a cascade of white blossoms dancing through the sky."

"Against a sky like this, I'd say it's more like a swarm of insects."

But how did it look to Luna's eyes? With her vision, perhaps snowflakes against a dark sky didn't look so bad. It occurred to Sol that everything she saw might look quite different to her companion. They might stare in the same direction and see two very different things.

"I wonder if I could ask you a question," Luna ventured hesitantly.

"Shoot."

"The way to Insomnia—no, the way to Lestallum. How many days' travel is it?"

"Hate to say it, but I really can't give you a precise number."

A vast expanse of sea stretched between the former lands of Niflheim and Lucis, where Lestallum was located. To get across, they'd need either a dropship or a watercraft of some sort. But dropships were reserved for patrols and reconnaissance; other uses weren't permitted. As far as ships capable of traversing open water, well . . . there were never enough hands available to keep the things in proper shape. And without many seaworthy vessels, it was likely that they'd make it to the port only to find it empty and have to wait.

"From what I hear, this area used to be about two days from the port. But we're making the trip hunting daemons along the way, so let's say four or five. Problem is, after we get there, we may be waiting for a while before there's a ship that can take us."

"And I suppose even once we're across, it will take several more days."

"More than that. The City of Light itself is the only place that's safe. Daemons lurk everywhere else, so it's slow going."

"Yes, I suppose that makes sense," Luna replied, in a voice so small Sol thought it might get carried off by the wind. They'd had to deal with three daemon encounters already, just to get to the site where they lost the cans. They'd narrowly managed to avoid two other packs by spotting the daemons before they themselves were spotted and speeding away on the bike. Three or four hours had gone by since they left Wael, but it certainly didn't feel like they'd managed to cover much ground.

"And daemons aren't the only things that'll slow us down. We gotta make time to rest, too."

Sol gently pressed on the brakes. Luna looked over with astonishment. She seemed to want to protest that she could go farther; she wasn't yet tired.

"Not for us," Sol explained. "For Regina."

Sol patted one handlebar as she said it. The engine had been pretty hot for a while now. It was well past time to let it rest. The bike was running again, but it had been a quick fix. She'd had to make do with whatever parts she could find, and Cindy, too, had made a point of telling her not to push the vehicle very hard.

"'Regina?'" Luna asked.

It wasn't until Luna chirped the name back that Sol realized what she'd done. *Ugh.* She hadn't meant to reveal that.

Sol had met Regina during one of her early missions. She'd been busy helping beat back the daemons, and bam, there it was: an old Niflheim-built motorcycle just abandoned there on the side of the road. It was love at first sight. Sol knew she had to ride it, and she begged Cindy to restore the machine to working condition. Cid shook his head as he muttered about it being the kind of thing a "do-nothin' bum" would ride, but he helped Cindy fix it up, and no sooner was it running than Sol was riding and thinking up the name she'd christen her new partner with.

"What, you got a problem with my bike's name?" she glared at Luna.

"Not at all," the Oracle responded.

Not that any other answer would have mattered. Rider and bike were inseparable now. Sol wasn't going to let anyone laugh at the fact that she'd named her bike—or at the name itself.

"No travel faster than the slowest member of the group," Sol said. "That's an ironclad rule among the Hunters."

Since departing Wael, they'd stuck exclusively to one particular route that ran parallel to a railway track. It was a fairly narrow road, offering much less space than the major thoroughfares, and at least for the portion they'd traveled thus far, it was poorly maintained. Lunafreya had assumed Sol chose the road to avoid encounters with daemons, but now she wasn't sure. They'd run into plenty so far. Why, then, travel along such a tedious route? It wasn't until the end of their first day that she finally understood.

Stations and signal cabins had been built along the track at regular intervals, so following the track meant they'd never want for a relatively safe place to spend the night. Along this route, they'd always have a roof under which to sleep, and the water lines servicing the buildings would enable them to drink and wash. According to Sol, only major stations were likely to see any upkeep and use as proper outposts, but even so, a tiny, unnamed signal cabin would serve well enough for one night's stay.

In the control room they were currently occupying, they found some tableware and folded blankets tucked away opposite the levers for the rail switches. There was even a small kerosene heater. A fine layer of dust coated everything, but aside from that, it was all in good enough condition to use.

Sol lit the heater, filling the tiny building with warmth and the reek of kerosene. Lunafreya, suddenly overcome with fatigue, realized that if she sat down, she might not stand back up. Better to take care of everything that needed to get done before resting.

"Shall I heat some water?" she asked.

Sol grunted in response, and Lunafreya began combing through the contents atop a set of small shelves. She found a small pot in which to heat water, as well as utensils for the night's canned meal. Then, her eyes happened to fall on a teapot hiding at the back of one shelf.

A teapot, she thought. *What an unusual find.* And if there was a teapot, then perhaps... Lunafreya's hands and eyes continued to search, eventually coming to rest upon a familiar rectangular metal shape. Loose-leaf tea. A bit of rust had begun to form on the outside of the tin, but when she popped off the top to check the contents, the tea itself seemed dry enough.

She turned back to face Sol at the heater and asked, "Would you mind if I put on some tea?"

"Tea?" Sol seemed surprised.

"I found some on one of the shelves."

"Sure, if you want."

It would be her first cup of tea in what felt like ages. Her heart leapt, and she offered silent thanks to whatever tea-loving engineer it was who had been stationed here in the past. Waiting for the pot to boil was an agonizing exercise in patience.

When the water was finally ready, Lunafreya poured a small amount into the teapot to let it warm. She dumped that water out, put in a few spoonfuls of the curled black leaves, then poured the hot water over them, this time filling the pot. Normally, she'd have used a bit of water to warm the teacups as well, but she decided it was better to place a limit on luxury. They'd boiled only so much water. Warming the teapot alone would have to do.

She looked inside the pot once to check that the leaves had properly unfurled in their scalding bath. Then when the brew was ready, she poured it into the cups. The unmistakable scent of rich black tea filled the room.

"Well, give it a try," Lunafreya said, and Sol lifted a cup to her lips. The younger woman's brow furrowed slightly.

"Kinda bitter," she said.

"Forgive me. I couldn't find any sugar."

Sol was right. The tea was rather strong, probably a blend meant to go with milk. Of course, to Lunafreya, even the bitterness of tea was a cherished taste.

"But it smells nice," Sol added. "Y'know, brings back memories or whatever."

Yes. It did bring back memories. This was a scent that reminded one of a world over which the sun still shone.

For a while, the two continued drinking in silence. It was a comfortable quiet, falling pleasantly in the small space. When the cups were empty and Lunafreya began to pour another serving, Sol suddenly spoke up.

"Where'd you learn that stuff?"

"How to brew tea?"

"No, no. The way you fight with that thing. I can tell you're not a complete beginner."

Sol pointed to the polearm resting against one wall. Lunafreya had found it among the items stored at Wael and had decided to allow herself to make use of it, fully intending to return it at the adventure's conclusion. It had an unusually stout shaft, probably designed as such for the sturdiness required by forces as mobile as the Hunters. But she'd quickly grown accustomed to it. They'd run into enough daemons in the course of the day to make sure of that.

"It was part of my training. All who serve as Oracle must be able to wield the Trident."

The Oracles of old had at times been asked to help quell or drive off daemons, and in fact, her physical training had extended beyond the use of weapons alone. She'd also been expected to build strength in her arms and legs. She'd not enjoyed it at the time, but afterward she was grateful. It had been crucial preparation for her role in aiding the True King.

The training had imparted both physical stamina and an ability to defend herself. She'd needed both while rousing the unruly gods and facing them on her own. She had a duty to fulfill and could not afford to collapse from fatigue. Still, she had not expected those skills to come in handy now, long after the fact.

Practice with a weapon enabled her to battle small daemons physically, without relying on the mysterious power of that first day. Lunafreya did not doubt the Draconian's gift, but each time she used it, a faint sense of dread accompanied the use. It had become all too apparent that the essence of the daemons was being drawn into her body.

Moreover, she'd come to understand something else: "daemons" weren't really daemons at all. They did not exist as their own separate class of beasts or monsters. Rather, they were host to other organisms within them, in thrall to the strange black miasma. Daemons didn't come into existence on their own. Other creatures were *made* into daemons. And it seemed most likely that the underlying cause was some manner of parasite—a scourge.

When Lunafreya used her power to pull the source of the disease into her own body, the daemon she faced would return to its former self. Yet perhaps because of weakness due to prolonged infestation, or perhaps because the infestation had begun in a corpse rather than a living creature, the creature's restored form lasted for but a moment. Purged of its infection, it would quickly turn into a cloud of dust and disperse.

The source of the illness, however, did not disperse. It remained lodged in Lunafreya's body, and as she eliminated more and more of the daemons, she became home to greater and greater quantities of the tiny parasite.

It left her with a looming concern: what would happen to her own body over time?

She wasn't able to get by without using the power whatsoever. Only the smallest of daemons could be vanquished with her spear and physical strength alone. For the ones that moved swiftly or possessed a stature exceeding her own, she had to rely on the power.

It had seemed to take everything she and Sol had to defeat the daemon of the day before, with its shape so evocative of a god of death. If they ever had to deal with an opponent stronger than that . . .

" . . . what I think it means?"

Lunafreya had been so lost in thought that she missed most of the question. Flustered, she said to Sol, "I beg your pardon. Could you repeat that?"

"Your training. I was asking what else you had to do besides learn how to fight."

Lunafreya thought back to the training ground. Ralmuell, she realized, was not so far from where they were now. It, too, was located somewhere in this narrow stretch of land lying between Eusciello and Succarpe.

"In the broadest sense," Lunafreya responded, "it was a regimen for me to strengthen both body and mind. To increase my physical strength, I ran and swam. To sharpen my focus, I spent many hours in meditation. In addition to that, I was introduced to the relics of the Oracles of the past, that I might know them more intimately. And there were the chants and the dances."

"Huh. Sounds kinda fun," Sol smirked.

"I suppose at times, I did rather enjoy myself."

Lunafreya had never shunned physical activity. Song, too, gave her joy. When she gave herself to the lyrics, bringing melody into the world with all she had, it always managed to drive the clouds of worry from her mind.

Of course, not all the training had been fun. It was almost always rigorous, designed to bring her to the verge of breaking. It was the surest way to sharpen her mind and build the endurance she would need.

"There were also periods of fasting. Those were rather difficult to endure. And the isolation for days at a time."

"Ugh. Well, that part sounds awful. I could never make it through that."

"Training is not training unless it requires you to endure."

Sol scrunched her face and made another disgusted sound. Lunafreya couldn't help but laugh at her companion's obvious distaste.

"So why'd you go through all of it in the first place? Like, what's the purpose of the training?"

The answer seemed so obvious Lunafreya wondered why anyone would ask. But the most basic questions sometimes had a way of getting at the heart of a matter and opening a path to deeper understanding. Sol's question gave her pause, and she considered how best to put her thoughts into words.

"Why, to prepare me to fulfill my duties as Oracle, of course."

"And what are your duties as Oracle?"

"To heed the words of the gods and aid the king."

"And that makes you happy?"

"It is not a question of happiness."

Sol's next question was even more bewildering. "Well, then is the compensation good?"

Lunafreya stared at Sol blankly.

"You know, compensation. Pay. They must pay you pretty well for all that work, right?"

"The Oracle's duties are a service to the people."

"So you work for *free*? Are you kidding me?! I mean, I guess maybe if it was something you enjoyed. Like, when you talked about the parts of the training you liked. That I get. But there's nothing fun about having to perform some public service. If you're not getting paid for it, why even bother?"

How could Lunafreya explain that it was not a question of choice? The Oracle's duties were mandated by the gods, and they must be carried out. It had always been that way, since long, long ago.

"Whatever," Sol said. "Guess it's just beyond me."

Lunafreya, for her part, found Sol's questions equally incomprehensible. Compensation? For her labors as Oracle? It seemed absurd.

The conversation ended without resolution, and they sat drinking the remainder of the tea in uneasy silence. After their usual dinner of one can each, they washed their own cups and utensils and set about their own tasks. Or rather, Sol began cleaning and checking her guns, while Lunafreya found herself with nothing in particular to do. It was still too early to sleep.

Suddenly she remembered the notebook from the day before. She'd forgotten to return it after Umbra's refusal. It wasn't until after they'd departed Wael that she realized the notebook was still among her belongings. As long as she had it, it seemed just as well to put it to use in keeping a record of the day's events. And though the signal cabin didn't boast nearly as many supplies as the outpost at Wael, it took only a quick look around the control room to find a pen.

Her scrawled message from before read, *I'm safe*.

Farther down the page, she noted her location. *Railway signal cabin.* And below that, she began her entry.

Dearest Noctis,
I am currently on a journey across the former lands of Niflheim, riding in the sidecar of a motorcycle driven by a hunter named Sol. My days are filled with new experiences, and though the difference in age between Sol and me is not so great, I've found our minds work in quite different ways. Already her companionship has yielded numerous surprises . . .

The following morning, before Luna woke, Sol slipped out of the control room for a moment alone. The rusty old door gave a harsh creak, but fortunately Luna didn't stir in the slightest.

Come to think of it, the Oracle had slept like a log the previous day, too. Maybe the travel wore her out. Or maybe she just wasn't a morning person. In any case, a bit of noise was apparently not enough to wake her. Not that Sol was complaining.

She took out her smartphone and flicked through her contacts. It didn't bug her so much to speak to Cindy in front of Luna, but conversations with family were a different matter. Better safe than accidentally overheard.

She *should* have called home the previous day, but it was a little late to feel guilty about it. The whole day, she'd been fuming, convinced that if a certain someone was worried, it was *their* responsibility to call and make sure everything was all right. It was the logic of a petulant child—an unfortunate tendency of hers, one that she knew undermined her own constant demands to be treated more like an adult.

It only made things worse that she'd let herself get separated from her comrades. She had been so certain she could mop up that pack of daemons on her own and so intent on proving herself a proper hunter in her own right.

At any rate, a couple of nights' sleep had brought things into perspective. It was on her to apologize. She was in for a scolding, but she'd stand up and take it like a woman.

Sol tapped the contact and waited, but the call didn't go through. Their phone was probably switched off. A letdown, but not out of the ordinary. The person Sol was trying to reach might be in the middle of planning an operation. Or maybe piloting the dropship. Signal interference was a legitimate risk and a smart one to eliminate in any situation that might require quickly issued commands. It was a funny little coincidence how Lucian smartphones and communication equipment aboard imperial dropships tended to get in each other's way.

"Welp, guess that's not happening," she muttered, and turned to go back inside.

Then she remembered there was someone else who deserved an apology. She looked back at her phone and brought up the contact. This call would *definitely* involve an angry earful, probably starting the second the call went through. The thought made her hesitate a moment before dialing. A bunch of angry shouting, first trying to ascertain whether she was safe, then demanding to know her current location. The fact that the yelling was born out of worry rather than real anger made it the harder to bear. But she bit her lip and dialed.

When the call connected, she was met with a different, much calmer voice.

"Well if it isn't the little lady!"

"Would you *please* stop calling me that?"

Wedge's insistence on "Lady S" was bad enough, but the way Biggs addressed her was absolutely *humiliating*. Lately, she'd finally managed to convince them to refer to her as "Sol," but every once in a while, for who knew what reason, they'd pull out those terribly embarrassing nicknames.

"Look," Sol continued, "I just called to say I'm sorry to make you worry. You, uh, already hear about it from Cindy?"

"Called us yesterday."

Honestly, Sol didn't even need to ask. The other day, she'd been so anxious to dump the two smothering babysitters that she lied to them. She told Biggs and Wedge that the rendezvous time with the hunters was an hour later than it actually was. After she'd given them the slip, they'd probably panicked and called everybody and anybody they could think of, desperate for any leads on where Sol might have been headed. Cindy was probably the first person they'd dialed—which meant that after yesterday's chat about the bike, Cindy had undoubtedly passed the news on to Biggs and Wedge.

"And what about Mom?" Sol asked.

"Lady A's, uh . . . "

There was the briefest pause, then, "She's busy planning an op, as it were."

"At the ruins?"

"That's right. She's just gone, as a matter of fact. On her way to reinforce the advance team."

Biggs's choice of words seemed to imply that the initial survey team had run into trouble. Surveys in former imperial territory, and especially excavations of ancient ruins, were a double-edged sword. They often yielded desperately needed resources, but danger was ever at the teams' backs.

Biggs continued, "But don't you worry. It'll all be fine. Wedge and I will rendezvous with her shortly."

"I wanna go, too!"

The situation bothered Sol. The fact that the advance team had called for assistance at all suggested something big had happened. And there had been that slight hesitation before Biggs answered her question.

"Where are you now?" Biggs asked.

"Just outside Wael, at the nearest signal station."

"Puts you a day or two out from Nohm, yeah? Head over and sit tight. Sure we'll have it all sorted soon after you arrive."

Nohm. The largest outpost in former imperial territory. The station house there was old, but it was a big, solid structure and there were always a few hunters posted there. It was close to the ruins, too.

"If I start out now, I can make it to Nohm tonight. Wait for me to—"

"Tonight? Maybe if you don't come across a single daemon on the way, but chance'd be a fine thing, eh? Don't push it."

"But—"

Biggs cut her off. "We'll be shoving off any moment. Won't have time to wait for you, so just take it slow."

This last statement suggested precisely what Sol didn't want to hear: Biggs and Wedge were probably already close to Nohm. If Sol stamped her feet and Biggs relented, she'd only end up delaying the rescue operation.

Sol mumbled sour agreement into the phone, to which Biggs replied, "There's a good girl. You take your time and play it safe, all right? If something happens to our little lady, *we're* the ones who have to answer to Lady A."

"I told you to quit calling me that!" Sol yelled into the phone, petulant child once more, and cut the call. The way their conversation had ended was par for the course, except this time the routine didn't do anything to help calm Sol down.

She had a feeling they needed to hurry to Nohm. It was time to wake up Luna and hit the road.

Perhaps because they occurred when she was on the cusp of waking, the dreams Lunafreya saw at dawn were always brief. The images in her mind were clear and crisp, but they lingered for only a moment. So she'd believed the same would be true of this dream. Gentiana stood before her now, but since she surely would be gone soon, Lunafreya's words spilled out in frenetic fashion.

"Gentiana! How I've been longing to see you! I would have liked it to be in the waking world, as with Umbra. But I'm delighted you're here now, even if only in dreams."

Lunafreya had been waiting eagerly for this reunion. There were so many things she wanted to say, and she needed to get them out before the dream ended.

"Tell me, did you know from the beginning? That the ring would take Noctis's life? Yes, I suppose you must have, but you kept silent for my sake. You did not wish to see me tormented by worry or anguish."

Gentiana smiled fondly. Lunafreya drew closer, only to find she was unable to reach out to the Messenger.

Of course I can't, she told herself. *This is a dream.*

"That is why," she continued, "I've decided to confront Ardyn. If I fight, I can drive away the darkness. The Star will be safe, and Noctis will not have to use the ring. It is my new calling, bestowed upon me by the Draconian. That he asked me must mean I am capable if I try."

Lunafreya paused, then added, "But still, I must confess I am frightened. I know I should not fear, but I find this power entrusted to me quite unnerving. What if my humanity should slip away?"

After another pause, Lunafreya realized something was amiss. She had carried on the entire conversation by herself. Gentiana had not spoken a word. At first, Lunafreya had assumed it was because she was in a dream. But now she was not so certain.

As she watched, Gentiana's lips moved, ever so slightly.

"Gentiana?" she asked. "Is something wrong?"

Before, the Messenger had been smiling. Now she seemed to be in pain. Her features were twisted with effort, as if she were desperately trying to relay something.

"What is it? Do you have a message for me?"

The Bladekeeper, she seemed to mouth. But Lunafreya was not certain. Again she tried to draw near, peering closely at the Messenger's face. Just then, several towering blades flew down before her eyes, forming a wall between Lunafreya and the Messenger.

"Gentiana!" she shouted with all her might, but all went black and silent.

Lunafreya wasn't sure which came first: the end of the dream, or the opening of her own eyes onto darkness as she returned to the waking world. When her mind was focused once again, she found herself in the cramped control room of the tiny signal cabin. She pulled her blanket more tightly around her body and shivered.

"What a peculiar dream," she said to herself.

She had long grown used to accepting the dreams for what they were; she could no better govern her dreams than her fate. Still, she had to wonder about her earlier visitation from the Bladekeeper. She hadn't thought to dismiss that first encounter as a mere dream.

The difference, she decided, was one of intimacy. The Draconian was not a being well known to her, but Gentiana she'd come to know more closely than perhaps anyone else in the world. That was why the encounter had felt unnatural and she'd been able to sense something amiss.

So perhaps it was not a dream. What if Gentiana *had* visited to relay some message, as the Draconian had before? Something might be preventing her from sharing that message.

Lunafreya tried to think. What could have happened to Gentiana? But just then, Sol interrupted her thoughts.

"Luna!"

The door of the control room flew open with a bang.

"Get yourself ready. And step on it. We're leaving."

"Has something happened?" Lunafreya asked. She rose and began to fold the blanket in haste, watching Sol's expression as she did so. The other woman appeared uncharacteristically anxious.

"It's nothing. Just hurry, okay?"

Lunafreya had yet to spend much time with Sol, but she had learned one thing about her companion: she had an occasional tendency to lie. And when she did, she did so poorly.

After a breakfast all but shoveled down their throats, they departed. They continued to follow the railway tracks. Sol was silent. Lunafreya wanted to ask what had happened, but Sol's entire demeanor warned her not to broach the subject.

Moreover, Sol appeared distracted. She was not focused on her driving, allowing Regina to bump over rocks and debris, and on several occasions she nearly ran the front wheel into a pothole, swerving only at the last second. Lunafreya was grateful that they had thus far avoided encountering any daemons, but she was nervous about what might transpire when they inevitably did. If Sol went into a fight as distracted as she was now, it would not go well for them.

Lunafreya did not know precisely how long they'd been on the road, but after a while, she waited for an opportune moment and ventured, "Perhaps we should take a break?"

As she'd feared, Sol seemed annoyed and replied curtly, "What? You need a break *already*?"

"I can continue. But mustn't we bear in mind the needs of the slowest member of the group?"

A flash of realization came to Sol's face, and Lunafreya was glad she'd managed to voice her concern effectively. Apparently, she had been right—Regina had nearly reached its limit.

The moment the motorcycle stopped, Sol hopped off and busied herself with a thorough check of its components. The process was accompanied by occasional clicks of Sol's tongue, as well as a few small sighs of relief.

Lunafreya did not know much about motorcycles, having just begun learning how to ride one. Still, the great care Sol paid to Regina was quite apparent, so whatever pressing matter was occupying Sol's mind, it was significant enough to cause her beloved Regina to slip from her mind.

The checkup seemed to have ended, but since Sol did not yet announce that it was time to depart, Lunafreya assumed that meant they'd be giving Regina some time to cool down.

They spent a few awkward moments in silence, neither having anything particular to do. Then Sol appeared to grow tired of the quiet and spoke, perhaps hoping merely to stave off boredom.

"Can I ask you something?" she began. "Your belief in the gods. Do you get anything out of it? Does it do you any good?"

Lunafreya had grown somewhat accustomed to these unexpected and unusual questions from her companion. Today, however, they seemed to include a touch of venom.

In fact, Sol did not even wait for Lunafreya to respond. "Is that what brought you back to life?" she spat. "Your faith in them?"

"No," Lunafreya replied. "I was bestowed life again that I might fulfill a new calling."

"And what calling is that?"

"To stop Ardyn Izunia. To drive the darkness from our world."

"Isn't that the king's job?"

"It was meant to be, yes. But it seems Ardyn has grown too powerful, and the intended fate of the world has gone off course."

"And *you're* the one they picked to fix the mess." Sol let out a small snort.

She continued, "So you're just gonna go along with whatever the gods say, huh? And you'll save the world all by yourself. I gotta say, that's the dumbest thing I've ever heard. There's no way. If the gods could send one person waltzing into Insomnia to put an end to all this, don't you think they'd have done it already? There've been a helluva lot of other people for the gods to choose from, all way stronger than you."

Sol capped off her outburst with, "If the gods planned to fix the world, why'd they let it end up like this in the first place?"

It was the anger behind the words that was the biggest surprise. It felt as if Sol were letting out some long pent-up frustration. Her tone was merciless, interrogating, and yet it also came across like a small child's tantrum.

"I do not know why I was chosen. Be that as it may, it is my calling. I must see it fulfilled."

"So you believe whatever the gods tell you?"

"As Oracle, naturally I must."

"So if you weren't the Oracle, you wouldn't have that faith? You wouldn't need to believe?"

At that, Lunafreya became aware of a new expression on Sol's face. She seemed to be on verge of tears.

"It is my opinion," Lunafreya answered carefully, "that each person has the right to adopt or reject faith as they see fit. But in my case—"

Sol cut in, her words more shouted than spoken. "I used to believe, too!"

"Sol..."

"I bought into all of it, right up until the day everything came crashing down. I was left with nothing. I begged them, you know. All of them. I begged them not to take it away."

Sol turned her face away, jaw clenched. The frustration in her profile was something Lunafreya had seen before. It hadn't been often, but every once in a while during her travels as Oracle, she'd caught sight of that expression. It was the face of those for whom prayers had gone unanswered and faith had been shattered. In Sol's eyes was the look of one who had long cursed the gods for her misfortune.

"Where were the gods then?" Sol asked. "What were they so busy with when *I* needed them? But who cares about the prayers of a child, right? They're beneath the notice of the mighty gods."

Among Lunafreya's duties as Oracle was to bring relief to those suffering from disease. But that did not mean she'd been able to help everyone. There were those for whom she did not arrive in time. Never had she faced open criticism from the friends or family of the deceased, yet there were times when people looked away as she approached, their anger and sorrow visibly held barely in check.

The gods did not deliver succor to everyone. To those struggling with loss, Lunafreya offered words of comfort as Oracle, ritual expressions and phatic utterances. Not the type of things Sol would want to hear now, but with those words unavailable, she did not know what else to say.

As Lunafreya fumbled for a response, Sol ended the conversation herself with, "Sorry, forget it. It's not like talking about it with you will change anything."

Then after a pause, "Pathetic. I sound like a little kid, expecting someone else to fix things for me."

Still turned away, Sol's face grew blank and hard. No trace of the earlier anger or tears remained. She merely bit her lower lip and muttered, "It's up to me. I won't let them die."

And then she was climbing onto the motorcycle and motioning for Lunafreya to get in the sidecar. She no longer seemed like a petulant child, or an adult who blamed the gods for allowing her loved ones to perish. Her demeanor was that of one determined to protect others through her own will and strength alone. She would not suffer loss again.

It made Lunafreya think.

What about me? she asked herself. *What have I wrought by my own strength alone?*

Perhaps she had not accomplished all that she believed she had. *So you're just gonna go along with whatever the gods say?* Sol's words had lodged deep in her breast, like a thorn that could not be pried free.

As soon as the exchange was over, Sol was already regretting her words. Why had she taken all that crap out on Luna? She'd acted like a little brat. It felt a lot like how she always seemed to end up behaving around her mother, but when she'd lashed out at the Oracle, there was another, slightly different dynamic at work.

It probably had to do with Luna's exasperating devotion to the gods. The Oracle never framed things in terms of herself—she was always thinking and talking about what the gods wanted or what was best for the Star. The woman never took a moment to think about what *she* wanted to do. Every action was based on some calling she was convinced she had to live up to. Sol couldn't wrap her head around it.

The only thing worse than someone who believed only in themselves was someone who was blindly devoted to a higher power. There was no guarantee that such an entity would be a force for good, but because people like that would never allow themselves to question their faith, they couldn't ever stop and reevaluate things with a critical eye.

When Sol was young, she'd known plenty of adults like that, those who unquestioningly placed their trust in their emperor and his vision for their nation. Not once did it occur to them that what was happening around them might not be for the best. As the emperor steered Niflheim toward its doom, they were all right there alongside him, up until the very end.

Sol's adoptive mother was different. She lived by her own rules. If you asked her why she went out of her way to help others, she'd laugh and say she only did it because she felt like it. There had been a time when Aranea let herself be constrained by orders, back when she'd been a soldier, but by the time she met Sol, she had left that part of her life behind.

That was why Sol had respected her mother, from the very first moment they'd met. As far back as Sol could remember, having her mother's approval had felt like the most important thing in the world.

Wait. Why was she thinking in the past tense?

This was Biggs's fault. The man couldn't lie worth a damn. She could tell from his voice alone that he'd been on the verge of panic. And now he had Sol fearing the worst, too.

Mom, please be safe. I'll be there soon.

She repeated the short prayer to herself for what must have been the hundredth time.

"Sol! We can't go this way! Stop!"

Sol snapped back to reality. A daemon was straight ahead of them, blocking the road. If she'd been paying attention, she'd have noticed it earlier, and they might have been able to circle around. It probably would have saved them some time, but it was too late now. The daemon had sighted them and was closing in fast.

Regina skidded to a stop, and Sol pulled out her shotgun. Luna jumped from the sidecar, spear held at the ready. Fortunately, this wasn't among the biggest daemons they'd come across, but neither would it go down easy.

Sol steadied her aim and let loose on the approaching enemy. The shower of hot metal slowed the daemon down some, but the wound was certainly not fatal.

"Luna!"

"I've got it!"

The daemon stumbled closer, now nearly in melee range. Luna flung her right hand out. The monster shuddered, and a stream of its sickening black miasma began flowing straight into her palm.

Sol stared in wonder. The Oracle seemed stronger than ever. In their early battles, Luna had played a supporting role by slowing the incoming daemons, which Sol then finished off with a shotgun shell at point-blank range or, if she were feeling particularly saucy, with a grenade thrown into a gaping jaw.

But lately, their roles had been reversed. Sol's barrages usually served to slow the creature, and Luna was the one to bring it down. As they traveled farther along the road, the number of powerful daemons seemed to increase, among them many for which gun and spear alone did not suffice.

The power to absorb the scourge seemed to take a toll on Luna. When the flow of miasma reached its peak, a wrinkle of pain would form on her brow, and she'd grit her teeth. The fact that Sol noticed such little changes in her expression at all was a clear signal of how their roles in battle had shifted.

And the burden on Luna wasn't limited to their time in battle alone. When the Oracle had been changing her clothes in Wael, Sol had snuck a quick peek at her back and saw that the woman's milky white skin was covered with sinister black patches. Now those patches were visible even at the edges of her collar and sleeves. In other words, whatever was happening to her, it had gotten that much worse in just a matter of days.

Sometimes, she even caught Luna with her hands pressed against her mouth as if in pain. She seemed determined not to let her symptoms show, but now that the two were spending nearly every moment together, it was impossible for Sol *not* to see signs of Luna's apparent agony.

Luna claimed that her power had been bestowed by one of the Six. If so, whichever god had given it sure had a sick sense of humor. Power that caused so much pain didn't seem like much of a gift, nor any way to motivate someone to carry out some divine calling. Why not give Luna another power that was easier to deal with or change the nature of the power so it didn't cause her agony? It didn't seem like something that would be hard for a god to do. So why was it necessary to let Luna suffer?

Whichever god had burdened Luna with such a thing must have been the same one who ignored Sol's own prayers as a child in Gralea. The gods had given no sign they were worthy of faith, and yet Luna went on believing despite her suffering. It was baffling.

They managed to fell the daemon, but after that, the creatures were everywhere along the road, pack after pack of them, as if openly mocking Sol's need for haste. In the end, they had to spend another night afield well short of Sol's destination.

They did not sleep at a minor outpost or even a signal cabin. They simply pitched a tent in a narrow space sheltered by a rock outcrop. To keep the daemons at bay, they placed portable lights at the edges of the camp and built a fire in the center. As one final precaution, they decided to take shifts awake, one keeping watch while the other slept.

Sol continued to be sparing with her words. Lunafreya learned only that their immediate destination was an outpost called Nohm. She was unable to discover why they were headed there or what they intended to do on arrival. Nor had she learned why Sol seemed so distracted and rushed. The other woman's decision not to share any of these things left Lunafreya feeling forlorn and insecure.

In battle, the pair had developed a strong rapport. They seemed to be well attuned to each other, and for the first time, Lunafreya clearly understood what it meant for two people to have each other's backs. However, although she felt that she could rely on Sol, she wasn't sure whether Sol felt the same way about her.

The night was quiet. So quiet that she could hear every little toss and turn from Sol as she slept in the tent. Both the firepit and the artificial lights seemed to be doing a commendable job—Luna sensed no trace of any daemons lurking nearby.

She turned away from the flames and opened the notebook. The light of the fire bothered her. Fortunately, she did not need it. Even at night in this perpetual darkness, she was able to read and write perfectly well without light.

During the day's breaks, there had been no appreciable amount of conversation. Lunafreya had used the free time to set down her scattered thoughts in the notebook.

Sol, for her part, seemed to be embarrassed about how she'd laid into Lunafreya. At the next break after their conversation and the one after, she'd simply sat in stubborn silence. Lunafreya, not wanting to press the girl, had stayed silent herself.

Unlike the short road breaks, Lunafreya now had a long, uninterrupted block of time—so long that she worried she might doze off. She decided it was better to keep herself busy than risk falling asleep while on watch.

Dearest Noctis,
It is my turn to keep watch, so here I am, tending the campfire. Sleeping outdoors like this is a new experience for me. What was it like for you on your first night camping at a haven? Perhaps you felt the same way that I feel now.

I was also in charge of the meal tonight. It seems I made too liberal a use of spices for my companion's liking. She went so far as to declare my sense of taste unrefined. Given that her own approach to cooking is quite lax, I hardly think her to be in a position to criticize.

Last night, we found ourselves with an abundance of free time from our arrival at the night's lodgings until it was time to go to sleep. We spent it in leisure, and Sol taught me a card game. Tonight, however, I suggested that we turn in early. She seems quite exhausted. I sense there is some great worry on her mind and that it has plagued her all day long. She is not her usual self.

I suppose I should mention that while Sol may be somewhat lacking in culinary skills, she is quite a proficient card player. I was impressed by her skill in planning and carefully executing each strategy for victory. Over the course of the evening, I managed not a single win. According to Sol, I am far too transparent in my intentions for my own good, and I let slip my hand too easily. At the time, I felt her accusations rather harsh and flatly refuted them.

She and I are slowly opening up to each other, but—perhaps because of this new power bestowed upon me, or perhaps because I have explained how I came to once again walk among the living—Sol continues to be wary of me.

Once Lunafreya touched nib to paper, the words poured forth in an endless torrent. She found herself unable to stop. There were so many things she wanted to tell Noctis, and she grew frustrated as her hand's pace fell far short of her mind's. For hours, she continued to sweep her pen across the pages, lost in thought. When she'd begun her watch, she'd worried she might not know what to do with herself or that she might fall asleep and let the fire die out. In truth, there was no need for concern. She was so immersed in her writing, she did not even realize it was time to change shifts until Sol came out of the tent.

It was already dawn when Sol felt her smartphone buzz. She fished it out of her pocket and checked the display: an incoming call from Gladiolus Amicitia.

She smiled. It was almost funny in a way—ten years ago, who could have imagined a citizen of Niflheim working together with a sworn Shield of the King?

If the man was reaching out to her now, odds were almost certain he wanted to ask about Luna. She answered his call.

"Can you talk?" Gladio asked.

"Yeah," Sol replied. She understood exactly what the question meant. "She's asleep in the tent. I'm outside."

He laughed. "You've always been a quick one."

Quick or not, it was hard for her to imagine any other meaning to his words under the circumstances. Once Sol had described her encounter with the Oracle to Cindy, the information had undoubtedly been relayed to Gladio and his comrades all but immediately.

"So what are your thoughts?" the Shield asked. "Think she's the real deal?"

"I still don't know. But that's what she claims."

"Noct would know," Gladio muttered. "He'd be able to tell right away."

"You really think so? Even he might not be able to know for sure, given the circumstances."

According to Luna, their last proper encounter had taken place while they were still children. Twelve years later, there had been a reunion of sorts, in Altissia, but he had only been part of the crowd as she addressed the people, her eyes meeting his from afar. If that was the extent of contact King Noctis had with the Oracle as an adult, would he truly know her so readily?

"Well," Sol said, "regardless of who she is, she's . . . "

Got my back, she was going to say but reconsidered. The woman's power was unsettling. There was no getting around that. Even if it'd been granted by the gods, as she claimed, from any objective viewpoint, it was the kind of thing you'd expect of a monster, not from someone you wanted to place your trust in.

She reached for another expression and finally settled on "She's proving helpful."

"Right. I'll pass the word on to Sania. She seems to think this self-proclaimed 'Oracle' and her powers, whatever they are, might make for some interesting scientific research."

Though Sol had just compared her power to that of a monster, hearing Luna described as a potential research subject was somehow disturbing. She wasn't sure exactly where that feeling was coming from, and she had barely begun to untangle it when she heard a rustling sound behind her. She turned to see Luna poking her head through the tent flap.

"All right, sounds good," Sol hurriedly said into the phone. "Talk to you later."

She cut the call and turned her gaze to the fire. For whatever reason, she couldn't bring herself to look Luna in the eye. How long had the other woman been awake? How much had she heard?

Finally, it dawned on her why she was avoiding the Oracle's gaze: it was from a sense of guilt.

From her seat in the sidecar, Lunafreya glanced over at Sol. The young woman's brow was still furrowed, the same troubled expression she'd worn all throughout the day before.

At least her driving seemed to be more focused. There was no way to avoid the daemons that ambushed them without warning from the roadsides, but by keeping a careful lookout, they could spot and circle around ones that appeared directly on the road ahead. Every time Lunafreya noticed a suspicious shape in the distance, she alerted Sol. Up until recently, she had not realized that between them, her vision at night was far superior. And now that she knew that fact, she wished she didn't. It was why she'd stayed quiet before, even though she thought it strange that Sol seemed not to notice the daemons Lunafreya could see so easily.

However, as Sol was clearly anxious to reach their destination, the fewer daemon encounters they had, the better. And so Lunafreya decided it was more important to do everything that she could to help rather than try to conceal her monstrous powers.

Thanks to Lunafreya's efforts, the time they spent dealing with daemons dropped dramatically, and they reached Nohm before evening.

Once she saw the station building at Nohm, it clicked. She'd been here before, prior to her ascension. It must have been ten years ago—or, rather, *twenty* years in this new world she'd awoken into. But the sight brought not a sense of nostalgia so much as one of unease. In the past, this station had been a lively place, with throngs of people filing into or out of the trains stopped at its numerous platforms. Not a hint of those days remained.

Even more disconcerting was the fact that every window of the station building was dark.

"Why are they . . . ?"

Sol, too, seemed unable to hide her confusion. Sol had been the one to tell her about Nohm, describing it as one of the more important outposts in the area, with a permanent Hunter garrison and windows always shining with light. She'd even talked about how relieved she always felt as she approached the place, seeing those reassuring lights as she pulled up to the building.

The lack of lights now had them both worried. When they walked closer, they saw several of the windows had been smashed.

"What could have happened here?"

"Isn't it obvious? The outpost was attacked."

Lunafreya's voice trembled. "May the gods watch over us."

Sol explained, "It doesn't happen a lot, but it's not unheard of. Sometimes daemons show up in force and wreak havoc on an outpost."

After Sol cautiously peered through several windows, she returned to the main entrance. She kicked the door in, gun held at the ready, and cautiously walked through the doorway. Lunafreya sensed no daemons inside, lying in ambush, but neither did she feel any presence of human life.

She followed after Sol, stepping inside the station building. What she saw was disconcerting. Every chair had been toppled over, the walls and tables punctured with so many bullet holes their surfaces resembled a wasp's nest. There were gouges and scorch marks on the floors. Clearly there had been a battle here, an intense one between hunter and daemon, and probably more than just one.

"Luna. Let's get moving."

Sol delivered the curt order and spun on her heel, heading back outside the building. Lunafreya hurried to follow. She would have liked to shut the door behind her, but the force of Sol's kick had bent the hinges, preventing it from closing properly.

"Where are we going?" she asked.

"Not sure yet."

As they walked, Sol pulled from her pocket the same small transceiver that Lunafreya had seen her use before, the thing she referred to as her "smartphone."

"I'll call in and find out where the next rendezvous point—"

Sol stopped mid-sentence with a gasp and came to an abrupt halt. Lunafreya's skin prickled as she picked up the sounds both of things crawling across the ground and of wings cutting through air. Vague shapes lurked in the darkness. She sensed they'd been surrounded.

The assault began from above. Sol didn't even have time to draw a gun, so Lunafreya flung her right hand up in haste. A repulsive sensation writhed its way along her arm, but she didn't have time to be disgusted by it now.

A shotgun blast rang out. Sol had managed to grab her primary weapon, but even that wasn't going to be enough to deal with this many enemies. Lunafreya realized that it was up to her to stop the daemons. She focused the power into her palms. The flying daemon that had grappled onto her arm crashed down right in front of her eyes.

It's all right. I can do this, she told herself.

She took down a daemon lunging in from the side, then swept forward to cover Sol's back. Her companion would not suffer even a single scratch; she swore it would be so.

She remembered the look in Sol's eyes when the young woman related how she'd been left with nothing, the broken sound of her voice when she'd demanded to know what had kept the gods from hearing her pleas. At the time Lunafreya had wished desperately to help, to do anything to understand and ease Sol's grief. She wanted to protect her new friend.

The moment the thought entered her mind, something inside her burst free. The very flow of time seemed to change. She could see the daemons about her frozen in mid-motion, and in this moment, she felt as though she could destroy any of them simply with a glance. The daemons in the air crashed to the ground, Lunafreya waving away the clouds of miasma they left behind, already intent on finding her next prey.

She continued to rip apart each and every black mass that lunged toward her. It was exhilaratingly easy, like crushing clumps of dirt between her fingers. She was hunting the daemons one by one—no, *cleansing* them from the world. Collecting trash, piece by piece.

Faster. More. She had to take *more*!

"Luna, what have you . . . ?"

At the sound of Sol's voice, she snapped back to reality. She looked around, but there were no more daemons.

She'd destroyed them. Every single one. With her own two hands.

Lunafreya's legs buckled, and she collapsed unconscious to the ground.

When Lunafreya had collapsed, it was not from fear. It wasn't until a while later that she understood why, but the cause of her weakness was the scale of what she'd done. She'd absorbed so much scourge in so little time her body was overwhelmed.

The darkness inside her would never dissipate. The more of the sickness she absorbed, the more sway it held over her. It pulsated and writhed within her, looking for any chance to take control.

Yet she still remained blessed with the healing powers of the Oracle. She'd been drawing on those powers unconsciously to help stay the tiny thrashing creatures within her.

That must have been the reason why she was chosen by the Draconian: her ability to withstand the scourge. A regular human being without divine powers of healing would simply succumb—once the scourge entered their body, they would quickly turn into a daemon. In contrast, the Oracle's power could counterbalance that of the scourge, which made her an ideal choice.

"Are you okay?" Sol peered into Lunafreya's eyes, handing her a mug with a steaming liquid inside. Lunafreya nodded weakly and accepted the hot drink.

After the battle at Nohm, Sol had apparently managed to carry the comatose Lunafreya back inside the station building. Not only that, she'd restarted the generator and restored light to the interior.

"I don't really know what I'm doing when it comes to making tea," Sol apologized. "Getting it right's harder than I thought."

"I am sure it is lovely. Thank you."

Lunafreya took a sip. The tea was in fact a bit more bitter than she cared for—which meant that for Sol, it must have been nearly undrinkable.

"The aroma is most pleasing," Lunafreya said, "As is the warmth."

Sol smiled and replied, "That's exactly what I thought. Figured you might appreciate it, especially now." Lunafreya realized it was true. Back at the signal cabin, where they'd found the teapot, Sol had fumbled for a way to compliment Lunafreya's efforts, eventually settling on the comforting smell.

"Do you think maybe . . . ?" Sol began, staring deep into the mug in her hand. "Do you think maybe, if you keep absorbing daemons the way you've been doing, you might lose your mind or something? Could you end up becoming one? If so . . . would it be better for all of us—you, me, the rest of humanity—if I killed you now?"

The words were sinister, but the tone was not. Sol made no movement to draw her guns. It was not the tense mood of that first evening over cups of tea, when Sol had still been careful to keep her weapons within easy reach.

"I wonder about that as well. Whether it is necessary for me to become a monster in order to stop them. I find myself... uncertain why the gods would put such a calling on my shoulders."

Lunafreya understood that the power she wielded was necessary to stop the daemons. But it seemed stopping the daemons might well cause her to become one. It was a terrifying thought that filled her with dread. She trusted in the gods, but still, she could not dispel her unease.

"Tell me," Sol said. "What do you want to do?"

"It is the duty of the Oracle to aid the king of Lucis, so I—"

"That's not what I asked," Sol cut in. "I don't care about the duty of the Oracle. I'm asking about *you*. The woman sitting in front of me. What does *Lunafreya* want to do? Y'know, stuff you like, that you're into but didn't get a chance to do before."

"I..." Lunafreya trailed off, uncertain how to answer.

"Isn't there *something*? Anything you wanna do not because you have to but 'cause you enjoy it?" Sol quirked a smile. "Hobbies? Clothes? Fine dining?"

She'd never even considered experimenting with her clothing. All she needed were garments that were clean and chaste, inoffensive to the people she would serve.

Although, there might have been one exception... A wedding dress. She'd had one once, and she'd been eagerly awaiting the day she might wear it, for on that day, she would stand beside Noctis and...

Sol seemed to read her mind. "For example," the younger woman said, "maybe you want to spend time with the king?"

Yes. She'd had one wish, which she'd hoped so desperately might be fulfilled but which had never been. She wanted to be with the person who was most dear to her, to spend her life together with the man she loved. She'd sacrificed that wish to her duty as the Oracle and had passed from the world with it unrealized. An empty, lonely, mournful feeling had filled her on that day. It had been so much worse than when they were torn away from each other as children in Tenebrae. She could feel the ache in her heart even now.

"I did once dream," Lunafreya said, "of spending my days together with Noctis. That would have been more than enough happiness for me."

"Well, look at that. So there *is* something you want for yourself."

"But . . . "

"So what's the problem? There's something you want, and now you've got a second shot at making it happen. How about instead of telling yourself you can't have it, you forget about the gods and this calling or whatever and focus on what *you* want out of life?"

Lunafreya hesitated. It was in order to fulfill this calling that she had been granted life anew. If she abandoned her duty, could not the god who bestowed that life just as easily take it away? And there was another, arguably more significant issue.

"I know not what I am anymore," Lunafreya confessed. "Am I human? A monster?"

She looked down at her open palms—the same palms that had drawn in more scourge than she cared to fathom. With a power like this, could she still be called human at all?

"I can't give you any answers about what exactly you are. But I do know what you've done. If it weren't for you, I'd be dead right now."

Sol's hesitation was marked, and her words carefully chosen. She didn't try to claim that Lunafreya was human in a facile attempt to reassure her. But neither did Sol seem inclined to deem her a monster outright.

"If you ask me, I say to hell with all this Oracle stuff. Who cares about some damn calling? The Oracle died ten years ago. The person I see before me right now is just a woman. Her name is Luna. She's crazy strong, but otherwise, she's a person like anyone else, and she wants to be back with the guy she loves."

On hearing Sol's words, Lunafreya felt the burden weighing her down lessen slightly. She was not free of her worries, and the physical pain and discomfort persisted as before. Not a thing had changed about her present situation, but even so, she felt a surge of determination to go on.

"Sol... thank you for your kind words. Once again, I find myself in your debt."

"Hey, could you, uh, cut it out with the 'I'm in your debt' stuff?"

"Why?"

She was reminded of the last time she'd said similar words to Sol. The younger woman had turned away then, clearly put out.

"It's the kind of thing people say before they up and die on you."

"What do you mean?"

"Do you really need me to spell it out for you?" Sol gave her a puzzled look, but then began to explain. "It's a jinx. You don't say all your thank-yous and good-byes, because if you do, there's no regret left to hold you back from dying."

Then, with a wrinkle across the bridge of her nose, she added, "Gods, how did you ever function before?"

"I understand now. I am again indebted for your thorough expla—"

"Stop already!"

Lunafreya, bewildered by her own mistake, brought a hand up to cover her mouth. Sol burst out laughing, and then Lunafreya was laughing too. She managed to keep her next thank-you silent, saying the words only in her heart.

It looked like Luna was feeling better. Maybe teasing out her true desires had helped put her mind at ease. She'd be fine for now, at least mentally—Sol had no idea what to make of her physical symptoms.

With Luna taken care of, the next thing to do was call Biggs and give him a rundown of what happened at Nohm. The outpost was critical to retaining their foothold in former imperial territory. Securing areas outside of Lestallum where people could live was one of the main goals of the Kingsglaive and everyone else who collaborated with them. So Nohm's complete loss was something they couldn't afford. They had to do whatever it took to make sure it wasn't overrun by daemons.

The nearby ruins were of interest because of the contents of a report on the empire's past activities. The ruins themselves were relics of Solheim, but apparently, one of the empire's old daemon-infused creations might be lurking within them. The goal was to eliminate the potential threat from the area and, at the same time, assess the feasibility of using the ancient structures as a settlement. A safe, easily defensible location in the former empire where people could live would allow them all to make more efficient use of the resources found there, as there were plenty of materials in the region that could not be transported to Lestallum.

"Sol! Are you all right?! Where are you?!" Biggs started shouting the moment the call connected. Sol winced and pulled the phone slightly away from her ear.

"We're safe in Nohm. But by the time we showed up, it was already empty."

"We heard about what happened. Some of the hunters managed to escape. What's it looking like now? The daemons still around?"

"We're all right. Luna took care of the daemons. What about Mom? Is she with you?"

There was another silence, just as in their previous call. It was more than Sol could bear, and she repeated her question, voice going shrill. "What about Mom?!"

"Lady A's squad is down in the ruins. They're surrounded by a pack of daemons that's blocking the way back out."

"Got it. We're on our way!"

"No need. We're already in the process of sealing the place up. Once that's done, we'll be pulling out of the area."

Sol couldn't believe what she was hearing. Seal up? Pull out? What was Biggs saying?

She felt the blood drain from her face.

"You're planning to leave them behind?!"

Biggs did not answer. Sol felt the draining blood surge back.

"The hell is wrong with you?! You think I'm just gonna stand by and let you do this?! I'm heading there now. I've got Luna with me, so—"

"Listen to me, Sol. These are orders from Lady A herself. She doesn't want anyone else going in there. This armor lurking down there—Sapphire Weapon, they're calling it—is too big a threat. Lady A says to seal off the entrance and get the hell out of the area. You've got to stand down on this one."

Sol had read the reports on Sapphire Weapon, so she knew how dangerous it was. But she still didn't want to accept the idea of... A lump formed at the back of her throat, and she found herself unable to speak. She knew her mother probably better than anyone else. If Aranea gave the order, she meant it.

Biggs filled the silence. "I'll pass word when we figure out the next rendezvous point. For now, sit tight in Nohm."

He ended the call, and Sol stood without moving, continuing to hold the phone in hand. Her thoughts wouldn't come together. One phrase from her childhood sounded over and over in her mind. *Please don't take them away. Please don't take them away.* Was she about to lose everything? Again? Just like that awful day ten years ago?

"Sol?" Lunafreya's voice came soft and gentle. "Is everything all right?"

"Um. Yeah. All good."

"Has something happened to your mother?"

At the note of concern in Luna's voice, Sol found herself almost ready to cry. She clenched her jaw, forcing down the welling emotion.

"She's in the depths of the ruins. Surrounded by daemons."

"Then we must hurry. Quickly, Sol! Let us go to her aid."

"We can't. She doesn't want anyone else following her in. I'm stuck out here."

When she said it, the words didn't even feel like hers. It was as if she were reading lines off a page of a script.

"What are you saying?" Lunafreya asked. "You told me before that you're going to make sure no one else dies."

Sol knew that already. She didn't need to hear it from someone else. Luna's hands grabbed at Sol's arms, but Sol batted them away in irritation.

"Look, there's some huge monster down there, one that even *she* wasn't able to take down. And now they're surrounded by a pack of daemons to boot. Me going down there isn't going to make the situation any better."

"You mustn't speak like that! You said it yourself on the phone. We're heading in there! You'll have me with you!"

It seemed Luna had been listening to Sol's half of the conversation with Biggs. Hardly a surprise, since Luna'd been standing right next to her. Which made it feel even worse for Sol to admit to herself that if Biggs hadn't cut her off, she'd intended to continue, "I've got Luna with me, so it'll be fine. *She* can take care of the daemons." Because here she was again, expecting someone else to fix things for her, just like a child. Now she felt thankful to Biggs for cutting her off and sickly relieved she hadn't let that last bit slip out where Luna could hear it.

"We've got to hurry. We shall finish off the daemons and save your mother, then—"

"Listen to yourself! You know better than anyone what absorbing the daemons does to you. If you keep on like this, next *you'll* be turning into a monster."

Asking for Luna's help was a step too far for Sol to take. She couldn't sacrifice someone else, not even for the sake of her own family. She wouldn't let someone else take on the burden that she should bear. Realizing that she'd been on the cusp of doing exactly that only strengthened her resolve.

"It does not matter. I will help you. Not because it is my calling, but because I wish to do so."

"Would you still say that if you knew who I really was to you? To your *family*?"

In M.E. 744, Emperor Iedolas Aldercapt of Niflheim had ordered the invasion of Fenestala Manor, home of the royal family of Tenebrae. The family of the Oracle. The assault claimed the life of the previous Oracle—Lunafreya's mother—and for four years afterward, Lunafreya had remained in the manor under lock and key. Her captivity had been on direct order from the emperor.

"I am Solara Aldercapt Antiquum, granddaughter of the late emperor of Niflheim. The man who killed your mother. Would you still help me now, knowing what my family has done to yours?"

Sol had always been vaguely aware of her own high status even from an early age, but how precisely she fit into the hierarchy of the empire had been explained to her only recently. Her adoptive mother had been the one to break the news. "Now that you're older," Aranea had begun, "there's something you should know."

The revelation had come suddenly and heavily. It felt like Aranea was delivering some deathbed secret—like she was preparing to leave Sol somehow. Sol had listened, but she'd grown sulky and defiant.

"Yeah, I know," she'd told her mother. "We're not really related, I get it."

She regretted those words now with all of her heart.

When she'd met Luna, she'd figured there was no reason to go out of her way to reveal her connection to the empire. They would only be spending a few days together at the most. But now, with Luna ready to sacrifice herself, it couldn't be kept secret any longer. Sol wasn't so cruel as to let the Oracle throw her life away for the sake of an enemy. Not for the descendant of someone who had so wounded her family.

Lunafreya's response took her aback.

"Granddaughter of the emperor or not, it does not matter to me. The person I see before me right now is just a woman. She is disconcertingly good at cards, a rather indifferent cook, and a bit stubborn, but she is still a person like any other, and her name is Sol."

"Luna . . . " Sol murmured.

"Before me stands someone in need. I could not fathom refusing to help when it is in my power to do so. If I were to simply walk away and let your mother be sealed up in the ruins, I could never forgive myself."

On receipt of Biggs's first message the other day, Sol had been almost frantic with worry. Who knew what might have happened to the survey team and those who had gone in to assist it? She'd taken her frustration out on Luna, saying horrible things to her, and yet, when they were surrounded by the daemons at Nohm, Luna had protected her as if it were the only thing to do.

And as a result, Luna had edged even closer toward becoming a daemon. Now responsibility for that lay on Sol's shoulders, too.

She looked at Luna. "I can't let you do it. I've already caused you enough trouble—"

"It is no hardship," Luna interrupted, words quiet yet firm. "I help because I wish to. Did you not hear me before?"

Their travels together had only lasted a few days, but during that time, Luna's words had always been truthful. The woman was too transparent for her own good, the type of person who always let her hand show. It was exasperating. But because she never lied and was always straightforward, her words held power. Luna wouldn't say something if she didn't believe it to be true. So her quiet statement pierced right to Sol's core.

"Luna . . . " she started.

Sol decided to be straightforward, too.

"I'm sorry. I need your help. I can't do this without your powers."

Luna smiled and nodded. "Then let us go. Together."

"Thanks, Luna. And whatever happens, I just want you to know—"

Luna cut her off. "No. Do not say any more. That is the kind of thing people say before they go and die on you."

They looked at each other and laughed.

On the road to the ruins, Sol finally shared the story of the day she lost everything. The day Gralea fell. Since the events had occurred after Lunafreya's death in Altissia, everything was news to her, from the revelation of Ardyn Izunia's hand in the destruction of the empire to the report of Emperor Iedolas's death.

"Daemons attacked the estate that day. Soon the whole place was overrun. Desperate to see to my safety, my lady mother . . . Heh. It sounds weird, saying it now. But that's what I used to call her. 'My lady mother.'"

Sol's real father—the imperial prince of Niflheim, Iedolas Aldercapt's son—had not been wed to Sol's mother. For a long time, the emperor had been unaware of the existence of his own granddaughter.

"The mom I have now, I met right after my escape. Ever since then, the day I became an orphan, she's always looked after me. We're not related by blood, but to me, she's my real mother."

"Then we must stop at nothing to ensure that she is safe."

"Yeah. You're right. We have to save her."

For a while afterward, Sol was quiet, and the motorcycle rolled on. But the silence was no longer awkward. There was no need for words said aloud. Lunafreya knew that she and Sol were thinking the same thing. They were headed toward the same future.

From the moment they'd arrived at Nohm and Sol had explained that there had been an incident at some ruins nearby, Lunafreya had suspected she knew which site it was. Now, as they drew near on Regina, her suspicions were confirmed.

"This is Ralmuell," Lunafreya murmured.

"Yeah, that's right. You been here before or something?"

"I have. For the first time when I was twelve years of age."

When Lunafreya explained that this was the location where she had performed her training in preparation to become the Oracle, Sol's eyes grew wide.

"I was taught that it was a temple from ancient times," Lunafreya explained, "but I had not realized that it rested atop a remnant site of the Solheim civilization."

The holy site of Ralmuell was said to be a place of communion between humanity and the gods. Citizens of Tenebrae often went to the ruins on pilgrimage, and the Oracle successors always trained there before ascension.

"If you trained here, then you must know the layout, right?"

"To some extent. As I understand it, there is a large underground cavern, but entry to that part of the site was forbidden."

"Know any shortcuts or side entrances? It'd be best if we can sneak in without being spotted. If Biggs and Wedge catch us, they'll stop us from going inside for sure."

"Biggs. Might that be whom you were speaking with earlier?"

Sol nodded. Lunafreya remembered the grief-stricken look as Sol had asked, *You're planning to leave them behind?!*

"Yes," Lunafreya said. "I know of a way we can get inside without being too conspicuous."

For the duration of her training, Lunafreya's contact with the pilgrims was carefully moderated, as she had not yet formally ascended as Oracle. She had made use of a passage that allowed entry to the training grounds without being seen by visitors.

Beyond the passage, too, she had learned of several small rooms and hidden staircases carved into the solid rock that allowed one to move about in secrecy. The existence of such things perhaps implied that there had always been, even from ancient times, those with untoward intentions who wished to see the Oracle and her words bent to their own nefarious ends.

They avoided the hunters watching the entrance and circled around farther back. To Lunafreya, everything about the temple grounds brought back memories. When they were inside, she gazed at the murals of the gods on the ceilings and of past Oracles on the walls.

At the time, it had occurred to Lunafreya that someday her likeness, too, would appear on one of these walls, but at the age of twelve the prospect had seemed like something so terribly distant it was hardly even real.

Things felt different now. She had lived one existence as the Oracle. She'd forged covenants with the gods at the cost of her life. She'd been killed by Ardyn. The temple walls were the same as when she was a girl, and yet now they carried a gravity she'd never apprehended before.

Lunafreya's mother had been killed suddenly and unjustly by the forces of Niflheim. Surely there were other Oracles of the past who had died untimely deaths, yet every Oracle on these walls was depicted with smiles overflowing with affection. How many tears did each of those smiles conceal?

The portrait furthest back was of the first Oracle. She appeared again by the doors leading to the sanctuary, this time as a statue silently guarding the entrance to the holy site. Her name was engraved on the pedestal upon which she stood: *Aera Mirus Fleuret.*

"Luna? Is something wrong?" Sol paused, a worried look on her face.

"It's nothing. This statue just caught my attention."

"She kinda looks like you, to be honest. Though I guess that makes sense. The first Oracle would've been one of your ancestors, right?"

Lunafreya thought she heard her name being called again. She looked up to meet the statue's eyes. For a brief moment, it seemed like those stone eyes were glistening with tears. The statue's outline began to grow indistinct, and Sol's anxious, repeated inquiries of "Luna?" faded away into the distance.

The gods blessed me with a power and a purpose: to cure people of what ails them.

The voice seemed familiar. Lunafreya felt certain she'd heard it somewhere before. The moment it reached her ears, her surroundings were bathed in golden light. Gone were the ancient murals and floor of stone. Gone completely were Sol's cries. Ears of wheat bowed in the wind, a field stretching on as far as the eye could see. On every side, the warm color of the harvest surrounded her.

Your devotion shall not go unnoticed. The gods will doubtless be watching over you.

The second voice was that of the first Oracle. For some reason, Lunafreya knew this with certainty.

So who did the voice other belong to? Who was the first speaker?

"Ardyn Lucis Caelum."

Her question was met with this immediate answer. Aera Mirus Fleuret, first to hold the title of Oracle, spoke directly into Lunafreya's mind.

"Such was the name of the man I loved," Aera said, "and the man meant to be our Founder King, ruling over the new nation of Lucis."

Ardyn? That was who she'd heard speaking? The voice was quite similar in tone to that of the Ardyn she knew, but her mind reeled at the implications. And what was this about the Founder King?

"Ardyn was chosen. He alone was bestowed with the power to heal those afflicted by the Starscourge."

Lunafreya's surroundings shifted once again. Now she saw a young woman in the throes of the scourge, chained atop a small wooden bedframe in a shed. Ardyn stood before her, his hand extended. He drew in the scourge, and the young woman was healed.

And there had been others, too. Soon, Lunafreya was witnessing scenes of innumerable lives delivered from the scourge by Ardyn's hands.

That power, Lunafreya thought. *It's the same as the power I've been given. But I've used mine only to destroy the daemons. I hadn't realized it could be used to heal as well.*

Lunafreya had brought comfort to the ill during her travels as Oracle. However, the powers she wielded in that role merely bolstered the recipient's innate capacity to heal. It was a world of difference from being able to remove the root of the scourge itself.

She witnessed Ardyn in his plain and simple garb, on an endless mission to treat the suffering people of his land. Never did he rest. She witnessed his growing conflict with his younger brother; after a disagreement about the best way to govern and aid the people, Ardyn was forced to run for his life. Even near the end, as the scourge ravaged his body, he labored on for the sake of his people. He was the very picture of a savior.

Ardyn desperately tried to contain the scourge that roiled inside his body. He feared that he might someday become a monster, and struggled against the worry that he might lose his own humanity. It was the same battle that Lunafreya had been fighting during these past few days of her returned life.

"Ultimately," Aera said, "Ardyn's calling as bestowed by the gods differed from what he believed himself fated to do."

Despite the fact that he had labored to heal the people of his land—no, *because* of it—he was ravaged by the scourge, rejected by the Crystal, erased from Lucian history, and imprisoned on the island of Angelgard. There, he was renamed "Adagium" and branded a monster. Entombed deep beneath the rocky shores, brooding over the unjust way he'd been treated, he had millennia to grow and foster his hatred. The woman he loved had been killed before his eyes. His happiness and future had been stripped away.

Nothing matters—none of it. Not the "blessed" gods above nor the accursed kings below. To hell with them all!

His words full of rage and malediction shook the surroundings.

Ardyn had put his faith in the gods and had given everything to his calling. Yet the gods did not heed his pleas. In fact, it was far worse than that—his fate as prescribed by the divine was of unparalleled cruelty.

It was because of what she'd been through that Lunafreya could understand his despair. She had been granted the same power, and she now struggled with the same fears.

How awful, she thought. *How could I have been so blind?*

"Please, you must stop Ardyn," Aera begged.

She appeared before Lunafreya now not as a lifeless statue, but as she had been in life. Upon her face was immeasurable sorrow.

"I beg of you. Deliver him from his long years of anguish."

Aera made no motion to wipe away her tears as she delivered her appeal.

Stay the Usurper.

So, too, the Draconian had commanded. The prospect of stopping Ardyn the Accursed seemed difficult enough. Now she was supposed to allay his suffering? Lunafreya did not know if she was capable of it.

"Why me?" she asked.

There was no answer. When she looked around, Aera was again a lifeless statue and Lunafreya stood right where she'd been before the vision. Directly before her was the pedestal inscribed with *Aera Mirus Fleuret*.

"Luna?" She could hear Sol's voice again.

"I . . . "

"Did that bother you? What I said about you looking like some ancient Oracle?"

Lunafreya remembered having heard such a comment, but it felt like quite some time had passed since Sol made it.

"No, that's not it at all."

"So you're not angry? You weren't ignoring me because you were mad about what I said?"

Apparently, the exchange with Aera had occurred within a brief instant. She'd seen Ardyn's past and heard the first Oracle's plea all in the blink of an eye.

"Are you feeling okay? And don't lie to me," Sol warned.

"No. I am fine."

Lunafreya met Sol's concerned expression with a smile.

"Come. We must hurry."

Had she truly had a vision? It had been far too vivid to dismiss as just a hallucination, but the revelation felt too earth-shattering to accept. She didn't wish for conclusive evidence so much as some sign to confirm what she'd seen was real and to help lead her to the truth.

At the back of the sanctuary was a small room, and inside that was a stairway that led underground. One level deeper into the earth, they found themselves at the entrance to the cavern.

"Beyond here, I can offer no guidance. This area was not open to us."

"So does that mean that it used to be sealed off? Like, there was some gate across the opening or a giant boulder rolled in front of it?"

"No. But there was always someone standing guard to keep people out."

The entrance to the cave and the stairway leading down to it looked the same as they had during her training. The only changes were the lack of a sentry and a faint light that seemed to emanate from the depths of the cavern. The survey team must have taken lights to set up along the way.

"So anyone who could get past the guard could just go right in?"

"Of course not. It was strictly forbidden. The cavern was not to be defiled by mortal hands."

"But didn't it being off-limits just make you that much more curious?"

"Among the citizens of Tenebrae, I doubt you would find many whose curiosity outweighed their respect for sacred ground."

Even Lunafreya could admit to the possibility of visitors with untoward intentions, who might have taken an opportunity to sack the ruins if one presented itself. But at the time, at least, sentries had proven sufficient to keep the cavern unsullied.

"In any case, let us make haste," she said. "We cannot afford to waste any more time."

The stairway leading down was narrow, which perhaps made the cavern seem all the more vast. The ceiling was so high as to make their voices echo eerily. Large piles of stone rubble littered the ground. They were clearly not the product of explosives meant for any survey. Great sections of the cavern walls had been blasted or torn away.

"Is this the work of a daemon?"

"Probably. Seems about what you'd expect from some giant daemon-powered magitek monster."

"The creation that waylaid the survey team?"

"Right. They call it Sapphire Weapon. Supposed to be a real tough customer."

According to Sol, it was yet another juggernaut developed by the Niflheim Empire. After its manufacture at a nearby research facility, it had presumably been sealed away in this cavern. Or the cavern may have been intended as a location for its first experimental activation. "Or there was some other screwed-up reason we'll never understand," Sol concluded.

The underground cavern was certainly large enough to serve as a testing space. But Sapphire Weapon was a variation of the armor used in the destruction of Insomnia. Diamond Weapon had toppled skyscrapers with ease. If a creation of similar magnitude had indeed been allowed to move about down here, it seemed nothing short of a miracle that the cavern itself had not collapsed.

"Still, it didn't have to go and open up huge holes in the place," Sol muttered, staring at a remarkably large depression in one wall. It might have been the result of some massive punch or kick. In any case, the result spoke for itself in terms of the sheer power behind whatever created it.

"Hey, come take a look at this."

Lunafreya looked over to find Sol peering into the depths of the hole. At a glance, it seemed to be just another element of the cavern wall, but as Lunafreya drew closer, she saw what Sol had noticed.

"It looks like something's buried back there," Sol said.

Lunafreya squinted. To Sol's human eyes, they were likely only vague shapes, but for Lunafreya, more accustomed to the dark, the outlines were clear. Weapons. A spear and a sword. And it looked like there might be more buried farther back.

"Why are these here?" she wondered aloud.

"What is it? What do you see?" Sol asked.

Lunafreya was unable to answer at first. The spear and sword were of unusually large size. So large that not even the empire's magitek creations would be able to wield them, let alone a human. The owner of these two weapons therefore must have been neither human nor daemon. They had in all likelihood belonged to one of the Messengers. If she had to guess, Odin.

When Lunafreya finally answered, she said, "Weapons, I believe. Ones that would have been used in the Great War of Old."

"What, you mean like the War of the Astrals? I thought that was just a story."

"It most certainly is not. The war truly happened. I have heard accounts of it from the Messengers."

Long ago, man had received the gift of fire, along with knowledge divine. Both had been bestowed by Ifrit, the Infernian. And with those gifts, man built a great and advanced civilization: Solheim. But the mortals grew arrogant. They turned against the god who had helped them to thrive and sought to drive him away. The Pyreburner, enraged, desired to put an end to mankind. This conflict between god and man would grow into a battle among the gods themselves, when first Shiva, the Glacian, and then the others intervened to safeguard the mortals.

In time, Bahamut, the Draconian, tired of the conflict, both of man against god and among the gods themselves. The Bladekeeper, inhabitant of the heavens and among the Six standing apart, attempted to bring an end not only to mankind but to the Star and the five gods who resided upon it. So great was his power that his ends were almost accomplished.

Four of the Six—Titan, Ramuh, Leviathan, and Shiva—defended against the Draconian's blow, and the Star and its people were safe.

In the end, all members of the Six retired in exhaustion, and the war ended with no clear victor or resolution.

"That's a lot different from the version I grew up hearing," Sol said, her head tilted to one side, as Lunafreya finished recounting the details.

"Much about the Great War of Old has been lost to time. Few today know its details."

When Lunafreya was young, she had constantly begged Gentiana to tell her stories of the gods. Ravus, her elder brother, had shown no interest, but Lunafreya loved to listen to Gentiana talk.

"The Great War of Old stemmed from mankind's rebellion against the divine. It is not a tale to pass down with pride."

"Right. I get it. It's the kind of thing people want to bury."

Lunafreya did not know who first labored to see the story covered up. The truth of Solheim's conceit would have appealed neither to Niflheim, seeking to return the glories of Solheim to the world, nor to Lucis, wardens of the divine gifts of Crystal and ring.

Whichever side was behind the cover-up, it had clearly made use of the natural hiding space afforded by this cavern deep underground. They'd buried away the unhappy relics of the war, then proclaimed the cave a holy site and constructed a place of worship above it, thereby discouraging unwanted exploration.

"The faith of the citizens of Tenebrae is great. If a place is said to be sacred, they can be trusted not to intrude. Whoever buried these artifacts abused that faith to ensure the truth would remain concealed."

"Well, can't blame 'em for wanting to cover up something like that. That doesn't make it anything you have to feel bad about, though. It's all ancient history, right?"

"I suppose . . ."

Lunafreya admitted to herself that Sol was probably right. At the very least, the modern survey team had either ignored or failed to notice the remnants of the War of the Astrals. They had neither connection to the line of the Oracle nor to Tenebrae. To them, this secret was irrelevant.

"So what if humans defied the gods and buried the truth? It's not like the gods did any better. Were they seriously going to let some stupid war escalate into the destruction of the entire world? Who even thinks that way?"

Here, too, Sol provided food for thought. What if it was not man's folly being hidden? Perhaps the truth that needed to be concealed was the narrowly averted fate of their star—that the gods might be petty enough to engage in pointless quarrels or reckless enough to destroy everything.

"Perhaps this is not a statement befitting the Oracle, but . . . in light of such knowledge, one cannot help but wonder whether the gods deserve our faith."

In her mind, Lunafreya heard Ardyn's words once more.

Nothing matters—none of it. Not the "blessed" gods above nor the accursed kings below.

They ended up paying a price for the time they spent lingering at the site of the buried weapons. Soon they were accosted again, this time not by daemons but by people.

"What are *you* doing here?!"

As soon as Sol heard the voice, her face scrunched up in dismay. A second angry shout joined the first. "Bloody hell, Sol, I thought I told you to stay out of here!"

Lunafreya immediately surmised the identity of the two men: Biggs and Wedge. Avoiding this encounter was precisely why she and Sol had opted to use the training ground's hidden entrance. Sol had thought that the two men would be busy helping seal off the entrance. Instead, here they were in the depths of the ruins. Clearly they had felt the same drive to assist Aranea. Even now, as work began on sealing the ruins, they'd ventured farther down into them hoping to perhaps carve a way through the pack of daemons encircling the trapped squad or locate some alternate route out.

"Enough with the heroics. Time to back it up to the surface. No hope of getting any deeper than this, anyway."

"But . . . !"

As Sol began to argue, Lunafreya placed a hand on her shoulder and stepped forward instead.

"Please let us pass. I journey here as part of a calling bestowed upon me by one of the Six."

In truth, her actions had not a thing to do with the new calling. Lunafreya doubted such a transparent lie would ensure them passage, but she decided to try anyway.

"Of course, miss," one of the men began in a placating tone, "However . . ."

She continued over him. "I have come to save the people trapped here using the divine powers granted to me."

She had no idea which of the two was Biggs and which Wedge, but both wore equally befuddled expressions. They turned to look at each other.

"It's all right," Sol offered. "You can trust Luna."

She said it with curt confidence as she stepped forward, now standing alongside Lunafreya.

"Please, you must allow me to fulfill my calling."

One of the men turned back to Lunafreya, shooting a dubious glance at her before asking, "Do you really think you have a chance?" Which was immediately echoed by the other's, "You think you'll be okay down there?"

"I do. I am sworn to protect this site sacred to the people of Tenebrae." Lunafreya placed a hand over her heart as she spoke and bowed her head. There was a tense pause, and then finally the two men seemed to assent. They stepped aside to allow Lunafreya and Sol to pass.

The two women made their way forward quickly. If they lingered, they risked having their bluff called. Spinning such tales was anything but Lunafreya's strong suit. Her constant losses during the card games with Sol had certainly attested to that.

When they were far enough away, Sol whispered into Lunafreya's ear, "Pretty impressive back there. Turns out you're a decent actress."

"Yes, I was quite pleased with the performance myself. It went much more smoothly than I had anticipated."

"Heh. Getting a big head now, too." Sol laughed, then after a glance forward, her face grew serious again, "Looks like we don't have any more time to chat."

Daemons. Undoubtedly some of the same pack that was keeping Aranea's squad from pulling back to the surface.

Lunafreya sensed Sol reaching for her shotgun. They had fought successfully together enough by now to be able to anticipate each other's moves—who would go where, who would provide cover when, and so forth.

The daemons were many and the quarters cramped, but neither posed a problem. The horde had been a thick black wall blocking their way, and now it was nothing but piles of fading dust. Beyond, they saw their destination. The furthest reaches of the cavern opened up even wider than before. *This* was clearly Sapphire Weapon's lair.

The air was frigid, perhaps because of the great depth beneath the earth, but if a shiver traveled up one of their spines, it was due to fear, not cold. The magitek armor towered before them, its overwhelming power obvious at a single glance.

Lunafreya and Sol gazed upon the monster's enormous maw—easily large enough to consume either of its challengers in a single gulp.

Just above that was a red protuberance, like some manner of tumor, located where the forehead would have been had the face been anything like a human's.

"That red orb up there. Is that its core?" Lunafreya asked.

She now felt grateful for the summary she'd received from Sol along the way explaining the makeup of the empire's giant, daemon-infused creations. That was how she'd known to look for the core, which was both a deadly weapon capable of emitting an infernal red beam, as well as a weak point whose destruction could stop the giant.

"You got it. Let's hope that thing doesn't light up, because if it does, we're in for more than just a pretty fireworks show."

They spoke in low voices while covering the remaining distance to the creature. For a while, it seemed like sticking close to the walls and moving quietly might get them surprisingly close. But in the end, reality was not so kind.

Sapphire Weapon turned and let out a roar.

"Looks like that's as far as our luck goes," Sol muttered indignantly.

This time, she produced a different weapon—one she'd brought along specially for the occasion.

"Time for Tiny to say bye-bye," she said, grenade launcher steady on her shoulder.

"Yes," Lunafreya chimed in. "Let us put an end to this. Together."

Using the sound of the firing projectile as her cue, Lunafreya began a flat-out sprint toward Sapphire Weapon. The grenade explosion shook the cavern but didn't seem to do much damage to its target. The juggernaut leaned slightly to one side, but that was the extent of the impact.

They'd have to stick with the fundamentals and create an opening for an assault on the core. Hopefully that would prove effective, but if not, they would be forced to try another course of action.

"Sol!" she called out, "Concentrate on the right leg!"

If they could restrict its movement, that might give Lunafreya a location from which to absorb the scourge.

"Heads up!" Sol called back. "Dodge left!"

Lunafreya dove forward and left, flattening herself to the ground. She felt a blast wave wash over her back. Sol's grenade had found the target exactly where Lunafreya wanted it, exploding on the monster's right leg.

Sapphire Weapon shook its massive limb, stamping its feet like an enormous toddler. Lunafreya had hoped Sol's attack might strip away part of the thick carapace shielding the creature's body. They were making progress, but a single grenade wasn't going to be sufficient.

"Again!" she called.

She backed off, avoiding the giant, crushing feet, then flung herself against the ground once more. Another explosion. Another hot wave rushing by. This time, the attack elicited an earsplitting, inhuman scream. Sol's shout confirmed, "It's working!"

Lunafreya jumped back to her feet and closed in. She saw where the carapace had been ripped away, exposing the inside of the magitek creation's leg. Flesh the color of rotten meat bulged out from the gash.

This is my chance, Lunafreya thought, and stretched out a palm. She felt the familiar numbness crawl along her right arm, then *wham*—she was flying backward. When she came to, she was lying on the ground, back stinging from the impact. She coughed.

"Luna!" Sol called. "Are you all right?!"

She held up a hand to halt Sol's dash forward.

"Keep going! I'm fine!"

Sapphire Weapon's wounds were already beginning to mend. They couldn't afford to let up on the assault. Not even for a moment.

"Incoming!" Sol shouted, and Luna rolled onto her stomach, shielding her face. Once the next blast wave had passed, she was up in an instant and running to where the grenade had hit.

This time, she managed to pull out a proper amount of scourge. Fire coursed through her arm. It felt like she might be consumed from the inside out. She grit her teeth against the searing pain and shouted back, "Sol! Don't stop! Keep firing!"

"Are you nuts?! I might hit you!"

"Just do it!"

Lunafreya's powers alone weren't going to be enough to stop Sapphire Weapon. And the monster's capacity to heal itself wasn't helping things.

"While I'm keeping it busy down here, aim for the core!" she shouted.

Sapphire Weapon was even stronger than they'd imagined. They'd have to fire on its weak point while simultaneously drawing out its daemonic energies. They didn't have any other choice.

But Lunafreya found herself flying backward once again, absorption interrupted.

"One more time!" she shouted to Sol.

First, the explosion on the right leg. Then the dash in to start pulling out the scourge—this time even more intensely than before. She had to keep the monster *still.*

She saw a first, second, then third projectile bound for Sapphire Weapon's head. While bracing against the impact and quake of the blast, Lunafreya let her power loose to an extent she never had before. Tremendous streams of scourge poured into her body. She couldn't stop the scream that tore from her throat, and gripping tight onto her consciousness, desperate to keep from fainting, she steeled herself against the torrent. A ceaseless drumming sound like the fall of a hard rain filled the space around her. Her ears rang so loudly she could hardly hear anything else.

As her vision began to cloud over, she saw one more projectile arcing from Sol directly toward the core.

Good, she thought. *There's the fatal blow.*

Suddenly, Lunafreya's body was thrown to the side. The world came back into focus. *No*, she realized, *I wasn't thrown. I've fallen.* Her hearing returned, and she found that someone was shouting her name. The numbness receded, and she could feel again. She realized arms were wrapped around her, propping her up.

"Luna! We did it! We finished it off!"

"Wonderful . . . " Lunafreya replied weakly.

Her breath came shallow, but her body continued to hold against the mass of scourge swarming inside. She'd done it. *They'd* done it. They'd succeeded in destroying Sapphire Weapon.

"Do not worry about me," Lunafreya said. "Go. Your mother needs you."

According to Biggs and Wedge, the order to withdraw was the last communication received from Aranea's unit. They were somewhere in the farthest depths of the ruins, surrounded by daemons, without any means of escape. They'd not been heard from since. As Lunafreya and Sol were now in the ruin's deepest chamber, Aranea had to be nearby.

"You must find her. Hurry," Lunafreya said. She could feel it. More than just a fear of what might be, it was a certainty: if Sol did not find her mother soon, it would be too late.

They'd challenged Sapphire Weapon, and no one else had joined the fray. If Sol's mother were able, would she not have rushed to her daughter's aid? The fact that she had not was an ill sign.

But Sol seemed already on the verge of tears.

"Luna," she said, her shoulders trembling slightly even as she stood straight and tall.

"Look . . . "

Sol pointed a shaking finger. Luna turned her head to look. The dust had settled, and Sapphire Weapon's hulking form was deteriorating. The expanse of the cavern was again visible, and there, in the direction indicated by Sol, stood another daemon. It was of height similar to Sol's, and it was—or at least, it had been—clearly female. On its back was a spear. Silver-white hair adorned the daemon's head. It was the same color Sol had mentioned when describing her mother's hair on the way to the ruins.

"It's Mom . . . " Sol said, slumping to the ground. "She . . . she's . . . "

Lunafreya's fears had been correct. Before them stood Aranea. Perhaps the mercenary had already known what was happening to her when she gave the order to withdraw and seal the entrance. Perhaps the scourge had been consuming her body even as the words left her mouth.

"Allow me to take care of this," Lunafreya said.

Her legs had been so weak she thought she might not walk again for some time, but resolve brought new strength. Lunafreya stood and headed toward the daemon Aranea.

She heard a faint rasping voice as she drew near. "Stay away."

It seemed the woman still retained some portion of her conscience.

"What do you mean, you'll take care of it?" Sol asked, voice trembling.

"I'll draw out the scourge. It's not too late. Once she's rid of the disease, she'll be back to normal."

Sol's eyes widened. For Lunafreya, too, it was a use of her new powers she hadn't considered before their arrival in this place. But there, before the statue of the first Oracle, Lunafreya had witnessed Ardyn's past. The man had once been hailed as a savior. With the same power that Lunafreya held now, he'd healed countless people.

"But you're weak," Sol protested. "You've already just drawn in all that—"

"I will be fine," Lunafreya cut her off. "After all, I am meant to save the world."

She turned to Sol's tear-streaked face and gave a smile. Ten years ago, the gods had failed to respond to this girl's fervent prayers. Sol had demanded to know whether they even heard or cared to answer. It was finally time to give her the answer she deserved.

"Luna, I'm sorry to ask you to do this for me," Sol sobbed. "But please... Please save her. She raised me. She's my only mother in this world!"

Lunafreya nodded. She turned back to face the daemon Aranea and stretched both arms wide in an embrace. She drew in the scourge—every part of her body absorbing it this time. She felt her breath catch in her throat. The tiny creatures already swarming in her body all began to thrash about at once. Lunafreya's shriek of pain came out as a guttural, beastly cry, and she clenched her teeth together.

Ardyn saved hundreds upon hundreds of lives. What about me? I still haven't saved a single one. If I manage nothing else with this life, let me at least save this one person so dear to Sol.

The scourge was flowing in even faster than before. The power was amplified to new heights, beyond Lunafreya's control. Darkness crept over her vision. Soon the world was painted black, and the only thing to penetrate her senses came with a strange clarity: a high-pitched cry of "Mom!"

Aranea's body was pulled away. That action, too, seemed to come from somewhere else. Lunafreya had not released her; though she willed her limbs to move, they remained still. But the scourge had all been drawn out. Of that, at least, she was certain.

"Sol? Where... ? What happened to me?"

This was a new voice, one Lunafreya did not know. She wanted to turn toward it, to confirm it was that of the person she hoped, but her neck was as stiff and unresponsive as her limbs.

The Oracle's body was no longer her own. But her vision slowly returned, and she looked as far as her unmoving eyes would allow, discovering patches of black-stained, disgustingly swollen skin. Her skin. Despair and regret snaked through her chest. She wished she had not seen.

"It was Luna! She saved you!" she heard Sol exclaim.

No, she wanted to scream, *don't look*. But her throat was frozen, too. She wanted to run, to leave this place and hide. She cursed her rigid arms and legs.

"Who's Luna?"

Aranea turned around, and Luna could see her face. She watched as the woman's expression shifted, filled half with fear and half with loathing.

Sol seemed to sense it, too.

"No! Mom! Stop!" she called, but Aranea was already brushing her daughter aside, one hand reaching for the lance at her back.

"Get the hell away from my daughter, you *monster*."

Blue sparks arced across Lunafreya's single frozen pane of vision. There was a horrible noise, together with the shock of impact.

And then there was nothing.

"The thing's a daemon, for gods' sake!"

Sol stood with her ear pressed against the hotel room door. Apparently, years ago the old Leville had been the lodgings of choice for Prince Noctis and his retinue whenever they passed through Lestallum. Now the building served as headquarters for the Kingsglaive and Hunters. Sol wondered how the prince—or rather, the king—might feel if he knew of the discussion happening in the building now, one meant to decide the fate of his long-lost fiancée.

"I think she's the real deal. Daemon-form or whatever, that's the Oracle in there."

Now Aranea was speaking. It was nice to hear her defending Luna, but Sol still thought bitterly of how things might have been different. If only her mother hadn't jumped to the conclusion that the woman she'd faced in the cavern was a monster.

No, Sol thought. *It was my fault. I didn't explain the situation well enough.* She should have begun by immediately telling her mother what had happened: Luna had drawn out the scourge. She'd saved Aranea. Or maybe this outcome could have been avoided if Sol had referred to her as "Lady Lunafreya, the Oracle," instead of by nickname alone.

At any rate, she'd failed to convey to her mother that Luna was a friend and ally. As a child, Aranea had lost her family to daemons, and her hatred of them was old and deep. When she saw what looked to be a daemon near Sol, she'd acted instinctively to protect her daughter. And who could blame her?

Once Sol realized what was happening, she'd raced to stop it and explain the situation. Sol's pained expression as she watched the scene unfold, along with the fact that Luna remained motionless, taking the full brunt of the Stoss Spear's first and only blow, seemed to make Aranea realize there had been a mistake, but it was too little too late.

Worse, Aranea's initial shouts had brought Glaives and hunters running. Once other people were involved, no amount of explanation or pleading was going to suffice.

After all, what they encountered on arrival was just some vaguely human-shaped *thing* wrapped entirely in pitch-black miasma. Lunafreya had been unable to speak or even stand by that point. The only reason she wasn't dispatched on sight was because Aranea had stepped in. "Sol claims this woman is the Oracle, and I can't say for certain that she's not," her mother had said. "This is a call we need to leave up to the brass." And so she'd urged them all to head back to Lestallum, where they'd settle the matter.

Lunafreya was slapped into restraints and carried back to Lestallum via dropship. Sol, not permitted to ride along, raced after them as fast as she could on Regina.

"If she truly is the Oracle, I assure you that's blood we don't want on our hands."

Aranea was doing everything she could to keep Luna alive. She seemed to feel no small amount of responsibility now that her own savior was bound and locked away. But the way Aranea said it—overemphasizing the word "truly"—seemed more for her own benefit than for the others engaged in the argument. Aranea was still struggling to convince herself. It was a bitter conflict between her hatred of daemons and the recognition that she owed this particular daemon her life, two strong emotions that were hard to reconcile.

In any case, the response to Aranea's sentiment was cold.

"We should dispose of it."

Short. Matter-of-fact. That would be Cor.

"Assuming she is the real deal, how do you account for her being here at all? Are we supposed to believe she came back to life? Ignis, you were there. You saw her die."

"Yes. Lady Lunafreya most certainly passed from the mortal realm. But . . ."

"But what?"

"I also witnessed something else. The Oracle's body seemed to, ah, *vanish* that day."

"It 'vanished'?" This next, rather charged exclamation was undoubtedly from Gladio. "What's that supposed to mean?"

"Precisely how it sounds."

"Now that you mention it, I do remember hearing they never found the body . . ."

"Even if she turns out to be the Oracle, that doesn't get around the fact that she's become a daemon. We need to get rid of her."

Sol crept away from the door. If things kept going the way they were,

Luna was in trouble. Sol had to find a way to save her. Simply breaking her out of confinement wouldn't be enough. Unlike the former empire, the area around Lestallum was well-populated. Any time spent lingering nearby would mean recapture and death for Luna. Someone would have to remain behind while Luna fled, to keep any potential pursuers occupied.

Luna had said she wanted to get to Insomnia. A journey like that required a pretty hefty supply of equipment and food. Fortunately, Sol had refueled Regina when she got into town, and had packed up some equipment and food as well. She'd had a hunch things might turn out this way, from the second she saw the cold and rough way the Glaives and hunters had handled Luna back in Ralmuell. That was why she'd been willing to push Regina to the limit on the road to Lestallum. She'd kept nearly constantly on the move, with only the bare minimum of breaks, then half threw herself and the bike onto a departing ferry. It was due to luck alone that Regina had managed the journey.

And as for Lunafreya, Sol owed her more than she might ever be able to repay.

She wouldn't let them kill her, no matter what. This was the woman who had answered her prayer, who had saved the only family Sol had left. Now it was Sol's turn to help see a wish fulfilled.

Lunafreya knew she was dreaming again. She was clothed in the pure white of her wedding dress. In her hands was a sylleblossom bouquet. Confetti swirled and danced through the air, and the scene was set to a chorus of cheers. Reaching out to take her hand was her beloved—the person she'd waited so long and so desperately to see. Her gaze traveled up from their joined hands, but before she could see his face, consciousness intervened.

Another dream, she thought. *Why do I continue to torture myself?*

She squeezed her eyes shut, not to return to sleep but to stave off tears that might know no end. She swore to herself that she would not cry. It was painful as ever to know that she would never be beside Noctis again, but she had managed to bring back the person who meant the world to Sol. That was a wonderful thing. A joyous thing. So there was no need for tears now. She would carry on with pride.

"Lady Lunafreya."

A familiar voice reached her ears, sudden and unexpected.

Lunafreya's eyes shot open. Her pitch went high with surprise. "Gentiana!"

Then after a moment, she asked, "Is this another dream?"

She was not in the hotel at Lestallum. Surrounding her was the same void as before, dark like the color of the deep sea. Gentiana's form floated amid the black, green, and blue haze.

"There is little time. Heed these words."

The High Messenger, always so calm and elegant, seemed unusually rushed.

"Do not be deceived by the Bladekeeper's words," Gentiana continued. "The Star is in peril, as are its people. To endeavor for the calling is to invite destruction complete."

Lunafreya's voice trembled. "Gentiana? What are you saying?"

"The flow of fate was altered when the Accursed turned from the gods. This much is truth. But the Oracle's new powers will not stay the Usurper. They have another purpose. The Bladekeeper seeks darkness, for which the Oracle is now a vessel. The Oracle is tasked with harvesting of all of the world's darkness, including that inside the Accursed."

"But why should that lead to the end of Eos and its people?"

Gentiana gave a single word in response. "Teraflare."

After a pause, she continued. "To cast it, the Bladekeeper seeks to increase his power by drawing on those of both daemon and Oracle.

Once before did blades supreme threaten the Star, but in that age long past, the power fell short. Destruction was stayed, the Bladekeeper's ends unrealized."

"The Great War of Old," Lunafreya murmured.

Bahamut, the Draconian, weary of the fighting between god and man, had endeavored to see everything wiped from existence. The other gods had held him back, just managing to spare the world its judgment. It was a story Lunafreya had heard from Gentiana countless times before.

She remembered a conversation she'd had with the Messenger when young.

"Gentiana, why did the Draconian try to destroy everything? Why would he want to do such a horrible thing?"

"Among the Six, the Bladekeeper stands apart. From the heavens high above, the Star and its lives seem distant."

"But I thought the gods protected the world. I thought they looked after all of us."

"Man is to god as flower is to man. When a girl walks among the fields of sylleblossoms, does she see each flower in its own right? Or is one the same as any other? Destruction wrought by the Bladekeeper is not vengeance against man. It is the work of a gardener, pulling from the field flowers among which disease has spread."

Horror swept through Lunafreya. Was *that* what Gentiana was implying?

"The Draconian. Does he again seek to reap us like flowers from a field?"

"Having failed once, the Bladekeeper will not fail again. The spell shall be charged with power overwhelming, that the disease of the field cannot spread again."

"And that is why the power to harvest the scourge was bestowed unto me, the Oracle?"

Gentiana nodded.

"But that's . . . " Lunafreya trailed off. She looked at her hands. The hands now intended by the God of War to help bring an end to Eos. "All this time, it has been the Draconian standing against us."

She remembered Ardyn, screaming his curses at the gods. Millennia ago, the man had placed all his faith in a presumed calling. He had given of his life only to be betrayed, then vowed to kill the god behind that treachery.

"We must convince the Draconian to abandon his plan," Luna proclaimed. "But how are we to sway him?"

"The will of a god is not easily bent."

Of course not. To Bahamut, they were merely flowers, riddled with pests and needing to be cut down.

"Do we have no choice but to defy him? If he cannot be swayed, our only other option is to stop him."

"Nor is the hand of a god easily stayed. The Bladekeeper exists twice over: once in this world, and once beyond. Though one should fall, return it shall, as long as the other remains."

"So he cannot be killed?"

Gentiana's voice grew even more hurried. "Hear me, Lady Lunafreya. The spell of the Bladekeeper requires strength immense. Stave off the first blow, and no more shall come. Strength sapped leads to slumber deep. The Star and its people may yet live on, even if the God of War cannot be defeated."

"The same as happened in the war so long ago?"

The outlines of Gentiana's form began to grow indistinct.

"The Messenger is discovered. There is no more . . . "

"Wait! Gentiana!"

The Messenger was fading, the deep haze beyond shimmering through her form. "The Oracle must choose her own future."

And then both words and form were gone. Lunafreya opened her eyes, and she was in the hotel at Lestallum, her hands and feet bound tight, body still limp and unresponsive. All as it was from the moment she fell asleep.

"The Draconian would destroy us," she murmured to herself.

It was beyond comprehension. The gods were committed to safeguarding Eos and all its inhabitants. Never once had she doubted that, not even when Gentiana had spoken of Bahamut's place as being above and distant from all, less attuned to mortal existence.

Long ago, the Draconian had bestowed upon Ardyn the power to act as a savior. Then he'd allowed the same man to be struck down, reviled by his kind as a terrible monster. The Bladekeeper did not hesitate to employ cruelty and cunning to see his will through. And now he was attempting to do the same to Lunafreya.

She and Ardyn were not unalike. They were both pious, dedicated in their faith to the gods, and blind to the plots that dictated the courses of their lives. They were both marionettes, made to dance as divine hands pleased, then cast aside when the play was over.

"It is unforgivable," she whispered to herself, new anger boiling to the surface. But she did not yet know how to proceed. She stared at the ceiling, scouring her mind for ideas.

It took Sol more time than she'd expected to locate Luna's makeshift holding cell. She'd assumed the room would be guarded, so she'd been on the lookout for manned doors. In the end, that hadn't provided much of a clue, since way too many of the hotel room doors had posted guards. Not that this was the result of some plan to throw off anyone intent on breaking the Oracle free—there were simply a lot of people and items that merited guarding. Which made sense, when she bothered to think about it. The hotel *was* the current HQ for all Hunter operational strategy, located at the very center of humanity's stronghold, the only source of order left on Eos.

"Rookie mistake." She shook her head, frustrated by her own naivety.

"And what mistake would that be?"

The sudden voice from behind her nearly launched Sol into the air.

"Mom?! What are you doing here? What about the meeting?"

The discussion hadn't exactly been going smoothly. Sol had figured both Aranea and the representatives from the Kingsglaive would still be holed up in their room for some time yet. That, too, was part of her plan, to make her move while the real threats were preoccupied. Some lowly sentry posted outside of Luna's door would be easily pickings.

She hadn't accounted for the possibility of running into her mother. This went way beyond a worst-case scenario.

"Kicked over a chair and got 'excused' from the rest of the debate," Aranea winked. "They sent me off to cool my head. Which gave me the opportunity I needed to come track down a certain little troublemaker. I had a feeling you'd be sneaking around by now."

"Please, you have to let us go. Luna's my friend. She needs my help," Sol begged.

My friend. The moment she said the words, there was a pain like a dagger wound deep in her heart. Sol finally understood. It wasn't because she owed Luna. It wasn't because of the things Luna had done for her. The reason she wanted to help was because Luna was important to her. Their time together had been short, but they were companions of the road now. They were friends.

"You're putting me in a tight spot here, y'know that?" Aranea said.

Then, "Hey. Don't start crying on me."

Aranea shoved a handkerchief up against Sol's nose. Sol realized tears were streaming down her face. Once more, she felt like a child.

"But, Mom, I . . . "

"Yeah, yeah. I get it."

Aranea's hand was warm on her head.

"Come with me."

Sol wiped the tears away with the handkerchief and followed. Once upon a time, she'd had to tilt her head back to see her mother's shoulders when she walked behind her. Now those shoulders were at eye level, and yet somehow Aranea still seemed so incredibly far above her. Once a mother, always a mother.

They stopped in front of an unguarded door. Sol was bursting with questions, but Aranea put an index finger to her lips.

Aranea knocked four times, then announced, "Good work in there." The pattern of knocks and the words seemed to be some manner of passphrase. The door swung open, and Sol saw that the guard was posted not outside in the hallway, but inside the room itself. He was a young man whom Sol didn't recognize, almost certainly at the bottom of the food chain around here.

"Sorry to bother you. Just wondering if I could ask you for a favor?" Aranea said.

"Me?"

"Yeah, I've got something you can help out with. Won't take more than a few minutes. The kid here'll watch the room till we get back."

Sol's head was already bowed low, in a most likely vain attempt to keep her tear-stained cheeks out of sight. She dipped it a bit farther in a curt nod.

"Thanks, Sol. Keep a sharp eye out, all right?"

Aranea casually slipped something into Sol's pocket, then led the guard out and down the hallway. Sol closed the door behind her with one hand and walked deeper into the room. Finally, she saw her.

"Luna!" she exclaimed. "I'm so sorry, Luna. I wanted to get here sooner."

"Sol!"

Luna lay on the bed, hands and feet still bound as before. Sol stuffed a hand into her pocket. She'd had a hunch about Aranea's little gift, and it proved correct. The locking device. Her mother must have planned it all out ahead of time.

"This is all my fault, Luna. I—"

"You needn't apologize. You believed in me, Sol. That was enough."

Tears traced their way down Luna's cheeks, black as ink. The ebony patches of skin once peeking out from her sleeves and collar had now crept down the backs of her hands and across her face.

"Of course I did. Obviously. What kind of friends don't trust each other?"

Sol pressed the button on the locking device. Luna's restraints snapped open with a dull click.

"Can you run?" Sol asked. "We need to get out of here before the watch returns."

"Won't letting me free cause more trouble for you?"

"You gave me my mother back. Now it's my turn to help you. You need a way to get to Insomnia, right?"

Luna nodded. Her hesitation was gone, and now determination shone through, clear as day.

Regina was parked at the edge of the city. They ran together through the streets. Finding Luna within the unfamiliar layout of the hotel had been trickier than she imagined, but when it came to the city itself, Sol was in her element. Nobody knew Lestallum better than she did.

Every shortcut, every corner to turn and alleyway to use to keep out of sight; she navigated them all without even having to think.

As they neared the bike, Sol explained, "Regina's already loaded up with food and equipment. A map, too. You've got this, right?"

She placed the helmet on Luna's head and adjusted the straps.

Luna lowered the goggles over her eyes. "I am in your debt, Sol."

A wrinkle formed at the bridge of Sol's nose.

"We've been over this already. That's what people say before they up and die on you."

"I know."

"So why are you—"

"Do not worry. I will not die. I swear it. So please, just let me say my thanks."

"All right, fine. Well I'm not gonna die, either. So when you get back, you better make me another cup of tea, okay? I'll be waiting."

Regina's engine roared to life. Sol saw Luna's lips move but couldn't make out the words. Then Luna and Regina were off, and Sol was waving with her arm held high as they rode into the distance.

When she could see them no longer, she turned around and drew her gun. Nobody would be following Luna. She'd see to that.

As she made her silent vow, the blare of emergency sirens began to fill the city of Lestallum.

On the road from Lestallum, Lunafreya was forced into occasional skirmishes with daemons. But she was thankful to find no trace of hunters or Glaives pursuing from behind. And, though she was still very much a novice on the motorcycle and her travels hardly swift, the skyline of the Crown City was growing undeniably closer. She realized she was now traveling the same road she'd walked along with the other evacuees the day Insomnia fell. Back then, she'd been so anxious to get out. Now, she was just as desperate to get back in. It was a strange feeling.

She stopped for a brief break just before the bridge leading across to the city proper. There, she added one final message to the notebook. Somehow, Umbra seemed to know. He was there before she'd even readied herself to call him.

"Hello, Umbra," she said. "When the time comes, please give this to Noctis."

The dog lifted his tail high, as if to say, *It will be done*. And then he was gone, vanished into the surrounding darkness.

Preparations were complete. She'd sorted out her feelings, and her mind was made up. Lunafreya's steps into the desolate Citadel were quick and sure.

On that day years ago, the Citadel had been filled with bullets, explosions, and the incessant drone of magitek engines. Lunafreya recalled the stench of gunpowder and blood. Those things, at least, had been evidence of people. Of life. Now she found only daemons as she made her way to the heart of the edifice. It was eerily quiet. There was no scent of blood anymore.

Slowly, she pushed open the final doorway.

Though ten years had passed, to Lunafreya, it seemed but a few months since she last stepped foot inside the throne room. But the vast space now looked drastically different.

"I'm afraid you're out of luck."

Ardyn's voice floated down from on high. Scant days ago, she might have been angered to find him lounging in smug satisfaction upon the throne. But not anymore. Now his boorish posture and lack of propriety were simply those of a tragic jester. She felt pity for the man.

"The one you hope to see is not here."

The erstwhile chancellor seemed to assume she had come for Noctis.

"Ah, but do pardon my surprise at this most unexpected development. How very nice it is to see you again, Lady Lunafreya."

Contrary to his words, Ardyn's tone lacked any trace of surprise. He seemed wholly unconcerned to find the woman he had killed with his own hands now returned to life.

Her words came measured. Precise. "You misunderstand. The one I am here for is you." The statement implied more: she was well aware that she would not find Noctis here. It was not yet time for them to be reunited.

"I have something I should like to discuss with you," she announced.

Ardyn's lips twitched ever so slightly.

"Ah! The Oracle would have words with me. And here I thought the gods had sent their pretty little marionette to do their bidding."

Wrong, she thought. *I do not desire to kill you, for you are as much a puppet to their will as I am. And now, I seek to clip my strings just as you do.*

Lunafreya stared into Ardyn's eyes.

Now came the gamble.

"I wonder if I might ask for your aid."

The Final Glaive

Myriad shadows writhed in the chill night air of the Citadel courtyard. Enemies were everywhere, but the certain knowledge that he would have to fight the hordes every step of the way elicited neither surprise, nor confusion, nor even the slightest trace of fear.

Step by step, he descended the great staircase. Gunfire erupted, waves of bullets flying from enemy barrels like swarms of angry insects. He wove his way between them, blade flashing into his hand as other opponents began to rush the stairs. Each clash was over as quickly as it began: one, then another, and another. Steel shrieked, and ash-colored automatons went rolling lifelessly down steps they had just ascended.

But something was amiss. A person—persons?—who should have been there with him was not.

Did I always fight alone?

Just as he felt the memory might be drawing within reach, a bullet grazed his ear, as if bent on preventing him from recollecting. He paid the injury little mind, simply turning to face the next incoming enemy, blade quick to send it flying.

The initial sense of unease, of dislocation, was growing.

These things I'm fighting. What are they?

Their armor was fashioned from some kind of lustrous dark metal. As he continued to cut his way through the endless ranks of empty, soulless suits, it occurred to him that they shared neither hue nor design with the magitek troops he'd known in some distant past. A black haze much like daemonic miasma emanated from their surfaces, an eerie aura like that of some ghostly apparition. Most disconcerting of all was the smell from their weapons, a thick, acrid stench of gunpowder. Niflheim's infantry had never used weapons like these.

Members of the horde continued marching up the steps, weapons firing wildly. Over and over again, he dispatched them with warp-strikes, a seemingly endless cycle of attack. He heard the thud of defeated foes falling, as well as the clatter as they tumbled back down the stairs. That, too, was different, not the same sound that defeated MTs made. The only thing these new foes seemed to share with the empire's automated infantry was an obnoxious degree of persistence.

A flash of red, then another. Half a moment after he saw the muzzle flashes, the unmistakable report of firearms resounded in his ears. But they were too slow, he thought dismissively, and their lack of aim made them little threat.

Where the hell am *I?*

It looked like the Citadel courtyard, but there were many small differences. The color of the place was wrong, or rather, it didn't *have* any color, just cold streaks of monochrome gray. His unease was transforming into alarm, into the distinct sensation that this world was not his own.

He pivoted on his heel, suddenly determined to confirm his suspicions. A few casual swipes of his weapon downed the enemies behind him, and then he was vaulting back up the steps he'd just managed to descend.

The memory returned abruptly. Ignis. He was nowhere to be found. Neither was Gladio or Prompto. Why had it taken him so long to mark their absence? That was far too strange. Something definitely wasn't right about this place.

He stepped inside the Citadel. It was dark and seemingly empty. He saw no one else. The sense of foreboding grew worse. This was the Citadel he knew, and yet at the same time, it was not.

He walked to the throne room doors, placed both hands upon the enormous handles, and pushed them open. Inside, he encountered a darkness even more profound, pierced by one faint beam of light that landed on the throne. Noctis was drawn to it. He climbed to the throne and sat.

This does not belong to me. But neither does it belong to another.

Straight after he had that thought, a voice boomed in his mind, seemingly coming from nowhere and everywhere at once. A voice with a force and gravity that were utterly inhuman.

Before the Chosen unfurls one possibility. To mortal mind, a dream.

Though man would choose, he has but one way forward. Ordained above is mortal fate.

To the Crystal, all possibility is memory, and all memory etched within.

The episode in the courtyard had felt half known to him and half strange. A possibility. A dream. If Noctis were entangled in a dream, that would account for the way the places and events had felt familiar and yet off. It would explain the mysterious absence of his companions.

Behold the heart of the Crystal, wherein lies the soul of the Star. It is in this place that the king will gain the power he needs.

Receive the memories inscribed in the Crystal, that the True King's calling may be fulfilled.

The word "calling" stirred something deep in his mind. He cast back through his memories—a place called Gralea, the imperial capital,

Zegnautus Keep—and then it all came flooding back. The endless hordes of magitek troopers and daemons. The battle that never seemed to end, no matter how many foes were slain.

"We're getting nowhere!" Gladio had shouted.

Then Prompto: "They just keep coming!"

"Noct, you must go on alone. If you can obtain the Crystal's power, we may yet be able to turn the tide. Elsewise, we are all like to perish here."

"Iggy's right. It's our only chance."

"We'll manage somehow! Just get moving!" With Prompto's final encouragement, all three were in agreement.

So Noctis had run. He left his three companions to fight by themselves and made his way to the Crystal alone. He ran until his chest was tight and his legs ached.

And then he was plunged into an absolute darkness that blotted out all the light of the world. All sound ceased, even that of his own breath. Touch, smell, and taste, too, were gone, and he was left with the solitary sensation that he was falling at an impossibly slow pace.

Please . . . Help me stop the daemons, he'd pleaded as he stretched out his hand.

He remembered it all now. This was the heart of the Crystal. He'd been dragged inside by a force that defied all resistance, and the last thing he'd seen before sinking inside was a face whose mere memory sparked rage: that of Ardyn Izunia.

Ardyn Lucis Caelum is my proper name, the man had said, looking Noctis straight in the eye.

Lucis Caelum? What could Ardyn have possibly meant by that?

As if responding to the questions now seething in his mind, the darkness faded and was replaced by the boundless, blinding light of the Crystal. The glittering peaked, then receded, gradually replaced by blue sky and green earth. Noctis found himself overlooking a landscape bearing no resemblance to any place he knew, but he felt a strange certainty that it was Eos of the distant past, in the age when the Crystal was brought to their star.

He saw a sanctuary in which the Crystal had been enshrined. Surrounding it were scattered homes and fields of wheat. The landscape began to change. Forests fast receded and the wilderness was tamed and tilled. The people grew in number. Noctis could see them, quotidian scenes swirling by at a dizzying pace. He witnessed the countless joys and sorrows of their lives. An inconceivable quantity of information flooded into his mind at once. The fact that he could make clear sense of it had to be thanks to the otherworldly Crystal in which he hung suspended.

Memories inscribed in the Crystal. That was how the scenes before him had been described. It seemed to have something to do with his calling as king—perhaps he'd need all the information recorded here. Perhaps it was important for him to understand what had happened in the beginning, when the Crystal and the Ring of Light were first brought to the land.

Two men came into focus, their names familiar. Ardyn. Somnus. Noctis saw that they were brothers, heirs to House Caelum, meant to support each another and rule the land together. To symbolize that bond, they were entrusted by their father and mother with a pair of weapons, two swords that were as one: the Rakshasa Blade and the Blade of the Mystic.

One parent and then the other departed from the world, and not long after, the two brothers stood in opposition. At its base, it was a matter of ideology. The two differed in opinion as to the proper mindset of a ruler. The younger deceived the older, and the older hated the younger for it.

Noctis had known nothing of this, and the knowledge stunned him. He had been so sure that Ardyn possessed not a shred of decency, that no matter how much he reviled the man, it would never be enough. Instead, he was now witnessing a man who was utterly selfless, consumed by the constant labor to relieve the suffering of his people.

Even more disorienting was the discovery that Ardyn had been in love. Her name was Aera Mirus Fleuret. The first Oracle. When the pair were together, talking and laughing, Ardyn was neither savior nor scelerat. He was simply an ordinary man.

Ordinary, too, were his desires. *Oh, Aera. Pray be with me always,* Noctis heard the man say. Ardyn dreamed of a simple happiness, one that had nothing to do with either star or god. It was a happiness every person should be able to know—and thus Ardyn had never for a moment thought it might be stolen away from him.

Was that why Ardyn had killed Luna? Because he knew firsthand the extent to which it would devastate Noctis?

It was still unforgivable. It didn't matter that Ardyn had been a savior laboring for his fellow man, and the death of his own love was no excuse. To claim an innocent life simply to see an enemy suffer was an act that lay far beyond the bounds of absolution.

But if Ardyn was beyond pardon, then so, too, was Somnus for the web of lies he used to ensnare his brother and ensure his own place as founder of the new nation. It was Somnus who had killed Aera and planted the evil seed that would culminate in Lunafreya's death.

And what about me? Noctis thought. *Don't I deserve some of the blame, too?*

The covenants had chipped away at Lunafreya's life. They were forged for Noctis, that the True King might be favored with blessings of the gods, and each one left Lunafreya weaker. Even had Ardyn's dagger not ended her life, the Oracle's time in the world would surely not have been much longer. Noctis, too, had played a part in her demise.

Sacrifice is unavoidable in the pursuit of a strong nation; that was the belief of the younger Caelum brother. If Noctis accepted Lunafreya's death as a necessary evil to see darkness purged from the Star, would that make him any different from Somnus?

Did he, then, have any right to condemn the actions of his forebears?

The memories of the Crystal swirled on, pushing Noctis's uncertainties aside.

He saw Ardyn, imprisoned in the depths of Angelgard. He saw Somnus, setting forth to exterminate daemons across the land. The citizens lived in peace and stability, and Lucis continued to grow as a nation.

Other rulers rose and fell, some more ruthless than Somnus, and others far too gentle. There was one who wore a mask throughout her life and reign. One suffered a tragic loss of the Oracle during his rule, taking up the Trident and duties in her stead. One brought Lucis an extraordinarily long era of peace. One was murdered on the very night of his ascendance to the throne.

Alongside Lucis rose other new and powerful nations. There was Tenebrae, ruled by House Fleuret, the bloodline of the Oracle and, like House Caelum, heir to powers bestowed by the gods. The Empire of Niflheim donned the mantle of Solheim, seeking to return magitek to the world. The Accordo Protectorate flourished through trade and grew wealthy.

The people of every nation were alike: they laughed, struggled, fought, and wished for happiness. Noctis saw that throughout the world, just as there were no two individuals exactly alike, neither were there any so different as to set themselves apart from all others. Every person resonated in some respect with every other, and in some respect, every person was unique.

The time allotted to any human passed swiftly and without mercy. Death came for all, leaving only lifeless husks to pile in the earth. The thoughts each mind held inside were lost forever, gone without a trace. Yet at the same time, the reality that they had once lived and walked among their fellow humans could not be denied.

A familiar face appeared, like driftwood surfacing in a muddy torrent: some two thousand years after the founding of Lucis, Ardyn was carried from the depths of his island prison. His recovery brought to Niflheim the means to produce their magitek infantry en masse. The empire's borders surged outward, and as Niflheim grew, Ardyn, too, accumulated power. The one man who controlled daemons ensured the spread of darkness throughout the world.

When the threat of all-consuming darkness seemed close at hand, Regis was chosen to stand among the ranks of the Kings of Yore. Around the same time, Noctis was born, and the Lucii pronounced him to be the True King.

Noctis saw his young self sleeping peacefully in his father's arms, still blissfully unaware of the burden of fate. He saw his father force back tears.

Though man would choose, he has but one way forward. Ordained above is mortal fate.

To the Crystal, all possibility is memory, and all memory etched within.

Perhaps, if Verstael had failed in his attempt to penetrate the depths of Angelgard, Ardyn would still be hanging from chains in his wretched stone cell. If Ardyn were still captive and the Crystal maintaining the silence of that age-old secret, the time foretold when darkness would cover the Star would still be far off.

Perhaps Regis would still have had the honor to stand as one of the Kings of Yore, but there would have been no need to name Noctis as the True King. He would have been merely another successor in the long line of Lucis, and his father would have lived free from the grief of knowing his son's bleak fate.

But neither, then, would Noctis have encountered the Marilith. There would have been no grave injury in his eighth year, no visit to Tenebrae to recover. No time spent with Lunafreya.

And that was not all. There would have been no marriage planned, no journey to Accordo with his friends. The nature of his companionship with Ignis and Gladio would have been different. More removed. More distant.

Without Ardyn, Verstael's forays into magitek would have been far less successful. No mass production of MTs. And that meant Prompto . . .

Prompto would not exist at all.

Queen Sylva Via Fleuret would still be alive and in good health, continuing her duties as Oracle. Her children, Lunafreya and Ravus, would still reside at Fenestala Manor in peace.

Behold the heart of the Crystal, wherein lies the soul of the Star. It is in this place that the king will gain the power he needs.

Ravus. Noctis had heard the words the high commander had spoken to Ignis.

"Even in death, the Oracle does not rest. Only once the darkness is dispelled is her calling truly fulfilled. And as in life, I know she will confront that challenge with a smile on her face."

They'd stood among the devastation in Altissia. The altar, like everything else in the city, lay crumbling in the wake of the Hydraean's trial. Between Ignis and Ravus lay Noctis's own unconscious form, sprawled across the flagstones.

Lunafreya was there, too. She was dead, yet somehow she arose and proceeded to the water's edge. As she walked, her feet did not tread upon the earth. To the Oracle, death did not mean dissolution. An Oracle's soul ascended in holy glory, joining the divine after its passage from the mortal realm. The Oracles received no burial, as they left nothing behind to intern.

"Oh, Sister… Please don't go." Ravus pleaded as she floated out over the water.

Ravus's words were thick with anguish. For the last remaining member of House Fleuret, this was a parting far more cruel than death. He would not be allowed to weep over his sister's lifeless form, robbed even of the chance to properly mourn her passing.

The Crystal swirled on to new memories, and Noctis observed the path that Lunafreya had walked in life. He saw Fenestala Manor in the wake of the occupation, Lunafreya standing before Gentiana with her head bowed.

"I have been confined to Fenestala and may no longer move about freely," she said. "But I have not forgot my vow as Oracle to forge a covenant with your mistress, Shiva. I intend to petition for imperial leave to travel, and once it is secure, I assure you I will fulfill my duty. So I would ask that you please entreat the Glacian for patience on my behalf."

"The Oracle seeks a covenant with the Frostbearer for the sake of the Crystal's Chosen, that he might have aid in the time of need soon to come?" Gentiana asked.

"That is my wish."

"Very well."

Gentiana's form began to change. She rose from the ground, arctic light pouring into her body until her skin shone icy blue. Lunafreya's eyes grew wide.

Noctis imagined the same look of shock on his face when he, too, had witnessed Gentiana's transformation.

"All this time," Lunafreya whispered, "the Glacian was at my side?"

Shiva's voice resounded in gentle proclamation, "Let the covenant be forged."

"My gratitude to the compassionate Glacian and the favor she shows mankind," Lunafreya responded. Noctis saw her cheeks flush with a mix of pride in completing one of her duties as Oracle and joy at knowing she had been watched over so closely since birth by one of the Six.

Some time later, Lunafreya was able to proceed to Ralmuell, the training ground for the Oracles. Once she had formally inherited the title, her days grew busy with journeys across the land to provide relief to the afflicted and to comfort the bereaved by performing the rites of requiem. It pained Noctis to think of the comfort and leisure in which he'd spent his own days around the same time.

Then came the fall of Insomnia. Regis entrusted the ring to Lunafreya, asking her to bear it safely to his son, and a certain pair of Glaives saw to the Oracle's safe evacuation from the city. Flames rose throughout Insomnia as Lunafreya fled, slipping between buildings on verge of collapse, speeding along crumbling roadways, her life ever in peril.

I'm sorry, Noctis thought. *Luna, I'm so sorry. I had no idea.*

After that long, harrowing night, Lunafreya journeyed on all by herself, ultimately making her way toward Accordo.

Noctis reflected on where he would have been during her struggles. Somewhere along his first journey beyond the walls of Insomnia, staring wide-eyed at the world and its many wonders, in the care of his close companions. When the Regalia had broken down shortly after their journey began, the four of them had taken turns pushing the car to Hammerhead, complaining all the way, but even then they'd still in some sense been enjoying themselves. Things were still lighthearted and fun.

Now Ravus's biting sarcasm—the anger he felt toward Noctis—no longer seemed so inexplicable or unwarranted.

Witness his splendor and glory. All hail the Chosen King, he'd sneered on confronting Noctis at Aracheole.

Ravus had watched his own flesh and blood dedicate her life to an ungrateful, ignorant child. Lunafreya expended her own existence for the sake of Noctis's success, and Noctis had regarded her sacrifice as nothing more than her ordained duty. When Ravus looked upon Noctis, he saw not a king but a coward who was undeserving of the title.

Looking back, he found it hard to imagine himself to be more lacking in understanding or maturity. Noctis had spent so much of his time sulking and moping, stuck in his own self-absorbed world, that he'd been unable to see the hands held out to him or the others supporting him from behind.

"How long will you remain the protected? The king entrusted the role of protector to you."

"Get a grip! Pull your head outta your ass already!"

He remembered the moments he'd been chastised first by Cor and then Gladio. Each time, he'd felt only defiance: he was trying as best he knew how. What gave them the right to criticize, and why did he have to put up with it?

In truth, he was running away. When he claimed to be trying his best, it was for his own benefit, to stave off the ugly truth that perhaps he *could* do better, and that he only wanted to make things easier for himself. His companions must have seen right through him, and still they were kind and patient enough to stand and fight by his side.

In Altissia, to save Noctis from Ardyn's malevolence, Ignis had gone so far as to chance the Ring of the Lucii. Noctis watched as the scene unfolded, Ignis declaring, "I swore an oath to stand with Noct and keep him safe. Whatever it takes, I *will* protect him!" The Kings of Yore descended. They approved of Ignis's devotion and lent him their power. But in exchange, they took his sight.

Upon Noctis's recovery, Ignis had refused to speak of the episode, knowing that it would weigh heavily on the young king's conscience. The advisor's lips stayed tightly sealed, enduring a darkened world while Noctis was blind even to his companion's compassion.

"Remember—those ain't your bodyguards, they're your brothers. Trust in 'em. Always."

At Caem, Cid's words struck him hard. It forced Noctis to think about what his friends were feeling and what they each had sacrificed. Through it all, they continued to hold their hands out to him. To trust his companions meant accepting their help with full knowledge of what it cost them. Accepting help without that regard was not building a relationship of trust. It was the act of a child, still hopelessly dependent on others.

Up to that point, Noctis had depended on others for nearly everything, and all the while, he'd sulked and complained. What could he offer back to those who had helped him nonetheless? What they had given him was priceless, beyond recompense.

Receive the memories inscribed in the Crystal, that the True King's calling may be fulfilled.

The visions spun once more, this time with intense speed. He saw himself in combat with Ardyn, the Accursed's fall to darkness now complete.

Was this the future? It had to be. Or at the very least, it was not the past, nor one of the possibilities of the past. Noctis's own aged appearance suggested this battle was impending, the Crystal hinting at a moment that was yet to come.

Then after Ardyn's defeat in Insomnia, Noctis saw himself upon the throne, wielding the Ring of Light and calling forth the Kings of Yore. He would finally destroy the Accursed's soul in the realm beyond, and Ardyn would perish once and for all.

Gather strength, O Chosen. The fate of this world falls to the King of Kings.

His Providence consecrated in the divine Light of the Crystal. So it is ordained—the revelation of Bahamut.

But the vision that unfolded alongside the Draconian's words was hard to accept. The Old Kings arrived, and there, on the throne, it was Noctis's own life that was ripped away. Blinding light burst forth from the ring, and the Chosen King was torn from his mortal flesh and carried to the Beyond. There, once Ardyn's end was wrought, Noctis's soul shattered into countless fragments of light, vanishing without trace.

A power greater than even that of the Six, purifying all by the Light of the Crystal and the glaives of rulers past. Only at the throne can the Chosen receive it, and only at the cost of a life: his own. The King of Kings shall be granted the power to banish the darkness, but the blood price must be paid. To cast out the Usurper and usher in dawn's light will cost the life of the Chosen. Many sacrificed all for the King, so must the King sacrifice himself for all. Now enter into Reflection, that the Light of Providence shine within.

When Noctis looked down, he was seated on a throne of kings—not the throne at Insomnia, but one situated here, inside the Crystal.

So it wasn't a dream, he thought. He stood and began to walk. His steps felt light and uncertain. How long had the vision lasted? He had no means to gauge time's passage. It had felt like only a moment, and it might have been so, but within that moment he'd observed two thousand years' worth of history. He'd watched as more people than he could ever count came into the world, lived their lives, and passed on. He'd known every one of their thoughts. Now all of it was at risk. If darkness shrouded the Star completely, all life would cease. And if the Star itself perished, there would be nothing left of man—not even artifacts or ruins to hint at what had once been.

I can save the Star . . . if I lay down my life.

With the darkness driven away and the safety of the Star ensured, the world of man would continue. Countless other joys and sorrows would fill the future. However . . .

Is that really how it ends for me?

Noctis brought his hands before his eyes. Use the ring, draw on the Crystal's power, and receive new strength. Then strike down Ardyn with these same hands. Securing the future was supposed to be as straightforward as that.

But . . . death. To be erased from the world. That was the fate that awaited him. It was terrifying, more so than he wanted to bear. He wanted to run, to never have to think of it again.

I can't. Now that I've seen what I've seen, I'll never be able to escape that knowledge or my fate.

He thought again of the endless faces recorded by the Crystal. They brought depth to concepts he'd assumed to be simple before. *The Star. Our world.* Behind those words stood every day lived by every life that was or had been, as well as every life yet to be.

If I abandon my calling, all of them will vanish.

At the same time, he couldn't help but note that he, too, was one of those lives. He'd been granted time on this star. His parents had eagerly awaited his arrival in the world. And though Noctis had lost his mother while still young, he'd been loved all the more by his deeply caring father. Ignis had been ever at his side, taking care of his every little need. Gladio, constantly honing himself for the day when he would serve as Noctis's Shield, was stern with him when necessary and at other times protective, like an impenetrable wall keeping Noctis from all harm. Prompto was there as a close friend, plain and simple, providing Noctis with invaluable time when he could forget his title and the burdens it imposed. Their journey together had been cut far too short.

I'll lose all of that. It'll all be gone.

He couldn't bear the thought. He did not want to die. He'd looked forward to the day when he could live together with those he cared about in a world that finally knew peace.

Yet without the True King's death, Eos had no future. To secure a tomorrow for everyone else, he had to give up his own.

It's not fair. I won't. I refuse!

The memories from the Crystal—the knowledge of myriad lives and deaths—once again swirled through his mind. He could never escape them. They were too heavy a burden to abandon.

A light shone as if to soothe his agitation. Noctis glanced up and found a familiar face staring back.

"Dad?"

Regis looked the same as he had in the last moment they'd been together, on the steps of the Citadel as he bid Noctis farewell. The king stood with sword in hand. His expression, too, was familiar: gentle, yet with a faint trace of sorrow. It was a sadness that appeared but for an instant, like a cloud momentarily passing across the face of the sun. It was fleeting, yet Noctis had never failed to notice it in days past. Nor did he miss it now.

"You knew all along, didn't you?" Noctis asked.

He recalled the vision shared by the Crystal, of his father on the day Noctis was revealed as the prophesized king.

"You cared for and looked after me, knowing exactly what my future held in store."

Noctis recalled the chiding comments of friends and relatives. *You're too soft on the prince*, they'd told Regis. Others questioned the king's decision to enroll Noctis in ordinary public schools. *Unsuitable for a prince's education*, they'd said. The criticism had poured in again from all sides when Regis allowed Noctis to begin living in an apartment on his own.

To Noctis, too, it had seemed nothing more than a father's doting on an only child. He'd assumed nothing deeper, certainly not that all those choices were born of a determination that Noctis derive the most joy possible from the short time he had.

"That was why you tried so hard to smile when you sent me away."

At the end, too, Regis's careful regard was apparent: he had arranged for Noctis to travel by car, to ensure that the journey would take time. The prince had been sent with a minimal retinue of three. The trip was one last chance for Noctis to forget his role as prince, to experience the wide world beyond Insomnia's walls, and to deepen his bonds of friendship. The smile given from father to son that day was a parting gift: well-wishes for the coming travels. For when they were inevitably over, so, too, would be the life of the traveler.

"I hated you for it at the time. You sent me away with a smile, and I couldn't imagine why. I'm sorry. It must have been painful for you."

A faint smile crossed Regis's lips. The late king shook his head, and then finally responded in words, "It is a parent's duty to feel concern for his child and to worry for his happiness. Those are feelings that needn't be returned. It is enough for the child to depend on his parents and let himself be treasured. With time, even moments of hardship or frustration are looked back upon fondly."

"Dad . . . "

"Now you are grown. The time for you to be dependent on others has come to an end. You are a man. A king."

His father had always been generous with praise throughout all of Noctis's childhood, and he'd always felt proud to have his father's approval. But all of that paled in comparison with the pride he felt now.

Then the smile faded from Regis's lips, and his tone grew stern.

"A king cannot lead by standing still. A king pushes onward always, accepting the consequences and never looking back."

Regis held out the grip of his glaive.

"Use it, to protect the one in your heart as well as the ones you love as brothers."

Noctis accepted the sword, feeling its weight. *Choose*, his father seemed to say. Not a choice of whether to yield to the fate placed upon him, but a choice of the future Noctis wished to see.

His options were by no means great in number. It was possible that, though he could not see it, he had no means to choose at all. But whatever path he walked, his father seemed to want him to walk it decisively and after much careful consideration.

"I understand," he said.

As if satisfied by Noctis's answer, Regis nodded and began to fade.

The things Noctis wanted to protect were clear. There were the people he cared about and everything connected to them. There was the kingdom he'd inherited from his father. The people he'd met during his travels, and the lands in which they lived. Everything was essential, and everything was integral. The loss of one brought emptiness and sorrow to others. If everyone and everything was connected in one great puzzle, then no piece could be neglected.

More than anything else, he did not want Lunafreya's sacrifice to be in vain. She'd expended her own life for the covenants. It was, he admitted, the one life he cared about above all others. He wished she could live again, but if that were not to be, he would at least see that evidence of her life persisted, that her memory might be carried forward into the future world.

With his father's sword in hand, Noctis lowered himself onto the throne in the Crystal and commanded himself to think. *Think well, that you might choose well.*

By the covenants awakened, the Six have seen the coming of the prophesied hour—a time when the Crystal shall have shed the entirety of its Light unto the ring. Only then, once the sacred ring is replete, can the True King complete his ascension.

Noctis heard the distant roar of thunder. For a moment, he believed he was having a dream about the Stormbringer. He opened his eyes, but the darkness beneath his lids was replaced by a darkness that seemed to envelop everything. *Perhaps,* he thought, *this, too, is a dream.*

As his eyes adjusted and his gaze swept about, Noctis realized he was on Angelgard. He'd seen this ancient stone prison before, in the visions shared by the Crystal. It was here that Ardyn had been sealed away by his brother. The roaring he heard, then, was of surf, not thunder.

He was not certain how long he'd lain there sleeping. Last he remembered, he was seated on the throne in the heart of the Crystal. Now he was here, seated atop cold stone.

Noctis stood. It was a strange sensation, as if he were making use of another's body rather than his own. The feeling lasted only for a moment, and by the time he was out of the cell itself and making his way to the outside, he felt his limbs moving as surely as they had in the past—or in truth, moreso than ever before.

He found that he knew the tunnel leading to the surface, though he'd never walked it himself. He had the Crystal's memories of Ardyn being led into his prison and then led back out by Verstael two millennia later. It was a simple, straightforward route, and the memories of the two journeys were more than enough to guide him to the surface.

Once outside, he was hit with the strong scent of the ocean. The sky was dark. He saw that in his absence, the daemons' influence had drawn a shroud over the whole world.

Be calm, he reassured himself. *You are the True King, and it is this very darkness you have come to banish.*

He descended the rocky slope down to the island's single cove. Even at a distance, he could see a ship moored there, as if awaiting the king's return. Noctis drew nearer and realized it was one he knew well: the royal vessel on which he'd made his journey from Caem to Altissia.

It felt like a reunion with an old friend. The ship was in good repair; someone, mortal or otherwise, must have kept an eye on it. It was precisely as he remembered it from when Cid's work was complete and they'd set off across the waves.

The royal vessel was not the only friend waiting. As Noctis approached the craft, he heard a familiar bark and friendly snuffle.

"Umbra!"

The dog seemed to appear from out of nowhere. He sat at Noctis's feet, and Noctis leaned down to pet the thick fur of his ruff. Umbra shook him away.

"What's the matter, boy?"

With one rear leg, the dog made several swipes at a spot farther back on his neck. Noctis followed the motions, realizing Umbra was carrying something. It was where he and Lunafreya used to tuck the notebook when sending messages back and forth.

The familiarity of the exchange hit him like an unexpected blow to the chest. The last time Noctis had squatted down like this to take the notebook from Umbra, he'd been at Cape Caem, just before boarding the same ship moored beside him now. Noctis had carefully opened the notebook's cover and flipped through the pages to Lunafreya's latest message: *Waiting for you in Altissia.*

Back then, he'd been so certain that he and Lunafreya would be reunited soon. No longer would theirs be a relationship confined to written words. They would finally be together in all ways, never to part again.

He recalled with vivid clarity the way his heart had leapt at the thought. It only made the current sting more painful. He recalled also the morning in Altissia when he realized that the notebook, the arrival of which had always delighted him, would now serve only as a constant reminder of loss.

Umbra shifted impatiently, unknowing of this inner turmoil. He nuzzled against Noctis's crouched figure, urging him to accept the delivery.

"All right, all right, cool it," Noctis told the dog.

He pulled the object free, realizing it to be a different, smaller notebook. He flipped it open to the first page, and on scanning it his eyes widened, a mix of surprise and confusion flooding his mind.

"How is this possible?" he wondered aloud.

Inside, in the same flowing script of the brief notes he'd seen countless times before, was written page after page crammed with thoughts, letters, and journal entries.

"Luna? She's alive?"

It was hard to believe, and yet the hand was unmistakable. The first message—*I'm safe*—was written in a hasty scrawl. She must have been in some great hurry as she began. But those were the only words that lacked the care and good form of Lunafreya's usual impeccable penmanship. Twelve years they'd exchanged messages; Noctis knew the shapes of her letters by heart. Her voice seemed to emanate from the words he read now. The more he read, the more certain he became: the notebook may have been different, but it was, beyond any doubt, something prepared by Lunafreya and meant for him.

There on the shores of Angelgard, Noctis read. He learned of Lunafreya's revival and of the new calling bestowed upon her. He learned of the world as it was now, devoid of daylight and uninhabited save for Lestallum and its environs. He read about Lunafreya's shock and bewilderment on waking into this new world. Of the new, inhuman power she'd gained. Of her travels through former imperial lands, felling daemons along the way. And of her new friend, a young woman named Sol. As Noctis scoured the pages, following every stroke of her pen, his vision began to blur, until finally his eyes were too full of tears to read further.

"Luna . . . " He wept. "She's . . . she's alive."

This whole time, he'd believed her lost. The one life he'd wanted to protect more than any other. When the Crystal had revealed the True King's calling, one thought had been more devastating than any other: though Noctis could promise a future to the world in exchange for his own life, it would be a future not graced with Lunafreya's presence.

But now he held evidence that she was alive.

"Thank . . . "

Thank the gods, he'd wanted to say, but his voice grew hoarse and thick with sobs. He traced a finger over the words of the notebook—the words that *she* had strung together, true and certain.

Wiping tears away with the back of his hand, he continued to read. Here and there, he found a date noted in small figures: 766. At first, he thought it was a mistake, but the number appeared over and over. Noctis's own journey with his friends had begun in M.E. 756. The scenes shared by the Crystal had spanned from ancient times up to that same year, which was to be expected, since Noctis had been drawn inside to learn of the past. The Draconian had shown glimpses of a future in which Noctis defeated Ardyn, but the god had given no hint of the year in which that event might take place.

"Ten years . . . " Noctis mumbled to himself.

He'd not imagined the Crystal might need so much time to pour its energy into the ring. There hadn't been the slightest notion that his calling might keep his companions waiting so long. Did they still have hope? Were they still awaiting his return?

If they had indeed waited all these years, then it was crucial that

Noctis hurry to find and rejoin them. They would fight side by side as brothers once again, and this time, Noctis would be ready to keep them safe. He would not only save his retainers and Lunafreya—he would see dawn returned to the world for all. Not one life more would be lost.

Noctis couldn't bear the thought of any more deaths. And Lunafreya . . . Never again would she have to offer up her own life for the sake of others, her duties as Oracle be damned.

"No longer will I abide a world in which there is such sacrifice," he vowed.

The writings of the notebook did not detail what Lunafreya's new calling might entail, but if that, too, involved her sacrificing her life, he would do anything and everything to prevent it. From now on, Noctis would see an end to all such things.

On the final page, he found written, *Waiting for you at the Citadel.*

A few pages earlier, there had been another passage that drew his attention. Lunafreya again mentioned the inhuman power she'd been given—a strength not meant for mortal hands—as well as her hesitation to use it. What did she mean? What was this power of which she wrote?

Thinking to send Umbra with that question, he found an empty space in which to write . . . then realized he had no pen at hand.

"Just my luck," he sighed, then realized that there was no need to write. They'd see each other soon. Noctis had his own business at the Citadel.

"Thanks, Umbra," he told the dog. "I'll give this back to Luna myself."

Umbra gave a single bark in response, signaling his understanding. After ruffling the thick fur around the dog's neck again, Noctis urged Umbra aboard the vessel and then hopped on himself.

When they pulled up alongside the pier at Galdin and disembarked, Noctis couldn't help but voice his surprise aloud.

"They really are all gone."

Not a soul was in sight. In the past, Galdin Quay had been a resort, bustling at all hours with all sorts of people come to enjoy a moment's respite from the daily grind. During the daytime, the blues of the sea and sky shone so intensely they were almost blinding. At night, dozens of lights lined the walkways and hung from the ceilings to keep the dark ever at bay. It was a place bright to both eyes and spirit.

Now not a single light was lit. Inky darkness covered everything. The pier stood lonely in the water, no longer host to vacationers enjoying casual spells of fishing. As man and dog walked along its planks, the only sound was of their own footfalls.

The instant Noctis had emerged from the stone corridors of Angelgard and observed the pervasive darkness that was not night, he'd suspected this world would be far different from the one he remembered. Lunafreya's account, too, had given warning: *uninhabited save for Lestallum.*

He'd grasped the concept intellectually, yet the reality still took him by surprise. The complete absence of people at Galdin Quay left him feeling as if perhaps everyone in the world had vanished, and now he alone was left. Even when he tried to reassure himself that this was not the case, unease still hung heavy upon him. Noctis heard nothing from the world aside from the rolling surf.

Then, without warning, Umbra was barking. Not a hostile bark, warning of danger, but a bark of recognition. Someone friendly was approaching.

"Welcome back, Your Majesty."

Words spoken aloud. A human voice other than his own. Noctis had to pause to be certain he'd not imagined it. He looked in the direction of the sound and could just make out someone running toward him.

"I'm not wrong, am I? You *are* the king, right?"

The speaker appeared to be a young woman about twenty years of age, more or less. A shotgun was strapped to her back, and Noctis presumed her to be carrying a variety of other armaments: as she drew near, he heard the clinking of a great deal of metal.

"Huh," the woman added. "You're a lot more handsome than I would have expected."

She stared at him without any hint of reserve. Noctis began to wonder if she might not be so unknown to him after all.

"And you might be . . . ?" he ventured.

"My name's Sol."

His hunch proved correct. So this was the companion of whom Lunafreya had written. The walking armory who was good at cards and bad at cooking.

"I was wondering how much longer you were going to keep me waiting," she said.

"You've been waiting here for a while?" Noctis asked.

He could see that it would take more than a few daemons to faze the young woman, yet it was still hard to fathom anyone waiting long in a place so desolate and devoid of all other souls. Clearly, Galdin was no longer any manner of haven.

"Don't get me wrong. It's not like I was here twenty-four/seven. But I've been coming by two or three times a day to check on the place."

She grinned. "Guess I ended up pretty lucky with the timing."

But the smile lingered only for a moment. Sol's next words were solemn.

"There's something you need to know," she began. "Luna's alive."

Had he heard it from Sol's lips before reading the notebook, it would have been too much to take in. Noctis would have been at a loss for words and quite likely unwilling to believe, his logical mind dismissing the possibility outright. It was fortunate, therefore, that

Umbra had reached him first, bearing that small but incontrovertible bit of proof.

"I know."

"You do?" Sol's surprise was apparent.

And well should she be surprised. Noctis and Lunafreya had never told anyone else of their quiet correspondence. There had been no explicit promise between the pair to keep the notebook and its contents secret, but as the messages continued, it naturally began to feel like something private, a matter shared only between the two young lovers and Umbra. If anyone else had been aware of it, perhaps Gentiana was the only one, but even of that Noctis wasn't certain.

"Talk about a letdown," Sol mumbled. "I thought you'd be blown away by the news."

"Sorry to disappoint you."

"Nothing gets past the king, huh?" she said. Then, "Anyway, we got bigger fish to fry. Come on. Car's this way."

Noctis recalled the location of the parking lot. He did not need Sol to lead the way but followed nonetheless. They passed through the quay's main building and crossed the narrow boardwalk, through drab surroundings of endless gray. The vibrant hues Noctis remembered of Galdin were nowhere to be found.

As they crossed from boardwalk to shore, Sol said, "You sure are trusting."

"Why wouldn't I be?" Noctis responded, perplexed by the comment.

Sol made a face, equally perplexed. "I mean, you don't even know me. You've never seen me before in your life."

"That doesn't mean I have any reason to doubt you. You're a friend of Luna's, aren't you?" To Noctis, that alone seemed reason enough to trust her. "Then, I believe you're here to help me."

At some point along the way, he realized Umbra was no longer with them. The dog seemed to have run off or vanished, as if his task was specifically to ensure Noctis's safe rendezvous with Sol, and now that his task was fulfilled, he was free to return to wherever it was he'd come from. It occurred to Noctis that the timing was too perfect to be a coincidence, and that was exactly why Umbra had come along on the vessel.

Sol began to speak but was interrupted by her smartphone. The ringtone was a familiar trill. For an instant, it had Noctis remembering an earlier time.

"Oh come on!" Sol was saying on the phone. "Your timing is almost *creepy*. How do you always seem to know right when stuff happens?"

Sol flicked her eyes at Noctis. Once more, Noctis felt a premonition about who was reaching out.

"That's right. I'm with him now," Sol said. "You wanna have a word with him?"

There could be no doubt now. Ignis, Gladio, or Prompto. So which of the three was holding the phone? Noctis felt certain it had to be one of them, but he couldn't make out the voice at the other end of the line.

"Huh? Oh. Yeah. We'll be there soon," Sol said, then breathed a small sigh as she slipped the phone back into her pocket.

"Who was that?" Noctis asked.

"Gladio. Says he's got some visitors, so he can't stay on the phone long. But they're near Hammerhead. We can meet up with them there." Sol added, "By 'visitors,' he meant they've got some daemons to take care of."

Noctis gave a small laugh. What a Gladio way to put it. He envisioned his sworn Shield in battle, the man's greatsword arcing effortlessly through the air. Then an unpleasant thought struck.

"Are all three of them okay?" Noctis asked.

Prompto would be at a considerable disadvantage in this new era of darkness, with his strong preference for guns. And if Ignis had not regained his sight, survival in a world overrun with daemons would be no easy feat.

What if one of them has . . . ?

Sol's interruption was merciful. "Of course they are. Could *anything* kill those three?" she laughed. "Prompto spends most of his time around Hammerhead, trying to impress Cindy. He helps out whenever she needs a little muscle on the road. Ignis hunts, too. Says if anything, *he's* more used to the darkness than we are."

It seemed clear that Sol was quite close with all three.

"They're gonna be real glad to see you. Not just your retainers, either. Everyone's been anxious for the king to return."

So they'd been waiting after all. For ten long years. Everyone in the world had carried on, believing that this day and this hour would come.

"We oughta hurry, too," Sol said. "Come on, jump in."

Noctis slid into the passenger seat at her urging. No sooner was his door closed than Sol had the vehicle in motion.

As Sol drove, she related the story of her encounter with Lunafreya and their first few days together.

"There I am, cruising down the highway on my bike, and out of nowhere this woman in white rolls right out onto the road."

"She *rolled* out onto the road?"

"I know, right? Figure she probably slipped off an embankment up above. She was in a real hurry." When Sol had slammed on the brakes, Lunafreya had jumped right into the sidecar without a word.

"She was being chased," Sol recounted, almost casually. "Apparently, the thing had been after her for a while. But that bike's an antique, y'know? Doesn't get the kind of speed you need to outrun a determined daemon. 'Specially not if you're lugging around extra weight. So I make a point of mentioning it to Luna—as a joke, right?—and guess what she does next."

"No idea."

"She goes, 'Right. What should I dump?' and flings the bag with all my food in it out onto the road."

Noctis snorted, at which Sol griped, "It was *not* funny. Food isn't easy to come by out in the wastelands. I was so mad I was fightin' back *tears*. The next day, we had to go back and pick it all up."

Sol began to talk about what a pain it had been, how they'd crawled around in the darkness on their hands and knees, picking up cans one by one. As she recounted the details, she mimicked their actions, stooping low and reaching her arms out to swipe up imaginary cans, not seeming to care that in reality, she was behind the wheel of a moving vehicle. According to Sol, Lunafreya had been much better at finding the cans.

"That was pretty much how it always went, right from the start. Luna was full of surprises. Same name as the dead Oracle. Then she tells me she *is* the dead Oracle. And then she turns out to be crazy strong, even though she's got that dainty little princess figure."

"What do you mean by 'crazy strong'?"

Lunafreya had mentioned in the journal entries that she was battling daemons alongside Sol. Noctis assumed she would've handled herself well enough given her training, but he wouldn't have expected this "walking armory" to describe the Oracle as an outlier in terms of physical strength.

"The way she fights, y'know?" Sol responded. "Packs a real punch. *Terrible* at cards, though. Oh, but there was this other game we played, and she was unbelievable at that one. Five Finger Fillet. You ever heard of it?"

Noctis had. "The game where you stab a knife between your fingers?"

It involved spreading one hand palm down against a table, then using the other hand to stab a blade down into the spaces between fingers, moving back and forth as quickly as possible. He'd played it with the guys on a road a few times. Ignis hadn't approved.

"It was *so* frustrating," Sol continued. "She claimed it was her first time, but she was going faster than me! Apparently, her brother was real good at it. She said she was just copying what she'd seen him do."

Noctis was surprised to hear that Ravus had played the game. It seemed the man had another side Noctis had never seen, far removed from the stiff, unapproachable high commander they'd encountered at Aracheole. Maybe Ravus was more easygoing in the presence of those he was close to. Or maybe he'd been another person entirely, before his mother died.

Sol kept on talking. "But the thing that *really* floored me was when Luna said she was gonna face off against Ardyn. Claimed it was her 'calling' ever since she came back to life."

Noctis turned involuntarily to look at Sol. "Did she really say that?"

The words gave Noctis a start; for a moment, he thought he must have misheard. Was that truly the new calling that Lunafreya had written about? How could *she* be the one destined to stop Ardyn? That was the True King's duty, bestowed upon him by the Draconian, inside the Crystal.

At Noctis's evident disbelief, Sol scrunched up her nose. "Please. Couldn't make this stuff up if I tried."

"Sorry. It just caught me off guard."

"Guess I can't blame you. I felt the same way. Told Luna that was a joke if I've ever heard one."

It was strange, though. Nowhere in the notebook had Lunafreya clearly spelled out what her new calling was, and she made no mention of going after Ardyn's life. If anything, she seemed to be suggesting the opposite, writing that she hoped to speak with Ardyn. Her message on the final page also told of the encounter with the soul of the first Oracle at Ralmuell, and of her plea to deliver Ardyn from his suffering.

He recalled the entry's words:

I imagine how painful it must be for you to think back on what Ardyn has done, but I beg for your understanding. I would attempt to speak with him. I think that perhaps . . . No, now is not the time. I shall explain in detail when we are reunited. Waiting for you at the Citadel.

And there was the question of why Lunafreya was approaching Ardyn at all. This was the man who had stabbed her at the altar in Altissia. Though the covenants she'd forged had already worn her life down to a thin edge, Ardyn had delivered the killing blow. Yet her words seemed to indicate an honest desire to communicate with him, rather than to seek revenge. Something pivotal must have happened for her feel that way.

If Sol's claim was correct and Lunafreya had indeed been called to *kill* Ardyn, the notebook's message was all the more troubling. It suggested that Lunafreya had turned her back on the gods' will. For one who had always lived a life of prayer and dedication to the gods, such a decision would not have been made lightly.

In the Crystal, Noctis had learned that the Ring of the Lucii provided the sole means to destroy the Immortal Accursed. Lunafreya wasn't in possession of the ring and neither was she a descendant of the Lucis Caelum line, able to wield it. He could see no logic in sending her to confront Ardyn. Why would the Six call on her to do so? Why send two people for a job that required one?

He then remembered another passage from the notebook, where Luna had mentioned the new, inhuman power she found herself possessing, as well as the disquiet it invited.

"Tell me," he asked Sol, "did Luna mention any sort of . . . new power she was able to use?"

He intentionally omitted the word "inhuman." Whatever this power was, he was reluctant to describe it the way Lunafreya had.

Sol stared straight ahead and answered stiffly. "Yeah. She can absorb the scourge."

The breath caught in Noctis's throat. There was only one other person who possessed power like that. And the Crystal had revealed the tragedy it had drawn down on him two thousand years ago.

"She claimed one of the gods gave it to her so she'd be able to face Ardyn."

"Do you know which god? Was it the Draconian?"

"I dunno. She never said."

Regardless of the source, Noctis wanted to know *why* Lunafreya had been given the power to draw the Starscourge. And why had she been commanded to kill the Accursed with the very same capability he possessed?

There was also the fact that Lunafreya was worried about using this ability. As Noctis understood it, the power would allow her to absorb the scourge but not to purge it. Each time she did so, the menace to which she was host would surge in strength. The Crystal's memories had made Ardyn's agony clear. To think of Lunafreya having to endure the same was intolerable. How could the gods do such a thing? Responsibility for killing Ardyn fell on the shoulders of the True King. Why drag Lunafreya into the equation?

"How much do you know about it?" Sol asked.

"About Luna's power? I guess I've got a pretty solid understanding."

As solid an understanding as anyone could have. He'd witnessed every detail of Ardyn's suffering two thousand years ago. Perhaps Noctis had already seen more of what would happen to Lunafreya than she had yet discovered for herself.

Another thought occurred to him. In the notebook, Lunafreya had mentioned an encounter with the soul of the first Oracle at Ralmuell.

Did Aera reveal to her the truth of what had transpired in their time? If so, that would explain Lunafreya's desire to speak with the Accursed. Ardyn was the only other person on the Star who knew firsthand what she was going through. Maybe now that she was privy to Ardyn's past, she no longer felt hatred toward the man at whose hands she had perished.

Or maybe Noctis was just grasping at straws.

The car came to a sudden stop, and Sol spoke again. "Listen, Your Majesty." She wore a grave expression. "You say you've got a pretty good grasp of what Luna's capable of. But there's something else you need to know. About the state she's in."

Noctis nodded for Sol to continue, but he could already imagine what she was going to say. The way she hesitated as she spoke. The fact that this detail was of such import that she felt she had to stop the car.

When Sol continued to fumble for words, Noctis ventured, "I take it . . . she's become a daemon?"

Sol's chest heaved with a barely contained sob, and she nodded.

"I'm sorry," she said. "It's all my fault. She was doing it for me, to save my mom's life, and . . . all she ever wanted was to see you again. To live by your side. She helped me even though she knew what it would do to her. I'm . . . I'm sorry."

"It's not your fault," Noctis said. "If someone is in need and it's within Luna's power to help . . . Well, we both know what kind of person she is. She doesn't hesitate. She just does it, no matter the consequences."

The expression on the young hunter's face shifted, now closer to surprise than tears.

"How . . . ?" she mumbled, the word seeming to escape from her throat of its own accord.

Then after another moment, "That's exactly how Luna put it. How did you know?"

"How could I not?"

After their sudden parting as children, Noctis and Lunafreya had never again spoke face-to-face. Yet a thread of written words had always kept them bonded.

No. *She* had kept them bonded. Lunafreya had worked to understand Noctis, and he'd done nothing to reciprocate. In that sense, too, he'd depended on her, as a child would. After he thought she was gone from the world, he'd lived with the regret of never becoming close enough to her to understand her tribulations. He would not make the same mistake again.

"Sol," he said, with sudden clarity of mind. "I'm not stopping at Hammerhead. I'm going straight on to the city. Pass the word on to Gladio and the others."

"You're not gonna wait for them? The garage is just up ahead."

"You said it yourself. Luna's anxious to see me. I can't keep her waiting."

Waiting for you. She'd written the same thing back then, as he and his companions prepared to embark for Altissia. She'd waited, but he hadn't made it in time.

He wouldn't make her wait again. *This* promise was one he would keep.

"All right, I'll let the guys know. You can bet good money they'll be racing after you as soon as they hear."

A mountain of problems to which he had no answers still loomed. He didn't know how he was going to protect Lunafreya. She had already turned. He might not be able to find a means to cure her of the scourge.

Still, inside the Crystal, he'd sworn that not another life would be lost. The only option was to move forward. He'd have to deal with everything as it came.

Maybe he was being too optimistic. The gods had always demanded that sacrifices be made. In the distant past, they'd chosen Ardyn, and the man gave his life that he might deliver his people from the Starscourge. Lunafreya had offered up her own to forge the covenants. Noctis, too, was commanded to lay down his life at the throne to deliver the Star from darkness. Yet even their sacrifices brought no certainty that the gods would save everyone. Ardyn had not been able to heal all of his people. Somnus, who refused to accept that some of those infected would be saved when others were not, had deemed it more fair to have everyone touched by the scourge killed. How much suffering could have been averted if the gods had deigned to decide that every life should be spared such a cruel fate?

By such thoughts, his path became clear. Fulfilling his calling was not enough in itself, and neither was driving away the darkness. Noctis had to see that *everyone* was delivered from peril, equally and without exception. Not a single life sacrificed. If the gods would not ensure that everyone could be saved, then it was up to him to do so, even as just a mortal king.

He would go to Insomnia. He would travel the path toward the future he wished to see—the path he'd promised his father he would take.

"I wonder if I might ask for your aid."

Lunafreya stared up at Ardyn. That was when she noticed the throne room's other occupants: several large puppets dangling from chains, each made to resemble some personage of importance to Lucis. A likeness of Regis hung among them. It made Lunafreya's heart ache. How would Noctis have felt if he'd been the one to encounter this display?

She resisted the urge to look away and, instead, kept her eyes trained on Ardyn.

"My aid," Ardyn drawled, a look of comically exaggerated surprise on his face. Then with a mocking little shrug, "Do you frequently invoke the aid of those whom you're sent to kill? What a charmingly unique habit."

"I have been commanded by the Draconian to confront and to slay you, that much is true. The life and strength I am given now are for that purpose."

"Of course they are. You—"

"However," she interjected, "I do not wish to kill you."

"And defy the duty bestowed upon you by your precious gods? How shocking." Ardyn pondered for a moment, then added, "Or rather, you would carry out your duty but can't bear the thought of bloodying your own hands and possibly dying in the attempt. So I am to chivalrously take my own life to spare you such hardships. Really, who knew what dark thoughts lurk behind that innocent countenance."

"That is not what I would ask from you. Your death serves only to further the Draconian's scheme. Please, you must believe me."

Ardyn's lips carried the same hint of a smile they always wore.

"What's this? A marionette that takes no joy in its master's success? I find that hard to fathom. Not that I have the least bit of interest in doing so."

"The Bladekeeper aims to purge the darkness and the rest of the Star along with it. Man, daemon, and everything else are all to be destroyed. For that purpose, he sends me to amass the scourge and—"

"Destroy everything, you say? How delightful! And here I thought I'd have to do everything myself, when it turns out I can just let the sword fanatic handle it for me."

"You would perish along with the rest of us."

"Your point being?"

Lunafreya's pleas landed on deaf ears. This was a complication she had not anticipated, that the difficulty would lie not in convincing Ardyn to help her but in persuading him to listen at all. A whisper of defeat wormed its way through her mind. No words of hers could reach him. No plea would penetrate his resolve.

Ardyn seemed to tire of the exchange. "Pray remember, Lady Lunafreya, that you call upon me uninvited."

"Please, I implore you. Hear my words."

"I'm afraid I'm not much for stories." Ardyn stood. "Now, I think it's time you take your leave, before my next guest arrives."

She saw his right arm rise. Just as it seemed their discussion might break down into violence, a voice echoed through Lunafreya's mind.

Please, you must stop Ardyn.

Aera's words.

I beg of you. Deliver him from his long years of anguish.

She could not give up yet.

"I am here at the behest of Aera Mirus Fleuret. She has asked me to help you find peace."

Ardyn froze. His ever-present smile melted away, and his face grew hard.

"If that name crosses your tongue again, I shall cut it out."

His lilting speech had turned harsh and flat, all traces of mirth now gone. Perhaps this was her chance to get through to him.

With voice bolder still, Lunafreya proclaimed, "At Ralmuell, I was graced by a visitation from Aera's spirit. She—"

"Be silent!"

Lunafreya had never once heard Ardyn raise his voice in anger. But the rage that twisted his features was a sight well familiar to her.

"I will not! Know this: Aera continues to suffer, and she continues to mourn for you. If you do not find peace, she will never find hers."

"I told you to be silent!"

They stood with gazes locked. Ardyn's burned with rage of frightening intensity. But she held firm, refusing to let herself look away. At the slightest sign of weakness, his ears would be closed to her words forevermore. She stared back at him resolutely, allowing her own eyes to pierce into Ardyn's, forgetting even to blink.

At long last, their deadlock broke; Ardyn was the one to flinch away. Lunafreya recalled Sol's comment back at the training grounds. *She kinda looks like you.* Ardyn likely found it excruciating to keep his eyes fixed on a likeness so close to that of Aera's.

His smile returned, though it seemed forced now. "Ifrit! Come!" he called.

No sooner were the words out of his mouth than a giant hand of flame rose from the ground before Lunafreya. She took an involuntary step back and recalled that among the scenes of the past shown to her by Bahamut, there had been one of Ardyn giving orders to the Infernian, the god's form marred with scourge.

"Be so kind as to entertain the Oracle for me. I have other, more pressing matters to attend to."

Ifrit's immense form, wreathed in flames, obstructed Lunafreya's view of the Usurper, but Ardyn's blithe tone seemed laced with a hint of vexation. She was uncertain if his smile still remained, but if she had to guess, probably not.

"If you'd rather not get burned, I suggest you run along home," he called from his spot near the throne.

Lunafreya had discovered the one topic that could provoke a response from Ardyn. He'd managed to kill Lunafreya once, in Altissia, but confronted with Aera's likeness once again, he hesitated. Aera and his memories of her were why Ardyn turned to the captive Pyreburner to drive Lunafreya away—he could not bear to do so himself.

"I shall remain here until you have listened to all I have to say," she announced.

She would not relent. No matter what happened, she would stay firmly planted in the Citadel. If Ardyn set the Infernian upon her, she would simply drive the god away. She reached for the polearm at her back—a weapon brought more out of a sense of precaution than any desire to use it—and readied for battle. She experienced a shiver of discouragement on realizing she'd fight this battle without Sol at her side, but fight she would, nonetheless. She had to.

Sol jumped out of the car at Hammerhead, and Noctis took the wheel, speeding toward Insomnia. The drive was uneventful, and before he knew it, he was outside the checkpoint for the Citadel courtyard. Leaving the vehicle, he approached the gates, found them unlocked, and pushed through.

This was where his journey had begun, so long ago. He'd passed through these same gates, riding in the Regalia together with Prompto, Gladio, and Ignis. Back then, the checkpoint had still been manned, with soldiers posted in shifts. The day was bright and clear. Blessed weather. His father was alive, and his friends with him. The Citadel and its surrounds were bustling with life as people went about their day.

It struck Noctis then just how much had been lost over the past ten years. He paused as a new concern pressed upon him, of whether all that had been taken away could ever truly be restored.

A king cannot lead by standing still. He remembered his father's words, and heartened, he hurried on through the checkpoint and into the courtyard proper.

The wide plaza stretched out before him, but the world's darkness left the place feeling drab, monochrome. Noctis realized he'd seen the courtyard like this once before: the dream in the Crystal, when he was first drawn into it. Endless ranks of unknown foes had filled this space, Noctis standing against them alone.

Enemies did not throng the courtyard now. Yet it seemed Noctis was still ordained to fight there, just with a different foe: as he traversed the space alone, there was a great clang and tremor of something metallic crashing into the ground. He instinctively dove to one side and flicked a glance back. A sword was lodged in the flagstones where he had just been. A moment later, in flash of blue light, the owner of the blade soared in—*warped* in, as if this adversary were a member of Noctis's own line.

"Great. So now I have to fight the Old Kings, too?" Noctis muttered to himself.

The warping would have been hint enough, but once Noctis saw the intricate suit of armor, he knew for certain.

Around the figure's thick platemail swirled the telltale black particles of miasma. Though once Noctis's ancestor, now this was also some manner of daemon. His opponent offered no confirmation of its own. It simply lurched forward in silence, bringing its great blade swinging down. Noctis's own glaive flashed into his hand, but no sooner had he repelled one blow than the next was incoming. The movements were swift, the attacks relentless. The strikes, too, confirmed his opponent's identity. This was one of the Kings of Yore. Or, more precisely, the soul of a king housed in a stone figure. An enemy far surpassing any of the daemons he'd previously battled, possessing strength and skill of another order.

When Noctis warped into the air above, the daemon king warped after him to cross swords in midair. If he stayed on the ground, the blows rained down from above, with gravity adding to their force and momentum. Any distance Noctis put between himself and his opponent could be crossed in an instant. Any attack he pressed might find only empty air as his opponent warped away.

This was what it meant to contend against the power of kings. Noctis gripped his sword, dedicating to the fight every bit of strength and skill he had.

The worst part of it was the constant awareness that he was alone.

No follow-up strikes from Gladio. No supporting fire from Prompto. No on-the-spot strategies from Ignis to turn the tide of battle.

Now more than ever, he longed to have his companions at his side. Somehow, in the dream shared by the Crystal, he'd been insensate to their absence, but here in the real world, it was at the forefront of his mind. He needed his three friends. They were irreplaceable.

But as king, there were things he had to face alone, and when that happened, as it did now, he would rise to the call. He could fight and win on his own—the Crystal's dream had shown him that. He would repel this foe, no longer dependent on others as he was in his youth. And if he fought alongside his companions again, he would guard their backs, not just rely on them to watch his. The dream had shown him he was ready for that, too.

He parried a blow from a greatsword that was nearly as long as Noctis was tall, then he rushed in at the enemy's heart, taking advantage of this tiniest gap in defense. He thrust his sword into a thin seam between the plates of armor, driving the blade deep, and then in the next split second, he was away, warping high into the air for another strike, this one from above.

The shriek of steel on stone filled the courtyard, followed by a cracking sound: fissures formed along the plates of the enemy's armor, and the daemon king fell to its knees. Noctis still held his weapon at the ready to fend off a counterattack, but his opponent made no attempt to rise back to its feet.

The contours of the stone figure grew hazy, and then it burst into a multitude of tiny particles dispersing into nothingness. When the ethereal mist cleared, a human form remained. Noctis was taken aback.

"Somnus Lucis Caelum . . . " he whispered.

It was a face he'd seen before, among the memories etched into the Crystal. This was the Founder King of Lucis, and Ardyn's younger brother. In the years following Somnus's summoning as part of the Old

Wall and his defeat at Ardyn's hands, Regis had ordered the statue of the Mystic reconstructed. It seemed Ardyn, on taking up residence in Insomnia in this darkened world, had alighted on the absurd notion of infesting the Mystic's avatar with the scourge. Perhaps he'd been eager to see it spar with the True King, once he finally arrived.

Somnus looked at Noctis and spoke. "Forgive my brother his sins, O Chosen. Anger and the scourge twist his senses. He thought to revel in the conflict between us, to watch as two so alike clash and inflict pain on one another."

"Sounds about right for Ardyn."

As Noctis looked into the other man's face, he had the strange sensation that he was seeing his own image, as in a mirror. Perhaps it wasn't so strange; they shared the same blood, after all. Ardyn had likely interpreted their similarity as a sign—the True King he longed to vanquish looked just like the brother for whom no amount of loathing would suffice. Thus the convoluted machinations to make them fight.

Noctis could see the torment filling Somnus's eyes.

"It was my own failing that turned my brother into what he is now," the Founder King said. "Of that, I am well aware. Still, I would beg of you. Stay his hand.

"Immersed in anger and hatred, he lives on immortal and knows not a moment's respite. Please, go forth. Restore the Light . . . and free my brother from his eternal curse."

Two brothers, as close as could be when children, driven apart by opposing ideals when adults. The relationship between the siblings had deteriorated until finally one died at the other's hands. Noctis knew that Somnus had regretted that outcome for the rest of his days.

"I will see it done," he vowed.

Somnus nodded. "You have my gratitude."

And then, with a faint smile shining through his melancholic expression, Somnus faded away.

The encounter with the Mystic brought a new question to the fore of Noctis's mind. The gods had given the power to draw the scourge to Ardyn alone. But why? It wasn't as if it could be given to only one person at time, or that Ardyn was the only one capable of wielding it. Both points were disproved by the fact that Lunafreya now possessed it as well.

If, in that age long past, the gods had bestowed such power on Somnus as well, perhaps the two brothers could have greeted the future together, even if their opinions had differed.

Or perhaps, if the power had been given to someone else entirely, and neither Ardyn nor Somnus wielded it, the outcome could have been different. The deadly struggle might have still claimed Ardyn's life, but the resulting hatred would not have persisted for millennia. Surely all would have been forgotten once the two men had both passed from the world.

Two brothers at odds, one with a power the other could never hope to possess. In the end, that was all it boiled down to. That difference between them had ultimately drawn a curtain of darkness across the world. The more Noctis thought it through, the more inept the gods seemed to be. Or perhaps it was simple arrogance: an inability of the Six to admit their own shortsightedness.

Perhaps Lunafreya was now being led along by that same blind arrogance. Or, more likely, yanked and dragged along, subject to all the accompanying suffering.

Plagued with doubts about the gods who gave him power, Noctis made haste toward the throne room.

She'd bitten off more than she could chew. Somewhere, in some corner of her mind, she knew that. To assume she might be able to pull every bit of infestation from the daemonified Infernian—it was as rash a plan as could be imagined. Still, she'd told herself she had to try. It was the only real means she had to face the deity.

"Ardyn!" she shouted, as the streams of scourge poured into her arms, "Is it not the Draconian who truly deserves your hate? Are you content to be but a cog in his machinations?!"

The words poured out of her in desperation. She had to get through to the man. The darkness was seething inside of her, and each time her mouth opened, she feared it might be the snarls and growls of a beast leaving her throat rather than words.

"Humanity brought to an end? The Star wiped from existence? How terribly convenient for me. Now if I could only find a way to eliminate that pesky god pulling all the strings. Then my revenge would be complete."

She saw the twisted smile on Ardyn's lips. In her struggle against the Infernian, she'd inadvertently drawn nearer to the throne.

"The Bladekeeper cannot be slain! He exists not only in our world, but also in the one beyond!"

Ardyn's eyes widened just slightly.

"We cannot hope to kill him," Lunafreya repeated, "But if we can convince him to cast his spell of destruction, he will be depleted and fall into deep slumber."

It would be like the Great War of Old. According to Gentiana, Teraflare could be cast only once. If they managed to survive the initial blast, they would be safe. Humanity would continue on.

By allowing the Bladekeeper to gather all the darkness into his spell, they could also rid the Star of the scourge. Four of the Six—Shiva, Ramuh, Titan, and Leviathan—had managed to protect Eos from Teraflare in the past. So long as they could manage the same feat again, Teraflare could be the key to ending the darkness.

"That is why," Lunafreya said to Ardyn, "I ask that you give to me the scourge that resides within you. I will pretend that I have slain you, appear to carry out the Draconian's calling . . . and . . . "

Lunafreya found herself unable to go on. Her breath caught with pain. Tears blurred her vision. In her warped field of view, she saw the face of the Pyreburner, twisted in similar anguish.

She remembered Gentiana's tales, and particularly one quiet story shared after Lunafreya had learned of the Messenger's true identity. The goddess always chose her words carefully, preferring modest expressions, but behind them was a clear and overflowing affection for humanity. As Lunafreya reviewed the story in her mind, it became clear just how much the members of the Six that resided on the Star shared in common with their mortal charges. Even the anger and hatred they experienced were feelings similar to those of humans.

At long last, the pain receded from the Infernian's visage. She seemed to have succeeded in freeing the god from the influence of the scourge. But it came at a cost: the agony burning within Lunafreya had increased several times over.

The Infernian turned toward Ardyn, who once again sat upon the throne. Anger twisted the god's features. Clearly, Ifrit was aware of his own loss of autonomy and of the fact that Ardyn had been behind his enslavement.

"Insolent mortal," spat the Pyreburner.

"Wait!" Lunafreya cried, fighting back against the strangling pain. To thwart the Draconian's plot to incinerate the Star and end all mankind, Ardyn's cooperation was absolutely essential. She couldn't afford a conflict between Ardyn and the Infernian. She had to stop them.

"God of Fire, I beseech you! Enter into covenant that the king might save our star!"

The fiery fist heading straight for Ardyn froze, and Ifrit turned to face the Oracle. Lunafreya found herself frozen as well, shocked by her own request. She'd been desperate for any means to prevent a fight, but the idea of using the covenant came out of nowhere.

Still, she continued, "It is I, Lunafreya, blood of the Oracle. In exchange for your release from the bonds of the scourge, lend your power to the Crystal's Chosen King."

It was all she could do to manage to stay on her feet. She forced her eyes wide. Tears were streaming from them now, and she could imagine the inky trails flowing down her cheeks.

"Let the king have your blessing!"

She had not previously forged a covenant with the Infernian—her demise in Altissia had come before she'd been able to make any attempt—and she'd always harbored a regret deep down at that failure of duty. Perhaps that was why the idea had come to her now.

"Please . . ."

Ages seemed to pass as she stood on trembling legs, caught between the heat of the flames before her and the agony of the scourge within. A moment in reality was for Lunafreya an eternity of torment.

The Infernian's gaze softened.

"So be it," he said. A curt answer, but sufficient all the same.

A chill wind blew through the throne room, and Lunafreya saw that the Infernian had departed.

She clenched her jaw, resisting the urge to slump to the floor. She knew that if her knees buckled now, she would not stand again, so she held on. Both her legs were nearly numb. The only thing she could feel was the aching of the scourge.

She heard a pair of hands begin to clap.

"Quite the show, Lady Lunafreya." Ardyn was standing again, his hands coming together with slow, dramatic sweeps. No trace remained of the hesitation and doubt she'd glimpsed before.

"And for your next act, you'll deceive a god?"

Lunafreya found it difficult to speak. She nodded instead.

"You and I shall put on a glorious performance, and when it's over, I'll be the one to fall on stage, is that it? A fascinating proposal. But I do have one question."

Ardyn's smile widened. It was an expression that had nothing to do with mirth.

"You've just gone past your limit. Now how will the show go on?"

And with that, her vision went black. Ardyn and everything else in the throne room disappeared. She heard the howling of a beast, and by the time she recognized it as her own voice, all was drowned in darkness.

Noctis heard a scream like that of a beast in pain. It seemed to be coming from just beyond the doors he sought to open. He flung them wide and rushed into the throne room, only to stop dead in his tracks. Some manner of creature lay writhing on the floor. From its jet-black skin rose the dark miasma of the daemons.

"I'm afraid you're out of luck," Ardyn's voice floated down from on high. "You've arrived just a moment too late."

"Ardyn!" Noctis growled.

"She couldn't wait for you any longer, you see."

The creature raised its head, arms and legs still limp on the floor.

Noctis gasped. "Luna!"

Lunafreya made no response to Noctis's voice. Her eyes were vacant. It was impossible to tell what she was looking at, or if she could see anything at all.

With the scourge's transformation, she hardly resembled the woman she was before. All the same, Noctis knew immediately that it was her.

He turned back to Ardyn. "What did you do to her?!"

"Now why would you think to blame this on me? I'm almost offended."

"Enough with the games!"

"I assure you, this is all of her own doing. She absorbed every last bit of scourge from the Infernian himself."

Lunafreya stumbled to her feet. When Noctis tried to rush to her side, she leapt away with inhuman speed, reaching down to snatch up a polearm that had fallen on the ground.

"Luna . . . " Noctis watched in disbelief as she leveled her weapon's blade directly at him. "Please! Stop this!"

She lunged, offering no word of explanation, or any indication that she'd heard his words, let alone comprehended them. Noctis dodged to the side, barely avoiding her thrust. It was clear her actions were not intended for show. She sought to take his life.

"Luna!" he shouted. "Can't you see it's me?!"

He'd managed to grab the spear's haft with one hand, gripping it tight. He needed to get the weapon away from her, before she got hurt.

But a mere moment after he'd laid his hand on the weapon, the world inverted before his eyes and his back slammed against the ground. He groaned in a mix of pain and disbelief. Somehow, she'd been able to lift and throw Noctis down effortlessly, in a show of overwhelming strength.

"Please . . . Luna, you have to snap out of it," he pleaded, rising from the floor and approaching her again.

Suddenly, a towering blade flew down from above, driven into the ground between them.

The Chosen's purpose is no more.

The words of the Draconian boomed throughout the throne room. The Bladekeeper himself made no appearance. There was only the massive blade and the stentorian voice.

Power is granted that darkness be banished and balance returned to the Star.

When mortals grow arrogant, seeking to repeat blasphemies of old, no longer are they worthy wards.

To cleanse the Star, all life must be swept away.

So it is ordained, and so shall it be.

"All life swept away?" Noctis repeated, uncomprehending. "But I thought you sent me here to . . ."

His mind needed time to catch up. Was this not the same deity he'd encountered in the Crystal? Still fresh in mind was his own calling, as delivered by the Draconian. The True King was to rid the Star of darkness at the cost of his own life. Had the Bladekeeper's intentions changed? If so, why?

Bahamut continued to speak. It seemed he would not offer answers or even pause to give Noctis time to comprehend.

The time is come. Let the power be unleashed, O Sovereign of the Scourge.

Lunafreya's body floated up into the air. That was the last thing Noctis saw, and as his consciousness slipped away, the last thing he felt was a tremendous force hurling him away.

When Ardyn's eyes reopened, it was to the scourge-darkened sky above. He was no longer in the throne room nor, it seemed, inside the Citadel at all. After another moment, he realized he was sprawled unceremoniously on the ground.

"Lovely," he announced dryly.

He shook his head and stood. He recalled seeing the Oracle release the darkness. He'd been thrown backward by the blast, and after that, he must have blacked out.

"Well, if nothing else, our dear Lady Lunafreya certainly set her sights high."

He looked up to find the Oracle—in Bahamut's words, the "Sovereign of the Scourge"—suspended high up in the sky. Around her swirled a vortex of black miasma.

A swarm of creatures flitted about the vortex. Birds or wyverns, he'd have guessed, until on closer inspection he saw that they possessed the same shape as the Bladekeeper himself. Avatars. Closer to the stature of a man than a god, dark in color, and singularly ominous. Dozens of them were circling the Oracle, protecting her, their black and gold coloration a disturbing echo of the royal colors of the hated Lucian line.

"Behold, the Goddess of Darkness," Ardyn mused.

The sky seemed to be darkest directly above the Citadel, right where Lunafreya was. This was the spot where all the Starscourge plaguing the world was to be drawn. All the dark power would be concentrated here for the Draconian's spell.

"Teraflare," Ardyn murmured. "The preparations are already underway."

The Draconian's plan, as relayed by the Oracle, had not come as much of a surprise. This was the type of dramatic solution the God of War was apt to prefer.

However, it was another of the woman's statements that bothered him.

The Bladekeeper cannot be slain! He exists not only in our world, but also in the one beyond!

That was a distressing revelation. Ardyn, his own soul trapped in the other realm, knew better than any other the truth of that consequent immortality and of the difficulty it would pose for any attempt on the Draconian's life. One could deal an infinite number of deaths to a foe with a soul stuck in the Beyond, but said foe would always rise again. To worsen matters, the Draconian's soul, unlike Ardyn's, was not held captive—the god was as free from restraint there as he was here in the mortal realm.

In short, a battle with Bahamut would be much harder than one with the Glacian or the Infernian. Neither the daemon-infused creations of the empire nor the hands through which flowed the controlling sting of the scourge would suffice to defeat the Draconian.

"Thus her proposal. The Bladekeeper casts his Teraflare, expends his energy, and falls into slumber. Ah, but if only it were so simple."

Lunafreya's notion was logical in the sense that history had unfolded in such a manner once before. But there was no guarantee that a reenactment of the War of the Astrals would culminate in the same result. This time, the Draconian's spell would be charged with all the darkness that now blanketed Eos.

There was another point to consider. At the conclusion of that ancient war, five of the Six had unquestionably fallen into slumber. Each had collapsed, depleted, somewhere upon the surface of the Star. But it was unclear whether Bahamut had slept. Tales told of him retiring to some place unknown; some posited that he'd been asleep high in the heavens. Of course there was no way to ascertain the truth of any of these claims. For ages, the god had simply been missing, without any clue as to his whereabouts or doings.

"The Lady Oracle might be willing to gamble, but I'd much rather take the sure bet," Ardyn mused aloud.

Put the god to sleep—that was the solution of a gentle soul. However, there were other options. Options that were more decisive. More *permanent*.

A violent shaking of the ground interrupted his reverie.

"Oh dear. What now?"

The Citadel, already half-destroyed, was quaking along with the earth. No, quaking *against* the earth, as if struggling to break free of it. Steel split and concrete crumbled. A great roar of wrenching and tearing materials drowned out all other sound. Everything was moving, but the Citadel most of all, in great jagged jerks toward ground and then sky.

When Ardyn managed to regain his balance, he murmured, "Moving the Crystal beyond the reach of man? Now that's not very sporting. I would say that I'd expected better of the Bladekeeper, except that would be an utter lie."

Dust billowed, and the Citadel in its entirety began rising into the air. The throne room hung in plain sight, its walls and ceiling blown away by the Oracle's earlier burst of dark energy.

Fissures tore through the large boulevard leading from the Citadel to downtown Insomnia. The ground shrieked as it ripped apart, and debris flew in all directions. The Citadel continued to rise, its great gates dangling limp, bars twisted like crumpled dollhouse ornaments.

"I suppose I should be grateful for the free ride. Stick with the throne, stick with the action."

A series of phantasmal leaps later, he was aboard the ascending island. So long as this was headed in Lunafreya's direction, Noctis wouldn't be far from hand.

"A family reunion in the sky. You won't keep me waiting this time, will you, Your Majesty?"

Ardyn, standing in the Citadel courtyard and staring down at the receding city streets, began to laugh.

Consciousness returned slowly, and for a while, the world was hazy. The ground beneath him was violently shuddering. It reminded him of that day at the Disc of Cauthess—a rumbling that rose from deep in the earth.

Cauthess. Right. He'd received Titan's blessing that day, thanks to Luna's covenant, and . . .

Luna.

The preceding moments reeled back through mind. Noctis jolted to his feet.

"Luna!" he cried, scanning his surroundings.

He wasn't in the throne room. In fact, he didn't seem to be inside the Citadel at all. He looked up to see the skyscraper moving ever higher: the whole structure was rising atop a small island of concrete and asphalt, as if it had been pulled up like a weed by some unseen force. The shaking of the earth he'd felt earlier must have come as the building was ripped from the ground.

Higher up, he saw a section of sky darker than its surroundings—a concentration of miasma denser than he'd ever seen before. In the center of the onyx circle was a humanlike figure: the daemon Lunafreya that both looked like his love and did not.

The scourge-tainted Oracle raised both hands high above her head and began to sing. It was a song Noctis had never heard before.

Lunafreya had often sung songs of old for him during his recovery at Tenebrae, measures passed down by the people of her homeland, with soothing, simple melodies.

There was nothing gentle about the song Noctis heard now. The tones were dissonant, harsh, and seemed to cause the very air to tremble, as if her voice might pierce the darkness itself. A moment later, light began to encircle Lunafreya. It was a light similar to that of the Armiger, but pure white and tracing the intricate lines of a casting circle in the space around her body.

"Is that . . . ?" Noctis said.

He recalled the words of the Draconian. *To cleanse the Star, all life must be swept away.* This had to be the beginnings of the Bladekeeper's spell of destruction absolute. As he stared up at the ominous vision, horror transmuted into urgency.

"I have to stop it!"

If the Draconian managed to complete the spell, the chances of recovering Lunafreya safely were slim. Noctis sprinted forward. He had to get up there. He had to stop the spell. The Citadel was gaining altitude. He didn't have much time.

He recognized his own unbecoming panic. Any trace of poise or cool was lost. Hours ago, he'd felt collected, ready to return home and fulfill his destiny. The clear and overwhelming images shared by the Crystal told him there was no other choice. He knew what he had to do, and nothing was going to throw him off course.

And yet here he was, panicking. Staying calm seemed an insurmountable task with Lunafreya's life once more at stake. He couldn't lose her. Not again. He remembered the pain in Altissia, when he regained consciousness only to learn of her death. His heart had seemed but a moment away from being ripped from his chest. The prospect of enduring that agony all over again left him terrified.

He ran with everything he had. A thrown blade and a warp brought him close to the rising Citadel. Next stop was the edge, and then he'd ride up into the sky, heading toward Lunafreya high above. Without other means to fly, it would be the easiest way up.

Unfortunately, Bahamut seemed to know it, too. As Noctis aimed for the lip of the rising island, he heard the sound of wings diving in. He turned, prepared to face an incoming pack of flying daemons. What he encountered was something quite different.

"It's the Draconian," he gasped.

Or if not the god himself, something quite similar. There was no mistaking the shape of the incoming assailants; they looked precisely like the god Noctis had observed inside the Crystal. However, they were much smaller in scale, perhaps twice Noctis's own stature, with splayed swords for wings and flexible tails like the supple leather of a whip. In their hands, they wielded greatswords.

There were several dozen, arranged in ordered ranks reminiscent of the empire's automated infantry. Whether these smaller Bladekeepers were incarnations or simply minions, Noctis was not certain, but they were undoubtedly created to execute the Bladekeeper's will. Avatars, perhaps. At any rate, this was no unordered mob of daemons; these foes behaved intelligently, clearly intending to strike at Noctis with co-ordinated tactics.

"Looks like someone doesn't want me near the Citadel," he muttered.

For what the avatars lacked in size compared to their master, they compensated for with speed and ferocity. The Royal Arms flashed into Noctis's hands. He parried blows and struck back, but it was clear he was at a disadvantage. There would be no swift victory against this many skilled opponents.

"Damn it!" he cursed, as another avatar swooped in.

Easily as troublesome as their greatswords were their bodies and wings. The avatars dove and twisted, not at all hesitant to try bodily slamming into Noctis, bladed wings sweeping forward to slice at his arms. He wouldn't be able to avoid every blow. A sharp pain ran through his biceps. Enough solid contact on his right, and he'd find it hard to wield his glaives to fight back.

At long last, he managed to fell one. But the rest continued to dive at him. His hard-won victory evaporated like a ladleful of water thrown upon hot coals. The avatars toyed with him, dictating the terms of the fight, and Noctis's fatigue mounted; despite the fact that he'd managed to slay one, it felt like there were more enemies now than there had been to start with.

All the while, the Citadel continued to rise. Soon, it would be at too great a distance for Noctis to reach with a warp. He had to cut this encounter short, but the number of opponents, their strength and coordination kept him pinned. He had to *think*.

A sudden call came from behind him. "Noct!"

An avatar's incoming sword rang with an impact and jerked off course. It took Noctis a moment to comprehend what had happened: a bullseye shot, dead center on the enemy's blade. Someone was firing at the creatures with a gun, and Noctis realized exactly who it was.

"Prompto! Glad you could make it!" he shouted in response. Before he could turn to confirm, he heard the whoosh and clang of a greatsword and then a heavy thud as something collapsed to the ground.

Noctis finally found a moment to shoot a glance over his shoulder. "Gladio! Long time no see!"

The sworn Shield lifted his massive blade to rest on one shoulder, the avatar that had been bearing down on Noctis's back now vanquished.

"Sure took your sweet time showing up," Gladio grinned.

"Look who's talking," Noctis responded.

"This is all quite heartwarming, but I'm afraid the happy reunion is going to have to wait," a third voice chimed in. Ignis.

The sound of wings slicing through the air reached their ears again. Three more enemies, inbound fast. Ignis was already crouched slightly, polearm held ready for the leap. For the vision he still lacked, his hearing seemed to have grown all the sharper. He was quicker to respond than anyone else.

"Hey, Ignis, instructions!"

Same words, same motions. Just like old times.

"Attack together on my signal," Ignis replied calmly.

The advisor had a strategy whipped up almost instantly. Everything flowed without a hitch, as if ten long years hadn't passed at all. The three companions assumed their formation around Noctis, as if they'd all done the same just days ago.

No. For Noctis, it seemed like yesterday, but his three retainers had ten years to prepare for this fight. Prompto's shots came faster and with more precision. Gladio's blows were more powerful than ever before. Even Ignis's movements were sharper, notwithstanding his lost eyesight. Noctis didn't have to ask how they'd spent the time in their king's absence. Here in battle, it felt like they'd spent every day of that decade right by his side.

Even so, the situation was growing worse.

"We're getting nowhere," Gladio growled in irritation. Their foes seemed to be growing in number. In all likelihood, the Draconian was summoning reinforcements.

"And they just keep coming!" came Prompto's frustrated follow-up.

"Heh. Talk about déjà vu."

"Now that you mention it . . . "

The exchange did seem familiar. Back at Zegnautus Keep, when they'd been surrounded by daemons, Ignis had instructed Noctis to go ahead on his own. Noctis had left the other three behind to fight, heading by himself to the chamber where the Crystal was kept.

Back then, the situation had seemed dire. This time, it seemed even worse. The fact that Lunafreya hung high above him, her life at stake, didn't make it any easier.

Suddenly there was a yell coming from loudspeakers above.

"Everyone! Get down!"

Sol's voice. The four men hit the ground as directed, without question or hesitation. An explosion shook the surroundings. They felt the scorching blast wash over their backs and heard the approaching drone of a dropship's engines.

"Hurry! Jump in!" Sol barked.

The dropship made a rapid descent, nearly slamming against the ground in a landing maneuver indicative either of incredible skill or brash disregard. Noctis wasn't about to complain. The offer to get away and end the stalemate was all too welcome.

"Just the kind of stunt I'd expect them to pull," Gladio snorted as he pushed himself to his feet. Apparently, he'd already figured out who was piloting, but there wasn't time to ask him. The dropship's hatch yawned open. Sol peeked out from one side.

"Figured you could use a hand, Your Majesty," she called, waving a hand to urge them aboard.

Inside, Noctis was confronted by another familiar face. "Aranea," he said. "Guess we've got you to thank for organizing the lift."

"It's been a while, Pretty Boy. Er, Majesty, I guess. Heard you were keeping an eye on the kid here."

Aranea's gaze shifted to Sol. So this was the "mother" Noctis had heard her mention in the car. And that meant the person Lunafreya had been determined to save—even in the face of her own imminent fall to the scourge—was Aranea.

Noctis replied, "I'd say Sol was the one keeping an—"

Eye on me, he'd intended to finish, but Aranea cut in.

"Let's save the chitchat. Wouldn't want you to bite your royal tongue."

Noctis soon realized what she meant. The craft climbed steep and fast, slamming backs and heads into seats. Noctis glanced forward at the cockpit and saw two more familiar faces: Wedge at the helm, Biggs sitting copilot.

"Take 'er to the roof, Wedge! As fast as she'll go!"

"On it."

The acceleration was so intense Noctis thought for a moment they might be crushed in their seats. A sudden sideways jolt was added to the mix, along with the sound of a violent collision. A shrill alarm rang throughout the craft.

"A hit," Wedge announced. "Damage to port."

They didn't bother flicking the display monitors over to the side-mounted cameras. What had happened was obvious enough. Bahamut's avatars were in close pursuit, and they clearly didn't have any reservations about ramming themselves against the dropship's hull. Firing the autocannon was out of the question. Aranea and the rest of the crew seemed to realize it, too. Lunafreya was out there.

The jolts continued, predictably enough. Every few moments, there was another impact against the hull, sending a shudder through the entire airframe. The attacks were relentless.

"Can't take much more of this, Lady A!" Biggs announced.

Aranea clicked her tongue in annoyance. "Looks like we're shit out of luck. Better set her down before we lose her."

"Over there." She pointed. The Citadel and its courtyard hung suspended just ahead. The courtyard gates and surrounding walls had fallen away. The once-smooth, stately flagstones were now a jagged mess over warped, uneven ground. But there was enough space for an emergency landing.

"You really think it's safe?" Prompto asked. "Putting the ship down th—"

Prompto cut himself off, hand flying to mouth and face twisting in pained grimace. Aranea's warning hadn't been a joke. The unpredictable shakes and jolts of the ship really did pose a threat. Gladio, Ignis, and even Sol sat tight-lipped. Only Aranea, Biggs, and Wedge spoke without concern, a clear indication of their long experience aboard the vessel.

"Mouths shut, heads back!" Aranea shouted. "This one's gonna be rough!"

Biggs's countdown began as the last word was out of her mouth. "Three . . . two . . . one . . ."

The impact of the craft rode a fine line between emergency landing and outright crash, but the dropship finally skidded to a stop. An unpleasant burning smell wafted through the cabin; it seemed like the propulsion system wouldn't be firing up again anytime soon.

Aranea sighed and said, "End of the line. Hate to say it, but it looks like you're on foot from here."

"Don't sweat it. This is a big help already," Noctis replied.

Without the dropship, he probably wouldn't have made it to the Citadel at all—it was already well beyond the range of a ground-based warp. And landing in the courtyard seemed to have brought them some measure of safety. As soon as the dropship slammed down, the flying avatars had ceased their assault. Maybe the Bladekeeper was loath to risk further damage to the Citadel and its precious crystalline cargo.

"You really saved our asses," Noctis added. He flicked his gaze to the cockpit's display. He saw the Citadel dead ahead on one panel, and on another, he could just make out Lunafreya, floating directly above the towers.

"Bet if we got up to the roof, we could reach her," Gladio said.

Prompto chimed in with agreement. "Race you to the top."

"In any case, getting into the shelter of the Citadel would seem to be in our best interest," Ignis said. "The Draconian has paused his assault, but it could resume at any moment."

Ignis wouldn't have seen the monitors—he must have surmised

the situation from Gladio and Prompto's exchange alone. And he was right. If the airborne foes were to strike again, Noctis and party would be at less of a disadvantage in the enclosed space of the Citadel than in the courtyard.

"As for us, guess we'll get busy on repairs," Aranea said and shrugged. Biggs and Wedge headed back toward the engine room.

Sol opened the hatch. Once they were outside, the extent of the damage to the dropship was obvious. Black smoke poured from the rear. If anything, it was a surprise the ship had held out long enough to save them from a real crash. That they'd managed any sort of emergency landing at all was a small miracle.

"Sorry, Your Majesty, but this is as far as I go," Sol said. "I've gotta help get the ship back in the air."

"Yeah, I figured. Don't worry. We'll take it from here."

In all likelihood, the Draconian's only concern was keeping Noctis from Lunafreya. With Noctis away from the ship, Aranea and the others would have the interval they needed to do their repairs and clear out of the area.

Noctis looked at Sol once more. "Actually, I've got a favor to ask. Once you've got this thing flying again, I want you to pull back to Lestallum."

"Huh? Why?"

"The people there need to be evacuated. I want you four to see to it."

All life must be swept away. Noctis couldn't shake the Bladekeeper's words from mind. At this point, it wasn't hard to imagine some massive blaze tearing across the surface of the Star. And if that *did* happen, evacuation would be easier said than done.

"I gotta admit, though, I have no idea where to ask you to take them."

To Noctis's relief, Ignis jumped in. This kind of thing was exactly within the royal advisor's domain.

"We'll be in touch as soon as we have a handle on the situation," Ignis said. "Until then, get preparations underway. Have the people ready to move at a moment's notice."

At Ignis's instructions, Sol gave a crisp, "Got it." Then she turned back to Noctis.

"Your Majesty, please do whatever it takes. Luna has to make it out of this okay."

"I'll save her. I promise."

He had sworn the same to himself countless times already.

Noctis and his companions broke away from the dropship and ran toward the Citadel. So far, their assumption that the Draconian didn't want any harm to come to the Crystal seemed to be holding up. There was no sign of the avatars.

But the state of the courtyard itself slowed their progress. It was canted down at a pronounced angle, with piles of debris and deep holes offering plenty of hazards. Further complication came from the fact that the Citadel was still rising, the intermittent jerks and shudders of the moving structure throwing them all off balance.

"You okay, Specs? I'm not walking too fast, am I?" Noctis asked.

When Ignis first lost his sight, Noctis had been slow to adapt. Gladio and Prompto had constantly been on Noctis's case for not accommodating their blinded companion's slower, less certain pace.

Noctis's question seemed to remind Ignis of that time, too. He gave a chuckle, insisting "It's no problem whatsoever, I assure you."

Noctis took a moment to watch his companion's progress more carefully and realized the rough terrain wasn't slowing him down at all.

Ignis hunts, too. Says if anything, he's *more used to the darkness than we are.*

When Sol had mentioned Ignis's reaction to the world gone dark, Noctis hadn't thought much of it. It seemed reasonable enough. Only now did it occur to him how much determination and effort must have gone into the smooth, natural gait Ignis walked with now, as well as how much time he must have spent honing his hearing, smell, and other senses to make up for the lost sight.

"If anything, we should pick up the pace," the advisor continued. "We must reach Lady—"

There, his words cut off. Noctis sensed it, too. Footsteps on the long stairway leading up to the Citadel doors. Someone had paused near the top. Noctis looked up. Even through the darkness, there was something about the man's presence that announced itself plainly for all to know.

"Oh, Noct . . . How I have waited for this," came the lilting voice.

Ardyn slowly made his way down the staircase, both arms flung wide as if to imply the king and his retinue would pass no farther.

"Out of my way, jester."

"Oh? And here I thought you came all this way to see *me*."

Mere hours ago, Ardyn's presumption would have been accurate. Noctis had been convinced of his calling to bring an end to Ardyn for the sake of the Star. But now the situation had changed.

Noctis's tone was cold. "I don't have time to play games with you."

"In a hurry, are we? Don't tell me. You think you have to go save your damsel in distress."

Ardyn pointed a finger toward the sky, at the point above the Citadel where Lunafreya was.

"Surely you wouldn't want to interrupt her," Ardyn continued. "You'd be spoiling her brilliant plan."

"What are you talking about?" Noctis grated out.

"Oh dear. You mean you haven't heard?"

Gladio drew his greatsword, clearly ready to pass by force. "Noct, don't listen to this asshole. Whatever comes out of his mouth is gonna be just another big, fat lie."

"Now you're starting to hurt my feelings. Lady Lunafreya approached me herself, in the hopes that I might aid her. It's nothing but the truth, cross my heart."

"Luna came to *you*?"

Time and time again, Noctis had fallen to the Usurper's deceptions. He knew it, and yet now he still hesitated. What if this time Ardyn was telling the truth? He recalled the notebook sent by Lunafreya. There, on the final page, she'd expressed her hope to speak with Ardyn.

His frustration boiled over into rage.

"Then, tell us!" Noctis snarled. "What was she planning?!"

"Noct, calm down!"

It was Prompto who reeled him back in—Prompto, who had been the victim of Ardyn's deceptions on board the train to Tenebrae. Nevermind that Noctis had ultimately been the cause of Prompto's suffering that day.

Ardyn obliged Noctis's question with an answer, seemingly unfazed by his anger. "A spell of ultimate destruction. Teraflare. She would provide the Bladekeeper with enough power to cast it. Look. It's already beginning."

He pointed up again, this time seeming to indicate the lines of the casting circle tracing through the dark sky. Already several massive swords had appeared, radiating from the circle's edge. The resemblance to Noctis's own spectral weapons was astonishing, yet they were clearly far more powerful than the arms in his arsenal.

"Lunafreya believes its casting will exhaust the Bladekeeper and send him off for a nice long nap," Ardyn explained. "She assumes that he is impervious to death, and that sleep is the best we can hope for in the fight against an opponent that exists both here and in the other world."

By "other world," Ardyn likely was referring to the Beyond. Noctis knew of it from what he'd learned inside the Crystal. Ardyn's own soul was trapped in that place, bringing him immortality in this world. That must be why Lunafreya thought Bahamut was impervious to death. And unlike Ardyn's, the Draconian's soul was likely not captive in the other realm.

"And so she came to me, asking that I give her the power of the scourge within me."

"Surprisingly reckless," Ignis murmured.

"Why, that's exactly what I thought," Ardyn said, nodding his head in a parody of grave concern. "Truly, I could not be more wholly in agreement. Who's to say our blade-loving friend will sleep as predicted? Or that we'll survive his spell at all? Lady Lunafreya claims the other gods will join together to resist the assault as they did long ago, but if you ask me, there's nothing more fickle than a god. And that is why . . . " Ardyn's words had been coming faster and faster, but here, he paused, and a wicked smile spread across his face, " . . . I think you ought to give me that ring."

With a flicker, Ardyn vanished from the top of the stairway.

"Take cover!" Noctis shouted. His three retainers each leapt off to one side. And no sooner had Noctis warped away than Ardyn reappeared right where they'd been standing, red blade in hand.

"How delightfully nimble!" Ardyn laughed.

"Son of a bitch," Gladio growled, making to rush at Ardyn from the side.

"Gladio, wait!" called Noctis.

Time was of the essence. He knew that overwhelming Ardyn as a team would be the swiftest course of action, that they should just force their way past him and continue on toward Lunafreya. But something inside Noctis told him to stay.

"I'll put an end to this," he announced.

His calling no longer held meaning; there was no reason to kill Ardyn when Bahamut endeavored to destroy all mankind. But calling or not, he had a score to settle. Not just for what Ardyn had done to him, but on behalf of all those whose lives he'd witnessed in the Crystal.

"This is a battle of kings." He looked back. Prompto nodded understanding.

Ignis responded, "As you wish, Your Majesty."

Ardyn smiled at Noctis. "Me, a king? You do me quite the honor. Are you sure that's all right?"

Noctis knew the title had once belonged to Ardyn, and he'd seen how it was stripped away from the other man. Ardyn had gone on to claim countless lives and amass a multitude of sins for which he could never fully atone, but that did not give Noctis any desire to deny the truth. Let Ardyn be known for what he was—a rightful king of Lucis.

"Let us begin," Noctis said, calling his blade to hand.

The shrill cry of steel on steel filled the courtyard. Noctis realized this was the first time he'd exchanged blows with Ardyn face-to-face. The events in Altissia unmasked Ardyn's malice, but still, king and chancellor had never found a chance to cross swords.

Though awash with scourge, hatred, and malice, Ardyn was nonetheless of Noctis's own line. The blood of Lucis flowed through the man's veins, and thus, as Noctis unleashed hell with the Royal Arms, so, too, did Ardyn.

Perhaps Ardyn had attempted to steal away the ring on the assumption that anyone of the line of Lucis would be able to draw on its power. If so, he probably intended to travel to the Beyond and slay Bahamut there. Before the fight, he'd mentioned how the Draconian existed in both realms, and that as long as one of the halves persisted, the god would never perish. Only a soul stripped of mortal flesh could enter the Beyond, a feat that could be accomplished by using the Ring of Light while seated on the throne of Lucis.

Adryn's soul, too, was in the Beyond, but in all likelihood, that alone would not suffice to contend against the Draconian. Noctis recalled the Crystal's vision of the future, of the way things were meant to be. In that future, he'd destroyed Ardyn's soul with one decisive attack. Ardyn had been unable to resist to any meaningful degree.

With mortal flesh intact, one could not cross over, and so the power of the Lucii was required to leave the body behind. Once crossed over, the soul alone could not properly fight, so again, the power of the Old Kings was needed. No matter which of the two worlds one was in, the power of the Ring of the Lucii would almost certainly be essential.

As Noctis's mind whirled, the fight with Ardyn raged on.

"*This* is the strength of the True King?" Irritation filled Ardyn's voice. "*This* is all the Draconian bestowed?!"

The course of the battle had shown the two to be almost evenly matched. Ardyn seemed unimpressed, as if the fight were wholly insufficient to appease two thousand years' worth of animosity.

"And the god tells me I'm to fall to this pathetic display," he cried. "What insult!"

Noctis recalled the Crystal's final vision of Ardyn, the man yelling with unbridled blood rage.

You say that I live only to die by the hand of the heir to an ill-gotten throne.

That *is the fate the gods have chosen to bestow upon me?!*

Not once have I begged the gods for such a blessing. And I do not intend to kneel before you now!

Nothing matters—none of it. Not the "blessed" gods above nor the accursed kings below. To hell with them all!

All that matters is I have my revenge.

I shall fell the gods.

Noctis had never seen a face so full of hatred in all his life. Of the two thousand years of history he'd seen within the Crystal, nothing came close.

"Insolent whelp!" Ardyn growled at Noctis. "You think ten years is a long time?!"

The fight was tense, and Noctis did not hold back. It wasn't simply a matter of dispatching his opponent anymore—now he had his own particular goals, which required keeping Ardyn alive. So he'd need to land a carefully targeted hit, one with just enough force to take the fight out of Ardyn.

"It is nothing to me! I have lived in darkness for ages!" Ardyn continued, his irritation growing hot.

"Believe me, I know," came Noctis's retort. "You've lived for two thousand years, every moment of which I've seen. I know every detail of your world."

With the Crystal's knowledge, the king was bound to act. The knowledge would weigh him down, end any thought of abandoning his fate, and fuel a sense of duty stronger even than the fear of death. That was why the Draconian had shared the memories recorded in the endless expanse of the Crystal. It was a tactic meant to render Noctis unable to flee his calling as True King. But the gods were gods. They did not know with certainty the mind of man. A burden meant to force one's actions might, if too overwhelming, compel its bearer to seek a different course. The weight on one's shoulders could be shifted and become a new source of strength. Such was the potential of human life.

When Noctis accepted his father's blade in the Crystal, the great burden he'd felt oppressed by changed. It was now the strength that would allow him to move forward without fear.

"Tell me," he asked Ardyn, "do you truly believe the theft of the ring and death of the Draconian will bring you deliverance?"

"Silence!" Ardyn grimaced. His finesse with the blade was gone, and he threw all his weight into each blow. "To hell with you accursed kings and your conniving gods!"

Noctis's comments had touched a nerve. It seemed Ardyn might have had a similar exchange with someone else already. The Accursed's attacks grew frantic, and his guard was down. When the fight began, Noctis had been pressed to find even the slightest opening. Now, Ardyn's movements were sloppy, and Noctis found himself with any number of chances to land his perfect blow.

"Deliverance means nothing to me! I am—!"

Noctis did not let him finish. Calling the Sword of the Father to hand, he thrust straight and true. When the hit landed, Noctis put all his force into it, hurling Ardyn to the ground. Ardyn lay face up, grip loosening from his own summoned blade.

"Do you wish to toy with my life? See me suffer?" The Accursed's voice was hoarse, his breath heavy.

He stared up at Noctis. "Is that why you do not strike at my heart? Finish this. Fulfill your calling. See? The Old Kings . . . they're waiting."

Noctis glanced up. The souls of the Kings of Yore were there, assembled in the courtyard. They must have appeared during the battle, sensing the ring's call close at hand.

Noctis looked back at Ardyn. "Not so long ago, I believed your death would bring an end to the darkness. I set forth to kill you so that dawn might come to the world once more."

Coming to terms with the act would have been another matter, but the execution would have been simple enough. Noctis had only to surrender his life. In exchange, both Ardyn's body and soul would be vanquished finally, and the darkness dispelled. That should have been enough.

"But I was wrong," Noctis continued. "The Draconian aims to bring an end to man and to the Star. Killing you won't change anything."

Once he'd realized that the calling bestowed by Bahamut was no longer relevant, Noctis began to focus on the bigger picture. He realized that it was up to him to ensure a future for the world, for the sake of all the things he'd witnessed inside the Crystal: the lives lived, the people inhabiting the world, and the sanctity of existence itself. That was the future Noctis wished to see.

He tugged his sword free from Ardyn's body. No black particles swirled from the wound. No sign of the usual rapid healing. Perhaps this was the power of the True King. If Noctis had aimed for his heart, the Ardyn in this world might already lay vanquished.

Noctis stared into Ardyn's eyes. "If you'd managed to gain the ring and cross over to the realm beyond, and if you'd managed to defeat the Draconian there, would Eos and its people be safe?"

Ardyn's words came between soft groans. "A possibility . . . perhaps. Not that it is any concern of mine."

If so, allowing Ardyn to cross over to the Beyond might be for the good of all, even if he were doing it for his own selfish reasons. But there was one problem.

"I won't stand for a world whose survival hinges on the sacrifices of others. Not even if that sacrifice is yours," said Noctis.

He would always hate Ardyn for killing Lunafreya, and the urge for revenge ran deep. Still, he was loath to use the man to achieve his own goals; the manipulation of others was the very root of the evil against which Noctis rebelled.

He continued, "Don't get me wrong. I'll never forget the things you did to my friends or the agony you caused Luna. I can't forgive you or let go of my hatred. But I want all the lives on this star to be saved, and you are one part of this world."

Ardyn's clenched jaw quivered. His eyes no longer held a trace of anger or loathing. In them, Noctis saw a flash of something else that was hard to place.

"And besides that," Noctis added, "I made a promise to the Mystic. He begged me to find a way to bring you peace."

Free my brother from his eternal curse, Somnus had pleaded.

Hatred and rage were not the only things that chained Ardyn. His undying body had also brought him long years of torment.

"I don't want there to be any more sacrifices, but if this will bring you peace, I'll allow it."

Noctis pulled the ring from his finger. Ardyn, face still contorted with pain, sat up. A breath escaped his lips, somewhere between sigh and wry laugh.

"How very regal you've become. A true king, indeed."

"Kings of Lucis!" Noctis called out to the specters assembled in the courtyard. "Hear my plea! I hereby entrust the Ring of Light to the man before me. Allow him to use it as you would allow me."

The royal souls floated in silence.

Noctis continued, "I know as do you the blasphemy I suggest. I know that you, whose powers stem from the divine, may be reluctant to do this. For with the ring, this man would endeavor to slay a god. But know this: the Bladekeeper works to bring an end to all mankind. Lucis and all else you labor to protect will be gone forever. Knowing that, would you still waver?!"

One of the thirteen moved forward.

"Rulers of House Caelum. Leaders of Lucis. Heed the plea of one brother for sake of another. Accept Ardyn Lucis Caelum as bearer of the ring."

The soul of the Mystic shed its great suit of armor. Ardyn's eyes widened. Among the thirteen, this one now stood not as an ancient king but as the man as he had been in life.

"Brother, may this serve as a small token of my penance."

"Somnus . . . " Ardyn whispered.

"I dare not hope to ever have your forgiveness. All the same, I will forever apologize for what I have done."

Ardyn's gaze remained fixed, features unmoving. Noctis had watched as Somnus offered an apology like this once before. Back then, he'd been rebuffed in rage. Ardyn's silence seemed as much a sign of reconciliation as might ever be hoped for.

Words from the other kings poured forth, all directed toward Ardyn.

"Man consumed by scourge is no longer man, and so . . . "

" . . . with our strength imparted . . . "

" . . . thou mayest but crumble to dust . . . "

" . . . or ignite with flame and burn alive . . . "

" . . . or suffer in agony equal to death . . . "

" . . . yet knowing that . . . "

" . . . wouldst thou still seek our power?"

Ardyn stood, his balance unsteady as he turned to face the Lucii. He spread his arms wide, his taste for theatrics apparently not dulled by his injuries.

"Crumble to dust, you say? Burn alive? Already have I lived through the worst agony this world has to offer. The pain of which you speak is nothing to me."

The thirteen kings glided closer to encircle Ardyn alone.

"Then so be it . . . "

" . . . thou shalt have our strength . . . "

" . . . to don the ring . . . "

" . . . and ascend the throne . . . "

" . . . where we will await thine arrival."

And here, Noctis saw that it was his father's turn. The thirteenth soul merely nodded without a word, and as if that had been the signal to depart, the Old Kings were gone and the courtyard silent.

Noctis held the ring out to Ardyn.

Ardyn grinned, "I must confess, it's been so long since I've been given a gift—almost two thousand years, in fact—that I've completely forgotten what to say." He gave another dramatic shrug, accepted the ring, then swept his arm to one side, inviting Noctis to make his way past.

"It's best not to keep a lady waiting, wouldn't you say?"

Noctis nodded, and then he was off and running. During the time it took to resolve the situation with Ardyn, the circle around Lunafreya had grown brighter, with more swords arrayed around it.

Inside the Citadel, they saw no trace of the Draconian's avatars. Perhaps damage to the structure and the Crystal it housed really was a risk that Bahamut could not tolerate. Noctis was thankful for not having to expend further time and stamina in battle, but whatever they had saved of both was quickly consumed by another challenge: movement.

Unsurprisingly, the Citadel's power systems were all offline. There were no lights. Doors locked tight by security fail-safes weren't going to open, so they had to backtrack and search for others that would. Between that and groping their way down dark corridors, the trek through the Citadel took time. And the final time sink quickly outweighed any previous frustration.

"Can someone remind me why we didn't just take the elevator?" Prompto let out a heavy sigh as the four trudged up flight after flight of an emergency stairway. "Y'know, instead of trying to climb our way to heaven one step at a time?"

Even Gladio was breathing hard, though apparently not so much as to forgo baiting Prompto. "Yeah, it's a damn mystery. Think it has anything to do with the Citadel being turned into a makeshift airship?"

"Right. Forgot about that," Prompto replied. Then, "Hey, Iggy, you doin' all right back there?"

"Tryin' to use Ignis to score a break? That's low."

"Am I that easy to read?"

"Like a billboard."

"Whatever. I'm fine. I could keep this up all day."

"We'll see about that. In case you hadn't noticed, there hasn't been a day in years."

The situation was dire, but on hearing his friends' banter, Noctis couldn't help but smile. The sense of urgency and worry did not lift, but they no longer seemed to weigh so heavily against Noctis's chest.

Looking back, very little of the journey they'd embarked on had gone as expected, and feelings among the four were hardly in perfect harmony the whole way. There had been disagreements, confrontations, and any number of tense moments. His sense of duty as the king had of course kept Noctis going, but even more important was the fact that he—that *all* of them—kept the faith that good times would follow bad. However much things hurt today, there would always be a tomorrow for them to heal. No matter how big the fight, they'd always reconcile.

"Noct." Ignis's hand landed lightly on Noctis's back. "It will be all right. We shall surely make it in time."

Just like now. His friends were the ones who helped him see that there was always hope.

"I know," he said and patted Ignis's shoulder in response.

When they finally reached the uppermost floor of the Citadel and emerged onto the roof, the darkness outside had grown so thick as to be stifling. The concentrated power of the scourge was palpable.

Lunafreya's strange song continued uninterrupted. The casting circle had begun to flicker at erratic intervals. It was plain that the spell was nearing completion. Teraflare was almost upon them.

"Great. We're here. Now how are we supposed to stop it?" Prompto asked uncertainly.

"No clue," responded Gladio. "But we gotta try. I'm guessing we can't just pick her up and walk on outta here."

The words had barely left his mouth when a whistling sound descended, like blades slicing through air. The avatars. It seemed Bahamut deemed the rooftop far enough away from the Crystal to risk a fight—or close enough to Lunafreya that there wasn't any other choice.

"Noct, you've no time for the riffraff. Leave them to us," Ignis instructed.

"Right," Noctis said, and hurled his sword at one of the foes gliding near. In a flash, he'd reached it and was aiming again. The only way he could get to Lunafreya was through warping, but she was too high above the rooftop to be in direct range. So he would have to go from enemy to enemy, using them like stepping stones through sky. As Noctis streaked from one foe to the next, he felt bladed wings brush against his arms and torso. Pain seared through him, but he did not slow. If he stopped, he would fall.

"Luna!" he cried. She was close now. But haste made him careless—an enemy he'd thought firmly within his grip suddenly twisted, and Noctis was tumbling through open air. By the time he realized what had happened, the wind was already roaring in his ears.

He tried to level his aim for another warp-strike but caught only air. He was falling too fast. Bitterness welled up within him. So this was how it ended. What a waste.

As his heart cried out that it was not ready for the end, a new voice boomed in his ears.

"Rise, O Chosen. The pact with the Oracle shall be honored."

A funnel of flame twisted about Noctis, breaking his fall.

"The Infernian?" Noctis wondered aloud. "Ifrit offers me aid?"

Before he could wonder why, a vision played in his mind. It was like the other times he'd received a divine blessing: he saw Lunafreya's labors as she forged the covenant. This time she stood face-to-face with the God of Fire. Her skin was the same inky black Noctis had seen in the throne room. Although she had already turned physically, at the time of the vision, she still seemed to retain consciousness. Noctis heard her plea, *Let the king have your blessing!*

It is I, Lunafreya, blood of the Oracle. In exchange for your release from the bonds of the scourge, lend your power to the Crystal's Chosen King.

She shouted it at the top of her lungs, her legs quaking beneath her. She was barely managing to stand. Every bit of strength in her body and soul was gathered tightly and expended for sake of the king, as she had always done. And now once again, as Noctis plummeted through open sky, it was Lunafreya's action that brought him aid.

This time, he would not lose her. He swore in his heart that he would see her safe.

"The revelation of Ifrit is at hand," the Infernian proclaimed, and Noctis felt himself rising high into the air, buoyed by the god's roaring flames. He was headed straight toward Lunafreya.

Noctis glanced down, seeing not only the Infernian below, but also Shiva, the Glacian.

"The gods have heard the Oracle's prayer. Let the Promised King receive aid divine," she announced.

And then the other gods of the trials appeared: Titan, the Archaean; Ramuh, the Fulgurian; and Leviathan, the Hydraean. The five gods that existed alongside the Star, gathered under darkened sky.

"Luna! I'm almost there!" Noctis called.

Another moment and he'd be at her side. Just a little farther . . .

The Darkness waxes full.

The Draconian's booming voice shook both heaven and earth. The intricate casting circles around Lunafreya expanded outward to touch the twelve summoned blades. From each of the blades came a blinding flare: each was as the sun at midday, a ball of burning light and heat.

Go forth, O Blades. Wreak destruction upon the foolish insolence below.

He was too late. Noctis looked on in horror as twelve orbs of fierce incandescence descended upon the land. The orbs grew brighter yet, until Noctis could keep his eyes open no longer.

"The time is come. Defend the Star!"

The Glacian's cry shook the surroundings. Noctis heard the rumble of earth, the crackle of lightning, the roar of waves, and the blaze of hellfire. Even with his eyes closed, bright white light filled his vision. He had no hope of seeing what was going on. He could only hear and feel the clash and collision of massive entities locked in battle.

Five gods fought against the catastrophe unleashed by the sixth. Though Noctis had been told it would be so, still he was frozen in shock. He hadn't arrived in time. Grief overcame him. He felt strength leave his limbs and his body fall limp.

The silence that followed fell suddenly and completely, as if all sound were gone from the world. Slowly, vision returned to Noctis's eyes. Far in the distance, he saw a crumbled mountain. The glowing red lava flowing around the rubble told him it had once been the Rock of Ravatogh. If so, that meant the vast empty space stretching out before the peak was once the ridged crater of the Disc of Cauthess. No trace of the Disc remained, as if the land there had been scooped away entirely. At the edge of the destruction, he saw the cityscape of Lestallum.

In the Great War of Old, four of the Six had managed to protect the Star from the threat of Teraflare. This time, five had resisted, and even then their combined power fell short of stopping it. Yet the gods had done well. They had averted complete devastation. That some portion of Eos still suffered was testament to the overwhelming intensity of Teraflare's power.

Their five divine saviors lay strewn across the land, facedown, unmoving. The Draconian's voice came down from on high, mocking their weariness and pain.

Mortal fools shielded by fools divine.

The five on the Star are spent, and to what end?

So be it. Since folly persists, those devoted to it may perish alongside their wards.

The Draconian's voice was firm and strong; he seemed untroubled by weakness or fatigue. Lunafreya's plan had failed. Teraflare had been cast, but the Draconian's strength had not been sapped. He had not drifted into slumber. The Bladekeeper, it seemed, was not so easily overcome.

Somehow, Noctis had been returned to the Citadel courtyard.

"Luna!" he called, scanning the surroundings. "Where are you?!"

He flicked his gaze up, to the place where the casting circle had been moments before. Lunafreya still hung there, her skin deathly pale, as if all the darkness she'd harbored had been drawn out and consumed by the terrible spell. New worry crept into Noctis's mind. What if the spell had sapped her vitality as well? Was she still alive? He tried to banish the dire thought from his mind, to focus on the moment.

Lunafreya's body lurched to one side.

"No!" Noctis shouted.

He ran across the courtyard. She was slipping from the sky, soon to plummet far to the ground below, discarded by the Draconian like garbage; her usefulness for the spell had been expended, and the god had no need of her now. Noctis's mind flared with anger at the god who allowed her to fall. The Bladekeeper saw them all as nothing more than pawns to be used and thrown away.

Noctis sprang into the air, leaping up off the edge of the Citadel's floating island. *Please let me catch her*, he begged silently, arms outstretched. He felt his fingertips graze Lunafreya's body and poured all his strength into his arms, reaching desperately to draw her in. Suddenly, her full weight was settled against his chest. He'd caught her. But now both of them were hurtling toward the ground far below.

Noctis twisted in the air to face the Citadel and flung his blade at it. Without a clear line of sight, he had no sense of where the sword lodged itself and thus no idea where they were warping.

With Lunafreya still held tight in his arms, he felt himself slam against a mercilessly hard surface. And then the world went dark.

She heard a voice calling her name yet again. *Luna*.

It was a voice she could not place at first.

A field of sylleblossoms extended in every direction, as far as the eye could see. The flowers gently bowed and nodded in the breeze. Lunafreya stood alone.

The sky was still dim but seemed to be growing brighter, as if dawn approached. But the flowers at her feet were not touched with morning dew, nor could she smell their fragrance. They were simply there in sight, the familiar blossoms fluttering in the wind.

This is a dream, she thought. *I'm almost certain of it*.

The light grew. It reminded her of her beloved, as if his smile had turned to rays of warmth.

"Noctis!" she cried out.

"Luna!" she heard him reply, and then she saw the Noctis she had known as a child, when she was twelve and he was eight. She looked down at herself and realized that she, too, was again a child.

"So you came to see me once more," she said.

"Yeah. Just like I said I would," he replied.

There was that smile she loved, the one that had been in her heart all these years, giving her strength, always and forever.

"It was all our friends," Noctis said. "They brought me to you."

He announced it with a hint of pride. *You are blessed to be surrounded by such wonderful people*, she began to say, when she realized that she, too, was blessed to have such good companions at her side.

"I . . . " She hesitated. "I, too, made it here thanks to much help from others."

A gust of wind snatched up some of the sylleblossoms, sending petals swirling about. Flower and light filled her vision, and she involuntarily shut her eyes against the glare. The wind stopped. Lunafreya opened her eyes.

Before her now stood the man. Oh, how she had longed to see him.

"My dearest Noctis . . . "

There was a mountain of things she wanted to tell him. She knew the time they had would not suffice for even a small portion, but she could at least say the most important.

"As Oracle, I lived bound to my calling before all. But now my eyes are open. In the short time I shared with Sol, I finally learned to value the words in my heart. And that is why . . . "

Noctis gave a nod, as if encouraging her to continue.

"That is why I was finally able to choose freedom, to dedicate my life to my own desires, rather than surrender it to calling or command. I was able to live for *me*."

"Luna . . . " His voice was soft and gentle.

Yes. This was Noctis's voice. This was how he sounded now that he was grown. She'd never had a chance to hear it before, but strangely, she somehow knew it already. Why?

"This may be our true and final parting, so please, allow me to speak from my heart."

It was strange that she should know his voice, but it did not matter. All she cared about was that he was here, before her eyes, and she'd been granted one last chance to tell him how she truly felt. It was all she could ask for.

"Noctis, would that I could live by your side."

The sylleblossoms began to blur, and the petals in the wind seemed to melt and wash away. Lunafreya sank, headed for the ocean floor.

"Noctis!" she cried, thrusting one hand out.

It was the moment she had died in Altissia, replaying all over again.

"Luna!"

But unlike that day in Altissia, this time she could hear him. His voice reached her with perfect clarity.

"Then live!" he shouted. "Stay with me forever!"

Lunafreya's eyes opened wide. She strained upward, reaching toward him with all her strength. She did not want to be pulled away from him. Not again. Not this time.

Her outstretched fingers swept through the water.

She felt them brush against something surprisingly warm.

Then live! Stay with me forever!

The sound of Noctis's own shout stirred him awake. He'd been with Lunafreya in a sylleblossom field, and then it had been that terrible day in Altissia, with her body sinking beneath the waves, his hand stretched out toward her.

Noctis, would that I could live by your side.

Had he imagined those words? Was it another dream? This time, he thought for certain he'd managed to grab hold of her hand. He remembered the feeling of her soft skin and delicate wrists.

"Noct, are you all right?"

He opened his eyes. A concerned-looking Prompto sat on the ground next to him, peering into his face. Beyond Prompto's shoulders, he saw Gladio and Ignis.

"I'm fine," he said, head beginning to clear. "How about you guys? Holding up?"

His Shield was the one to answer. "Remember who you're talking to. Who's gonna stop the three of us?"

Noctis tried to lift himself upright. That was when he realized he was still holding Lunafreya securely in his arms.

"Luna?!" he exclaimed in surprise.

Her eyes were shut, and her face was deathly pale. Noctis pressed his fingers to her neck. Her pulse felt weak and somewhat erratic, but it was there. Lunafreya was unconscious but alive. She was *alive.*

Relief swept through Noctis's body. He'd managed to make it after all. This time, he'd gotten her back.

"Are you able to stand?" Ignis asked.

"Yeah."

He didn't have time to be sitting around. He gently laid Lunafreya on the ground beside him, then hauled himself to his feet.

"Looks like you guys took a beating."

All three of his retainers were badly bruised and scratched. On recovering consciousness, Noctis's first thought had been of their safety. Gladio had brushed off his concern with his usual brazen air, but Noctis wasn't fooled. Their battle with the avatars wouldn't have been an easy one.

"Mind looking after Luna for a bit?" asked Noctis.

The battle wasn't over yet. Bahamut had neither fallen into slumber nor depleted his strength. However, it occurred to Noctis that the conspicuous absence of the avatars in the sky suggested that Teraflare had drained the Draconian more than he was letting on.

It was Prompto who voiced the group's concern.

"We'll take care of her," he began, but added, "You sure you're gonna be all right on your own?"

Noctis needed to take the fight to the sky. To get up there, he'd have to warp. He would've preferred to take his companions along, but it wasn't an option. They'd have to stay behind.

Noctis gave a decisive nod. "Yeah. I got this."

He had a promise to Lunafreya to uphold. One he had made way back when they were kids, sitting beside each other in the manor at Tenebrae. Lunafreya had explained that only the True King, anointed by the Crystal, could purge the Star of its scourge.

She'd promised to help him see it through, and he'd responded, *I won't let you down.*

When he'd said it, a glow of happiness touched Lunafreya's cheeks.

Today, he'd see that promise kept, along with their new promise, to be together forevermore.

Noctis set his sights on the Bladekeeper, floating proudly in the sky high above.

"Irony. The one thing of which life is never in short supply," Ardyn grumbled, as he climbed the steps to the Lucian throne.

He'd never had the honor of sitting the throne. In fact, it was the denial of it that had prompted him to walk the path of darkness, stained red with blood. As he awaited Noctis's return from the Crystal, he'd established himself in Insomnia, making a point of lounging upon the throne as an affront to all, to emphasize that it was merely a chair like any other. That it was not his place to sit was the sum of its appeal.

But now he was ascending it in truth.

"And that the True King would allow it," he mused. "Even after two thousand years, it seems life can still manage to provide a surprise or two."

He settled down onto the seat.

"He cannot forgive and continues to hate. Yet he would see me find peace. My, how the wayward prince has grown."

He recalled Noctis as he had appeared during their first encounter at Galdin. The young prince had been almost an entirely different person.

I can't forgive you or let go of my hatred. But I want all the lives on this star to be saved, and you are one part of this world.

Those words had struck him deeply. Noctis was but a whelp, yet Ardyn, with two millennia at his disposal, had never been able to find it in his heart to offer Lucis quarter despite his hatred. Noctis's magnanimity seemed only to emphasize Ardyn's own shortcomings.

Still, he wasn't headed to the throne now to anoint himself the hero. Not after all these years. He would use the ring, yes, but not for Noctis or for the world or for anyone else. This was an act taken to fulfill his own selfish ends.

"My revenge is finally at hand," he muttered as he slipped the ring upon his finger.

"Kings of Lucis . . . come to me!"

He thrust his sword down at his feet. The Lucii appeared, weapons in hand, each in turn charging directly at Ardyn.

It was like a blue-white flame boring a hole straight through his chest. In the courtyard, he'd claimed to have lived through the worst agony the world had to offer, vainglorious of everything he'd endured. Not a moment of it compared to the pain he suffered now. Not even the false Aera with her false Trident conjured up by the Draconian had managed to impart such torment.

At each stab from the spectral monarchs, his consciousness very nearly left him. The kings had warned he might crumble to dust, and now Ardyn understood that it was no metaphorical threat.

Still, he had to endure. He could not faint yet.

"This . . . will not . . . stay me," he said through gritted teeth.

He forced his eyes open against the pain. Above him only the Mystic remained, hovering still.

"Come at me, Somnus!"

And then, when the Blade of the Mystic pierced his heart, he heard a faint whisper.

"Farewell, Brother."

The sky was still dark, and Noctis was not sure why. Wasn't all the scourge supposed to have been drawn into Teraflare? Though the spell had been executed, darkness persisted.

Either the Draconian's spell hadn't been fully charged, or the pall cast over the Star was so thick that even the Bladekeeper's attack could not consume it all.

As Noctis approached the Bladekeeper, the god's voice resounded in the dark sky.

Still the mortal fool would persist in his defiance.

A wayward king seeks to turn god-gifted strength against the selfsame god.

Abandon such folly. What can one frail creature hope to do against the divine?

Noctis tightened his grip on his sword, undeterred by the Bladekeeper's derision.

He shouted back, "I do not pretend my power is my own! But it is no gift of yours!"

In all likelihood, the ring itself had been fashioned by the Draconian. But the power gathered within was of the kings of Lucis. It was a power born of mortal life and death. The ancient monarchs each gathered this strength, honed it, and passed it on from one generation to the next.

Though not almighty gods, humans were by no means frail. Noctis recalled the many past foes over whom he thought he might never prevail. He had persevered, slowly amassing strength, until each foe that once intimidated him was easily surpassed.

"Watch as the mortals you mock prove your own undoing. This is one battle I refuse to lose," Noctis growled. He hurled his blade straight at the Draconian, warping in for a strike. It was similar to his strategy against the Hydraean during the trial in Altissia. Back then, it had been all he could do to cling to the Tidemother's scales.

The blade drove deep into the Draconian's shoulder. Not a moment later, Noctis was knocked away by a force far beyond that of the Hydraean. Bahamut's strike was too swift and too powerful to phase through or parry.

Noctis plummeted. Soon he would slam against the ground below. Death's embrace was at hand, and there was nothing he could do.

And then, when all seemed lost, his fall was arrested. He hung suspended in the sky.

Noctis looked down. He saw the Infernian, risen again to stop Noctis's plunge. The rest of the Six, too, struggled upright to rejoin the fray.

"Five more are the gods who watch this star," rumbled the Infernian. "And they abide none who seek to harm the world. Not even the sixth."

The five deities were weak from countering Teraflare. Noctis could see that almost all of their strength was spent. Still they stood and continued to lend their aid.

"Fly, O Chosen," the Glacian called, her hands spilling waves of countless ice shards across the sky. Noctis warped from one to the next, once more approaching the Draconian to strike.

It was a pattern he repeated over and over: a strike at the vast deity, a leap back to safety, then up the icy steps again.

When the Draconian swung one giant arm to knock away the ice, the Hydraean swooped in to carry Noctis back up. When Noctis struck again, his blade found home together with bolts of judgment issued from the Fulgurian's staff. The Archaean's great fists served as shields to drive back the Draconian's counterattacks, and a whirl of hellfire enveloped the Draconian's lustrous black mail in searing tendrils of flame. The Glacian unleashed a new wave of ice shards for Noctis to climb.

He attacked relentlessly together with the power of the five gods. Again and again, he executed a sequence of swings, thrusts, and warps. His fatigue mounted, but never did he waver in the assault.

Everything I have, he told himself, the mantra already repeated in his mind more times than he could count. Nothing would be held back.

Finally, the Draconian seemed to falter under the incessant assault. There was a loud, sharp sound, and a crack traced its way across the god's mask. This was their chance.

"God of Fire and Goddess of Ice," Noctis called, "Lend my blade fury!"

Gelid wind and infernal flame wrapped Noctis's glaive with redoubled power. When the blow connected with the Draconian's mask, the crack snaked from one edge to the other. Then the mask was broken and falling away with a terrible shrieking noise of rent metal. Noctis saw the face behind it and froze.

At first, the only word he managed to utter was, "How . . . ?"

It was a visage he'd not laid eyes upon directly, but the similarity was undeniable. It was like Somnus's face. It was like Noctis's own.

"Was it all planned? From the very beginning?" murmured Noctis.

Had Somnus been fashioned in the god's own image to serve as Founder King? Or had it been coincidence? Perhaps the younger brother of House Caelum had simply grown up to look so much like the Bladekeeper as to garner the god's favor. The workings of the Draconian's mind were something Noctis might never grasp. Regardless, the resemblance was clear. The countenances of the first and final kings of Lucis were eerily similar to Bahamut's own.

Anger at the god swept through Noctis once more. "How long do you expect us to abide the games you play with our lives?!"

A god who treated the mortals he watched over as merely tools or playthings was not deserving of faith. Someone had to stop the Bladekeeper, and Noctis would be the one to do it, shared likeness be damned. He lifted his glaive high and rushed in.

I know this place, Ardyn thought. He'd seen it once, in the future shared by the Draconian, wherein Ardyn died at Noctis's hands. But the sense of familiarity didn't derive from just the vision. Somehow, he'd known this place for ages. He'd not seen it with his eyes, but his soul had been trapped here for millennia.

He seemed to be gently falling through space but knew not whether the sensation was real or imagined. Before his eyes floated the Draconian—the one that existed here in the world beyond.

Begone. This is no place for the Accursed to tread.

"Believe me," said Ardyn, "of that much I am *painfully* aware."

He clenched the hand wearing the ring into a fist, and slowly and deliberately held it forward. The world before his eyes wavered as the thirteen Kings of Yore shimmered into view. Twelve hovered in formation. The last was at Ardyn's side in a silent gesture of fraternal support.

"Hmph. Who could have foreseen a day when I'd ask *you* for aid?" Ardyn said.

"My sword is yours, Ardyn. Today we fight as brothers."

Ardyn.

They'd still been taking turns at chess when Somnus last called him by name. Two boys so inseparable that a day spent apart invited jests of impending rain from a clear sky. Brothers.

"Today we fight to end it all."

Their childhood rapport. Their contesting ideals. The hatred in the wake of betrayal. All of it would be gone.

The power of kings flowed into Ardyn via the ring. Then, in a burst of light fierce enough to rend Ardyn's soul, the thirteen shot forth, converging into a spearpoint thrust, an arrow flying true, a savage bullet lusting for the heart. They ripped into the Draconian's armored chest with such force that by the time the god flinched, the battle was already won. Perhaps it had all occurred in an instant, too quickly for Bahamut to react. Or perhaps on this side, souls were simply unable to twist and dodge as freely as desired.

Insolent fool. With the death of the Bladekeeper comes the loss of the Crystal. All of the Six shall fall.

Why persist in this fatuity?

"You ask . . . as if I give a damn," came Ardyn's labored response.

Let the gods perish. Let the iniquitous Crystal break into a million pieces and Ardyn's soul with it. Naught else mattered.

"As if... this isn't what I've wanted... all along."

Consciousness was fading along with his soul. Next he would shatter, and soon after, the shards would vanish into nothing. Ardyn knew and welcomed his fate. If every memory of his existence should disappear forever, all the better.

"Nay, my love. Even if all others forget your name, I will always remember."

Ardyn flinched. "Aera? Is it truly you?"

Another illusion. Surely it had to be. Another product of his wretched imagination. But whether false or true, at least Aera was here before his eyes. He once more admired her golden hair, fluttering in the breeze, and gazed into her eyes the color of the sea, the loveliest color he'd known in all his days.

"Oh, Aera," he told her. "Pray be with me always."

And in that final moment of existence, as his soul crumbled to dust and began to disperse, Aera spoke, and Ardyn heard her.

The darkness split. Fissures ran through the sky itself, and shards of the heavens began to rain down upon them.

"What's happening?!" Noctis cried.

The Star—their very world—shuddered and screamed. Between the cracks in the sky, something else shone through. It was the color of the deep sea. A color Noctis had seen before.

"That's the realm beyond. Why is it... ?"

He could guess one thing with confidence: Ardyn must have managed to defeat the Draconian.

One foolish act trumped by another greater still.

Such havoc serves only to harm those who wreak it.

Without the guidance of the Light, mankind will fail, doomed ever to repeat the cycle of folly.

The Bladekeeper's voice resounded with intensity anew. But to Noctis's ears, it was the obstreperous posturing of one on the verge of death.

Always have mortals lived under patronage divine.

Though guided by the Light, they war among themselves and defile the Star.

How could mortals hope to survive alone in a godless world?

If divine patronage meant man was subject to destruction at a god's whim, then they were better off without it. They'd been treated as tools, disposed of once their utility was over. If the gods thought such selfishness to be guidance, it was better for mankind to live on alone.

Noctis looked upon the Bladekeeper and said, "We may be foolish and repeat our mistakes, but we do not stand still. Mankind is always moving forward."

And then he gripped his glaive and yelled a battle cry, sending himself hurtling toward the Bladekeeper with one final warp-strike. He felt the impact shudder down the length of his blade. A crack snaked its way through the god's armor plating as in the mask before. When the blade was lodged deep, and it felt as though it could go no farther, Noctis leaned into the grip with all his might. A wail of pain erupted from the Bladekeeper. Noctis held the glaive tight as the god thrashed against him.

And suddenly, the sword was free, and the Bladekeeper was fading, his mammoth form breaking apart into countless tiny fragments. The lustrous black armor fell with an ear-splitting clangor. The deity shuddered and spasmed, as if determined to fight to the bitter end. Finally the thrashing quieted, and the Draconian lay still.

There was a roaring sound, and Noctis looked up to see all the scourge in the sky and across the world rushing in great, sweeping waves toward the Citadel. They amassed at a point of blinding brightness: the Crystal. As the Crystal drew in the darkness and shed its blue light, the Citadel began to shake violently.

"The whole thing's gonna fall," Noctis muttered.

The shaking grew more violent still. Noctis saw his companions and Lunafreya down on the jagged expanse of the courtyard. If the Citadel fell, they'd have little chance of survival. Even if the Citadel stayed afloat, the intensity of the vibrations might send them flying off the side.

He had to act quickly.

"God of Earth! Lend me your strength!" called Noctis.

The darkness continued to flood into the Crystal like a foul current. It seemed the stone was intent on consuming every last bit of the Starscourge. It wrenched itself free of the Citadel, shooting through the structure's walls, then flew high into the air. The darkness followed, still flowing in as the Crystal shed its intense rays of light.

The light grew and spread, and the darkness steadily shrank away.

Then at the moment when all darkness and light had become one, the Crystal shattered. Particles of darkness and shards of light scattered together throughout the sky, then melted away into nothingness. The border between this world and the Beyond trembled, grew thin, and then vanished altogether.

With another great shudder, the Citadel started to crumble. The walls, floors, ceilings, and stairways were being ripped apart into a rain of debris that hurtled toward the earth.

"Hurry!" Noctis called, as he rode the Archaean's massive palm to the edge of the courtyard. He jumped down, gathering Lunafreya in his arms and lifting her up to Titan's palm. Prompto sprang onto Titan's hand, pulling Ignis up after him. Gladio climbed on next. The courtyard began to wrench apart, and Noctis threw his glaive onto the Archaean's palm in a warp-strike, the great flagstones falling away not a moment later.

Titan ferried them safely to the ground. As they were dropped off, they looked to the sky and saw the now abandoned Citadel, a mere husk of its former glory, plummet to the ground.

For a good while, the narrow escape left them all quiet. Gladio's lips were pursed tight. Even Prompto's usual garrulity had vanished; he seemed to have forgotten how to speak at all as he watched the Citadel meet its demise. Ignis, though unable to see the fall, would have known what happened from the rumbling and crashing of the impact. His head was bowed as if in silent prayer.

Lunafreya still lay unconscious. Dark thoughts reared their ugly heads in Noctis's mind, whispering that she might never awaken. After all, it was the Draconian who had granted Lunafreya new life. With the god dead, would she not perish, too?

From behind, he heard the voice of the Glacian. "O Chosen King."

He turned to find her in her guise as Messenger.

"The time for parting is nigh. The world is now in mortal hands. No more gods. No Crystal."

"Gentiana . . . "

"Under the king's rule, the Star shall surely . . . "

Gentiana trailed off, as if another thought had occurred to her. She turned, lowering one porcelain white hand to brush her fingertips across Lunafreya's eyelids.

"A farewell gift, O King. Blessings for a friend."

And with those words, Lunafreya's eyelids twitched ever so gently.

"Luna!" cried Noctis.

Lunafreya opened her eyes.

"Noctis . . . " she whispered.

Oh, thank the gods, he tried to say, but found himself unable to speak. He simply held Lunafreya in silence. He thought he heard a whispering voice say, *May happiness fill your life together,* but when Noctis looked up, Gentiana was already gone.

In Tenebrae, the Messenger had once told a young Noctis that it was "heartening to see the future king and the Oracle enjoy such familiarity." The Messenger had smiled as she said the words, and he could still remember her gentle eyes upon him even now.

"Thanks, Gentiana. For everything."

Tears welled up in Lunafreya's eyes.

"Oh, dear Gentiana . . . thank you."

Gentiana had left them with one last irreplaceable gift. Not as a goddess watching over the Star, but as a friend. Noctis gently held Lunafreya's hand, vowing in his heart that he would never let her go and never lose her again, come what may.

Their quiet moment was interrupted by a sudden loud shout from Prompto. "Check it out! Over there!"

They turned to find him standing nearby, and followed the line of his outstretched arm. Noctis squinted as a bright light struck his eyes. An incandescent strip peeked over the horizon, slowly rising into the arc of a circle that shone ever brighter.

"Is that . . . ?" Lunafreya asked in a small whisper.

Noctis turned to look into her eyes. He opened his mouth to answer, only for Gladio to grunt a response from behind. "The dawn."

Noctis looked up in surprise, then narrowed his eyes in exaggerated displeasure.

"Wow. Way to ruin the moment. Pretty sure *I* was supposed to say that."

Ignis chuckled, and then Noctis, Prompto, Gladio, and Lunafreya were laughing, too, a brightness of spirit that filled the air as all welcomed the first morning light to grace the Star in years.

M.E. 76?

Darkness has departed, and dawn again shines upon the world. The Six and the Crystal are no more. The two realms are become one. And the mysterious powers once bestowed upon mankind have ceased to function.

The once grand expanse of Insomnia is now an immense crater in the ground. The Crown City's loss is softened, if only slightly, by its long years spent abandoned; no loss of life accompanied the devastation.

Efforts to rebuild it have yet to materialize, hindered by the city's remote location and connection to the mainland by means of a single bridge. However, in an era without god or Crystal, the purpose around which Insomnia formed is also gone. For the time being, the recovery of Eos's other regions is more pressing. It may be decades hence when buildings stand again in Insomnia and people fill its streets. Even then, the shape the city takes will likely bear little resemblance to the Crown City of the Kingdom of Lucis.

At one edge of Insomnia's crater are the remains of the Citadel. It has towered there ever since its plummet from on high, visible even across the water in Leide. One is hard-pressed not to see it as a funerary monument for the abandoned city and fallen kingdom.

Across the continent lies Lestallum, a bustling city forced to grow denser still during its time serving as the last bastion of human civilization. Though partially damaged by Teraflare, clever and rapid preparations for evacuation ensured that nearly all its people escaped harm. That the EXINERIS power plant was spared any damage at all ensured the city's steady recovery following the attack.

The territories of the former Niflheim Empire are now freed from ice and snow, the warming perhaps induced by Teraflare's immense heat or as a consequence of the Glacian's departure. The tundra is now a vast wetland, a ready source of fertile ground for the settlers who are sure to surge in number with time.

Tenebrae, having escaped the brunt of the world's destruction, is the city that revived most rapidly and true to its legacy. Care was paid first to the old Fenestala Manor and its surround, a testament to the faith and devotion of the Tenebrean people.

Altissia, the splendid City on the Sea, rises in defiance of its many suffered misfortunes. Already half-destroyed by the Hydraean's trial and deteriorated from a decade's abandonment, the city was again ravaged as Teraflare wreaked havoc upon the Star's tides.

Despite its catastrophes, Altissia's recovery has been astonishingly swift. Demolished waterways are reconstructed, damaged buildings repaired, lost structures rebuilt. Perhaps most heartening of all is the restoration of the lovely bridges found throughout the city. The people of Altissia accomplished this in less than a year following dawn's return to the world.

Camelia Claustra, the ever capable First Secretary of the Accordo Protectorate, played no small part in that triumph. But another factor of significance may have been at play. In the days before the darkness spread, Altissia had been chosen as the site for the marriage of Noctis Lucis Caelum and Lunafreya Nox Fleuret. A decade later, that dream would finally be realized. Surely awareness of the celebration to come lifted the city's spirits and bolstered its resolve to see the recovery hastened. Or perhaps such an interpretation is simply the fond delusion of a doting parent.

A new wedding dress was commissioned, its design matching the one of ten years earlier. The patterns for the dress, the legacy of a master dressmaker, were carried personally from Altissia to Lestallum in the evacuation during the years of darkness. They'd been kept safe in the City of Light until the return of the dawn.

Preparation of the cake was entrusted to Coctura Arlund, head chef at Mother of Pearl in Galdin Quay. She came up with a new recipe for the occasion, splendid in both taste and appearance.

On the day of the ceremony, crowds thronged outside Palazzo Altemeria. Many were the residents of Altissia in attendance, along with an untold number of travelers from Tenebrae, Gralea, Lestallum, and all manner of places far and wide. Cheers resounded for the newlywed couple, symbol of the peace, on their emergence from the palace.

Present at the ceremony were the many dear friends and companions of the bride and groom. On the right side of the aisle were many who helped see my son through his long journey from Insomnia to Altissia.

On the left stood those who had served House Fleuret at Fenestala Manor. Among them was one young woman grown beyond recognition; a decade ago she must have been but a child. Now she stood with tears welling in her eyes and cheeks flushed with pride, as overjoyed by the occasion as the happy bride herself.

I thought to ask Ravus who the young woman might be, but alas, he was overwhelmed by the occasion and not for words. The sight of his dearest sister walking down the aisle in a dress of pure white doubtlessly affected him greatly. Thus, I have saved my inquiry for a future occasion, of which we are sure to have many.

That I might see Noctis take Lunafreya's hand in his and watch as the two of them take their first steps in matrimony was a joy beyond any dream. That joy was redoubled by the sight of so many who wished them well.

I owe all of you my eternal gratitude.

To Cor, for your long and steadfast watch over the Crown City. It was the labors of the Crownsguard that allowed Insomnia to endure against the daemons until return of her king. I can only imagine your ordeals during the years of night. You forever have my thanks.

To Cid, for guiding my wayward, untraveled son. I eagerly await the time when we might sit together again, drinking until the dawn. However, I hope that day will not come too soon. Please, if you would, look after my son a while longer.

To Cindy, for breathing renewed life into the Regalia. Seeing the car again brought Noctis great joy, and though his own appreciation is already effusive, I would offer mine as well.

To Gladiolus, for the stern discipline you brought to Noctis's life, patiently bearing his protests and complaints; and to Ignis, for ever and always supporting Noctis as both a friend and an elder brother; and to dear Prompto, for being at Noctis's side because of the person he is and not his title. To you three, I cannot express thanks enough. You have done more for Noctis and for me than you may ever know.

To Lunafreya, for seeing the ring to my son, and for standing beside him in the struggle to ensure a future for the world. As I am sure you must also see, the wayward boy has grown into a man of whom I could not be more proud. Please watch over him for me. Now and forevermore.

And to Noctis, my son, congratulations. May the future you two share be overflowing with joy.

The End

Concept Art and Illustrations

Featuring commentary from the *Final Fantasy XV* Development Team, the art and information provided herein refer to the content of this novel and the planning materials of the downloadable content games.

A piece of key art used in brainstorming sessions during the early development of *FFXV*, this illustration depicts Lunafreya as she emerges from death in Noctis's hour of need, assisting the True King by way of an ultimate spell during the game's final battle. Though the image didn't make it into the main game, it had a profound and lasting impression on the development team, and it was slated for use as the key art depicting the final battle in *Episode Noctis*.

A moment shared between Ardyn and Aera at the height of their love. This scene serves a pivotal function in *Episode Ardyn*, as it provides a glimpse of a completely new side to the titular character, who displays a tenderness impossible to imagine of him at the time of the main game. The relationship between Ardyn and Aera corresponds to that of Noctis and Lunafreya, which is what prompted the decision to surround the pair with fields of wheat, implying themes of life and abundance, and reminiscent of the field of sylleblossoms in Tenebrae.

Verstael retrieving Ardyn from his cell on Angelgard. Though this scene does not appear in the animated short film "Episode Ardyn: Prologue," it is enacted in the DLC, where it serves to mark the transition from the opening narrative to actual gameplay.

Produced during the early development stage of *Episode Ardyn*, this illustration depicts Ardyn's determination to have his revenge on his brother, Somnus, and the Kingdom of Lucis, even if it means succumbing to darkness.

The development team's main goal in producing *Episode Ardyn* was to provide a more nuanced glimpse of the titular character, revealing emotions and expressions far removed from what we see of him at the time of the main game. Having already come to know the sardonic, nonchalant Ardyn of Noctis's era, we now experience the unbridled anger he feels toward his brother, Somnus, reminisce with him about happy times with Aera, and grieve with him over her death. By sharing these new facets of Ardyn's personality, the team hoped to allow players to enjoy and

Design for Somnus began with reference to Noctis. The True King served as a base from which the design team developed a harsher, more pragmatic individual who could serve as a foil to the Ardyn of the past. Ultimately, Somnus's character would settle as one that shared a number of visual similarities with Noctis while possessing a vastly contrasting personality.

Ifrit frozen in ice. After discovery by Verstael at the Rock of Ravatogh, where the Infernian had slumbered since the Great War of Old, the Astral was kept encased in ice and transported to an imperial research facility, where his body would be subjected to Verstael's experiments and used to further the empire's magiteknology.

WALL AMPLIFIER

Concept art for the devices used to amplify the strength of the Wall manifested by the ruler of Lucis. Early in the development of *FFXV*, the original idea was that the amplifiers themselves would project the barrier. The energy drawn from a Guardian enshrined within would travel from the central dias up through a channel in the ceiling and out of the top of the structure.

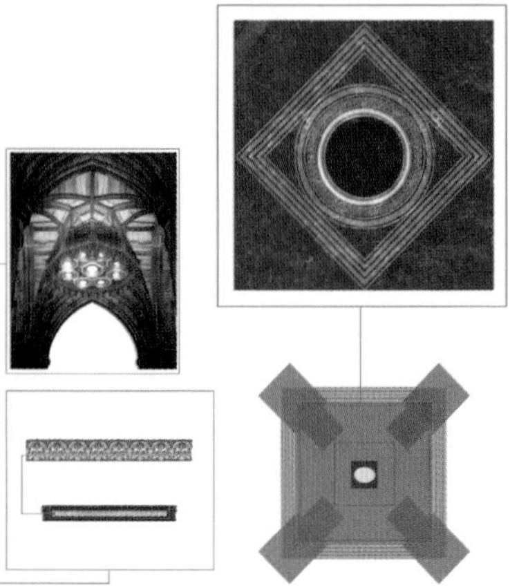

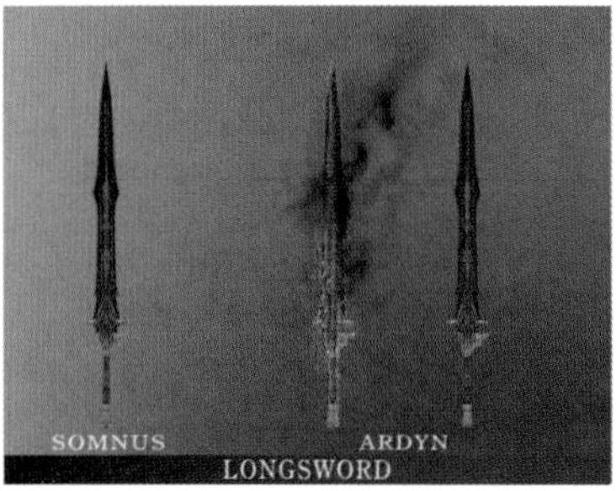

The sword wielded by Somnus would ultimately continue on with the Lucian line as one of the Royal Arms. A second blade of matching design was entrusted to Somnus's elder brother, Ardyn, the two weapons twins in all but color. But as Ardyn began to absorb power from the daemons, his sword would go on to possess sinister properties and appearance.

Stationed around Insomnia to thwart enemy invasion, Guardians are protectors of the Crown City modeled after the Kings of Yore. As they exist separately from the Old Wall, they do not have access to Royal Arms. Shuriken- and mace-style weapons newly designed for the *Comrades* multiplayer expansion make an additional appearance in *Episode Ardyn* as Guardian-specific armaments.

Two pieces of early development concept art for *Episode Ardyn*. From the outset, the development team aimed to convey the busy, lively atmosphere of the Founder's Day Festival, which players would enter as Ardyn and be allowed to roam free and cause chaos with all the character's powers unleashed. The concept of playing as the villain and having an opportunity to wreak havoc in the world of *FFXV* was extremely well received across the development team.

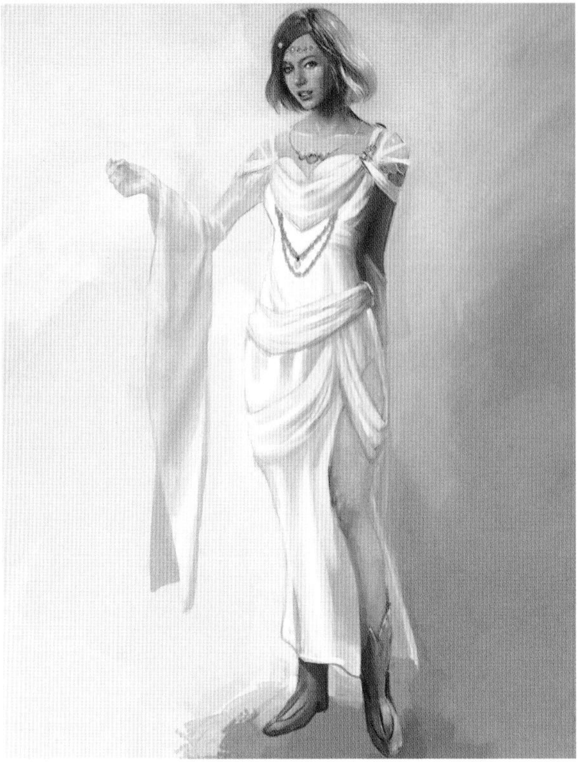

Aera plays a pivotal role in the story as the only woman Ardyn truly loves. As the design team worked to capture the special essence of her character, numerous parallels were drawn with Lunafreya, including many elements of her physical appearance.

Aera is the first Oracle, as well as o
of Lunafreya's ancestors. As describ
in the *Cosmogony*, Aera was bestow
with the ability to commune with t
gods and was thereafter known as t
Oracle, serving as link between heav
and earth. Though she was slain
the hands of Somnus, her kin wou
carry on her calling, with a member
House Fleuret always serving to fill t
role of Oracle.

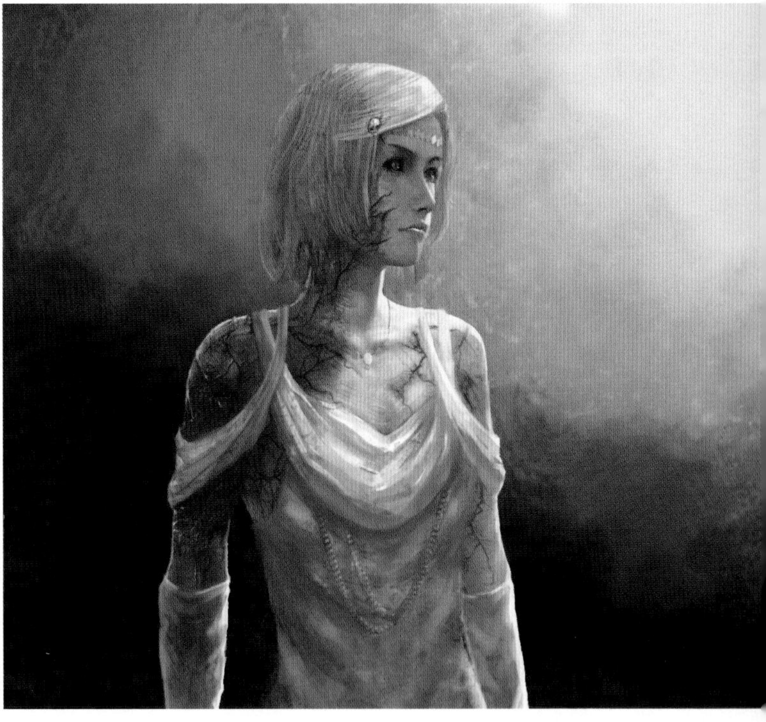

Ardyn on the loose amid the chaos of Insomnia. Appropriately, the name of this piece is "Conditioned to Hate," a title which it shares with the battle theme that plays during the assault on Insomnia during *Episode Ardyn*. The theme is a perfect musical companion to this particular piece of art.

After learning that his younger brother continues to protect Insomnia as one part of the Old Wall, Ardyn threatens the life of King Regis, determined to force Somnus to appear. This piece depicts the moment when Regis's life seems all but lost, and the Ring of the Lucii begins to emit its light and call forth Somnus.

Concept art drawn during scenario development for *Episode Aranea*. It depicts the commodore positioned on a rooftop, looking out across the imperial capital of Gralea. The DLC episode was to be based around the fall of Niflheim, featuring action-focused gameplay in which players would be free to navigate Gralea in a manner befitting a dragoon, leaping from one location to the next.

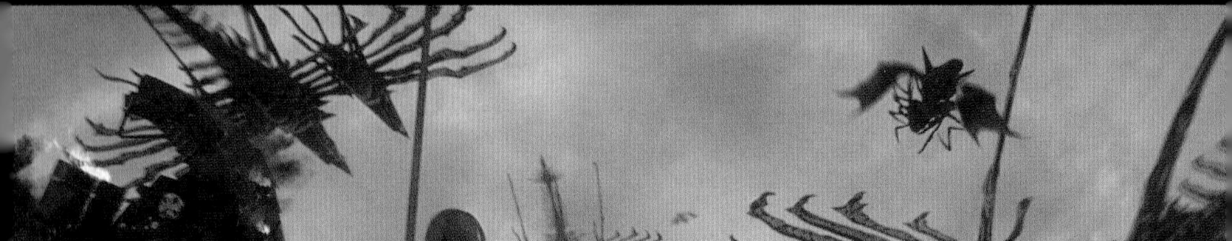

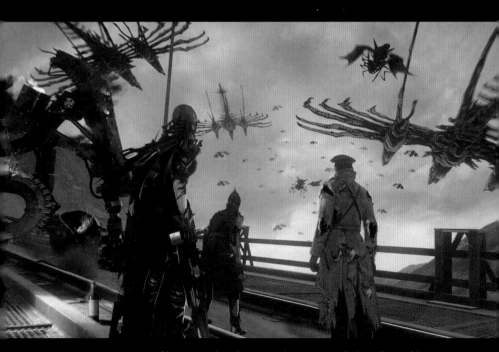

Aranea accompanied by Biggs and Wedge. The two men are ever by her side to aid her cause, and Aranea places immense trust in them. The wine bottle at their feet is one set aside by Biggs for celebration of a job well done at the end of the episode's long and sleepless ordeal.

At the behest of the emperor amid the havoc of Gralea's fall, Loqi secretly sees to the safety of the young girl known as Sol, then entrusts her to Aranea as the commodore departs the capital. After learning the girl's true identity as sole successor to the imperial throne, Aranea comes to serve as Sol's guardian, and the two spend the following ten years with the closeness of parent and child, even as darkness consumes the world.

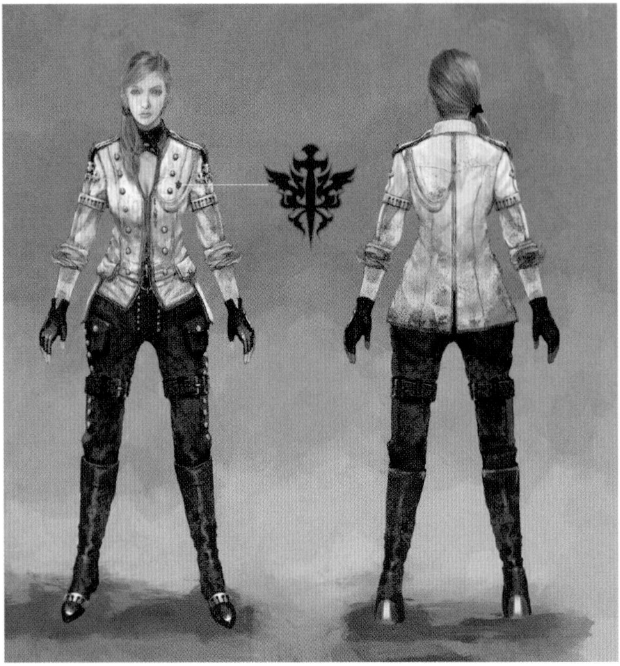

"The end of days for the Niflheim Empire, and the worst day of Aranea's life." Thus went the planned tagline for *Episode Aranea*, which was to follow the story of an exhausted Commodore Highwind, who, at the end of an already grueling day of work, is thrust into the chaos of a crumbling empire. With that context in mind, the commodore's attire was to be relatively casual, providing a striking contrast to her appearance in the main game.

Solara Aldercapt Antiquum, aka Sol, is Iedolas's granddaughter, though never publicly revealed as such. Sol was eight years old when Gralea fell under Ardyn's assault. By that point, Iedolas had been aware of her existence for several years. However, he did not feel he could name a girl of such tender years as his successor and instead had a trusted retainer see that she was kept safely hidden.

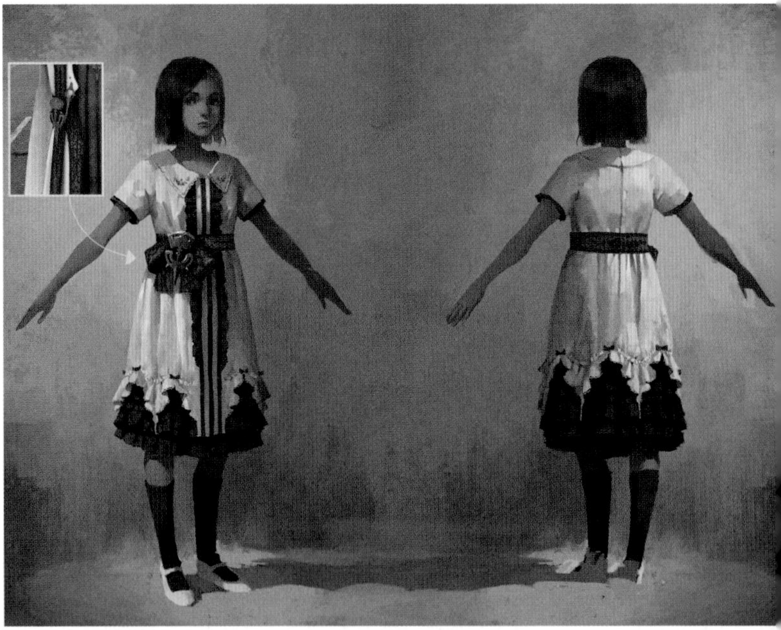

Biggs Callux (right) and Wedge Kincaid (left) are members of Aranea's imperial squadron and close associates of hers since their mercenary days.

Biggs is loquacious, tending toward coarse and sarcastic speech, but on occasion he reveals a bit of a bashful streak and difficulty putting his true feelings into words. He also has a tendency to grow skittish and fretful in tense situations. Still, Biggs is typically optimistic and boisterous, always looking forward to a good drink to celebrate a job well done.

Wedge is taciturn and, in stark contrast to Biggs's gregarious personality, retains a cautious, apprehensive, and frugal approach to life. At his core, however, he stands firm, able to confidently express his views and be there as a courageous, dependable ally when the need arises. He is apparently just as fond as Biggs is of a good drink but chooses to abstain, since when drunk, he's liable to act in quite the opposite manner of his usual self, becoming both talkative and merry.

The gameplay experience in *Episode Aranea* was to be even more action oriented than that of the main game. The spear pictured here was conceived of as a prototype weapon of Niflheimian origin, which players would wield as Aranea to battle daemons and magitek foes. A highly versatile armament, it would transform into different configurations at a single button press, acting as both melee and ranged weapons as well as a shield.

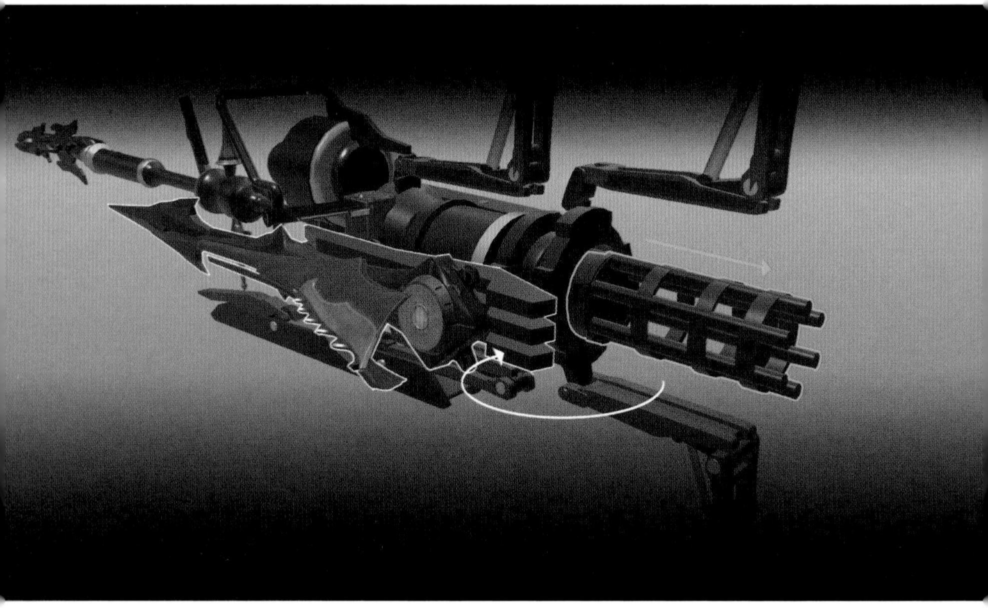

Aranea's spear in its Gatling configuration. The pictured asset was used in the modeler to design and demonstrate the various transformation sequences used to shift the spear between its different configurations. Pictured here is the set of rotating barrels that would extend from the front of the weapon, able to pummel opponents with a sustained volley of bullets at long range.

Aranea's spear in its Barrier mode configuration. The spear point opens wide, emitting a powerful energy discharge from the onboard magitek engine to kill the momentum of enemy attacks and thus protect the user.

The spear's Blast attack is pictured here. When fighting against the party with the Stoss Spear in the main game, Aranea is occasionally seen shifting the weapon's magitek engine into overdrive, discharging explosive red energy with each thrust and dive. Similar attacks were to be available in *Episode Aranea*, but without the need for putting the spear's engine into overdrive, allowing for on-demand energy bursts that would hurl enemies away.

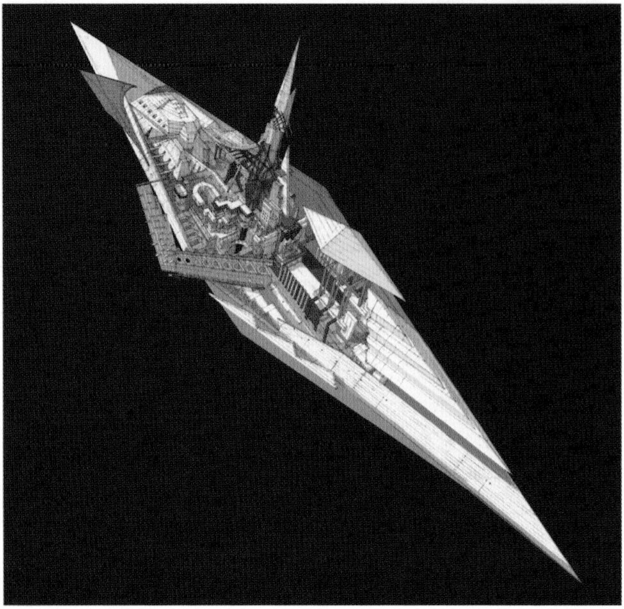

A rendering of the exterior of Ze tus Keep, the imperial megafortre floats high above the Niflheim En capital city of Gralea. This is the colossal mazelike structure that p must struggle their way through Chapter 13 of the main game.

A depiction of the top of Zeg Keep. This is the location Aranea to in pursuit of Diamond Weapon her episode—and where she inste an unexpected run-in with Char Ardyn Izunia.

Diamond Weapon is a daemon-infused magitek armor developed by Chief Verstael Besithia. It also makes an appearance in the movie *Kingsglaive: Final Fantasy XV*. Ardyn makes use of this weapon to ravage the imperial capital of Gralea, after which he sends it toward Tenebrae. Aranea and her squadmates manage to stop and destroy the monster.

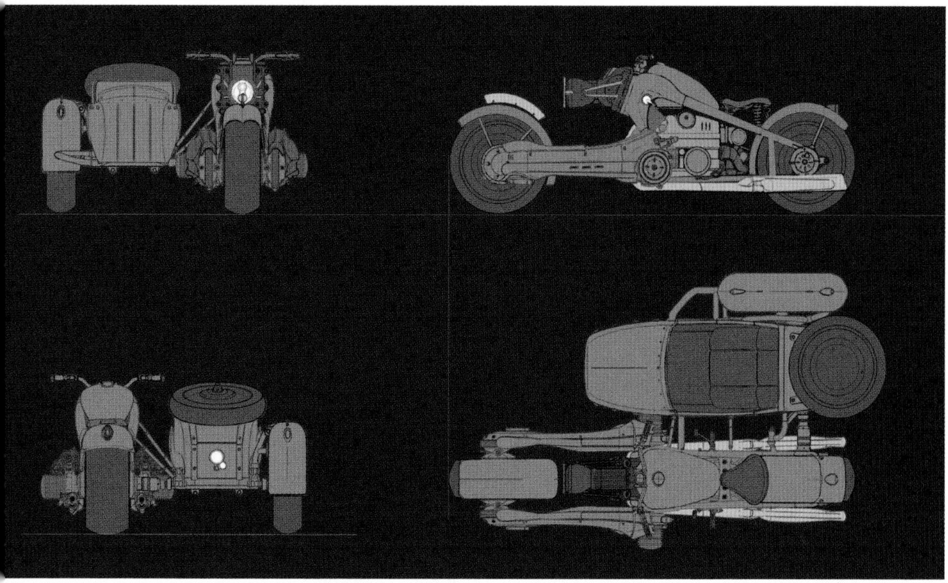

As *Episode Lunafreya* was to be the story of Lunafreya and Sol's shared travels, the team hoped to present it as a journey of close female friends and thereby complement the scenario of the main game. The choice of a motorcycle as their mode of transportation felt like a perfect way to signify the rugged, unwavering conviction of both protagonists as they make their journey.

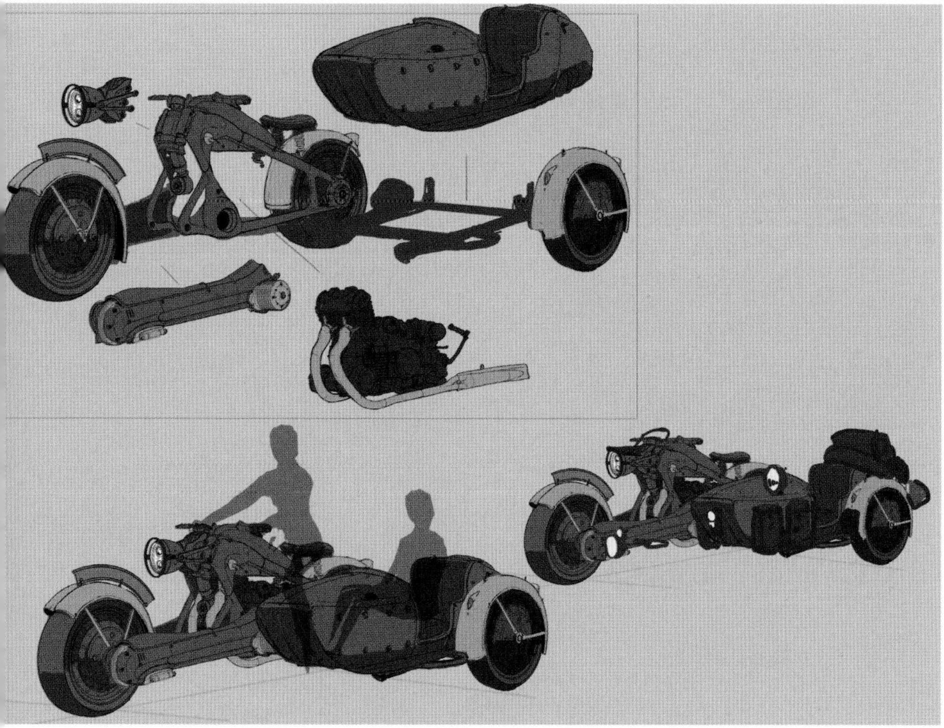

Immediately after her death in Altissia, Lunafreya was granted the power of the Starscourge by Bahamut and returned to the living world in a body filled with daemonic power. From there, she fell into a long slumber, her body slowly recovering from its fatal wound, until finally she

From the early stages of planning, *Episode Lunafreya* was to feature the titular character wielding daemonic power nearly equal to that of Ardyn. Lunafreya was to have been resurrected by the Draconian, the power bestowed upon her enabling her to fulfill her new calling.

Sol as she was designed to appear during *Episode Lunafreya*, set several years after the events of *Episode Aranea*. Sol was taken in and raised by Aranea, and by the time she appears here, she has grown into a strong and confident young woman. An initial plan, later scrapped, called for Sol to have a prosthetic arm, thus the design seen in this illustration. *Episode Lunafreya* was to show Lunafreya and Sol traveling and growing together. Given her position as heir to the Niflheim Empire and her close relationship with her adoptive mother, Aranea, Sol was to occupy a critical role in the arc of the new DLC.

Concept art for Lunafreya's awakening at the beginning of *Episode Lunafreya*. It depicts the light she first looks upon after being called from her watery grave back to the mortal realm.

Concept art depicting the impending final battle in *Episode Noctis*. The four heroes prepare to face off against Bahamut, God of War. One proposal had players swapping between the four characters over the course of the battle. While the combination of Noctis, Lunafreya, Aranea, and Ardyn seems rather strange at first glance, this piece helped the dev team realize that from the standpoint of character archetypes, it really wasn't too unusual in terms of conventional Japanese role-playing-game party configurations: the prince, the princess, the female dragoon, and the mysterious stranger.

This piece was created by the art team to help generate ideas for the ending to *The Dawn of the Future*. It depicts a funeral procession held for Ardyn. The team had always intended for Ardyn to receive proper recognition for his life and place in history at the conclusion of *Episode Noctis*. This illustration helped solidify the form that recognition would take, inspiring the planned inclusion of a final funeral scene for the man originally meant to become the Founder King.

As with the illustration above, this piece was provided to assist in generating ideas for the ending of *The Dawn of the Future*. Titled "Reunion at Daybreak," it is meant to depict the moment when all is complete and the dawn draws nigh, and the realization sinks in for Noctis that the woman he loves is still alive.

Another piece provided by the art team to help generate ideas for the ending to *The Dawn of the Future*. It depicts a funeral held for Ardyn. In the background stand Lunafreya, Noctis, and their friends. As Ardyn leaves behind no corpse, the casket is empty.

A piece meant to portray a happy ending befitting the grand arc now brought to a close. When planning the new DLC, the development team began by asking themselves what kind of conclusion fans of *FFXV* might want to see. The art team was asked to provide an assortment of images depicting appropriate finales to the DLC arc, of which this one stood out most prominently. It shows the characters spending a peaceful day, years after the events of the main game. It suggests numerous new possibilities to excite fan imaginations. Present here are Noctis and Lunafreya's children, along with an older Ignis, Prompto, and Gladiolus. Also seen is Ardyn, who displays another unexpected side to himself as he enjoys playing with the children.

Another piece created by the art team to help generate ideas for the ending of *The Dawn of the Future*. No clue has been provided as to the names of Noctis and Lunafreya's two children; it is a detail the team has decided to leave up to the creativity and imagination of the fans.

Square Enix Cafe Collaboration
LUNCHEON MATS AND COASTERS

The following pages are a compilation of all illustrations used on the *FFXV*-themed placemats and drink coasters included with orders served during limited-time promotional events held at Square Enix Cafe locations.

Note: The designs shown are those used at Square Enix Cafe Tokyo. Some mat and coaster designs varied slightly on items provided at Square Enix Cafe Osaka and Square Enix Cafe Shanghai. However, the underlying artwork used to develop those designs is the same.

Luncheon Mats

SET I

SQUARE ENIX
CAFE
FINAL FANTASY XV

SET 2

SQUARE ENIX CAFE
FINAL FANTASY XV

SQUARE ENIX CAFE
FINAL FANTASY XV

SQUARE ENIX CAFE
FINAL FANTASY XV

SQUARE ENIX CAFE
FINAL FANTASY XV

SQUARE ENIX CAFE
FINAL FANTASY XV

SQUARE ENIX CAFE
FINAL FANTASY XV

SQUARE ENIX CAFE
FINAL FANTASY XV

SET 3

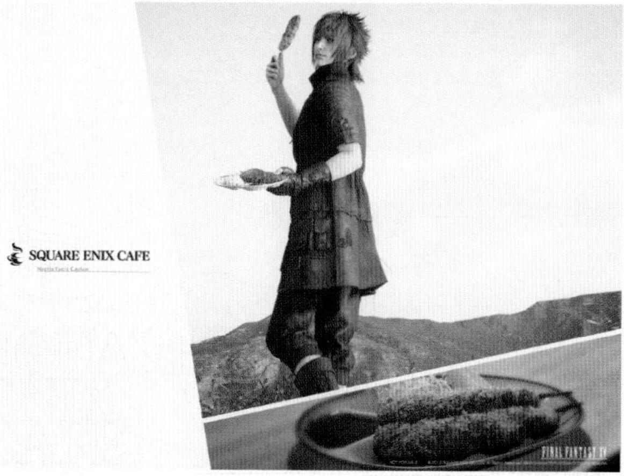
SQUARE ENIX CAFE
FINAL FANTASY XV

SQUARE ENIX CAFE

Ignis Scientia

SQUARE ENIX CAFE

Gladiolus Amicitia

SQUARE ENIX CAFE

Prompto Argentum

SQUARE ENIX CAFE
FINAL FANTASY XV

SET 4

SQUARE ENIX CAFE
FINAL FANTASY XV

SQUARE ENIX CAFE
FINAL FANTASY XV

SQUARE ENIX CAFE
FINAL FANTASY XV

SQUARE ENIX CAFE
FINAL FANTASY XV

SQUARE ENIX CAFE
FINAL FANTASY XV

SET 5

FINAL FANTASY XV

FINAL FANTASY XV

VITTLES
Chef's Favorite
COME
FINAL FANTASY XV

FINAL FANTASY XV

KINGSGLAIVE
FINAL FANTASY XV

SET 6

SQUARE ENIX CAFE
FINAL FANTASY XV

SQUARE ENIX CAFE
FINAL FANTASY XV

SQUARE ENIX CAFE
FINAL FANTASY XV

SQUARE ENIX CAFE
FINAL FANTASY XV

SQUARE ENIX CAFE
FINAL FANTASY XV

SQUARE ENIX CAFE
FINAL FANTASY XV

SET 7

FINAL FANTASY XV
SQUARE ENIX CAFE

FINAL FANTASY XV
SQUARE ENIX CAFE

FINAL FANTASY XV
SQUARE ENIX CAFE

FINAL FANTASY XV
SQUARE ENIX CAFE

FINAL FANTASY XV
SQUARE ENIX CAFE

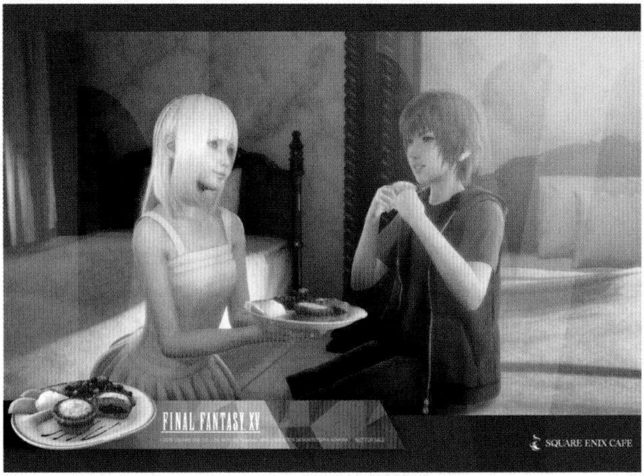
FINAL FANTASY XV
SQUARE ENIX CAFE

Coasters

SET 1

SET 2

SET 3

ET 4

SQUARE ENIX CAFE
FINAL FANTASY XV
SQUARE ENIX CAFE
FINAL FANTASY XV
SQUARE ENIX CAFE
FINAL FANTASY XV
SQUARE ENIX CAFE
FINAL FANTASY XV
SQUARE ENIX CAFE
FINAL FANTASY XV
SQUARE ENIX CAFE
FINAL FANTASY XV

ET 5

SQUARE ENIX CAFE
SQUARE ENIX CAFE
SQUARE ENIX CAFE
SQUARE ENIX CAFE
SQUARE ENIX CAFE
SQUARE ENIX CAFE

SQUARE ENIX CAFE

SQUARE ENIX CAFE

SET 6

SQUARE ENIX CAFE
FINAL FANTASY XV

SQUARE ENIX CAFE
FINAL FANTASY XV

SQUARE ENIX CAFE
FINAL FANTASY

SQUARE ENIX CAFE
FINAL FANTASY XV

SQUARE ENIX CAFE
FINAL FANTASY XV

SQUARE ENIX CAFE
FINAL FANTASY

SQUARE ENIX CAFE
FINAL FANTASY XV

SQUARE ENIX CAFE
FINAL FANTASY XV

Square Enix Cafe
Final Fantasy XV *Collaboration Timeline*

SESSION 1	October 1, 2016–October 23, 2016
SESSION 2	November 14, 2016–December 15, 2016
SESSION 3	December 26, 2016–January 22, 2017
SESSION 4	March 25, 2017–April 21, 2017
SESSION 5	September 16, 2017–October 13, 2017
SESSION 6	March 3, 2018–April 6, 2018
SESSION 7	November 17, 2018–December 14, 2018

Note: The limited-edition original luncheon mats featured here were provided with orders of the corresponding *FFXV*-themed entrées or desserts served during each session. One limited-edition original coaster was provided at random with orders of *FFXV*-themed beverages.

FINAL FANTASY XV
The Dawn of the Future

ISBN: 978-1-64609-000-6

Library of Congress Cataloging-in-Publication data is on file with the publisher.

Printed in the U.S.A.

10 9 8 7 6 5 4

SQUARE ENIX
BOOKS
www.square-enix-books.com